MW00616879

AVID

READER

PRESS

Also by Derek B. Miller

Norwegian by Night
The Girl in Green
American by Day
Radio Life
Quiet Time (An Audible Original Novel)
How to Find Your Way in the Dark

THE
CURSE of
PIETRO
HOUDINI

A Novel

Derek B. Miller

AVID READER PRESS

New York   London   Toronto   Sydney   New Delhi

AVID READER PRESS
An Imprint of Simon & Schuster, Inc.
1230 Avenue of the Americas
New York, NY 10020

This book is a work of fiction. Any references to historical events, real people, or real places are used fictitiously. Other names, characters, places, and events are products of the author's imagination, and any resemblance to actual events or places or persons, living or dead, is entirely coincidental.

Copyright © 2024 by Derek B. Miller

All rights reserved, including the right to reproduce this book or portions thereof in any form whatsoever. For information, address Avid Reader Press Subsidiary Rights Department, 1230 Avenue of the Americas, New York, NY 10020.

First Avid Reader Press hardcover edition January 2024

AVID READER PRESS and colophon are trademarks of Simon & Schuster, Inc.

Simon & Schuster: Celebrating 100 Years of Publishing in 2024

For information about special discounts for bulk purchases, please contact Simon & Schuster Special Sales at 1-866-506-1949 or business@simonandschuster.com.

The Simon & Schuster Speakers Bureau can bring authors to your live event. For more information or to book an event, contact the Simon & Schuster Speakers Bureau at 1-866-248-3049 or visit our website at www.simonspeakers.com.

Interior design by Wendy Blum

Manufactured in the United States of America

1   3   5   7   9   10   8   6   4   2

Library of Congress Cataloging-in-Publication Data has been applied for.

ISBN 978-1-6680-2088-3
ISBN 978-1-6680-2090-6 (ebook)

Inspired by many actual events

Do you care, do you care, do you heed these things,
O God, from your throne in high heaven?
My city is perishing,
ending in fire and onrushing flame.

—Chorus, *The Trojan Women*, Euripides, 415 BC

AUTHOR'S NOTE

BEFORE THE AMERICANS BOMBED OUR abbey at Montecassino in 1944—the same abbey founded by St. Benedict in 529 AD—I stole three paintings from the Nazis who were stealing them from the monks. I was fourteen years old. The story of how three Tiziano paintings from the Renaissance survived the war is therefore the story of how I survived, and the story of how I survived is the story of Pietro Houdini and his curse.

I was contacted in March 1979 by the Italian Ministry of Cultural Heritage and Activities about conferring on me the silver Medaglia ai Benemeriti della Cultura e Dell'arte—the Italian Medal of Merit for Culture and Art—for saving the paintings. The medal came with a request: they wanted me to write the story of how it all came to pass. I was reluctant. They were insistent. I tried to warn them that this was not a hero's story. It was a survivor's story. "What's the difference?" they asked. "Honor and mercy," I said. They didn't understand.

I'd brought the three paintings to the attention of the authorities on an autumn day in 1973. I did this by walking along the paths through the green gardens outside the Museo di Capodimonte in Naples, past the bug-eyed fish on the Fontana del Belvedere, and into the front door. I was holding three cardboard tubes.

"I'm here to see the director of the museum," I said to a woman who looked properly officious. Her slack face was a provocation, so I said: "Under my arm are three Tiziano paintings that were lost in time to the archives of Montecassino Abbey but were saved by a young girl and an aging man in 1943 before the Nazis could steal them and the Allies could bomb them. They are studies for three of the six poesie paintings, which, I assume you know, are among the greatest masterpieces of the Renaissance. I'll be in the café until I'm not."

Despite my being rather well dressed, they didn't believe me, of course. I watched the director approach me ten minutes later in his three-piece suit and pocket square. He looked me over, assessed my wristwatch, considered my shoes and the likely cost of my hairdo, and tried to decide if I came from a family worth talking to; such is Italy.

"Montecassino," I said, holding my cup.

He looked at the tubes beside me on a chair. If anything convinced him to take me seriously it was probably the German writing on the tubes (*Inhalt, Qualität, Herkunft, Bestimmungsort*) or, perhaps, the swastikas.

"Come with me, please," he said as though it was his idea.

Before the curator of the relevant collection, a master of art restoration, a bureaucratic-looking man I took to be a lawyer, and two armed guards, the director—Dr. Giacomo Esposito—placed the tubes on an enormous table in a room of marble and wooden cabinets. One by one he opened the tubes. The backs of the canvases made his eyes open wide, and the master of art restoration became flushed. The fabric emerging from the Nazi tubes was exactly what I claimed it was.

Their faces, however, became drawn and then agitated when they opened each one and saw what Pietro had done to them.

"What . . . what is this?"

"Oh. Yes. That. You see, the paintings are hidden, Dr. Esposito," I said gently. "To escape, everything was hidden. The paintings. Me. Pietro Houdini, of course. Also Dino and Lucia, Harald and Ada. The abbot had to hide in the crypt. I think even Tobias had to hide himself from God. Only Ferrari, our mule, faced it all directly. It was a war, you see.

"To understand what you have here, you are going to have to patiently uncover what is hidden to reveal the mystery and the value within. If you do that, as I learned, the rewards are beyond measure."

"Is this a game?" he said to me.

"If it is, we are all a part of it," I replied.

WHAT FOLLOWS IS MY WAY of explaining what came to be. It is a story about war, sex, violence, transformation, and death; some of it I learned at the time, some I learned later and wove throughout as needed. It is a story that has convinced me of the truth of a paradox that I cannot reconcile: I am now certain—I *know*—that we are a part of something larger; something mystical and beyond the realm of human understanding that impinges on our stories and our lives. But I also know that being part of something larger does not mean we are part of something *good*; something just, fair, or virtuous. I cannot reconcile these truths. What it means to me—what it means for me—is there is no bottom when we fall into tragedy. This may help explain how I managed to save three paintings from oblivion. It may also explain how I was responsible for the destruction of the abbey at Montecassino.

—Bologna, October 17, 1980

PART I

PIETRO HOUDINI CLAIMED THAT LIFE clung to him like a curse and if he could escape it he would. His namesake—the Hungarian, the American, the Jew, the illusionist—died in 1926, a full seventeen years before Pietro and I met in the dirt by the side of the road in an Italian village beneath the long shadow of the abbey of Montecassino. I was bloodied and blue, lying in a gutter, and he was standing above me, white and glowing and pristine like a marble god.

In his late fifties, Pietro seemed immortal to me. He had a mane of long, thick white hair to his shoulders, a close beard, an angular face, and a muscular body.

He reached out his hand and I took it.

I had been in the gutter because I had been an orphan fleeing south from Rome after the bombings and I never stopped until a group of boys assaulted me, choked me, and left me for dead.

Pietro had been standing over me for reasons of his own, some of them soon to be announced and declared, others hidden and protected until the very end. He carried a brown suitcase and a canvas shoulder bag and, he said, was on his way through the town of Cassino and to the abbey itself to see the abbot after a long trip from Bologna. He had seen the boys kicking me and ran them off with a wave of his hand.

"Are you planning to stay there?" he'd asked me in a northern accent I found sophisticated and comforting. "Or are you going to get up?"

I could see that he was not a normal man. His clothes were not the drab browns of the countryside and his eyes were not the browns of most Italians. Instead his suit was white and his eyes were blue. His skin was not the pinkish hue of the northerners but had the bronze of people baked by the summer sun. The wrinkles around his eyes and on his forehead spoke more of wear than years and I felt his presence to be dramatic and theatrical and magnetic: as though my eyes couldn't help but fall on him, and when they did—like being drawn to a performer under a spotlight onstage—I was unable to break away because of the promise of some inexplicable drama yet to come.

I was right about all of it.

PIETRO HOUDINI FOUND ME ON the fifth of August 1943. My parents had been nice and gentle people with roots up north and extended family in the south, some of whom I knew and liked. My mother's sister lived in Naples with a second husband whose name I'd forgotten, and I had a younger cousin named Arturo I had met only twice. My father had taught finance and accounting at Sapienza University, and on the evening before I fled Rome, my mother and I met him near his office. The plan was to carry on to a party for some of their friends. I remember hearing the planes moments before we joined him in the wide piazza near the entrance to the school.

I had heard planes before and I was generally scared of them. There was a story passing through northern Italy at the time, a story that had come down to Rome. It was about a plane called *Pippo*. It was understood to be Allied and it was something to fear. It was not a normal plane. It was a supernatural one. A *mystical* plane. The fascist newspapers covered the stories about *Pippo* too. I still don't know why. Nevertheless, those stories confirmed or created or re-created everything Italians feared most about the dark.

"Is that *Pippo*, Mamma?" I asked, inquiring after the mysterious plane that could only be heard and never seen.

"Probably," she had answered, because—for all the anxiety *Pippo* created—*Pippo* never did anything. *Pippo* never showed up.

But it was not *Pippo*. It was not one plane—not *the* plane—but many. The Allies had come, not to liberate us from Mussolini's tyranny and Hitler's twisted alliance with us, but to bomb us.

I knew, in some manner, that the Americans were our enemies but I didn't really believe it. Not until I saw it. Looking up, I saw the bomb doors open and the black cylinders fall out. I saw the explosions in the city not far from me and I . . . didn't understand.

I *knew* what was happening. But I had never seen buildings fall or balls of fire in a city. I had never experienced the industrial force of hatred and revenge. I could not absorb the notion that my country, Italy, had *wanted* this. Had *asked* for this. That the timeless buildings were simply gone. That we (me, my mother, my father, the people I saw running) were guilty of something. I may not have been raised a proper Catholic but the core teachings were the very lifeblood of the Italian people and were therefore inescapable. I *knew* that we were punished for guilt, not for innocence.

A stray bomb—caught by the wind—landed at our feet in San Lorenzo, near the university. When the air raid sirens started, my parents had instinctively thrust me ahead toward a building with a bomb shelter in it, and I had run in that direction, assuming they were right behind me, but they had stopped to take the hands of an aging friend. A moment later they were all dead from falling rubble.

I ran back and dug for them through the debris.

I found them.

My mother's butterfly clip. My father's watch.

I RAN SOUTH FOLLOWING THE VIA MERULANA. I had no money or suitcase. I saw a truck full of people and they waved to me to join them. I had no idea then—how could I?—that Rome would be declared an open city only a month later and I would have been safer there than where I was headed.

My clothes were ripped and dusty and foul, so a woman on the truck gave me some of her son's clothes out of pity. I put on a white shirt and waistcoat and cap.

When the truck finally stopped a hundred kilometers south with the last of the people who wanted to go that far, I stood by the side of the road near Frosinone and then continued walking. My aunt was in that direction and my dead parents were behind me. That created a line I followed.

I walked. I slept. I walked more. I stayed with kind people for days at a time. I got as far as the village of Cassino in early August before someone put his hands around my throat.

The cause of that fight and what they wanted doesn't matter now. What matters is they didn't get it, and soon after the skirmish was over, Pietro found me broken by the side of the road. It was a good thing he didn't ask my name in that moment because, there in the filth and blood, I hadn't decided on one yet. I had decided only that the old me was gone and so was my history.

The old me was an only child who was raised uneventfully in Rome to loving parents who shielded me from the wider politics of Mussolini's Italy and the war all around us.

The old me had been studious and had a few close friends at school, but had never been especially popular or admired.

The old me was comfortable in the company of adults and liked to listen and pretend I understood everything happening around me even when the topics turned to matters far beyond my comprehension.

That me had been happy because I had been sheltered from what would later cause me the greatest pain.

However:

That other me had been weak and I wanted to be strong. The other me was vulnerable and I wanted to be a warrior. The other me had been taught that being weak and vulnerable was a product of my birth and that it could never change because I was born inferior and lacked the creativity and courage for greatness.

That was the person I was committed to leaving behind in the gutter as my parents had been left in the rubble below.

I was a newborn without a name; a child who matured on the spot.

He was big but he was not a threatening presence. He sounded educated, which to me meant safe.

"Who are you under all that?" he asked.

"Just a boy," I said.

What he said next—I think—was *maschio*. It means "manly" or "masculine." I suppose he was speaking to himself. Perhaps he was being sarcastic. I don't know. Through my ringing ears, though, I heard "Massimo." Or was it the other way around? Did he say "massimo" and I nervously heard "maschio"? Either way, what I said aloud was "Massimo."

He reached down and pulled me up and repeated: "Massimo."

Did he name me or did I name myself? Regardless, the transformation was nearly complete.

My face was as soft as a baby's, my shoulders slender. My eyes too big. But now my name was maximum, the *top*, the *peak*; all to describe a half-dead child with snot running down a broken nose and blood mixing with the salt of tears.

"Just a boy?" he asked.

"Yes," I said.

"All right, Massimo," he said, looking me over. "I am Pietro Houdini. Chemist. Painter. Scholar. Master artist and confidant of the Vatican." He looked up the mountain at the abbey for emphasis or affirmation. Its walls were white and reflected the sun. It was a vibrant thing as though the light came from inside it. "I have time. I will take you home."

"No!" I yelled.

This confused him. I could see by the way he flinched that he misunderstood. He thought I'd felt threatened by him, like he might be a new attacker. But I was never afraid of Pietro Houdini. It was the word "home" that had terrified me. I would never go back to Rome. Rome was haunted by death and I needed to go south. To go *away*.

"You already decided not to stay here. So . . . where?" he asked.

"Naples," I said.

"Naples," he repeated as if to confirm my order at a café. "Where are your parents?"

I didn't answer.

After a long-enough time for him to understand the words not spoken he said, "So . . . Naples."

"Yes. I will go there or I will die," I explained.

He nodded his understanding, not at the value of my words but at the intractability of my ideas, my determination, and this new encounter that he could not explain but could also not ignore.

He responded gently: "Whether you are going to Naples or not, my friend, you are not going now. The Allies have won the battle for North Africa. Now they are fighting in Sicily. They are coming for Naples. Racing them is not a good idea. One should never be anywhere near soldiers fresh from combat, my young Massimo."

He stood there with his arms crossed over his chest and his eyes looking to heaven for intervention or guidance or—at the very least—to ensure there was a witness.

"You are alone?"

I didn't answer that either. The word "yes" was not available because of its finality.

Pietro Houdini stood silently and stared at me, asking a question I couldn't hear. It was hot and his body was perfectly still. His mind, I felt, was building a plan as big as a cathedral.

When the plan was finished he said, "Okay. You will come with me. You will not understand this but the monks of Montecassino have re-

6

quested my presence to help protect one of the greatest repositories of art in Western civilization. War is bad for culture, as it happens. That place, up there, is one thousand, four hundred, and fourteen years old. It is a fortress filled with wonders. They tore down the temple of Apollo to erect it. He was the god of war. I suspect he remains angry. I also suspect that the abbey has a very good wine cellar that is poorly guarded and shamefully catalogued, all of which is to my great benefit. If one needs to stay out of sight and wait for a dark moment to pass, there are worse places than a fortified wine cellar on a mountaintop. Believe me, I've checked.

"So," he continued. "You and I share the same problem and the same destination, which is why the abbey is the only solution for the moment. If you come with me there are conditions. So listen. No talking when we get there. Talking is for me. You listen or else pretend to listen. You will be doing a great deal of listening and pretending to listen. Now . . . fix your cap, Massimo. You'll want to tuck that hair in and then get it cut. Secrets and lies are illusions and one must commit to the illusion if it is to work! This is why I am called Houdini."

He started off and I followed him. Bruised, limp, weak. For the next two hours I dragged myself up a five-hundred-meter mountain without ever asking—without even wondering—why he wanted me to come. Following Pietro Houdini seemed the most natural act in the world.

THE WHITE BEAST AND ITS walls came into view through the trees like a mirage—ancient and foreboding—and then disappeared.

"The foundations were raised in 529 AD," Pietro said, sensing but overintellectualizing my curiosity. "That was the same year the Christian emperor Justinian closed Plato's Academy in Athens by defunding it, thereby ensuring the downfall of what they considered pagan philosophy. Symbolically, my young Massimo, the intellectual life of the West shifted from the academy to the cloisters. To right *there*. It wouldn't return to the academy until the pagans found their voices again in the Renaissance, all without my help! Up there," he added, "is where St. Benedict wrote his *Rule* and monastic life began. Every monk you've ever seen got his ideas about how to live from an old document written right up there. Its significance to the Christian mind can't be overstated. We are going to call it home for a little while. It is an island in a rising sea of despair. You may think you've seen hard times, but harder still are coming. Math does not lie."

I was intimidated and awed when I arrived at the top. From the bottom the abbey had looked like a toy, a dollhouse. But when I was standing beside it the walls were as heavy and thick as those of a castle. The windows were small and there was only one way inside, through an archway with the word "PAX" inscribed at the top.

PEACE.

It looked more like a threat or a command than a prayer.

Peace . . . *or else.*

My father—perhaps as a joke, because fathers lie to their children for humor—had led me to believe that voices live inside rock. When I was little, maybe six, he took me to the Pantheon in Rome. Inside was the domed roof with the hole in the top where the rain had been pouring in since 128 AD (long before Montecassino was built). When you stand beneath that dome, toward the sides, you can hear whispers. They come from all over the room, but when I was a child I did not believe they came from the other people. I was certain—and my father confirmed it—that the words came from the rocks, and they spoke in Latin and Greek and Hebrew and other ancient and exciting languages because it was not the rocks speaking but instead the remembered words spoken in there by the dead. Rocks did not speak, but instead retained the sounds, the very vibrations, of every word spoken in their presence. Somehow, when forces aligned, those words were released and if you listened carefully you could hear the conversations of the dead. "Not ghosts," my father said. "The past. Which is far more interesting."

To me, Montecassino was made of the same rock. Standing there, however, I sensed more: Unlike the Pantheon, which was a dead place and a museum and a tourist attraction, this monastery was no relic, no ruin. It was alive. Words were being spoken in those languages even now, and so many more. Inside the rock were the stories of fifteen hundred years; stories that were not trapped in the cloisters but had already broken free long ago to change the world. Outside the entrance I could feel the pulse of the world thumping beneath the floors and I could already hear the whisperings of the crypts.

In Cassino, I had had no idea any of this was up here: a fortress in the clouds. For someone who wanted to hide as I did, there was perhaps no better place.

When we entered the compound through the archway, the scorching sun reflected off the sandstone, making the air shimmer and become heavy. Through the archways to my left I saw the brown and green of the valley dotted by the small villages below. Around me there were monks, like back in Rome.

"I'm thirsty," I said to Pietro, hiding the rest of my concerns.

"I know."

"I need to pee."

"We will get water in and out of you soon."

"I have to go *now*," I said.

"We will *now* meet the abbot," he said with my emphasis. "He is very old. Old enough to have shrunk. There will be an exchange of papers and blessings. Your relief will be that much greater when all is done." He turned to me, looking serious. "Again: be quiet and, no matter what I say, you contradict nothing or there will be no food, water, or toilet for you."

The old man arrived a few minutes later dressed in the black robes of the other monks. He must have been eighty years old. Two other monks flanked him, their hands clasped inside their long sleeves.

Pietro said something in Latin, or what I assumed was Latin because it wasn't Italian and it involved monks. The abbot responded in kind. Pietro handed the abbot a letter, which had been sealed. The monk opened it and read it immediately. It looked very official and had many stamps. When the abbot nodded, Pietro introduced me in Italian as Massimo (no family name) and then christened me a second time that day by giving me a title: *assistente del maestro di restauro e conservazione*—assistant to the master of art restoration and conservation. This is how I was introduced to the monks—a teenager, my eyes black and swollen, two blue handprints around my neck. One by one they shook my thin hand and welcomed me to this house of God with not a question asked.

Such were the times:

Assistente.

Maestro.

I thought it was a joke but the monks accepted it, and after my needs were met and I was fed, I was led to a room where I then slept for more than twelve hours.

Maestro Houdini kept his other promise and put me to work the next day, rising at seven in the morning, long after the first prayers by the monks.

So BEGAN A PERIOD OF peace and healing and exploration.

But also delay.

ON THE VERY FIRST DAY Pietro came into my room and saw that I was fed, washed, and rested, he said, "Stay here. You will have work to do soon enough. Before that I must prepare my tools and establish my authority and presence here so whatever I choose to do later will not be questioned. Magic, my young friend, is all about preparation. And illusion is about drama. More on this another time. Now I must go."

Five minutes after he left, so did I. Who wouldn't?

There was no map of the monastery. No guide. It was not a shape that one can easily describe and its layout lacked the symmetry one expects to find in a great cathedral. No, this was a place unlike any other place. As I snuck out of my room and ventured into the halls and corridors, archives and basilica, along the outer walls, and deep into the labyrinths below—some of vaulted gray stone and dust and others of mosaics of blues and golds—I came to imagine the place as a mighty ship.

Unfortunately, the only mighty ship I knew by name was the *Titanic*.

Imagine a ship on a sea of green grass at the highest point of a mountain with nothing else surrounding it. From its decks one could see all around without obstruction; the village of Cassino below, the road that snaked its way up and down, the fields and flowers outside, the tiny goat paths leading to further mysteries in the hills and forests beyond.

The ship itself was made of white stone except the lower parts of the walls where the foundations flared outward like a fortress and the glimmering abbey above gave way to ten million stones below. The roof was made of reddish and orange tiles, even the basilica in the middle and toward the prow. The two exceptions were the green domes: one above the church and the other near the outer walls.

On either side of the nave—all safe within the walls—were two cloisters with green parks in the middle and archways that led to walkways around them. At the entrance to the basilica itself was a massive stone patio with a fountain in the middle. Leaving it behind, I would walk under the porticos and come to the top of the enormous staircase; a staircase as wide as the church itself that went down toward the back of the ship, passed between the statues of St. Benedict on one side and his sister,

Scholastica, on the other, passed the fountain from which the monks still drew water, to my favorite outside spot: the archways that looked westward and over the rolling hills that masked any sign of human life.

It was not the outer walls of the monastery, however, that liked to talk. It was the interior walls. It was the walls of the museum that no one frequented but me, and the archive rooms with the tens of thousands of papers and books and manuscripts and scrolls. It was the dark corners where secrets had been exchanged over the millennia, and where everything undocumented and hidden had produced their force.

The voices grew louder the deeper I went.

There were stairs. Too many to mention. I would open a wooden door and find stairs. I would see a wrought iron gate and behind it were stairs. There were stairs behind bookcases like in the old stories of haunted houses and there were stairs going down into places too dark to visit.

On that first day I covered as much ground as a child could and it was a miracle I even found the surface again. Over the months to follow, the abbey of Montecassino would become the building—the structure—I knew best in the world, better than my school in Rome. Better than the halls of the university where I would explore, bored, waiting for my father to emerge from one overwrought meeting or another.

"ARE YOU READY?" PIETRO ASKED me in the morning.

"For what?"

"Work. Perhaps you've heard of it?"

"What work?"

"You are the *assistente del maestro di restauro e conservazione*. Or have you forgotten already?"

"You were serious?"

"As far as you are aware, we are here to protect and safeguard the art of Montecassino from the challenges posed by the war around us. The rumbling. The pollution. The unforeseen."

"How?" I asked.

"I'll worry about that."

"I want to go to Naples," I said, though after four days in the peace and excitement of the monastery I was no longer so sure.

"No one's stopping you. But your timing is poor. Is someone waiting for you?"

I admitted they were not but I had people there.

"Are you certain they are there?"

I admitted I was not. But where else would they be?

The obvious answer—dead—eluded me then.

"I suggest you wait for the right moment," he said to me.

"When is that?"

"Moments present themselves. That's what makes them moments."

I didn't understand and the blankness on my face must have been readable because he responded to my silence: "The ancient Greeks had two words for time. One was '*chronos.*' That was like . . . time passing. Minutes and hours and such. The other was '*kairos.*' That meant the right or opportune moment, like the perfect instant to loose an arrow. Today we have lost that distinction but the Greeks were right, as usual. Put your trust in *kairos*, not *chronos*, Massimo. There really are opportune moments if you open yourself to seeing them. Now: I see from your shirt that you've had breakfast. So . . . if you're not leaving immediately, we can go be productive, yes?"

PIETRO HOUDINI MENTIONED THE CURSE to me a month later when we were in the abbey on a hot Wednesday morning in late September, deep underground in one of the vaults. Pietro was touching up a fresco and I was doing whatever he told me to do. On that day, like most other days, I was cleaning the already-clean brushes and listening to him talk. My sense of urgency to go south was suspended if not gone. I was content to be out of Rome with a comfortable place to hide.

The particular fresco he was working on was called *The Annunciation*. Maybe a third of it remained on the wall. I remember it having pinks and yellows and presenting a summer day with one figure standing before another, bent at the knee. I was fourteen and only marginally a Catholic. My father was a professor and secretly leaned toward the socialists in our fascist Italy. I didn't properly understand the figures in the fresco or what they meant. Angels and saints, I supposed.

The vaults were generally cool because they were deep underground but this one was hot because of the powerful lamps he used to illuminate the cave and its paintings. Pietro was shirtless and caked in the dust kicked up by our presence. Our bodies were both damp, my own shirt soaked.

I understood, to a point, the work he was doing because he had explained it when I first followed him down one of those long staircases into the first of several vaults we'd work in. Already, though, I had some suspicions that he might not be who he said he was. Rather than worrying me, it was a comfort. It meant—in this respect at least—he was more like me than other people were.

"When I'm not with you I'm usually up in the archives doing some homework. There are some, shall we say, items I'm trying to find that are related, shall we say, to my southern journey. Unfortunately, the monks have not done a terribly good job classifying their loot. So it's a bit of a project. When I'm with you, we're doing this," he said, as though it were obvious. "If the painting does not flake and is only dirty," he said, "there is no need to take risks by using paint. It is enough to put five drops of lemon juice into a teacup of lukewarm water and then—using a cotton ball—moisten the cotton and dab the oils. They will come alive as you do. Later, after it is dry, I dissolve half a teaspoon of sodium carbonate crystals in a cup of warm water. And then I dab the surface, being careful not to remove any of the paint that might flake. If it does flake, I keep it to myself and tell no one."

Other days we would catalogue art upstairs, or else check the mountings on paintings so they might not fall off if the world started to shake. Other times—rather arbitrarily, I thought—he'd remove some other pieces from the walls and wrap them in fabric and box them.

It all seemed madcap to me, but his actions and my understanding mattered far less than our time together and the words spoken. Our best conversations—or I should say, his best oratory—were always underground, when we were most isolated, most protected, and most alone.

He spoke as he worked and I watched. At times his topics were informational. Other times he rambled. Pietro Houdini had the sorted mind of a scientist but the spirit of a shaman who had seen too much and expected to see much more of it. Rather than recoil into silence as others might—as many did during that war—he exploded into words. The man I knew was a thinker and a storyteller and a liar who had as little reverence for the facts as P. T. Barnum. And yet, his dedication to *truth*—to God's own truth, a truth Pietro claimed to know and I now believe he did—was bottomless. "Bottomless" was a good word too: I hear him now falling endlessly towards the truth and leaving behind him the wake of an eternal scream.

Everything was fodder for Pietro's tall tales and exaggerations, but it was his radical capacity to live that eventually kept us all alive as long as it could.

"I met a most interesting monk the other day," he said as I watched him do next to nothing: dabbing a single square of a blue mosaic tile for what seemed like hours. "His name is Tobias. I put him in his early thirties but he barely needs to shave, making me think he's younger, and yet his magnanimous spirit makes me feel he's older. I therefore have no idea and because I have no idea I chose not to ask because the uncertainty is fun.

"He comes from Aosta, south of Geneva and west of Milan. I have always thought of Aosta as ugly and industrial and I said so, but he insists to me that the center has a charm I have not experienced, that the people have a warmth I have not felt, and the scent of the alpine glaciers reaches them on just the right days and accentuates the taste of the food. I believe none of this but I found his attempt to defend the city noble and it touched me because it carries with it the unstated premise that the entire population will be better off if only he can convince me of what he sincerely believes. I find that self-sacrificing as well as flattering. So I now have complete faith in him."

"Why?"

"Why? *Why?* There he is, willing to risk ridicule and contradiction only to raise the reputation of a people who cannot even hear or benefit from his efforts. This is the heart of a good man. Misguided, perhaps, but . . . he's a monk, so one expects that sort of thing. When he isn't roused about the magic of Aosta he likes to talk about music. He was telling me," he added, "about the music collection here at Montecassino. It is a fascinating subject! Most of the music is considered profane—that is, not sacred or religious music—because the collection was formed organically through the donations of various collectors, most of whom were Neapolitan families, mostly between the years of 1837 and 1839. Normally all the nineteenth-century books and private documents are kept deep, deep underground in the cellars that no one ever visits. But in this case, a special room was selected in 1838 to house the entire music collection. Ten thousand manuscripts! No one had any idea what was down there. Which composers were down there. Whether operas and arias and symphonies were down there that were otherwise lost to the entire world. Imagine. One single copy of an opera that has never been heard and that might inspire generations of other musicians; might bring joy and light and tragedy and understanding to millions. In a single spot below our feet right now.

"Well, as it happens, I was not the first one to think about this. Tobias said that a Benedictine monk and organist named Don Luigi De Sario arrived and he took it upon himself to check that all the music was indeed ordered by the name of the composer, was correctly classified, and had a proper location number. Tobias says there is music going back to the sixteenth century! He says there are a number of first editions including Breitkopf editions of Mozart operas as well as an F. A. Hoffmeister from Vienna. No one knows they're here. I think I might steal one before we leave. In any event, all of this has a funny way of making me think about paperwork. It is the scientist in me, alas. I see the absence of order, and I feel the hunger to differentiate what is different, to build classification systems, to build an index! Oh, the allure of a fine index is something a child cannot understand, so I will confess this to God later rather than burden you. To see everything in your reach, and have it under such control, is a feeling of power that borders on the . . . well. Again, you are but a child. The Germans," he said, pointing at the ceiling because all Germans everywhere were upstairs, "understand this kind of elation, but for them it is a relief and not a joy. Joy is not for them. This is why these particular Germans cannot be trusted."

There was more.

More dates. More names. More great events ("Did you know that in 1936, only a few years ago, they discovered the first Latin Passion play, written right here at the abbey, that preceded the earliest one known by more than two hundred years? It came into being because of a new concentration on Christ's human suffering. It culminated in new religious art. Right here, Massimo!"). More testimonials ("This is not only a repository, or a place of idle prayer, Massimo. It is a cultural center where the West produced its most significant works . . ."). More people and their views. More reasons to tell God or, under no circumstances, admit something to Him.

It was all incomprehensible and thoroughly hypnotic.

I didn't wear a watch, but I knew it was shortly after Terce, or mid-morning prayer at the abbey, on that hot Wednesday morning when Pietro made that statement that seized my attention and imagination. I knew this because the Benedictines held to a rigid schedule that I had learned quickly on arrival so I could make sense of the bells and movement around me. Second prayer was at nine. Even though I couldn't see or hear them above us, I could *feel* them at prayer. I would like to say that I could sense their words traveling to God but that was not the sensation I had. Rather, it felt as though the abbey was emptied as the monks turned away from corporeal matters, and as the spirits of the monks faced the divine, I became more free to breathe; free to move and escape the scrutiny of questioning eyes and the curious attention of the adults.

FROM MY ARRIVAL AT MONTECASSINO that August until that particularly hot Wednesday I had rarely spoken and only listened. I had little to say and no desire to talk. When I was restless I would explore the abbey (inside and out, top to bottom, hiding from the monks like they were wraiths). My silence had not been a problem because Pietro had done enough talking for both of us. I spent most of my time that late summer cleaning brushes and listening. Those were my two jobs. "Keep cleaning the brushes, especially if you hear someone coming. And listen to me talk. You don't have to pay attention. There will be no test. But you must feign interest at all times."

I liked both of my jobs. The brushes were beautiful instruments made of sable. When no one was looking I would run their soft bristles across my face the way I had seen my mother apply makeup. I had never felt anything so luxurious. Making them wet seemed a shame but they felt the same once they were dry again, so it didn't pain me. The brushes—aside from their contact with my skin—were never dirty because never once did he use them to touch the surface of a painting or mosaic or fresco. Not a single time, in those early days, did I see the man paint anything at all; not in those early days, and certainly not to restore anything. Instead, he applied his cocktails of chemical solutions to the frescos with damp cloths, or else he closed off rooms to the monks and staff and visitors with the pronouncement that it was their *breath* that was causing the deterioration:

"Your life is killing them," he said. "You may enjoy them or you may save them, but you cannot do both." Other times we would place buckets of salts in damp rooms to dry out the air and regulate the moisture. All of this was work of a sort, but none of it involved painting and none of it was work as I would ever have so named it before. And if it was work— which it appeared to be—how did it work? Pietro's actions seemed like those of an alchemist and his ramblings part of an incantation.

What was happening, though, was being done with flair.

That September morning I watched him work and listened to him talk and through his ramblings I found my own voice again; as though his curiosity and interest and words were a current and I had no choice but eventually to submit and start talking too.

When I did it was not in the only-child voice I had had with my parents in Rome, not the one that insisted, that yelled to friends, that blathered about the other children at school, or the voice that accompanied my slaps on the table when I was certain—*certain* the way only a fourteen-year-old during a world war could be certain—about whatever damn thing I'd been certain about. No. That voice was silenced. The one that returned to me (that came to me?) was a smaller one but far more powerful. It was a *questioning* voice. A voice of inquiry. Pietro called it "the voice of creation" because it was questions that created possibility.

I wanted to know about that word he used when he made his pronouncement: curse.

I believed in curses as much as I believed in spiders and clouds and bombs. These things were real. If Pietro was cursed I wanted to know about it. More than that: I wanted to know how it *worked*. How curses worked seemed important.

PIETRO WAS IN A MOOD that morning and it wasn't because he'd been affected by his own rant or because the Benedictines were at prayer. Rather, he was in a mood because the Germans were back.

THEY HAD BEEN COMING TO see the abbot over the last few days and the visits were on Pietro's mind. He hated the German soldiers, like everyone else did, but something about their presence *annoyed* him. He had seen two German officers start to "haunt the abbey" (his phrase) and he had heard they were asking for the abbot. He didn't know why and he wanted to. He sensed it was important. If it involved Montecassino, he said, it had to be important. ("Nothing insignificant has ever happened here, including us, Massimo. Believe me. We are already part of the history of this place.")

I couldn't make sense of his frustration. The Germans were everywhere, weren't they? Why not here? Consequently, his mind was going in one direction while mine was going in another and his hands were busy while mine were idle. The inharmonious mood forced me to speak. After all, I took his pronouncement about the curse at face value. It never crossed my mind that maybe he *wasn't* cursed. After all, I certainly was. My parents had been. Italy was clearly cursed. Probably the entire world was. It was a world war, I'd heard. Such a thing can't happen naturally.

Pietro seemed to have some insight into how it all worked and I needed to know.

Curious as I was about the curse, I was still too scared of the answer to ask it directly so I started someplace else with my newfound inquisitiveness: "Is that why you chose his name? Houdini's?"

"What?" he said, his hands stopping. He turned to me as if aware of my presence for the first time. It was reasonable. Perhaps I had only just arrived.

"You said that life clings to you like a curse and you would escape it if you could. Houdini was a master of escape. Is that why you chose that name? Because he too was a master of illusion and escape?"

"You think Houdini is not my real name?"

I smiled for the first time since the bombing. Not because his question was funny but because it was so outrageous. "Houdini isn't a real name," I said. "Is it?"

"It was Harry's name. Why not mine?"

"I heard he made it up."

"Who told you that?"

"My father."

"Did he like Harry Houdini?"

"Yes."

"Your father was right. And so are you. Well done."

"Are you escaping from something?"

"You want to know my secrets," he said, as though it were a fact. He was sitting on the three-legged stool and relaxing his heavy body on his knees. He raised his finger to his head and spun it around. "I see the mechanisms moving. When I found you in Cassino, you were struck silent. Then you found your voice. Small things, 'I'm thirsty, I'm tired.' Then you started requesting things. 'Pass the salt.' You're a child, you don't see this, but these are the steps of recovery. Finally you asked the big ones. 'Who are you, what are we doing here?' You're returning. This is good. Your grief and pain about your parents and your injuries will remain, but your journey through purgatory is coming to an end. Now, as you step further into the light, you move beyond mere needs and statements of fact into the highest form of consciousness. You know what this is?"

I shook my head.

"Curiosity. Yes, yes, of course a squirrel can be curious and we don't consider her intelligent, but we do consider her *well*. Conscious. Alive. Aware. The curious mind is the living mind. Have you ever seen a puppy?"

I nodded.

"Their minds are everywhere. *This* is interesting and so is that. *That* is even *more* interesting! Eyes everywhere, paws tripping over each other, up on a leg, down the leg to chase a pigeon, ears at attention, and the nose. Oh, the nose! In this, in that. Curiosity everywhere. Every moment. No time for study or reflection or contemplation. No time for reasoning or solving problems. But we are not talking about utility here. We are talking about the beating pulse of life. Curiosity is life, Massimo. This is why nothing sleeps more deeply than a puppy or a baby. Because living makes you tired. So now, here *you* come. Asking your first questions and they are about my name. Fine. Houdini *was* a master of escape. Good for you. Perhaps I would like to be. But there are differences between us. He was tormented more by death than life. He declared once that if he could find his way back from the other side he would. For ten years his wife, Bess, waited in séances on Harry's birthday for her beloved to reappear. He never did."

"But . . . you *chose* his name, right? What's your real name?"

"You want to know about my real name?" he then asked, as if called back from a reverie. "You're the first one brave enough to ask. I thought you were going to ask me why you wash the brushes we never use."

"I want to know that, too."

"What else?"

"I want to know about the curse."

"What curse?"

"You said life clings to you like a curse. Is there a curse or is that a . . ."

"Metaphor."

"Right," I said, though I wasn't sure. I had forgotten the word.

"So. Your silence has been a ruse. All this time you have been assembling your questions for an assault."

I said nothing. I hadn't thought of it that way, but perhaps that was what I'd been doing.

It was often like that with Pietro.

"Let's start easy and work upward. We clean the brushes for the monks," Pietro said as he shifted focus from the black of an angel's hair to the golden tips of her wings. "They check on our progress, and when they do, they see the frescos, they see the brighter colors, and they naturally look to the brushes, and their minds connect all the pieces. They are theologians by profession, Massimo; they have faith in *coherence*. They apply it to everything. It's adorable. So, to them, the brushes must play a role. To support their faith, we keep them clean and wet and moving so as not to confuse them. This is the assurance they crave and these are tough times. No need to become a new burden on their souls. This is my attitude. Right now their souls are burdened by two German officers who keep showing up and there is a mystery afoot as to why. Montecassino is not like other places. There is a commanding position over the Liri Valley, which is the only way to get to Rome from the south with tanks. There is also treasure here. Treasure that would make pirates weep and Nazis drool."

Before Pietro answered my other questions, however, the abbot surprised us by coming down the long flight of stone stairs. He came with questions of his own for Pietro. It turned out they answered mine, after a fashion.

THE ABBOT PAUSED AT THE bottom, having successfully descended the treacherous steps, and he placed his hand against the wall to steady himself or possibly the abbey, which I'm sure he took to be moving. Pietro and I glanced at each other and without a word it was clear we both suspected that his visit had something to do with the German officers. Pietro stopped cleaning the black hair of the girl and stood to receive the abbot. On surveying the environment, the abbot politely but also pointedly asked, "Why do you need an assistant?"

I remember being dumbfounded that he was curious about me. Who was I? No one. I ate little, said less, and caused no trouble. Why should a man who negotiates with empires and God care about me?

Pietro nodded in confirmation that he had understood the abbot's question. He took it as proof that the monks were irritated. Rather than calm the abbot, however, he did the opposite: "If my mouth is not moving, my hands will freeze up and the movement of my hands is what saves your frescos. My hands and mouth are connected and they move in concert with one another, producing words and deeds together just as the cellist moves the bow across the strings. The sound does not exist without the movement, and the movement cannot help but create sound. This is what humans are. Words and deeds. There is nothing else. They can no more be separated than the spirit removed from the body."

It was an odd thing to say to a monk who spent most of his life in comparative silence.

"This does not answer my question," said the abbot.

"I need an assistant because I need *assistance*. I need an assistant to talk to as I work. There is a great deal to be done here. The art of Montecassino is world-famous and the danger to it is real. Without an assistant, God might think I am talking to Him. Given the dearth of mercy in the world—and the things I am inclined to say about it—it is better for everyone if God not be the audience for my pontifications and rants. Such words, Father, coming from deep inside the abbey, might be mistaken for prayer and this would be good for no one. I suggest you consider the boy part of the war effort and our investment in him an act of mercy on our Lord and Savior."

"How is the boy a mercy for the Lord?" the abbot asked.

"By listening to me, and being the audience for my words, he is freeing the Lord from distraction. He is making it possible for God to concentrate on something other than me."

"The world burns, Maestro Houdini," the abbot said to Pietro. "You think your voice can attract the interest of the Almighty to the point of distraction?"

Without a laugh or a smile Pietro said, "Yes."

I believed him. He had made clear to the abbot and me that God listened to Pietro Houdini unless Pietro Houdini was speaking to me. I was there to clean the brushes so the monks would remain calm. I was there to listen to Pietro to keep God calm. I was there to protect God from Pietro Houdini, the man who wanted to escape.

"I can see in your eyes that you did not walk all the way down here to talk about the boy. You want to talk about the Germans, but then you looked at us and thought better of it. So I will take the burden off you. Who are the Germans, Father?" Pietro asked him as Archabbot Gregorio Diamare paused at the bottom of the stairs he was about to mount and prepared himself.

"They just want to talk," he answered.

"About what?"

"Art."

"What about art?"

"I'm still listening, Maestro. Thank you for caring and for your continued assistance."

"This conversation isn't over, Abbot," Pietro said to the abbot's shadowed legs as they labored up the stairs.

To our mutual surprise, the legs answered: "I'm sure it has only just begun, Signore Houdini."

Alone again, Pietro turned back to the mosaic. I too looked at it, but I wasn't interested in the mosaic: I was interested in what Pietro might be looking at.

The Annunciation got its name from the moment when the archangel Gabriel told the Virgin Mary she was pregnant with the Lord. The word itself—annunciation—means to *pronounce*: to make a declaration. Had Mary asked the Lord what was happening to her body? What had brought on the changes, as she had done nothing new herself? Had Mary even inquired? If not, why not? If so, why do we credit Gabriel and the Lord with a pronouncement rather than Mary with her question? Maybe this moment was a response to her. Maybe it was an apology.

Surely she deserved one.

Has a god ever apologized to a woman?

This was the question I was on by the time Pietro started answering anything. He was a little behind me:

"No. Houdini is not my name, but Pietro is. I didn't choose the name Houdini," he said without his usual glib tone, picking up the thread of our prior discussion. "You do not choose a name from the darkness of war. When the darkness sees you, it announces your name to you and you accept." He wiped the sweat from his forehead with his arm. His shoulders sank slightly. "As best as I can tell, it is much the way that writers choose the names of their characters. They seem to step out of the void and demand to be recognized. The difference is that a nom de guerre comes from the dark whereas in literature the characters emerge out of the light."

Which kind of name was Massimo, I wondered? Pietro had chosen my name, had he not? Was he the exorcist who had extracted my nom de guerre from the darkness? Or had I done it myself by hearing him incorrectly? Did my new identity emerge, therefore, out of my own internal hell? Or maybe—possibly—was my new name a *fiction* and not a *lie*? Was Pietro Houdini my author and was Massimo his blessed creation that sanctified the secret I had only half formed myself? Could it be, as I hoped, that Massimo and Houdini were characters in a wonderful story yet to be written that would see us through the war?

Either way, I was filled with new questions now and, therefore, as Pietro had explained to me, with life.

IN THE COMPANY OF TWO painted saints and a shirtless sinner, in that deep vault below the summit of Montecassino, I found not only questions but my first answers. I learned that I was both a blessed and cursed thing occupying a unique and inexplicable position between Pietro and God. I learned too that I was not to be alone in that space; something else was there occupying it with me. Whatever it was felt bigger than coincidence but smaller than destiny. I felt that I was doing what I was *supposed* to be doing; that I was caught up in something real and significant and that the people around me had been waiting for me to arrive and that whatever was going to happen next—with the abbot, with the Germans, with Pietro, with the art—was now free to progress because I was there to participate.

In Rome I was subject to the forces of the war and *Pippo* haunted my nights.

In Montecassino I was now an actor and my days were safe inside the walls of the abbey.

In Rome I was a girl whose parents were dead and I was afraid.

At Montecassino I was a boy called Massimo and I was strong and alive and so was everyone and everything around me.

MY QUESTIONS CONTINUED AS LIFE returned and I settled into being Massimo and the assistant to the Maestro. Pietro Houdini, though pleased with this, did not exactly reward me with a rush of facts and honesty. Rather, they dripped out of him, and my thirst was not sated.

For one thing, I did not take his pronouncements about his new name as a complete answer. He had provided only an explanation of where "Houdini" had come from. I wanted to know who he *really was*. That would take more time, and only after some dramatic events involving murder and arson. These were still the quiet days.

That day—the day of my awakening—Pietro finished his work on the mosaics (such as it was) and wiped his face and neck with a cloth. As he started packing up the materials into his work box he shook his head again. I felt that he was recalling his unsatisfactory conversation with the abbot and in that moment I wanted to make him feel better and, perhaps, myself too.

He saw me looking up at the ceiling and through the rock, through the abbey, to the source of the footfalls up above that we could both feel but not hear.

He smiled.

"Ask me. I'm prepared to talk, but only if you're clever enough to ask the right questions. Otherwise, what's in it for me? I'm too old to share your sense of wonder. But I can enjoy the company of a good detective. So: start simply but directly."

"The Germans," I said.

"Yes. The Germans. But Germans are people from Germany. Nothing more or less. They are not a question."

I was confused by this. He tried warming me up.

"What do you think of the Germans?" he asked me.

"Their language is ugly. It sounds like a doctor's handwriting."

"Ah," Pietro said, pushing away the notion. "In fact their language is quite eloquent, rich, and very good for both opera and science, which is a unique combination. You think it's ugly because their soldiers are mean, which is fair enough, but it is mainly because you are Italian and Italian is the most beautiful language in the world. English is flat and listless though inventive and precise. French can make claims to beauty, I admit, but it is not *inviting*. The French want their beauty to themselves and the foreigner can feel it in every conversation. Alas for them, beauty that is hoarded can never glow as brightly as beauty shared. Beauty is nothing without love and generosity, Massimo. No one sees a flower and hides it. But if a foreigner speaks even ten words of Italian we embrace him like a lost relative whose soul has returned to us. In this way, French loses to Italian. German is painful to your young ears because it is a language of creation and destruction. More than anything it is a language of *time*. German never lets you forget time and therefore mortality. That, more than anything, is what makes it both honest and cruel. But in that space there is a wistfulness. A realization that moments are precious. You start to see the precision of their language as an attempt to not miss anything. From that perspective, you can begin to hear the love."

I had nothing to say about this so I waited. Waiting always worked with Pietro:

"So," he jumped in. "What is a better question? What should a young detective ask?"

One of the reasons it was warm down there was because of the flood lamp. An industrial thing, it cast a penetrating cone of light at the wall that, for all I could tell, was half the power of the sun. The cleaner the wall became from Pietro's efforts, the more it reflected the light and the cave glittered with the flecks of gold leaf from long ago. This also meant Pietro's face and beard and torso were lit on one side whereas the other was in comparative darkness.

"Why are the Germans here?" I asked.

"Brava. Or bravo as you now prefer," he said, both revealing and forgetting himself. "What kinds of Germans? I see no dentists or taxi drivers."

"Soldiers."

"Indeed. Why are the German soldiers here. Now. That word . . . 'here.' Where did you mean? Earth? Italy?"

"Why are German soldiers in the monastery?" I said. And because the incongruity—the specificity of the thing—was too much to ignore I added, "And why does one of them have a red Fiat convertible?"

Pietro lowered his voice conspiratorially. "Good. Very good. Not only soldiers, Massimo. Officers. Those are good questions. This place is filled with monks. Most are here for life, with a few visiting for one reason or another. So why are there German officers here to consult with the abbot and why does the abbot wear these consultations like a yoke that is so heavy he can think of nothing else to openly complain about than a child in the cellar playing with brushes? These are also my questions. They are the questions we are going to ask Brother Tobias over dinner tonight. We will ask Brother Tobias because I rather like him. You see, beyond being a music lover like all the best people, his soul is torn between St. Benedict's admonition for silence and a peasant's unstoppable need to gossip. This makes him conflicted, complex, and fun to torment. We are becoming friends. He also takes my confessions. He is the only priest I tell. My sins are the deepest and most interesting of all the people here. He's the kind of man who appreciates things like that, and there is really no point in pouring forth to an audience that doesn't appreciate you.

"You and I will take the side of the devil tonight and encourage his desire to talk. Have you ever seen a pail tip over? Yes? It will be like that. Once he begins to talk, no force will be able to hold back the flood of words. But! And this is important: I need you to not interrupt him or correct me. You and I are after something specific, my young detective. We need to nudge him into revealing what he considers a secret. If we nudge him in the wrong direction we risk the words of Brother Tobias spilling out on the wrong side. This would be very bad for us because knowledge is precious during a war. So are words, even if they come loose and easy. We cannot trick him into revelation more than once."

Pietro snapped his fingers. "Are you getting this? Your face is listless."

"Yes," I said.

"So we have the mystery of the German soldiers to solve, and you seem set on uncovering my own secrets. So be it. But there is also a problem, which is different from a mystery. That problem is your future and safety. Now, like you, I am determined to get to Naples, which is either a great coincidence or we have both been drawn together by a force outside ourselves, which is what I suspect.

"You only happened upon the abbey by happenstance. I, however, have come to Montecassino for very specific reasons, because passing through the abbey is essential for my mission, which must end in Naples for not one but two very specific reasons that I am not—at the moment—at liberty to reveal. But for you . . . I am not convinced that Naples is the direction for you to travel. Maybe someday, but not now and not soon. Perhaps when the war is over."

I started to object but he raised a finger and his look was severe. "You must understand, Massimo, that the battlefront is not safe for you. If you travel south, you will meet the front. If you stay here, the front will meet you because the Allies are coming and the Germans are dug in and waiting for them. So you can't stay here or you will die. Everyone in the valley below is going to die. The view from the Chiostro del

Bramante—where the statues are outside—is painful to me because, like Cassandra, I know what is about to happen yet I cannot stop it. What looks to be peace is only the calm before death. It makes me sad. I have considered the wisdom of sending you off into the countryside alone but Italy has lost its mind. There's martial law all over the country, and new resistance movements and partisans are harassing the Germans who are coming down here to man the front. There are Axis planes overhead and Allied bombers. There are criminals and gangs, opportunists and fools. There is no certainty anymore, Massimo. There is no knowing who the enemy is or where the danger may come from. The inexperienced will consider this the fog of war and look for the patterns within. But I know the truth, which is that the chaos is the pattern. It is very hard for certain minds to accept that conclusion. This is now a land without heroes and villains."

He drew a deep breath and pressed on: "We Italians are not good at uncertainty though sometimes I think we invented it. I think our discomfort is because we are Catholic. We sin—gloriously and creatively—and then we recognize our failings and ask forgiveness. In the confessional we receive it. And then . . . confident . . . our discomfort is lifted. That is what gives us the peace needed to repeat our sins. Repetition is part of our culture too. In our dance, our music, our meals, our arguments, our lovers, our politics. We keep coming back for more. Learning is not for us. We have been surrounded by water and nearly impassable mountains for centuries so we have learned that when we reach our limits it's time to turn around and go back and repeat. As a hobby, this is fine. But not now. Not for a child in war. Not for you. Out there is a nation without a strong sense of who it is, and without the bonds of a shared story, a shared vision, a nation comes apart like a molecule without strong bonds. Going south is a mistake for anyone right now and going alone into the countryside is also a mistake. I think you need to go back north once we satisfy our curiosity about the German soldiers and the abbey."

"I will not go back to Rome," I said.

He continued as though my statement was not the fact it was.

"I have business in Naples. Family matters. There is someone down there I need to assist if I can, and someone else I need to see if fate allows. Most phone lines are down between north and south and those that are open are monitored by the German occupiers and other fascists. I cannot even risk sending word. I therefore have no choice but to go. You, however, need safety. You think it's in Naples but it is not. Between this mountaintop and Naples is the southern flank of the war, which is coming toward us, and around us are the defensive positions of the Axis war machine. The Allies are a supernatural force. The Germans, fortified into the mountains here, are a supernatural barrier. The explosion will be catastrophic."

He leaned forward. His voice was grave and there was no softness in his message:

"The German officers who are up those stairs milling around the abbey know that Sicily has fallen to the Allies. That was the seventeenth of August. On the third of September they made landfall on the mainland. Two weeks ago, on the first of October, they took Naples. Right now the Allies are moving northward from Naples to Rome and will cross this mountain. The man controlling the Gustav Line—controlling us—is named Fridolin von Senger und Etterlin," he said in a perfect German accent as far as I could tell. "He is no ordinary man. A good man or a bad one I can't say, but he is a refined man and a professional soldier prepared to fight for Germany. I'm told he was a Rhodes Scholar who studied at Oxford. He speaks English and French and, most interestingly, is a lay member of the order of the Benedictines.

"I know this because he took command here a few days ago and I saw the Germans in the villages acting busy in a way they had not been busy before. During one of my strolls, I asked one of them about it. 'You seem to be in a good mood. What makes today special? Is the war over?' and the soldiers laughed at my joke and were pleased to hear their mother tongue in a foreign place, so one of them told me about Senger. They think he is a good leader who had just fought in Sicily and then commanded the forces in Sardinia and Corsica. 'But he lost,' I said to provoke them a bit, and they said, 'Perhaps, but he fought well and everything he is doing feels right.' He was a hero of the Great War, one of them told me. What this tells us, Massimo, is that the Fates have taken an interest in us by placing Senger here," he said.

By *here* I thought he meant the abbey.

"A religious man fighting for the Nazis? And a Catholic no less? And not only a Catholic but a Benedictine? A Benedictine commanding the forces at the foot of the hills where St. Benedict established the order? Such things are beyond the imagination of Carl Jung. Have you heard of him? No, of course not. You're a child. I'll explain it another time if an explanation exists at all. What you need to know is that forces are at play on our lives, and those forces play more deeply on our lives the harder we live. All around us is tragedy, dear Massimo. With more tragedy yet to come. But as the teller of the *Iliad* and the *Odyssey* knew, the function of tragedy is to force us to acknowledge what is of value, and—if we are attentive and open to guidance—to prevent it if we are brave enough and not restrained from doing so by the gods."

Pietro now took my questions from me and finished the journey alone:

"The soldiers said that Senger has sworn to the abbot—this is Gregorio Diamare, the man you met on your first day here and the one who came down to the vault—that the Germans will not use the abbey as a military base. Now, it's too soon to know whether he will keep this promise but it deepens my questions. Who are the officers? They came yesterday and today. There are intense negotiations taking place. Why? About what? Do the Germans want to move weapons here? It is a fortress. But it is also a place of God. It is also a museum and a treasure trove. If they did use this structure as a base, it would make Senger a liar and that is not his reputation. Or maybe it has nothing to do with military affairs. That is when I started thinking about why I'm here. You see, at the risk of being crass, this monastery is nothing but a chest full of loot ready for the taking. If he took it, it would make Senger a thief, which is also not his reputation. We need to know, my young detective, who these new German officers are and how they might affect our respective plans. Are they working with Senger or against him? Under his orders or not? Are they here to secure a military base or to convince the abbot he is secure? Or are they casing the place and deciding what to steal? I want to know. Lesson number one in this war is: Keep your eyes on the Nazis. So. How do you feel?"

Hungry, I said.

A COOL BLUE EVENING AWAITED us when we emerged into the Chiostro del Bramante from the deep vault. Bramante was Pietro's favorite of the cloisters because it commanded the best view from the abbey: out to the southwest over the Liri Valley. I stood next to him as he donned a white shirt and buttoned enough of it so it wouldn't fly away. It caught the last rays of orange sunlight and made him glow.

"What do you see?" he asked me.

See?

I saw an arch. I saw hills. I saw villages in the valleys. I saw clouds. I saw the sun dropping and I saw night coming. I saw what was in front of me. I also saw my mother's body under the rubble. How dusty her coat was. The butterfly clip I took from her hair and placed in my pocket. Or did I? I couldn't remember. And my father, who was supposed to protect her. I saw him, too. The man who was tasked with catching bombs, holding back the walls of the buildings, and keeping the sky from falling using the hands he used to turn pages and wind his wristwatch every morning at the edge of his bed.

What did I see?

I saw what she saw. I saw what he saw. I answered Pietro, not for myself, but for them.

"Nothing," I said.

"What I see," Pietro said, his white hair blowing, "is how our sun, which is setting, is the same sun that is high in the sky over the great city of New York and may even be shining its morning light over the metropolis of Los Angeles. That is the city where they make movies for our entertainment, and they are doing so right *now* as though nothing is happening anywhere else. So I suppose what I am seeing—rather at odds with your 'nothing'—is that the world is round and yet very disconnected."

This annoyed me, even as a fourteen-year-old. It was pedantic and philosophical and had nothing to do with anything. I held my tongue, though, because I thought it was only another instance of his incessant talking. I didn't know he would remember this spot and this moment and everything about me much later.

"I have never been to those places, of course," he added, shaking off a chill. The orange sun was now so low on the horizon it was under the clouds and illuminated them from beneath, turning the sky to gold leaf and the heavens into a pool of flame. "But you will go," he said with prescience.

"Go where?"

"To America. To New York and Los Angeles. To the *future.*"

These were words without meaning to me.

"Come now," Pietro said, placing a hand on my shoulder. "You mentioned food."

THE DINING HALL WAS BEAUTIFUL. The ceilings were painted with the stories of Matthew, and the star over Bethlehem shone down on the monks, day and night. It smelled like stew. It seemed reasonable that a thousand years of stew made it smell like stew all the time.

Brother Tobias—Pietro's friend and confessor—was tall and lanky and when he spread his arms he made me think of the cranes I had seen flying over the Villa Borghese in Rome. I felt that he might be made of rubber and that he could be bent and contorted but never broken because his limbs contained no hard materials. His smile was wide and genuine, and I was surprised to see a look of affection and warmth on the face of a monk.

In Rome I was afraid of them. They had always seemed absorbed in their own world. They talked about esoterica if they spoke at all and they looked grave. If one of them looked at me it was always without a smile or a *buon giorno.* My father had told me to ignore them because they meant no harm and—while not friendly, it was true—their lives were harder than they looked.

"Because they wear black in the sun?"

"We can start there," he answered.

At the abbey, they generally ignored me. Pietro said this was because the abbot had told them to, and at the abbey, the abbot was like a king.

Brother Tobias, however, did the opposite. He welcomed Pietro and me at the door with wide and open arms and a call of "*Orso y Massimo!*"

It had been Tobias who had started referring to Pietro as the *orso polare,* or polar bear, of Montecassino. The moniker had spread. It was not a bad name. With Pietro's wide shoulders, swaying white hair, and glassy blue eyes he looked to have been born in a blizzard—his first breaths drawn from glacial mist, blue water running through his veins instead of red blood. I liked this version of him and I hoped nothing would prove it wrong.

Pietro received Tobias with a hug and they both patted my head. During September I had listened to Pietro regale Tobias with stories of history and philosophy and theology, and together they had tried to outdo each other on their knowledge of the monastery. I had thought Pietro was there to restore and protect the paintings. It hadn't occurred to me that

Pietro might have other, more strategic plans. It should have, though. His annoyance at the Germans and his concern with their plans should have been a clue; that and his constant hints, which I had ignored.

There were about thirty monks around us eating in silence.

Pietro had explained that the monks had taken vows of stability, and given the quiet, I presumed that Benedict must have considered talking a very destabilizing force in human relations.

He was probably right. Still, I liked the comforting sound of people talking.

We sat. We were presented with plates of broth from boiled chicken, a few bits of meat, a spoonful of rice, brown bread, and some greens that may or may not have been vegetables (Italy was starving to death and we were not so we did not discuss the food). Pietro did not ask Tobias about the Germans. Instead, he started talking about the Berbers and Jews and events from very long ago.

Evidently, the monks' vows of silence did not extend to guests. Or at least not to Pietro Houdini.

I had never heard of Berbers and had not given any thought to Jews. I knew about Italy's racial laws against the Jews because everyone talked about it but my parents had been dismissive and said Mussolini was putting on a show for Hitler. "Jewish Italians are Italians like us. We disagree about the legacy and meaning of Jesus, who was himself a Jew. These differences do not make people more or less Italian. They make them more or less Catholic, which they are not claiming to be. Don't listen to any of that," my father had said.

My father was dismissive because he thought that things that don't make sense don't matter, when in fact they are the things that matter most.

Pietro often talked about the distant past as though it were immediate and present because to him it was. To him, the past was alive in every word, every gesture, every argument, every premise that made it possible for two people to connect. If people could speak meaningfully about anything, he thought, it was because someone—at *some time*—had made it possible. Otherwise, like two dogs, we'd only interact but not communicate.

For these reasons and others he surely never explained, conversations were all of a piece and the time between "then" and "now" was but the space between two words because both ideas and feelings—feelings of love and hate, pride and humiliation—all last far longer than empires:

"Something is happening here at the abbey with those Germans, Tobias," he said with a mischievous smile. "And I think I know what that something is. I heard a rumor," he said, as though he'd overheard it at a café and the subject was titillating and urgent, "that the reason Spain and all of Christendom fell to the Moors between 711 and 1492 was because of the treachery of Count Giuliano."

Pietro sliced his chicken and speared a kidney bean to give it texture if not taste.

"Cervantes alludes to this in *Don Quixote*. As the story goes—and I don't know if it's true but consider the world turning in this way, dear Tobias— Don Rodrigo was the last of the Visigoth rulers of Spain and under his charge was the too-young and too-beautiful Florinda, daughter of Count Giuliano. Through surely no fault of her own," said Pietro, sipping from a mug of beer brewed somewhere downstairs, "she became pregnant by the treacherous Rodrigo. Giuliano was so outraged he betrayed Rodrigo to the Moors and with that betrayal went Spain and all of Christendom! This provoked the Battle of Guadalete in 711, which is when Granada fell and the faith was pushed back for eight hundred years. Of course, you should know all this, Brother Tobias," he said, drinking the rest of his beer in a mighty gulp, "because the story of Guadalete was written right here in the *Historia Langobardorum* by Paul the Deacon. And when I say 'right here,' I am not being figurative. It is said he wrote the history here at Montecassino, in the abbey, around the year of our Lord 790. Perhaps at this very table, my dear Tobias. Why not? Perhaps your own bottom is sitting on the same piece of wood."

"This is true?" Tobias asked.

This had nothing to do with anything as far as I could tell. Not Germans. Not fascists. Not the crates we had seen arrive from Naples. Not the frescos.

Not even the bad stew.

This was how the men talked:

"Everything I say is true as far as I know or care," Pietro continued. "Now, there is more: In my view, much of the Catholic hatred of the Jews began then. The Church had already been very hard on the people of its parent religion, so the Iberian Jews—Paul the Deacon tells us—allied with the Moors and provided warriors to fight alongside them. The Jews fought so well, in fact, and there were so many of them, that in the aftermath of the victory the Jews were commissioned to garrison Seville, Córdoba, and Toledo. Today, we push the Jews around or throw them out of Italy. Back then? They were Spain's masters. I think we're still holding a grudge. Despite this being Italy and not Spain. But, as you know, with Franco and Mussolini it's fascists all around now.

"Of course, the reason I tell you all this," Pietro said, nodding to himself as if in agreement with his own decision to get to the point, "is not because I wonder about the Moors but because I have to wonder why your fellow Catholics here seem so keen on cooperating with the Jew-hating Nazis who have rolled up in their fancy cars—one of them being a stolen Italian car. They're scheming, Tobias. I know it. You know it. And you know what it is whereas I don't." He leaned forward to whisper his question. "What is it? Is the abbot holding a very obscure Catholic grudge against the Jews, Brother Tobias? Are they toasting their demise in there? Because that is not what Jesus would be doing."

We were seated on long benches at the enormous wooden table. No one else was interested in our conversation, or at least they gave no outward proof of it. I remember looking at Pietro's hands then, his fingers knotted together. Every muscle and vein in its place. They were always cool to the touch and smooth as though he'd been sculpted.

"They are not talking about Jews," Tobias said. "The abbot is a compassionate and kind and—"

Pietro opened his palms, receptive to new information and a change of mind.

Tobias stopped defending the abbot and leaned closer.

"They are talking about art."

"Art. What about art?"

"The Germans want to take it away."

"Take what to where?" Pietro asked.

Tobias raised his eyebrows as though this were an answer.

"Who are the two German officers, Tobias?"

"There are three, actually. One is called König. I will return to him. The one with the sports car is called Max Becker. The other's name is Schlegel."

"Sound like a pastry."

"Close," Tobias said, leaning in conspiratorially, the pail tipping as Pietro had predicted. "He's an *oberstleutnant*—a lieutenant colonel—and he is, indeed, from Vienna. He's a Roman Catholic, which is unexpected. Yesterday, he drove up here on his own authority and asked to speak with Father Gregorio. They sat together drinking tea. He was very pleasant and respectful. He said that he was worried about the monastery and everything inside it and that—with the abbot's permission, of course—he would like to organize transport of all the art and manuscripts to the Vatican for safekeeping until the war is over."

Pietro was used to being the one who told the most outlandish stories.

"*All* the art and manuscripts?" Pietro asked.

"Yes."

"Do you have any idea how much art there is, and how many manuscripts there are?"

"More or less."

"Because I do. I've been reading the inventories and archives."

"I'm sure."

"You heard this with your own ears?" Pietro asked.

Brother Tobias had volunteered to help with the tea and, after leaving the room, had lingered in the adjoining one, where sound carried off the thousand-year-old walls as gently as a choirboy's voice lifted itself directly to the ears of God.

"You do realize," Pietro said, his eyes now looking very much like those of an *orso polare*, "that I am *maestro di restauro e conservazione* and confidant of the Vatican? How in the name of all that is holy are you having these conversations with Topfenstrudel Schlegel without me?"

"I . . . ah—"

"There are *seventy thousand manuscripts* in the monastery," Pietro said. "There are over one thousand, two hundred handwritten documents from scribes, many in the Beneventan script, a calligraphy that dominated for over five hundred years. It is *irreplaceable* to the history of the world. There are books and private collections, not to mention a music library built in the nineteenth century. Leaving all that aside—leaving aside the breviaries and their hand-painted pages," he said, "the illuminations, the original works brought here from Constantinople when Abbot Desiderius, of all people, imported their mosaic workers around 1070 AD—leaving *all* that aside, the abbey is now in possession of art objects from the National Roman Museum, galleries in Florence, the great cathedral of San Gennaro in Naples, and *all* the treasures of the Abbey of the Virgin near Mercogliano, including silver and gold and ancient gems from the Roman collection. And this is off the top of my head! I don't even know what else. All of that was moved *here* for safekeeping from the war. Why? Because even Charles de Bourbon—that asshole—spared Montecassino when he sacked Rome in 1527!"

"Well, yes, but—" began Brother Tobias, unsuccessfully.

"There are original works by Marcus Cicero, Horace, Virgil, Ovid, and Seneca," he said, tapping the table because his mouth was moving.

"We have cult objects. We have original relics of Benedict of Nursia. I have seen paintings by El Greco, Raphael, Tiziano, Van Dyck. More. Why do I know this? Because there's an inventory I was studying the other day and I have an excellent memory."

"Ah!" said Tobias, injecting himself into Pietro's rant. "The inventory. Yes, that reminds me. The third man is Truman König. He's the paper man. A real clipboard Nazi. He keeps asking about the paperwork that lists all the art and archives. He's looking for it."

"I'll bet he is."

"Where is it?"

"I might have it. I might not."

"Why?"

"I don't see any reason they should know what's here. I also like the idea of König becoming anxious. He is, after all, German. Incomplete lists make them twitch. Why would I make that stop?"

"You're going to need to share them with him at some point," Tobias said.

"Perhaps. But not until I make some corrections."

"Corrections?"

Pietro looked at Tobias with a stone face and Tobias took his meaning.

"You're going to take things off the inventory and hide them?"

Pietro wanted Tobias to come to the answer himself: "This monastery, right now, is one of the greatest repositories of culture on earth. It has no security, no particular expertise, no weapons, and no locks. The Germans are now politely asking for all of it while making it sound like they are doing *you* a favor: to protect it from the war *they* started. And you are inclined to agree, Brother Tobias?"

"Oberstleutnant Schlegel," Tobias said with emphasis, "says that it is all in danger. He is not König. He is soft-spoken and sounds reasonable. He is acting without military authority. He risks a court-martial for this. You must admit that with the Gustav Line traversing the abbey, the art *is* in danger here. It's why we invited you in the first place. To help us keep it safe. He seems quite sincere. And perhaps moving it is the way to keep it safe."

"He sincerely wants your loot," said Pietro.

"I think he wants to save it for posterity," said Brother Tobias.

"Aryan posterity. And König?"

"That is certainly *his* goal, but I don't think Becker and Schlegel feel that way. It changes nothing, though. The art and the treasure need to leave the abbey. We are duty bound to protect it."

"The monks are agreed?"

"No," Tobias admitted. "There is terrible disagreement."

"If what you are saying is true, Tobias, we are currently discussing the greatest art heist in the history of the world over very, very thin soup."

"Father Diamare is going to convene a monastic discussion about it," Tobias explained. "No one is taking this lightly, Maestro. I suspect the abbot will ask for your help too, because the journey by lorry to Rome will be bumpy and it's important that—"

Pietro raised a giant paw to make Tobias stop.

"Let me get this straight," he said, "because too much here is crooked and everyone has the same name. General Fridolin von Senger und Etterlin is in charge of this region. He is a Benedictine and a Roman Catholic and has assured the abbot that the Germans will not violate the abbey's neutrality. But the Austrian whose name is not Senger but *Schlegel* evidently doesn't agree because he secretly wants to move all the art on the pretext that it is dangerous here and the abbey itself is a likely target whatever Senger's assurance. How Schlegel might plan to do this we have no idea, but such is the impulse. So the first possibility is that General von Senger is lying and *does* plan to put troops here, which will ensure we are an Allied target, and that would make Schlegel's urgency logical because he wants to get the treasure out before we're destroyed and so is the art. Or else—and this is the second possibility—the general is telling the truth and thinks we'll all be safe and it is Schlegel who is lying so he can steal the art; perhaps he is stealing it for himself, because he is a mastermind, or he is in the service of Hitler under secret instructions by Göring or . . . we don't know. Alternatively—and this is hard for me to believe—the Germans are not coordinated, and Schlegel and von Senger, despite the similarity of their names, are two hands working separately. One way or another, the pieces don't fit, Tobias. And then we have Dr. Becker, who, I'm being led to believe, showed up in his own little red car with the same idea? You see all this, yes? The strangeness coupled to the unfettered audacity of it all? Dare I say it in this context but . . . yes . . . the chutzpah of these Germans."

"What do you think the answer is?" Tobias asked, his meal completely untouched.

"I think we face a mystery and also a problem. The mystery is unsolvable with the information we have. The *problem*, however, is nothing less than staying alive at the front line of the coming war and—if we're feeling magnanimous—trying to save a bit of the art of Western civilization for a post-Aryan rainy day. Here's what I'm sure about: if it's time for the art to leave, it's time for *us* to leave too."

"I can't leave," Tobias said, sitting back.

"This isn't a prison."

"I took a vow. I plan to stay here until I die."

Pietro raised his eyebrows.

"That's not what I meant. I meant . . . forever."

"Forever is over."

"I don't think it works like—"

"I don't know Schlegel's motives and perhaps I never will," Pietro continued. "Maybe he didn't ask for permission from Senger because he's a master thief setting himself up after the Nazis lose the war. Or maybe he thought it would contradict Senger and make him look bad, which is good because he hates Senger. Or maybe Senger really sent him because he's a good soldier and will keep his promise not to use the abbey as a fortress but . . . if the Allies don't believe it, and they absolutely will not, by the way . . . he knows they'll attack, so better to be safe than sorry with the art." Pietro paused but very briefly. His mind worked almost as fast as his mouth: "Or maybe Schlegel's acting first knowing Senger will come around if he can present a solution rather than a problem by securing the abbot's blessing first, which will make everyone look good. Actually, that's not a bad analysis. Anyway, he is going to need a lot of trucks. A *lot* of trucks. And they all belong to Senger because they really belong to Göring. All I know for sure is that Nazis like art more than people and generally speaking they hate art. If the art's going, so are we. We need to save who and what we can."

"Be careful, Maestro," Tobias whispered.

"Of what?"

"The Nazis, Pietro. König is looking for you."

THAT NIGHT PIETRO KNOCKED AT my door. I wasn't asleep. I was staring at the ceiling listening intently for the telltale vibrations of the plane that I was certain had followed me—like my own, personal storm cloud—from Rome. My hand was placed against the ancient stones so I could feel it before I could hear it.

I tried to picture *Pippo*, picture the monster that was following me. I wanted to give it form and convince myself it was made of the same earthly things that I saw around me—the metal and rivets, the stone, the wood. But the more I tried to picture *Pippo*, the more he slipped away. It was like trying to imagine evil. I think evil is something that assumes a form but does not have one itself. It was no surprise to me that *Pippo* could never be seen and only heard; the monster in the basement. The doom that follows us through the woods.

What would I have done if *Pippo* had found me?

I would have been terrified. Beyond that, I didn't know.

Like the monks who lived there, I had a small room to myself. It was a rectangle meant for little more than sleeping, prayer, and meditation. There was a single bed, a night table, a desk and chair, a lamp, a dresser with three drawers for my few personal effects, and a locker with no lock. It was clean and comfortable enough. The lights were out across the abbey in accordance with the blackout rules. There were curtains over the windows so the bombers could not check their locations against the terrain. I don't know how long I'd been lying like that when I heard the knock.

"Who is it?" I said, pulling the blanket up to my neck.

"Massimo," Pietro said. "It's me."

He opened the door, his eyes sparkling in the light of the candle he was holding. The lines in his face ran deeper.

"I've been thinking, Massimo," he said to me, seating himself in the chair, "that if Father Gregorio agrees to Schlegel's plan, there will be trucks going to Rome. I have no doubt the Nazis are going to steal much of the art. But I suspect some of it will surely get to its purported destination. I think this because Hitler and Göring love their propaganda and this will be a victory for them. Art is a visual thing. Monks, trucks, art, the Vatican. The journalists will not be able to stop themselves. I suspect we can get some of the monks on one of the trucks. The Nazis will not kill the monks. If I pack a truck with many monks and the most worthless art it will surely get to the Vatican. I would like to put you on that truck with Brother Tobias. North is the direction for you. Back to Rome. He can come back when you are safe. You know him now. He's a good man."

"No!" I said, almost shouting.

"Rome is safer than here and much safer than the south."

"No!"

His shoulders slumped. "Massimo, be reasonable. There is a war coming here and there are trucks driving away. The best way to stay out of the lion's mouth now is to ride on its back. Go with the Nazis. The Nazis will keep you safe. You hear the sentences this war is making me say? It is unnatural. Your parents must have had friends in Rome and I'm sure that—"

"I'm staying with you. We're going to Naples!"

"Naples is on the other side of a great wall of fire."

I crossed my arms.

"I will get you onto a truck," he said very gently. "I have money. A lot of money. I will give you more than you will need for years. You and the grown-ups in Rome can use it to keep yourselves safe. The Germans' plan can work to our advantage if we look with new eyes. Okay?"

It was not okay. I said that if I could not stay with Pietro Houdini I would kill myself.

Pietro, at the end of his capacity to lecture and plead, blew out the candle. He sat there in the chair as I waited for *Pippo* to arrive and Pietro to leave. Neither happened.

After minutes that felt like hours in that blackness I saw the shape of him nod. I could feel his resignation. He had reached an agreement with himself.

"*Allora,*" he said, preparing himself for the revelation to come. "I don't know if Schlegel is a thief or a saint or both. Or Becker. What I do know is that I am a thief and no saint. I steal time. I steal love, I steal promises and dreams, I steal entire lives, which is one of the reasons I need to get to Naples and return some of what I stole before it is too late. Around us are mankind's greatest treasures. I therefore think nothing of stealing the Nazis' own plan right out from under their arrogant noses. They want to steal the art from Montecassino? Fine. You and I are going to steal it from *them*. If the monks are prepared to give it away, why not give it to us? Ours will be the first art heist inside an art heist in the history of the world. But it is small consolation because in truth I would like to be the man to thwart their heist. I would like to concoct a brilliant plan to turn all those trucks to a new destination, where my team of fellow thieves are all dressed like German soldiers and the real ones off-load it all and put it on a ship of my people, and that ship then turns out to sea—the Adriatic, I think—and together, as seaborne pirates, we smuggle a thousand years of history to an island, the island where Odysseus was trapped by the nymph Calypso, and we wait out the war drinking nectar and eating ambrosia until we return to Rome at the end of it all as heroes! Heroes who will be met with accolades and awards, redemption and love, a few flittering eyelashes and a medal to hang around our necks. Champions of Italy! Of course we'd take a few choice objects. Nothing of immense historical or emotional value. Maybe some ancient gold coins that will be worth, at least, their weight and probably ten times that. We'll take some of the paintings too but my favorite kind: paintings no one knows exists because they are not catalogued and so won't be missed but will be cherished when they surface, when I donate them in my will to the museum. I am still trying to figure out which ones. I have to choose them wisely."

Pietro was starting to confuse me because his fantasy now started to sound like something he was actually doing.

"And hide them," he continued. "How does one hide a painting?" he muttered to himself. "Perhaps the gods will help. Not this one, necessarily. Not the one bleeding on the cross. No. Not the one behind that God either. I'm taking about the ones Homer described. The ones who stood on the beach at Troy. The ones who pick sides and change the winds. The ones who reward audacity. Those gods. The ones I understand."

I HAD THOUGHT THIS WAS more useless talk. I was wrong. Inside that speech was his past, our present, and my future.

* * *

"THERE IS A TRAGEDY CLOSING in on us, Massimo, and I have an idea. A crazy idea. If we do this together, Massimo—and I'm not promising yet that we will—we will need to leave the vestiges of our selves behind and become one with the war itself. We will need to lie, cheat, steal, fight, kill, and sin our way to Naples. We will hold our own lives as precious above all others. We will trust no one but each other, and we will try to remember that in this country, at this time, there is no way to tell friend from foe. You would prefer all of this rather than return to Rome?"

I said I would.

And I did. But I had no idea. If I had known, I would have trusted the Nazis, traveled with the monks, and faced my own grief.

But I was only a child.

PIETRO WOULD COME WAKE ME every morning. I was often up by the time he did though I would never leave the room, preferring instead to watch the light from the sun track across my wall as I tried not to think of home and the bedroom I once had and the stuffed bear that was still there, all alone, as I also tried to convince myself I'd outgrown both its affection for me and mine for it. Whenever I did think of home my thoughts soon slipped to my mother's arm sticking out of the rubble and my father's broken back, open eyes, and ticking watch.

PIETRO WAS LATE IN COMING that morning. He was usually there by the time the sunlight caught up to a little dimple on the wall that I'd made bigger since moving into that room in August. The walls were old and therefore brittle. It was tempting to put my fingernail in the little hole and make matters worse. I fought the impulse but was easily defeated.

By the time the dimple was cast in shadow again by the wandering sun I decided to get up and venture out on my own. I knew it was an important day because the monks had had their deliberations with the abbot about the Germans' proposition. Decisions had been made by night. With the sunrise came a new truth. Something was going to happen.

Pietro's room was nearby. I was starting to grow less fearful of the monks through familiarity and routine, and also because Tobias was kind, and if he was kind, it suggested the others might be too. Still, I preferred to avoid them. I did not trust worlds composed entirely of men.

I left the room barefoot and went searching for him. The stones in the hall were cold and the walls were thick. When I faced Pietro's door I paused for a moment, uncertain of what to do, because if he wasn't in there I'd be alone again and the idea scared me. It scared me so much in fact that I started knocking too hard and too fast. I didn't stop until he whipped open the door.

"Massimo," he said, as though recalling my existence out of a long-forgotten past; a former student from decades gone. "Oh. Yes, of course. Come in. I forgot about time."

I stepped inside a room that was all but identical to mine except for the smell of something burning. The window was wide open, which was necessary, because the ceiling was nearly obscured by a thick cloud of smoke rising up from a steel bucket beside his bed. On the desk was a lit candle.

"Sit down," he said, pointing to the edge of the bed as he sat himself at the desk.

"The Germans are back. Have you seen them?" he asked me.

I shook my head.

"Well, they're back." He picked up a pencil that was worn halfway down. I saw a small penknife on the desk he'd been using to whittle it to a point, over and over again. He'd been burning whatever he'd been writing.

A burnt offering to his preferred gods.

"The monks have a radio," Pietro said. "Vatican Radio reported that the Allies have been bombing Naples. They're going to invade the mainland. The telephone lines are down and . . . I don't know what's happening."

I had thought he was going to tell me about the monks' decision regarding the art, not this. I did not have to wait long for the stories to align.

"My wife's name is Oriana. She is younger than me. She's only forty-eight whereas I am fifty-seven. Forty-eight may sound ancient to you, but she looks thirty-five, which is indistinguishable from twenty-nine except there is knowledge and experience in a thirty-five-year-old woman's face that the porcelain perfection of the twenty-nine-year-old lacks because it isn't there. Oriana is a thinker, a fighter, a lover—not that this is any of your business and you are too young to hear it, but it must be said and so I am saying it."

Pietro rolled the pencil back and forth very slowly on the desk. Because it was not round but octagonal, it created a slow beat like a third heart in the room as he spoke.

The smoke was visible like a cloud at eye level. Inside it were the plans to . . . something . . . that he had burned up and I was now breathing in. He had either burned them because they were failures or else because they'd been perfect and he didn't want anyone to see them. Even after breathing them in I couldn't tell which was true.

"Oriana did not like fascism. And she did not like Il Duce. She was not quiet about either of these facts, especially after I made some poor decisions that redirected her energies from saving us as a couple and toward saving Italy itself, which she took to be the easier of the two tasks. For all this I only have myself to blame. Perhaps someday I will find the courage or the desperation to tell you about that but not yet. So: against my preferences, and at first, she became a member of Giustizia e Libertà. Later, when it was outlawed, she continued her often subtle resistance in other ways including journalism about the Spanish Civil War and the dangers of Franco. To be against Franco was to be against Hitler and also Mussolini. It was a delicate position. She was called a Communist because no one is ever called a democrat when resisting fascists, which is, if anyone cares, the tragedy of our century. In fact she was no lover of Stalin or Moscow. Rather, Oriana was a woman who believed in the human heart, in love, in kindness, in decency, in freedom of speech, in faith, and in the creative genius of our species. She would not be silent in demanding it all because for her it was all of a piece, and this humanist agenda is the *true* revolutionary agenda and humanity's only hope. Leaving aside her beauty, her wit, her patience, I married her because she was a woman who burned with her own inner passions and fueled them with her own thoughts. She was every truth about women that fascists simply can't believe. She cut through history the way a mighty ship cuts through the surf. I picture her chest breaking the thick of the storm.

"As it happens—and you might as well learn this now—having opinions gets you into trouble. In fact, having desires of any kind gets you into trouble, which is why life itself is troublesome, but opinions are less tolerated than desires because there is, ultimately, no excuse for them. Before the police came to take her away, we spoke quickly. We knew they took people like her to the islands south of Sicily. We knew that when the Allies arrived, they would free them.

"If she has not been killed, Massimo, she will be free right now. Either way, the imprisonment of her body and mind is surely over. I cannot impose on you the extent to which I need to see her again or else die trying. Before she was captured we chose Naples as our meeting place. It is a spot we both know well. A building, a café, a table inside the galleria. We said we would return every Thursday afternoon until contact was made or we died there sipping our last vermouths. Now that you and I are agreed on our shared destination you deserve to know why I'm going. So there it is. For me this is a holy mission. It is a quest for love, even if that love is unrequited. And whenever men are set on a holy mission, the Fates—far older than any Christian or Jewish God—take pity on the pilgrim and they lay solutions at his feet. I believe the Fates have put the Germans here to enact some bold and mystical plan."

"I'm not going north in the trucks," I said, misunderstanding him.

"No. It is not their trucks that interest me anymore. It is their slavish trust in paperwork that has my mind working. I hate everything about the Nazis, Massimo, except for one thing: their predictability."

Pietro waved his hand through the dissipating smoke. "These are my plans. No, no, it's not a metaphor. Sometimes the act of writing things down helps commit them to memory. I did and then burned them immediately." He brushed ash from his hands and wiped the rest on his trousers. "It will involve me painting. An old hobby that I took up again with zeal about six years ago. This plan of mine owes a great deal to the Nazis, in fact. You see, there was once a grand exhibition called *Degenerate Art*," he said. "*Die ausstellung Entartete Kunst* and I was there! With Oriana. It was put up by Der Führer himself in the latter half of 1937. There was no war yet, of course, just lots and lots of Nazis. Of course, who was I to complain, as it was our very own Duce who coined the term 'fascist'? Anyway . . . off we went, curious and adventurous. Who didn't want to see all the world's degenerate art in one place? It was very convenient!

"The trains between Bologna and Munich are fabulous. You pass through the Italian Alps into Ticino, where the Swiss speak Italian. From there, on to Interlaken in the Bernese Oberland, where the majesty of the scenery is beyond the need for words, and from there—on to Munich, which is filled with words . . . though for a decade all placed in the wrong order. It's a long journey, but the kind of train journey that stirs the imagination. Anyway, onward we went to very neat and tidy if philosophically deranged Munich.

"This was an exhibit of over *half a million works of art* confiscated by the Nazis as part of their merciless war on everything that insulted the 'German feeling'—whatever that is—and by failing to conform to whatever it was Hitler considered good about his *own* work. At least that's my theory. I've heard people say Hitler was a failed artist and his work was no good. It's true he didn't get into the school he wanted, but his stuff is perfectly serviceable, actually. It's just devoid of humanity. Of empathy. Of life. It's still and unyielding. They're exercises rather than achievements. Anyway, I think it was a childish act of revenge. Picasso, Chagall, Kandinsky . . . all degenerate in his eyes and therefore they should be in everyone else's. His list of degenerates was endless. And their value was priceless. It was that exhibit that inspired me and Oriana to begin painting again!

Our feeling was, if you aspire to degenerate art you might achieve your goals, and I'm nothing if not tenacious. And now here we are. Hitler's hatred and pettiness inspired love and dedication. The Nazis' plan to steal Montecassino's art gave us the idea of stealing it from them. And how will I hide it? By painting over it! You see how it works? The pieces of our lives are all connected, Massimo. In this, I *know* the Fates are with me. I *know* we are part of something bigger. But are they with *you*? Are you caught up in something bigger than yourself? I think you are. I feel it. You are the key to the entire story.

"And now, my dear friend, your brushes will finally need proper washing. I am going to work fast and in watercolor, which we miraculously have here. I found them already. We have much to do and choices to make before this Truman König becomes a problem for us. Step one is finding the *right* paintings we want to steal. This . . . is going to take some doing. But I think they will speak to us, and when they do, we will have to open our hearts to hear what they are saying. The paintings we steal will be divinely inspired, dear Massimo. They will be our guide. Somehow—and I don't know how—we will have to put our trust in them."

FOR THE NEXT SIX HOURS, Pietro allowed me to join in his rummaging through the art of the abbey of Montecassino. This was the sort of activity he used to do on his own, but now we were thieves sharing a destiny and so I was a part of it. We spent most of our time in an archive room to the west of the basilica. It had ten-meter vaulted ceilings and enormous wooden shelves and cabinets that reached so high we needed to use ladders. There were paintings inside the cabinets; many were framed but some stacked. Pietro frowned and occasionally lectured about this because he was displeased with the monks' care of the world's immortal remains.

It was around this time I started to suspect he was lying about being a confidant of the Vatican. I was too naive to be political but it occurred to me that usually you don't complain so much about your friends.

We both sneezed constantly. Pietro liked to swear. It started in Italian. Moved to English, and finally—after about forty sneezes—moved on to German. I did not understand the swearing in German. But it was definitely the most elaborate and used the most consonants. If I didn't know better, I'd have sworn he was threatening the dust and trying to scare it off.

The lighting inside was poor because most of the bulbs were burned out and had not been replaced on account of shortages and rationing. We relied on the natural light coming from the tall, narrow windows to find . . . whatever it was Pietro was looking for.

"What *are* we looking for?" I finally asked him after an hour of watching him search. I had been assigned to hold a mirror and we used it to reflect the sunlight into the area he was searching. It helped, but the mirror was large and encased in a wooden frame, so it was heavy. I often had to hold it at awkward angles and I found the job tiring.

"We're looking for works of art that meet certain specified criteria. And of course we need some of the gold. But that's easy. That's in the box over there."

I wasn't interested in the gold. I wanted to know what "criteria" meant and I said so.

"It means we're looking for a few items of immense value that the Nazis might not notice are missing; that I can disguise in quite an ingenious manner, as I alluded to in my chambers and if I do say so myself; and if there are any records of the paintings I need to be able to erase them from the inventory papers. In mathematics, this is called a 'set problem.' We are looking for the set of paintings that meet all criteria. It's a very small set among a very large archive and the task needs to be achieved in a very short period of time because Nazis are slithering through the halls of the abbey. I need to work hard and get very lucky."

"Papers?"

"The inventory papers are supposed to list what's stored here at Montecassino. They probably don't. Still, the Germans will use those as a kind of checklist while they rush to fill their trucks. I don't want the Nazis to know what's here; otherwise they'll know what's missing because, for all their faults, they're rather good at deduction. My plan is to take these inventory papers"—he pointed vaguely toward a table near the end of the room—"and then use the relevant chemicals to ruin the bottom edges such that the last three to five items there will be erased and therefore protected from the Germans."

He was on the fourth rung of the ladder with his head tilted, looking at the paintings that were stacked like framed maps in the cabinet. He continued to flip through them studying the archives for the ones that corresponded to those listed at the bottoms of the pages. I continued to point the sun in his direction.

"I do look forward to seeing König's face when he sees all that."

I saw Pietro smile to himself.

"Oh, he'll know the papers were destroyed on purpose but what can he do? Nothing. Who can he blame? No one. Where else will he have to look? Nowhere. You see, the reason paper deteriorates is because acids from inside and outside the paper break apart the glucose chains in what's called acid hydrolysis, which in turn creates more acids and . . . it's a vicious circle. Newer paper is often worse quality than paper from hundreds of years ago, so it's little surprise that newer papers will have more deterioration. The good news is that most of the inventory lists are rather recent. Chemistry is a very handy science, Massimo. Don't let anyone tell you otherwise. Ah, here's the last one!"

Given how much there was to explore and how specific Pietro's criteria, it was nearly miraculous that he found any works of art that fit them at all. But there they were. After six hours, four hundred sneezes, and a trilingual epic poem of epithets against the Germans, Pietro Houdini had his paintings, paintings that seemed to have been willed into our hands so that we might live more intensely and find solutions in the tempest to come.

"These are good. These will do nicely," Pietro said, climbing down from the ladder and placing the three framed paintings against two long tables so we could stand back and examine them. "Tiziano. All three. That one is *Perseus and Andromeda*. The middle is *Venus and Adonis*. And the last is the saddest of them all, I think. *Diana and Actaeon*. The three that are missing from the set are the *Danaë*, *Diana and Callisto*, and of course *The Rape of Europa*, where Zeus turns into a bull and steals the poor princess away and takes her to Crete, where she gives birth to Minos and, from Minos, all of Western civilization. This is our story. Awful, no? I have never been surprised at your choice to become Massimo. Your logic is clear but . . . as I suspect you'll find . . . also very situational. Anyway. Tiziano. Have you heard of him?"

Had I? I had no idea. I was fourteen and had visited a thousand museums and seen a million paintings in Rome, and those of a period all looked the same.

"They all look the same," I said.

"How do you mean?"

"The colors are always dark and the babies are fat."

"Ah, the cherubs. That's not very charitable. Try 'corpulent,'" he said. "It's a nicer word. "Or 'succulent' if you're a cannibal."

"No," I said, answering Pietro's actual question. "I've never heard of him." I found that freeing Pietro to talk was always easier than trying to restrain him.

"Never heard of him. That's depressing. Well, I won't bore you at length, but briefly and by way of introduction: Tiziano was a Venetian painter at the beginning and middle of the 1500s when Venice was perfect," Pietro said, putting his hands in his pockets and indicating the paintings with his chin. "At one point, the young King Philip the Second of Spain commissioned him to create six paintings. Ovid had a long poem called *Metamorphoses* and Tiziano wanted to capture some of that magic.

All six paintings are inspired by him and the Greek and Roman myths about transformation. Not all of them good, I should add.

"King Philip was a young man in his twenties and had a reputation as a womanizer. Tiziano was one of the greatest painters ever born to create images of female flesh and bodies and movement. He luxuriated in painting the female shape and raised it to something sublime and beloved. He moved the painting of his era from lines and balanced compositions to color and drama and asymmetry. Some say he painted directly from the bodies of Venetian courtesans. And some say that Philip would stare at these erotic paintings only in private."

I made a face at this.

"Maybe that was a bit too far. Anyway. As lush and warm and sensual as they are, they are not love scenes in any proper sense. In these stories there was no communion. No choice. No shared exaltation. No promise of mutual joy. They were stories about flesh and power and the unfairness of the gods and the unfairness they too suffer. I fear what these pictures portend for us but I feel they are the right ones."

I looked at the pictures and didn't understand them. *Perseus and Andromeda* showed a man flying through the air with a sword, about to attack a sea monster to save a girl who was chained to the rocks. *Venus and Adonis* presented a fat pink woman trying to keep a hunter from running away for some reason. *Diana and Actaeon* didn't make any sense at all. A handsome young man pulled aside a red curtain in the middle of a forest to reveal a bathing scene with a bunch of girls.

They were okay, I guessed.

I'd seen better.

"Because they are studies that the master used to prepare the final versions, they reveal to us early elements that might never have finally appeared in the finished pieces. I'd have to compare them to know. If we did compare them, we could witness the decisions Tiziano made and, if we can become one with his mind, possibly understand those choices and therefore how history was made. To me, looking at these paintings—which I'm certain no one knows exist but us—is like reading Marcus Aurelius's *Meditations*. You've heard of those?"

I didn't even bother to answer.

"This is the distinct violence of the fascist educational system. They steal the pieces from Roman culture they like and casually discard the rest. But removing colors from a painting is to ruin the painting. It is to undermine it. The *Meditations* are the thoughts of a Roman emperor that were never intended for publication. The term 'diary' is anachronistic but . . . it was a diary. In that book is honesty. Truth. Sincerity. Formative thinking. A touch of trepidation. A lot of hubris. A look inside the life and mind of a great man written in private. That's what we see here in Tiziano's studies if you know how to see. These versions are, if anything, even more erotic than the final ones, which I find exciting. They are more . . . intimate. For now, dear Massimo, it is enough for you to know this: these three paintings are formative and priceless. And now . . . they belong to us because we're going to steal them. In fact, consider them stolen. Having been stolen, they have also been saved because these are not the sort of thing you hand over to someone like Truman König."

We emerged from the stifling archives in the mid-afternoon with our three finds, which Pietro had removed from their wooden frames, carefully rolled up, and then placed inside three cardboard tubes. Outside the air smelled sweet, free of dust and history. There was a breeze. I closed my eyes and let the wind blow around me to remove the stagnation of the centuries from my hair and clothing and spirit. Pietro, for his part, extracted a cigarette from his pocket and lit it using a soldier's trench lighter.

When the *orso polare* breathed out it looked like his frosty breath rather than smoke.

There were several Germans milling around in the cloister smoking and they paid no attention to us. Pietro walked us out of the PAX exit, where we both saw that Schlegel's Mercedes was parked. Pietro flicked his cigarette away and said, "Walk with me, Massimo."

We crossed the cobblestone mosaic patio in front of the entrance and loitered by the trees and away from ears. "You have a new assignment," I was told. "Your time holding the mirror and listening to my rants has come to an end. Now it becomes more challenging because it involves other people."

He walked me several hundred meters down the road and stopped us on the hillside by a copse of pines.

"This is what you are going to do. It is important and I cannot do it myself as I have other matters to deal with. Have you ever built a house of cards? Yes? Then you know that the first cards need to be placed very carefully and if they are not secure all of it will collapse, hence the metaphor. We are about to set up the first cards. I am going to ask you to do something that might seem a bit mad, but I strongly suspect—since your face is known here—it is not dangerous and will draw the least suspicion. Also, even children must play a part in the drama of Europe's future, I regret to say. So: I need you to walk into the hills beyond the herb gardens and the flowers and the livestock and find me a solitary German soldier manning a defensive position. It is quiet now, so he will not be agitated. You must find me one who is alone. If he asks what you are doing, say you live in the abbey. You are curious and want to know what's happening. You like taking walks. You're a child and one he has perhaps seen. You don't need complex reasons for your actions. If he wants to talk . . . talk. Where are you from? What do you eat in the army? Keep the topics pointless.

"You do speak some English, don't you, Massimo? Some of the Germans speak English. The more educated they are, the more English they speak."

"A little," I said. It was almost true.

"When you find this German, you say that your uncle speaks German and wants to talk to him. That's me, in case you aren't paying attention. Afterward, you come back to me. He and I will need to have a talk."

Pietro turned to leave me there but I grasped his arm. "What do you want from this German?"

He hesitated, not because he didn't know the answer but because he clearly couldn't decide whether to tell me. After a pause he said, quite simply, "A gun. I want a gun. There are three ways to get a gun in a war. You can find one. Someone can give you one. Or you can take one. The first is unlikely before the fighting and the third is very dangerous. I'm therefore going for option two and I'm hoping to buy one. Naples is far. It is very unlikely we can get there without shooting someone. So . . . a gun."

Done, he walked back up the hill to the abbey without ever turning back to me.

ALONE, I LOOKED OUT AT the surrounding hills. I knew there were Germans. Everyone did. The problem was, they scared me. The Americans did too, but only in an abstract way. The Americans were the men on propaganda posters threatening Italian women. I remember one with an airplane above an evil American with a flag for a scarf who was standing over the dead body of a child who was maybe three years old. It read, "*i delitti inumani dei 'gangsters piloti' radiano per sempre gli stati uniti dal consorzio civile*"—"inhuman crimes of 'gangster pilots' forever remove the United States from civil society." But I had never actually seen these men. What I had seen were German soldiers. I had heard their language. I had heard the stories and I remembered what my parents had taught me about Hitler and the Nazis. They were not abstract to me. They were over there, on that hill. After staring off into the distance for five minutes—which may have been a small lifetime—I decided that if Pietro wanted a gun there was no reason I couldn't get one from an Italian. After all, I spoke Italian.

THE VILLAGE OF CASSINO WAS an eight-kilometer walk down a thin mountain road of switchbacks—the same road we climbed to reach the abbey. It sat on the valley floor under the shadows of the triangular hills that surrounded it, and—at the time—under the majestic eye of the monastery, which seemed to watch over it and define its character.

It was a town like so many others. Most of the buildings in the center were erected in the 1800s and only a few stories high. There was an Esso gas station on the corner where the proprietor had placed two large white pots for seasonal plants. The streets were wide and in the late-summer mornings the Italians drew all the curtains in all the balcony doors to keep the interiors cool.

Long before the front line came this far north, Cassino was already a ghost town. The men had all gone off to fight and the old seldom ventured out. The women did everything and the children—I knew firsthand—ran feral in the streets because school was irregular and felt pointless in the face of national catastrophe and the absence of a future. They had been raised to respect men and men only, and with no men left behind it was a place without discipline.

I sensed, from the moment I entered the town, I had made a mistake. Pietro had given me a simple assignment: find a nonthreatening, solitary German and report back so he could talk to the man later. Standing alone and looking around the village I realized I had made myself unnecessarily vulnerable and taken on a task without direction. I didn't even know for certain why I was there. Had it been fear of the Germans? Or did I have a desire to impress Pietro? Or had the notion of finding a gun myself and walking these streets and maybe encountering the boys who had beaten me held a kind of perverse attraction?

Honestly, what would I have done? Shot four children in the chest?

I stopped in the middle of the street, which had no cars, feeling both useless and far from my room at the abbey. I also felt thirsty and hungry because almost ten kilometers in the hot Italian sun is enough to wilt a spine. I found a café on the left side of the street and walked inside. It was cooler in there and dark. I was surprised to smell coffee because Pietro had said only soldiers had coffee. But that was when I saw the two German officers at a back table, their shirts open, and each with a coffee and liquor. They looked at me and their eyes sized me up.

"What do you want?" one of them said to me in Italian words and a Nazi accent.

"My aunt," I said, before realizing I had said anything.

He had a pistol on his belt and silver insignia on his shoulders. I didn't know the ranks at the time. Still: the colors and shapes of their badges and clothes burned into my mind because we remember what we fear.

He nodded his head toward the staircase, uninterested.

I was trapped in my lie. I walked to the staircase without a plan and started mounting it not knowing what was upstairs, knowing only that I was moving farther from the exit. I could have run for the door but it felt impossible. I sensed they would have chased me. Or shot me for sport. These men had been allies to Italy so recently but were now our occupiers. They had turned on us with no hesitation or remorse. It was beyond our understanding and made our hatred that much deeper.

* * *

THERE WAS NO FIGHTING IN Cassino, though. The town was quiet and the Germans sipped glasses of local *amari* beside the last of their espressos.

THE STAIRS WERE OLD, WOODEN, and worn. I trotted up and turned the corner to the left, where I found a closed door. I was tempted to stand there for a few minutes in complete silence, pretend I'd spoken to my aunt, and then race back down the stairs and bolt outside. Surely the soldiers wouldn't have cared about my business at that point.

I had resigned myself to this plan when the door opened.

A woman in her thirties stood over me. She had thick black hair, deep brown eyes, and a face that might have been beautiful once if the world had not extracted her happiness from her like a scent from a flower. She looked at me first with alarm but then, on looking closer, she seemed to see something else in me; something the soldiers had missed in their arrogance and haste.

"Who are you? There's nothing for you here."

I looked down the stairs to where the men sat and spoke German to each other.

"Please," I whispered, turning back at her.

Refusing me might have created a scene and so she let me in and closed the door behind her.

The bedroom was decorated simply. A red bedspread beside a lamp. A boy of about ten years old was sitting there reading a ripped newspaper and beside him—sprawled out—was a girl of seven or eight. She was holding court with four stuffed animals and, as best as I could tell, she was explaining to them that there was no tea left but there was beer. I found this odd but said nothing.

When the door was closed she tore into me quietly: "Who the hell are you? You have no right to be here. I am not looking after some orphan girl. Whatever brought you—"

"Boy," I said, interrupting.

"'Boy' . . . what?"

"I'm a boy."

"I'm a dolphin."

"I'm a boy," I said again.

The woman sighed and her shoulders sank. Whatever bravado had inflated her shape was now released. Her frame collapsed into the moment. "You need a haircut and new clothes if being a boy is your primary defense," she concluded.

I didn't care about those things. I was on a mission from Pietro Houdini: "I need a gun," I whispered.

The woman stared at me without emotion for long enough that my thoughts actually did turn to what she'd said.

I had forgotten that my hair was growing, and Pietro never commented on my appearance. I had bound my small breasts close to my body using strips from bedsheets and I was dressed in trousers, a shirt, and Italian army boots. But the softness of me—of my neck and shoulders, my thin wrists and high cheekbones, my lips and my eyes—was a permanent betrayal. I stood there in the middle of a war believing that words alone could define the truth and serve as a defense. It had never occurred to me that my new identity might be a negotiated thing.

"A gun and a haircut," I said, accepting her point.

"And how, exactly, would you pay for either?"

"Gold," I said to the woman, thinking about my morning with the paintings.

"Gold," she repeated. "And where is this gold?"

I walked to the window and extended my arm as far as it would go: "There," I said, pointing to the abbey of Montecassino.

WEARING NEW CLOTHES, WITH A backpack filled with more, and a haircut that helped, I was back at the monastery, passing through the main gate. The Mercedes was gone and most of the monks were in the church for Compline prayer. I knew Pietro wouldn't be there but I wasn't sure where to find him.

Back in my room, I studied my new face in the tiny mirror. The Italian field jacket that formerly belonged to Bella's missing husband was too big on my shoulders. I liked the way it hung around me, though; I felt as though it were hugging me and protecting me. I looked at my new haircut and agreed that the illusion was more convincing. I didn't feel bigger or stronger but I did feel, somehow, invisible. I felt that I would walk around and be noticed but not seen. Not singled out for attention. I liked the feeling. I liked being Massimo.

With a new look and a new plan in my head, I turned back to the door and noticed the message tacked to the wood on the inside.

"Meet me in the third vault."

It was Pietro's handwriting; we had numbered the rooms and chambers in the abbey because I had proved incapable of memorizing their proper names, which were in either Gibberish or Latin, a distinction lost on me.

Compline—or eighth prayer—takes place at seven o'clock in the evening and generally the monks slept after that; they had to be up for

68

the Matins prayer at two in the morning. After Matins came Lauds, or the dawn prayer, at five. Luckily, neither Pietro nor I were expected to keep such hours and the result of these parallel schedules was that the nights at the monastery—between seven in the evening and two in the morning—belonged to us. These were the hours we looked for things to steal, hatched our plans, and spoke most freely. They were also the hours when spying eyes were easiest to spot and footsteps could be heard far off, tapping through the stone corridors.

I skipped down the familiar staircase, buoyed by the solution I had found for the problem Pietro had confided in me, so when I entered the room and found him painting—with actual paint and using my perfectly cleaned brushes—I was momentarily stunned, but I was not nearly as surprised as when he turned to look at me, studied me up and down, and then became more angry than I had ever seen him.

"You fool!" he yelled, the shout echoing off the walls and booming into my ears. "Where the hell have you been? You've been gone all day! Look at yourself! You were given one small task. Look for a German in places I knew Germans would be! An hour's activity, two at the most. Now? Eight hours you're missing! Eight hours unreachable. Was it eight hours? I lost track! I don't even know! Do you have any idea what could happen to a child in a space of time that long? Do you? You have no idea. Your kidneys could have been sold to the Turks by now! And who were you with? Who turned you into a shrunken Italian soldier? Hmm? How in the name of all the saints did you get a haircut and go shopping? Did you even *find* a German?"

Then he had a deeper idea.

"Did you even *look* for a German?"

He tossed his paintbrush into the water, and when he did I caught a glimpse of what he was doing. He was painting a mountain scene—a bit like the view from the cloister—directly on *top* of an ugly painting I'd never seen before. I couldn't understand why he would paint on another painting rather than use the back of the canvas, which was completely blank.

He exhaled and shook his head without gesturing toward me.

"Where?" he said. "Just tell me."

"The village."

"Cassino."

"Yes."

"And you went there because . . . why?"

"They speak Italian."

"Uh-huh. You have heard the story of the fool who went looking for his keys beneath the streetlamp? A man finds him and says, 'What did you lose, friend?' and he says, 'My keys.' 'Right here, below the lamp?' the man asks. 'No, over there by the bench.' 'So why are you looking here?' the man asks. And the fool answers, 'Because this is where the light is.'"

"There are Germans everywhere," I said in my defense.

"How many Germans did you find?"

"Two. Officers. In a café."

"I told you to find one. Alone. Who ideally wasn't an officer but some kid who wanted to make a few lira selling a weapon he didn't need. Did they cut your hair?"

"No. The woman who owns the café cut my hair and gave me some old clothes. She will get us a gun. Two guns."

"Will she. And where are these guns?"

"On the belts of the officers."

Pietro froze.

I watched him for a long time. I think it was only the spark of a new idea that reanimated him.

"And Lady Macbeth's plan is . . . what?"

"We will poison them and then take their guns," I said as though it were a fact. "She will keep one and we will keep the other. We will pay her with gold."

Pietro rinsed his paintbrush in the water and then dried it on the leg of his trousers. With nothing else to do and no further way to avoid the conversation he sank lower into his stool.

I seemed to be having this effect on people.

He looked me over even more closely that time. He wasn't looking at the hair or the new jacket, but into my soul. I don't know what he saw.

"Let's hear it," he said.

For the next twenty minutes I spelled out my ideas with the clarity of a bank robber.

MY PLAN WAS UNCHARACTERISTICALLY DIABOLICAL. Not that I truly understood what I was proposing. There is a difference between imagining something and actually experiencing it. What I was doing was concocting a story the way that Pietro strung sentences and ideas together. The impact, the reality, the emotion, the consequences—these did not exist for me. My plan was a solution to a puzzle and nothing more, a way to take the guns away from the men who scared me. I was comfortable with this because I didn't want to be scared anymore. I hated those who scared me and I wanted power over them.

This was the way Mussolini had taught me to feel and these were the kinds of actions that Italian culture validated.

For boys.

"YOU ARE A CHEMIST," I explained. "You will brew a poison and I will give it to the *signora*. She will put it into the *amari*, where it will dissolve with the alcohol. The Germans know that good alcohol is hard to find now, so if it tastes strange they will not care and drink it anyway. She will use extra sugar, which she has hidden away, and they will drink it all. And then they will die and we will take their guns."

"Mm," he said. "And they will obediently drop dead, will they? Like in the crime movies?"

I had never seen a crime movie.

"Yes," I said.

"And when there are two dead German officers on the floor of this café, what will happen next?"

"We take the guns and pay her the gold."

"Yes, yes, but . . . the dead soldiers?"

I didn't understand the question. What did it matter what happened to the dead men? They were dead. We had the guns. It was over, wasn't it?

He could see my confusion. He paused to think more about what I said because this had not been his plan. His plan had been to receive a gun given willingly. His plan had no dead bodies. My plan was different. For him to choose mine, he needed a reason.

"Okay, let's skip that for a moment," he said. "How big are these men? Are they my size?"

I had thought he was trying to measure the amount of poison we would need. He wasn't. He was several steps ahead of that, like a chess master.

"They were sitting but one had shoulders like yours. He was younger. The other was skinny."

"The big one," he said. "With the shoulders. Did he have a gray jacket?"

"Yes, Maestro."

"Right. Well. On his shoulders there must have been straps. Try to remember, Massimo. The straps indicate rank. Try to remember what you saw."

I remembered them well. "The skinny one had red straps with gold diamonds and the number eight."

Pietro shook his head. Whatever that meant, it wasn't ideal. I wanted to please him, though. I wanted the Fates to work their magic and prove they were with me too: "The big one, though, had two pips and no number."

"No number?" he said, his voice rising slightly. "That's a captain without designating the division. That means more flexibility for us. Same size as me? More or less?"

I shrugged.

"When do these men go to the café?" he asked.

"Almost every day."

"How do you know this?"

"She said they never leave."

"This woman—the proprietor. How old is she?"

I said I didn't know. But her two children were younger than me.

"Is she attractive?"

I said she looked sad.

He accepted this as an answer.

His mind was doing math—building a formula—that my inexperience prevented me from performing. He was thinking about who they were, what they were doing there, how often they came, what kind of expectations they would have, how guarded they would be when faced with change, when being handed a drink, when starting to die.

Afterward: what to do with the bodies. And what of the woman and children? She lived there. How was that supposed to work?

"This was her idea, I suppose?" he concluded.

"Yes." It was partly true.

"Why do you want to kill these men?" he asked me. "You barely know that woman. You don't know those men at all. Now you're a killer?"

I didn't answer. What I did not feel was any sense of remorse at my decision or even trepidation. To me, pressing forward no matter the cost felt right. Even reasonable. This was how I would get to my family in

Naples and how Pietro Houdini would see his beloved wife, Oriana, who he said was waiting for him at a café.

Which didn't exactly explain why he wanted to steal the art from the Nazis who were stealing it from the monks, but I didn't mind. I assumed everything would become clear in time. What I knew was this: "We are on a quest of love," I said. "They are not."

Did this convince him to take this riskier path? All I know is he waited a long time before saying, "All right, We'll do it your way."

WE NEEDED GOLD AND WE needed poison. Luckily, we were in a Benedictine abbey.

Brother Tobias often worked in the kitchen and that meant he spent considerable time in the herbarium, in the libraries, and growing plants in the surrounding hills. It was Tobias who had told Pietro about the plants that grew around the abbey and why there was such variation. Over the centuries—explained Tobias to Pietro, and now Pietro to me—the abbey had been a partner in trade with other monasteries and institutions of learning. Alchemy had given way to chemistry only a few hundred years ago. Back then and to my young mind, several centuries had seemed a long time, but according to Pietro even Sir Isaac Newton had dedicated much of his life to alchemy and the occult.

Pietro told me about this as we snuck outside into the dark, keeping our voices very low so that the monks and God and the Nazis wouldn't be able to hear us: all of whom were very close.

"I read it in the newspaper last year," Pietro whispered as we crossed through the cloister under a starlit sky toward the fields beyond. The stars were very bright because the villages were all blacked out. The Germans in the woods—like the crickets—were silent. Everyone was very disciplined. The feeling of the night was nothing like peace.

"This way," he said.

On his shoulder was a bag and in his hand was an Italian military flashlight with a small wire handle. It swung from his fingers like a lantern.

"What I read was that John Maynard Keynes bought a collection of Isaac Newton's papers on auction." We walked down a path I hadn't noticed before. It led into the southern-facing hills that had been terraced into small fields. "Most of the papers turned out to be studies of the occult. You'd think most of it would be about science but no. Superstition, alchemy, magic, wishful thinking. Brilliant speculations, all of them, but not science. The man wanted to turn lead into gold like everyone else. But we are not out here for the gold at the moment. That's inside. What we need is poison."

His gold story finished, he turned his encyclopedic knowledge of trivia to facts about killing people:

"Over the centuries, a vast number of herbs of medicinal value passed through here and were often planted because the healing arts were still only arts then, not a science. As a chemist I took classes on pharmaceuticals and as students we used to talk about poisons and explosives and love potions. This was the way of universities in my day. I suspect it will never change. What was I saying? Oh yes, the abbey still has many seeds and samples. But more important, much of it still grows here on the hills. One of those plants that is very easy to identify is called monkshood. Yes, yes, the irony. It's also called wolfsbane. You know it?"

I shook my head. I knew nothing. Not the people he mentioned, not alchemy, not plants. I would, however, remember it all:

"I come here with Tobias from time to time for a nice stroll because he loves botany and herbs. I noticed it then. It had never occurred to me that these magnificent purple flowers that have grown here since the time of the ancient Romans would get me a gun. It's a strange form of transformation—a flower into a gun. There they are! Come on."

Pietro and I walked off the path, beyond the tended herb gardens, and into the edges of the terraced fields. I followed the terrible brightness of his flashlight, which I wished he would turn off because I was scared of who or what might see us. The Germans, yes. But I wasn't as afraid of them as I was of *Pippo* and the bombers.

By the end of the tree line, beneath Pietro's feet, were purple flowers. Not many, and not a sea of them, but flowers all the same. It was not spring, which is when I thought flowers grew, but in Italy the hills alight with new growth throughout the year. Pietro stopped and withdrew heavy leather gloves from his bag and picked a tall stalk of purple flowers. I had a sense of awe because my plan had now burst into life with color.

"Do. Not. Touch. Are we clear? Not with your hands, your feet, or your tongue. Don't touch. *Aconitum napellus*. The most magnificent hue of purple, isn't it?" He picked many and shoved them into his satchel.

"From these I make a liquid that I dissolve into a bottle of . . . something. The monks will have a locally made *amaro* someplace in the cellars. I once read that Medea tried to kill Theseus with this, not wanting her husband to recognize his estranged son. Likewise, Alexander the Great was offered a poisoned princess who had it on her lips—somehow. I don't remember how that one worked."

"What do you mean?"

"I mean. How could the poisoned princess have it on her lips and not die, if kissing her would make Alexander die?"

"I don't know," I said. "How?"

"I don't know. That was my point."

That is when I heard *Pippo*.

THERE ARE MANY PLANES IN any theater of war. But the sound *Pippo* made was different. It was a stuttering sound. The sound of something inside the clouds scratching and struggling to get out. It was also the sound the monsters made under my bed when I was little: a grumbled breathing, an anxious tap. *Pippo* was up above, just out of sight, and I knew it was looking for me because I had escaped and my escape had given it a purpose. Its eyes wanted to see me and I couldn't let that happen.

"DOWN, DOWN!" I YELLED, AND I ran at Pietro, who was so shocked at my yelling, he didn't even move. With all my speed I dove into him, knocking him to the ground amid the flowers. We hit the ground hard, rolled twice, and then tumbled from one terrace to the next, dropping a meter onto the land below and then rolling some more, over and over with an audible *umph* from him each time his back hit the ground.

"What the hell are you doing?" he managed to grunt.

Pippo was overhead. I didn't care what Pietro was asking. I needed to keep us safe. I could hear the plane circling but couldn't see any lights in the sky. We needed to hide but there was no place to go. I wanted to push us directly into the earth itself and hide beneath the poison flowers named for monks and wolves.

I tried putting a hand over his mouth but he'd have none of that. "It's a random scout plane. They pass by all the time. You think an airplane can hear me yell? Now get off me before I throw you off!"

I did stand up but not because he told me to. The flashlight was on above us, giving away our position, illuminating the entire monastery, and providing *Pippo* a complete map of Italy so he could destroy us all.

I clawed at the ground trying to reach the flashlight, which was growing before my eyes into a spotlight. I was convinced that bombs were going to drop on us at any moment and the mountaintop itself would explode around us. Risking bold movements, I leaped up onto the higher terrace and pounced on the flashlight, curling around it in a fetal position as I tried to figure out how the infernal thing worked.

I couldn't.

I knew, in my head, that there was a slide button on it but I couldn't find it so I sprang open the clip that held it together.

The giant battery fell out and disappeared into the shadows.

After that the world became very quiet. I realized, only in that moment, that *Pippo* was gone.

Pietro stood, brushed himself off, and then walked back to the main path with a new fistful of flowers.

He was very angry.

I followed several meters behind like a bad dog. I knew he was in no mood to talk.

When we reentered the monastery, Pietro pointed toward the staircase in the direction of my chamber. "Go to bed!"

"I want to stay with you."

"No. Not tonight. You are an electric wire. There is too much happening in your mind. You'll wake the entire abbey. I have things to do in silence and that means without you. Go. Sleep. Tomorrow we find out what's happening with Schlegel and Becker and the art and what that asshole König is up to. I need to prepare a poison tonight and also damage the inventory with the other elixir as I try to find a hiding place for the Tizianos. I'm *busy*. Events are moving fast now. And once they properly begin, Massimo, they will not stop. This is war. And war is gravity."

PIETRO MUST HAVE WORKED THROUGH the night, because when he roused me the next morning he looked exhausted. This was October 17, 1943; a Sunday. The sleeping chambers in the abbey were on the eastern side so the morning light would ease the rousing of the monks. This was by the decree of St. Benedict himself. The west side was for more public business. As Pietro settled himself into the chair by my desk I looked up and saw that the sunlight was far past my little dimple on the wall.

"What time is it?" I asked.

"Almost ten o'clock. The monks were asking about you, and I said you had some tummy issues and it was best if we let you sleep it off as you'd been making frequent trips to the toilet during the night."

"Did you have to say so much?" I asked.

"Better to add the little details," he answered.

I saw that his fingertips were blackened and his face was gaunt.

"Did you sleep?" I asked him.

"Not much. I am in a race against König even though we have never met. He's looking for me and these papers. I can feel it, like prey knows it is hunted. But I am ready. If I can, there will be time tonight." He did not look optimistic about this.

I looked to the door and Pietro sensed why.

"Schlegel is back with his friends," Pietro offered. "According to Brother Tobias—who missed his true vocation as a spy—he and the abbot have reached an agreement, which is to give the Germans everything they want. I suspect the Germans will agree to these terms. The interesting part is that General Fridolin von Senger und Etterlin—I do like saying his name—is now on board with this idea and is sending Hermann Göring's Parachute Panzer Division up here with a hundred trucks or more to start moving everything out. König will be at the front of the convoy. He will want his inventory. He will pack everything accordingly. Everything he can find, anyway."

"Maestro," I said, because I was about to do something I had never done. "Why are you really stealing those paintings?"

Pietro's shoulders were slackened and I felt guilt at asking him something sensitive at a moment he was weakened, but I was growing stronger and this was what the strong do.

"Massimo," he said, "I am very aware that I am withholding information from you. My name, for one. Certain facts and histories about my relationship with Oriana. Even why I need these paintings and who I have to give them to. But you need to trust that I have my reasons, and whatever games I might be playing, I will never turn on you or abandon you, or use you as a pawn in my machinations. Can that be enough for now? There is so much to be done if we're to survive what's coming."

"What do you mean when you say life clings to you like a curse?"

"I mean . . . life is inexplicably attracted to me, dear Massimo. And I ruin it. But I don't want to."

"I don't understand."

"You're fourteen. There's time."

"What are we going to do next?" I asked.

"I'm going to look for him, of course. When I find him, I will be exasperated and ask where on earth he has been, on vacation? There's too much work to do for him to be absent like this! He will object and mutter something in Nazi and I will reply in Italian and wave off his logic as meaningless stupidity. I will demand he return to the task at hand. I will explain that the pages are damaged and I have been scouring the abbey in the most unlikely and hidden places to find another copy, but I failed and this is the best we have. He will not believe me and I will enjoy that. If König thinks he can do a better job in the time we have, I will be glad to watch and learn. Meanwhile, the Allies are coming to the Liri Valley and the trucks and art need to go."

I had nothing to say about this. I was more concerned with the escape and the murder and the guns, all of which seemed more tangible and pressing.

Pietro and I both turned our attention to the knapsack he had settled down into the corner.

"You didn't find a place to hide everything?"

"I did, actually, yes. I'm going there soon. Inside that bag is a lot of money, gold, art, and poison. And a few snacks." We both continued to stare at it as though it might move. "The life of the panzer division is going to get busy for at least a few weeks depending on the speed and efficiency at which they work and the resources they plan to allocate. I still wonder if any of it will go to the Vatican or whether all of it will go north to Germany and Austria but what is certain is that those trucks will go north and the Allies—assuming they find out about this, and they will—will not bomb them."

"Why not?"

"They want the Germans going north, not south. Also, they probably know about all this by now and they don't want to be seen as destroying all the art."

"Don't they actually not want to destroy it?"

"That's a fine distinction for a young mind and . . . I hope so. I hope, indeed, they don't want to harm it, and not only avoid handing a propaganda coup to the Third Reich. Their motives notwithstanding, the trucks will not be harmed."

This was his way of telling me that he still wanted me on the trucks.

I decided not to contradict him in that moment because there seemed to be no point. We had a busy day ahead because we had men to kill.

THE WEATHER WAS TURNING. IT had been cool the night before as we'd gathered up the purple flowers but it was warmer come midday. The sky was slate gray and low over our heads. The colors of the world around us were dampened as we walked down the winding road from the abbey and into Cassino, nonchalant, as though we were taking a stroll to consider a fine point of philosophy or to reflect on the advice of a dear friend. As we walked, large German army trucks with canvas tarps roared up slowly, their diesel engines grumbling about the steep incline and their massive wheels turning sharply into corners designed for goats.

As they drove up, we went down, a descent into some forthcoming hell and we knew it. I wonder, sometimes, whether there had been another way to get those guns and make our escape south, and of course the answer must be yes but only in that phantasmal manner where circumstances always twist to support our ambitions and on the day of the race it never rains.

At the time we had no other solution and Pietro had an idea about us traveling west—to the coast—before the Allies appeared in the valley. We needed the guns now. And so, as in all wars, it went as it went.

IT WAS AFTER NOON WHEN we arrived at the café in town. The town was occupied by the Germans but not policed and they were not using it as a garrison. Cassino, at the time, was more than a village; it was the home to some twenty thousand people who spoke in *sotto voce* and whose eyes studied the patterns in the dust more than the possibilities in the clouds. The natural scenery during our walk was beautiful but the pleasure was tainted by our knowledge of the Germans in the hills who were using them as cover for the violence to come.

Were there snipers out there? Artillery? Legions of demons?

We paused outside the café door and Pietro said to me, "This is it?"

"Yes."

"They think she's your aunt?"

"Yes."

"Is there a back door?"

"I don't think so," I said.

"You ready?" he asked.

I said I was. I wasn't even sure what the question meant.

"As discussed: We will walk inside together. You go directly up the stairs; do not even acknowledge them if they are there. I will come in after and distract them. If the woman and children are there you tell them now is the time. The children should walk straight out and you will go with them. The woman is to stay up there, ideally. You understand? The children are your responsibility, Massimo. That is why you are here. That and the chain. Once the kids are outside the café, she may come down." He reached into his satchel and withdraw a chain half a meter long with an open padlock on the end. "Once you are outside, you will put this through the two handles and lock it. Once it's locked, you and the children run. Go back to the monastery. I know it's a long walk but do it and don't worry about me. If she leaves with the kids, the officers will be suspicious. If three children leave it means nothing to them."

"How will she get out?" I asked.

"She'll go out the bathroom window. Or some other window. I don't know. That's not your problem. You lock the door and take the children to safety."

"What about you?"

"I have to get them to drink the elixir."

"You could give the bottle to her," I said, more alarmed now that I was actually there and looking at it all and feeling it.

This had been mad. I was scared. Pietro had wanted a gun, nothing more. I had walked him into this. Now I wanted it to stop. He could be killed, and then what? What would I have?

"She could give it them and then leave," I added. "We go back later for the guns."

"It might not work that easily, Massimo. And she knows that. We both need to be in there," he said, placing the chain and lock on the ground by the door for when I would need them. "Take these," he said, handing me some strangely heavy coins with rough edges. "They are for her. As you promised. Here we go. Remember: You go straight up the stairs. Don't even look at them. I'll follow."

The doors were partly ajar and I pushed them forward.

I don't know if I was surprised to see them or not. Even now I can't piece it all together. It was a Sunday, but I knew nothing of how German officers spent their time in those days. For whatever reason, on whatever schedule, there they were, each with a beer in an unlabeled bottle, drinking what must have been a limited supply. The men looked at us as we walked in. Pietro ushered me upstairs as expected and then—to my surprise—approached the Germans. I could hear him, for a moment, before I knocked. His spoken German was effortless and fluid.

I heard a chair being pulled out and a bottle land on the table. I heard positive grunts from the officers.

Trying to focus on my task as though it could protect me, I knocked on the door to the bedroom but did not wait for an answer. I pushed down on the handle and pressed it open. I saw the woman in a nightshirt though it was the afternoon. The bed was rumpled. Her eye makeup had run down her cheeks and she was smoking a cigarette. She turned to look at me without any expression.

Not waiting, I walked to her and removed the gold from my pocket and put it on the end table beside a bright green pack of German cigarettes with a large number 5 on them.

She looked at the coins. There were seven of them.

"They're pure gold," I said. "Fifteen hundred years old. That's about thirty grams. They're worth ten times that amount to collectors. I'm supposed to take the children. Where are they?"

She placed the coins on a bureau. "They aren't here," she said.

"Good," I said, though I was confused.

"Is it happening?" she asked me.

"Yes," I said with more urgency now. "I was supposed to take the kids and lock the door. You are supposed to stay here for a bit and then climb out the window. Get ready."

"I'm staying," she said, pulling on her cigarette and blowing the smoke out slowly.

"We have to go. Please," I said, looking around for a dress or something she could wear.

"I'm staying. You go."

"I have to lock the door," I said. "Please, I have to do it now. There won't be another chance."

"There is no chance at all. They won't let me go even if I climb out the window. They need to die. You're a child. You don't understand. Go out and lock us in. This is the only way."

I didn't know what to do. But then I recalled what Pietro had said. *We will need to lie, cheat, steal, fight, kill, and sin our way to Naples.*

Had he meant this literally? Had it only been hyperbole? I had thought it was the loose talk of an Italian man convincing himself to be brave in the face of fear. Whatever Pietro's intentions had been, to me they were a guide and in that moment of fear they turned me as though by hand, and once my direction was clear I rushed out the door, down the stairs, and past the table where I saw that dreaded bottle was open

86

and the three men were laughing as the two Germans drank the amber liquor in shots.

I remember the bottle glowing purple, the way neon signs burst out of the night.

No one stopped me or even called out as I rushed past and closed the doors behind me. The coins on the table, the posture of the men; uniforms and guns and booze and cigarette smoke, wooden tables and black cloth. Shot glasses and cutlery. It was every scene from every table in every war. I don't know whether they heard the chain wrapping around the mighty door pull and me locking them in.

Once the padlock was secure, I should have run. I wanted to. I had planned on it. But I couldn't. I was transfixed by the doors, unable to turn my eyes away. I should have done what Pietro had told me. I know this. I should have been a half kilometer up the road by then, the horrible events to come behind me.

I REMEMBER EVERY LAST DETAIL. Every texture, smell, and play of the light and shadow inside that café.

PIETRO HOUDINI HAD SAID THAT natural wolfsbane usually takes several hours to kill but he'd modified the poison somehow because he was a professor of chemistry and he knew how to accelerate the effects. By how much, though, he couldn't be sure. "I'll need to sit with them. It could take some time," he had explained. "Plenty of time for you and the children to disappear."

So he sat with them and they drank together, laughing and speaking in German as the men consumed the poison and Pietro pretended to.

Outside, I could still hear their tone and feel the mood despite not understanding the conversation. They were *men drinking*. They were *all* men drinking to me. Men drinking was something I had seen many, many times. Men on the street in Rome. Men in uniform leaning into bars and tapping them and slapping them and guffawing at their own jokes; smoke in the air, women with legs crossed at tables, bartenders busy, waitresses grabbed, lies being told, rumors spread, insults hurled, punches thrown.

I had misunderstood Pietro, though. When he said it didn't take effect immediately and it could take time, I thought he meant for death. But what he'd meant was the dying.

I imagined there was going to be a calm delay and then, like scared goats, the men would freeze up and tip over—stone-cold dead—at the same time.

That isn't what happened.

The skinny one lurched up from his seat first. He was wearing no cap and his collar was open. As he stood, he grabbed his stomach. Pietro had his back to me and when the skinny one stood he did too, reaching out an arm in support but not touching the man. His companion, less empathetic and assuming the man was joking, took another shot from the open bottle and made some comment that antagonized the skinny man and made him pound the table. Pietro held up his hands, stepped backward, and went for the bar, where he poured water into a pitcher as the second man's face turned grave, and then, clutching the table, he also stood up, the poison having affected him, too.

He was not only bigger, though. He was also smarter. It was his face that changed from confusion to rage as he came to the realization of what was happening.

He grabbed the edge of the table and flipped it forward, sending the glowing purple bottle of poison toward me before it smashed on the ground, where I expected the floor itself to melt.

Poison works faster on the lean. I could sense the wolfsbane saturating the thinner man's blood and rushing directly to his heart. As the big one got angry, the thin one lost his will to fight almost immediately, and instead of focusing on the bottle or the table or Pietro he cradled his stomach and reached out for the wall. His last clever act was to stick his fingers down his own throat with his free hand and try to vomit up the death he had consumed. But it was too late. He dropped to the floor clutching his abdomen.

The big man, though; that was a different matter.

Fighting the nausea and pain, the strong man stepped toward Pietro while unsnapping the flap that covered his gun. Pietro had nowhere to hide and the thin wood paneling of the bar would have been no match for the bullets from the officer's Luger. The gun was on the officer's right side but so was the wall and he needed the wall for support as he walked, so he removed it and switched it to his left hand.

The skinny man thrashed. Foam came out of his mouth during his death throes but the strong man paid no attention. He aimed at Pietro using his left hand to wield the Luger.

I was certain Pietro was going to die.

The panic coursed through me. I couldn't watch Pietro get shot. I couldn't see his lifeless body on the ground. I couldn't be alone again.

That is when I picked up a rock and smashed the glass.

I had never done anything like that before but it was all I could think to do. The window only cracked and did not shatter but the sound was enough to startle the poisoned man, who turned toward me and fired a wild shot at me instead of Pietro, blowing out the window a meter away from my head.

I flinched. I might have ducked but I didn't have the sense to get down and stay down. I needed to see, to watch. And what I saw was Pietro trying to decide what to do; whether to attack the man with the gun or try to flee, somewhere, somehow.

But there was nowhere to go. He was stuck behind the paper-thin bar.

The dying man pivoted back toward Pietro. He tried to take aim as he fought the shortness of his own breath and need to double over. Staggering, his gun hand swaying. His strategy for dying was to get closer to what killed him. Closer and closer to Pietro until there was no way to miss because the gun would be pressed into the center of his chest and the bullet would pass through his heart and into the wall beyond, where it could testify forever to his vengeance.

With his next step, though, everything changed because he had reached the gap where the staircase began and there was no more wall to lean against. Instead—and quite unexpectedly—his right hand came free from the wall and instead of finding only air it landed on the left shoulder of the woman, who had come down the stairs.

I HAD, UNTIL THAT MOMENT, thought of women as the peacekeepers. The ones to break up the fight. The gentler sex, which tries to appeal for calm. I had been raised to believe that women were one step closer to God than men. More civilized. More in control. And also weaker. They were not born for the struggle or combat or victory. Theirs was the way of peace and cooperation and kindness and, ultimately, submission and defeat and service. This was the culture of fascists. The culture of men. It was the reason I became Massimo.

I think some part of the German officer believed it too. Some part of him must have believed that raping her had made them connected. I think that is why he paused, because he thought something tender was passing between them in his moment of pain.

He was wrong.

With one hand on her shoulder and the other clutching his pistol, he and the woman looked into each other's eyes. In that misunderstood intimacy, she thrust a steak knife directly between his ribs and into his heart.

The officer looked down for only the briefest of moments, during which Pietro leaped forward from behind the bar and swiftly took his gun away.

The woman released her hand from the blade. All three of us watched the man drop to a knee and then topple forward, driving the blade farther into his own chest.

Still outside and looking in, I saw Pietro place the gun into his knapsack and then flip over the man to remove the remaining magazine from his holster. The skinny man was already immobile. I don't know whether he was dead yet. Pietro did the same with him, removing both the gun and the extra magazine.

From the ground I saw him pick up the two gold coins that had fallen and press them into the woman's hand. She did not look at the gold and instead watched the two Germans. Her face was entirely impassive.

That is when Pietro took in his broader surroundings and noticed me on the other side of the bullet-shattered glass.

"What did you see?" he asked through the shards.

"Everything."

He tossed me the key. "Unlock it. Quickly. It's time to go."

I did as I was told and dropped the chain, lock, and key to the ground.

"Down the street. Go. Now. Run."

He did not turn to see if I went, and it is a good thing because I didn't. I was unable to move, whether from fear or the unnamed compulsion that forces us to experience a story through to the end.

I heard him tell the woman to get out. "Go!" he yelled to her, but she did not move; she wasn't finished watching the men die.

Or, perhaps, be dead.

Either way, she wanted more.

Pietro vanished behind the bar and soon emerged with four bottles of strong alcohol. He snapped his fingers and the woman looked at him. Without a word, she nodded. Turning to the task, he poured three of the bottles over the bodies of the men and splashed more through the rest of the café. He then placed a soaked rag into the top of the fourth and handed the woman a match. "The German military police will find them. Sooner or later and no matter what we do. There's no avoiding it. No lie we can tell will account for the missing guns and the Germans will notice they're gone. I was going to use that one's coat but I can't anymore because of the blood. If you're here, they will interrogate you and will not stop until you say something interesting—true or not. You can't stay. You need to go. But . . . it's your café. Only you can burn it down. Even this has rules."

She nodded. He lit the rag and handed her the bottle but she refused it. Instead she took his match and dropped it onto the strong man's body with the indifference of a smoker. The flames caught and the man did not move when they did.

Pietro hurled the Molotov cocktail at the back wall and the burning began.

At this point I backed away. I saw the tablecloths catch the flames and I watched the blue edge expand along the rivulets of booze to find the other man, who also did not flinch when he started to burn. I was surprised—if surprise was still possible—at how much smoke filled the café even before the flames were visible outside. Pietro walked out with his bag over his shoulder and the woman in tow, his fist clenching the fabric of her dress by her upper right arm. She staggered like a drunk.

He pushed her out the door, and once she started moving she stayed in motion, walking with purpose and direction down a street and then disappearing from our sight.

Pietro turned to me next but his countenance changed when heads starting appearing in windows. I think, now, that no one had come outside to look earlier because of the gunshots. One instinctively avoids gunshots. But fire is another matter. Fire spreads. It calls. It is orange and people like to watch things burn.

Pietro felt the eyes on us, and being the quick thinker he was, he pointed to the café and shouted, "Fire!" as though he had discovered it rather than started it.

Once he was certain that their attention was on the fire and not us, we moved swiftly to a side street and then to another and then to another still so that our secondary roads became tertiary and soon we were buried in the village and away from our past.

PIETRO DID NOT TALK TO me for the first several kilometers as we hiked back up to the monastery. I had expected him to give me an earful about not doing what I was told and disobeying him and being too close to the danger but instead he reached down and held my hand. When he did, my pulse began to slow and that made me realize my heart had been beating as though I'd been running. My mouth was dry and my eyes—I felt—were open too wide.

"I was in the Great War," he said. "I was a twenty-nine-year-old officer. These were not my first deaths and not my worst."

"Mine either," I said.

Pietro did not lecture me on the trenches or the gas they used. The machine guns and the barbed wire. The terrible fear. The futility of it all. Instead, he stopped talking because there was nothing else to say.

The walk back took us nearly three hours. We had no water and we smelled of smoke. We were passed by no fewer than a half dozen German army trucks on the way. By the fourth I had been almost ready to flag one down and ask for a ride, and I think Pietro sensed that because he gave me a stern look. From then on I kept my eyes on my feet.

We arrived at the monastery wilted. Sunday is usually a day of prayer and rest. There was no sign of that. Pietro called over a man called Brother Bartolomeo, who was dressed in his traditional black hooded cloak. He was significantly older than Pietro and also smaller. I had had few encounters with him but I thought of him as gentle, scholastic, and soft-spoken. He had been at Montecassino for over forty years.

"*Buon giorno*, Maestro Houdini," he said with a wry smile—either because Houdini wasn't his real name or because it was obviously not a good day. "How are you?"

"Busy," said Pietro.

"The abbot is looking for you," said the monk. "And so is König. König also has men looking for you. I think they are suspicious about why the paperwork has not been handed over to them."

"And the abbot wants to talk sense into me before I cause any trouble," he said, slightly out of breath and clearly disappointed that the strain of the day—and probably his experience with Germans—was not over.

"The abbot is in the archives."

"With Menschenfresser König?"

"I suspect so."

"I need to clean and collect myself. Please tell the abbot that I'm on my way and will be there presently."

Before the two men parted, though, Pietro gently took hold of Bartolomeo's cloak and asked, "Have you seen Brother Tobias?"

"I believe he's taking confession," he said.

"Yes," said Pietro. "This would be a good day for it."

Pietro took me by the hand and gently guided me through the commotion of the monks and soldiers who were now busy assembling the crates that would be used to transport the wealth of nations from the halls of Montecassino to whatever destination the Germans decided to take them.

In the distance I saw Dr. Becker—the man with the red car who I sometimes confused with Schlegel—with his hands in his pockets standing on the steps between the statues of Benedict and Scholastica. He did not look pleased with himself but rather . . . saddened, somehow. Having just orchestrated two murders, though, I may not have been attuned to a normal range of human emotions.

I then saw Schlegel himself. He was more animated and was pointing and directing and managing the process. I wanted to see malice and deception in his face but I couldn't. He simply looked like a person trying to get things done. I turned away because the moral ambiguity of his intentions unnerved me and I was already very shaky.

There was a great deal of shouting around us as we made our way up the stairs of the cloister, past Becker, and toward the basilica. There were many instructions in Italian, also German, but mostly in English because that was the language the Germans and monks had in common. My eyes were everywhere; partly because of the blood pumping through my brain in the wake of events and also because I could not shake the feeling that I was watching the building of an ark or something equally monumental.

Montecassino's basilica was constructed the same year the Pantheon in Rome became a church. That building had a hole in the roof and on stormy days my father and I liked to go there and watch the water pour down as a column. This place was not like that. Here, the ceiling was vaulted in gold. There were marble columns that upheld the serenity and terror of faith. The floor was rose and white and gray and polished, I assumed, by thousands of feet over thousands of years and the walls, too, were polished down and gleaming from the constant slew of words and prayers and confessions that brushed along their surfaces.

Pietro marched to the confessional and I shuffled along quickly behind him. The booth was open so he stepped inside and closed the door. I'm certain he knew I had taken a seat on the step nearby and would therefore hear every word. I think he wanted me to. In my state, however, none of that mattered. It would have been impossible for me to leave his side.

His voice was even and direct: "Bless me, Father, for I have sinned. It has been . . . perhaps three weeks since my last confession." I heard Brother Tobias greet him and welcome him and ask to hear his sins. And so Pietro listed them: "Today I killed two German officers in the town—not because they had repeatedly raped the woman who helped me kill them, which they had—but rather because they had something I needed and it was the only way to take it. Actually, on reflection, I think I only killed one of them as the other died by other means . . . but I'm being pedantic. My acts were sins but I feel I'm losing my sense of what is right and wrong in a world where God Himself has—if not abandoned the weak and the humble entirely—at least turned over the reins of earthly guidance to madmen and devils. And so I find it hard to ask for absolution, which is perhaps another form of sin. I find it easy to recognize my own trespasses but find my heart is hardened against contrition, and while I sense a better way I can't imagine where to look for it; not when others depend on me for life itself, which surely must be the greatest good and the highest means of honoring the Lord if He still has reverence for the life He created and insisted was good."

They spoke more, and much in this vein. Pietro confessed like he spoke: without equivocation, without apology, with self-awareness, and with an eye toward a state of being—a condition of the spirit—that seemed to be on the other side of a moat or a mountain or a curse.

When the men finished speaking they emerged from their respective sides of the confessional. I did not confess and no one asked me to. Together, all three of us walked outside to the Loggia del Paradiso, which looked out over the valley. The sun was going down and I knew Pietro was headed to the abbot and König now that he had washed the stains of blood and poison from his hands.

Before we broke with his company, Tobias whispered to Pietro, "Do the Germans know who you really are?"

"No," he answered.

WHEN IF EVER HAS THE birthright of a civilization been packed up and shipped out before the eyes of a child?

Dr. Becker was gone and as Pietro, too, had disappeared to his chambers to rest before facing his next drama of the day, I sat myself between the statues and looked down at the men in uniform or black robes who marched back and forth from the archives and museum where Pietro and I had found the Tizianos, across the cloister in front of me, and out the PAX exit to the waiting trucks.

They marched with boxes and crates. They carried paintings in frames and others rolled under their arms for packing later. They carried books and tomes, sculptures and artifacts, maps and spells and curses and secrets and mysteries and promises and the laments of saints.

They carried the spirit and soul of the monastery, and in every step I felt a violation for which I had no word.

Perhaps there was no word.

I had overheard Tobias tell Pietro that monks take a vow of stability. I wondered, as I watched the art move in front of me, what such a vow could mean in a time and place like this.

YOU HAVE TO TRY TO picture it in your mind: the paintings by Leonardo da Vinci, Domenico Tintoretto, Domenico Ghirlandaio, Pieter Bruegel the Elder, Tiziano, and Raphael all being carried from stage left out the door at stage right. There was the moment before me, but also the moment as unique spectacle in the sweeping history of civilization itself. When had there been such a moment? Ever? Consider the past *eight thousand years* and hold them loosely in your palm. With a finger, separate out the glorious cultures across the millennia and from one continent to the next and consider who has plundered them and how. Parse them like so many pieces of sea glass: the wars and conquerors, conquistadors and *reconquistas*; the thieves and vandals and tomb raiders from the Mayans to the Mongols to the Moors. When has such a thing happened?

Never.

Try to visualize the Library of Alexandria and, instead of burning to the ground, its contents being relocated to Jerusalem or Tripoli or Khartoum. That is the scale of what I was seeing. Try to imagine moving the left wing of the Louvre or the right wing of the Met. They moved some of the art from the Prado during the Spanish Civil War in the thirties, but it was nothing compared to this.

This was beyond the ability to imagine. The closest you can come to imagining it is watching the thing itself. And even then, you wouldn't believe it.

AFTER A TIME THAT WOULD have been impossible to measure, Pietro joined me in the cloister. He was in his white suit again and his shirt was open, like an artist. Instead of a hammer and chisel he held his papers. He looked clean and he smelled good. Whatever had happened in Cassino wasn't visible on his face now, and after his confession, perhaps it was not inside him either.

"I have to go talk to the saint and the sinner. Can you manage by yourself a little longer?"

I said I could. Tobias had given me bread with some cured ham and a large bottle of water. I was not clean but I felt all right and watching the Germans work had calmed me down; watching people absorbed in work created the comforting illusion that they weren't looking for something else to do like arrest or kill me.

"Will you be long?" I asked.

"No. I already told you what I'm going to say to him. We'll probably be speaking English or German so you won't understand anyway. He will be like the sea monster in the painting. I told you what it was about, yes?"

He hadn't. Only its name. It wouldn't have mattered. When he was in the mood to speak, he did.

"Perseus and Andromeda and the sea monster. Andromeda was the daughter of an Ethiopian king named Cepheus and the queen called Cassiopeia. For some reason Tiziano painted her as pale as a nervous Irishman caught with his hand in the till rather than dark like the Ethiopian princess she was but . . . that's another matter. Somehow, Cassiopeia was overheard bragging about her daughter's beauty and how the girl was even more lovely than the Nereids, the sea nymphs. Now, the nymphs heard this and complained to Poseidon, who unleashed a sea monster named Cetus to ravage the Ethiopian coast as a punishment for the insult. Well, the king was devastated and he appealed to Zeus for help and Zeus—being Zeus—said the king needed to sacrifice poor Andromeda to the sea monster as the only way to appease Poseidon. So that's what happened. They chained the innocent girl to the rocks and there she was, about to die, when Perseus flew over in his winged sandals and found her there. He was so enraptured by her beauty that he killed the monster and married the girl. Our friend Tiziano—a slave to drama as the best of us are—captures the exact moment of the rescue and the beheading of the monster. I'm not sure that König is our sea monster. He feels more like a snake, and in this case, there is no Andromeda tied to a rock. So maybe ours is still out there. But already we can feel the paintings drawing life toward them and focusing our minds on myth and magic, tragedy and beauty, love and violence, heroism and treachery. They are all around us, dear Massimo. We must be vigilant."

I watched the art go by. I saw the monks stand like dark trees in a copse and witness their home vandalized; experience the consequences of their decisions and know they were helpless to protest what they themselves had agreed to set into motion.

An impossible decision. I suppose they made it because they had faith.

PIETRO RETURNED FROM HIS MEETING with König and the abbot rather agitated, and in no mood to discuss it. More than that I didn't know. I had always expected to meet this König devil, as he loomed so large in my consciousness and was so central to our preparations. That didn't happen, though. The monster never appeared, at least not to me.

Pietro sat down on the steps beside me and looked at the pictures passing from stage left to stage right. Everyone was busy. We were the audience.

"How long have you been watching this?" he asked me.

"The whole time."

"See anything good?" he asked.

I smiled, not at his joke, but at the realization that he was still able to make a joke and so maybe everything would be okay.

Together we watched. After ten minutes Pietro walked down to the man in charge and introduced himself, and soon all the movers were coming out of the monastery facing the art in our direction: "For inspection," Pietro said to me with a wink.

There we sat, surrounded by swastikas and crosses, each of us with blood on our hands and secrets in our hearts.

In a strange way, though, I felt like a king.

A bit later he dug into his satchel and pulled out two green apples. He handed me one. He crunched and chewed and then I crunched and chewed, and together—synchronized to the steps of the workers—we crunched and chewed.

A Raphael passed by, upside down.

We crunched and chewed.

We stopped when Brother Tobias approached.

"How are you two doing?" he asked. "How was your meeting with König and the abbot?"

"We are having a challenging day as I explained in confession."

"I was being polite," Tobias said.

"As for the meeting, I enjoyed watching König eat his outrage about the condition of the papers I handed him. So that was a fleeting pleasure." He took another bite and spoke as he chewed. "You monks . . . you're all convinced this is a good idea?" He waved at the madness below, near and far.

"Not all of us, no," Tobias said. "I would describe the conversation we had as . . . agitated," he said, sitting down beside us and placing his arms on his knees and leaning forward. "The gravity of what we're seeing here is not lost on us, Signor Houdini. Do not think us fools for this decision. But the story is complex and so are the actors. I've spoken more with Dr. Becker. He studied art history at university before becoming a doctor and he spent three years on an archaeological expedition in Persia. His passion is Anglo-American literature. I find him refined and quite pleasant."

"This is the one with the sports car?"

"Yes."

"He's a Nazi fighting for Hitler," Pietro said. "The fact that Nazis know good wine from bad only makes all this worse. You see that, yes? It also proves that people easily mistake refinement for virtue."

"I'm not that easily fooled, Maestro. He's a doctor who was assigned here," Tobias went on, defending him. "I don't take him for a Nazi and he doesn't want this war. I know zealots. He's not one of them. His wife and children are in Berlin. You may have noticed," the monk said with a bit of an edge, "that we're not all completely in charge of our destinies."

"I had noticed that, yes," admitted Pietro. "Though some of us make more virtuous decisions than others."

Brother Tobias blinked very, very slowly at him.

"Fine," Pietro conceded. "Then take yourself as an example! The point remains."

Tobias continued: "It was indeed Becker's Fiat *cabrio* in the parking lot. Apparently, while stationed in Sicily, he dug it out of the rubble of an abandoned house near Catania. One way or another, he managed to get it started and on board the ferry from Messina to Reggio Calabria during the German evacuation of the island in mid-August. At that point, he was driving it—I imagine with the top down—during the bombing of Pompeii, and barely escaped strafing by one of the Allied aircraft who, again I have to assume, couldn't pass on the opportunity to shoot at a German officer in a red Italian convertible."

"That's a lovely story," Pietro said. "Except you forgot why the house was nothing but rubble and you ignored who the rightful owner might be and why he was absent. Otherwise, a very glamorous event."

"I'm trying to reveal his *personhood*, signore. I'm trying to remind you that there is a man beneath the uniform."

"The Nazis are stealing your stuff, Tobias. Rather inefficiently, in my opinion."

"They're moving it, Pietro. Whether they're stealing it is debatable or, more to the point, unknowable. I doubt even these soldiers know. If it survives, anywhere, there is a chance it can be recovered. What really turned us around, Pietro," the monk said, "is that Cassino was already bombed on the tenth of September. You know this. You were here and you saw the explosions and smelled the fires. What Captain Becker and Lieutenant Colonel Schlegel also showed us—with obvious omissions, of course—is how the line for their defensive fortifications runs directly around Montecassino. They also reminded us that the definition of 'precision bombing' by the Allies is 'within five miles' and they suggested that placing our faith in the accuracy of Americans flying B-17s and B-25s is a faith placed in the wrong direction. Personally, I found these arguments convincing. The Germans are going to allow us to ride along with them to Rome, confirm that the crates have arrived, and return to the abbey with the empty trucks."

"What about König?" Pietro said.

"What about him?"

"I might make concessions for Schlegel and Becker. Even Senger on this particular subject. But I've looked at König. I've looked in his eyes. He's here to shop for Hitler. He's the devil."

"Like I said," Tobias answered, "they're going to let us ride along on the trucks, and for the record, Pietro, I'm not making a case for Nazis. I am not a fool. I am only reminding you that individuals can and often do defy assumptions, defy orders, defy cultural expectations and even," he added rather pointedly in a way I didn't yet understand, "family relations."

"That was uncalled for," Pietro said.

"I think I've earned some latitude to speak my mind. And my point stands. Stay away from it, Pietro Houdini. Please. Those who know your real name also know who you are married to. They know what happened to Oriana, and they know why. They also know that the Germans have terrible leverage over the man with that name. So do all the Italians. What almost no one knows is what that man looks like . . ."

"I shunned the spotlight in my youth."

"Good thing, otherwise you wouldn't have much of a chance now. Nor, I suspect, would your wife. Or . . . the other one in Naples you're going to visit."

"I suspect not," he said with a sniff. "Who else knows?"

"Only me."

"I told you in confession. You can't tell anyone."

"I learned all this long before you confessed. Be that as it may, do you honestly think I would tell anyone?"

"No. I love you and trust you with my life. But you mentioned my wife and it spooked me. I'm sorry. How did you figure it out?"

"When you got here I called the University of Bologna to report on your safe arrival. The phones still worked going northward and I didn't suspect the fascists would care even if they were listening. Well . . . I should say I called to report on the maestro's arrival. The university, however, was surprised by this. They said it was very unlikely he was here because he disappeared in 1940 because he is Jewish. Now, it came as a bit of a surprise that I referred to the maestro as Pietro Houdini rather than Professor Rosselli—the real maestro's name—but together we wondered if, perhaps, Professor Rosselli had decided to risk the journey out of a sense of duty to the art, which by reputation was possible. It seemed reasonable he might assume another name for the task. I described you. They said they didn't know anyone named Houdini. They did know another Pietro, however, from the Department of Chemistry, who fit my description perfectly."

"How did you describe me?"

"An opinionated but charming polar bear with a big personality and a beautiful accent."

"Go on."

"König is suspicious of you, Pietro. Don't stay too long. Your false papers—the ones you presented to the abbot—gave you a reason to be here. That reason is now being loaded onto a truck. I won't be able to protect you if the truth comes out. Nor will the abbot."

The monk stood to leave. As he wiped the dust from his hands he said, "Oh, with all this talk I almost forgot the reason I came looking for you. Your guests have arrived."

"My guests?" Pietro asked.

"A woman and two young children?"

"Ah," Pietro said. "Have they now."

WE WERE NOT EXPECTING GUESTS. I certainly wasn't. It was going to be evening soon. The sun was already turning orange and the edges of the clouds were black.

Pietro stood quickly and walked even faster, chucking his apple core into an open crate of paintings. I tried to keep up, but with shorter legs I had to jog. As with most visitors to the monastery, they were waiting by the entrance cloister.

PAX.

It was an inauspicious place for three murderers to meet.

Pietro walked out onto the stone patio outside the entrance with wide-open arms and kissed the woman on each cheek as though she were an old friend. He patted the head of each child. He ushered me over to be a babysitter as he gently but firmly pulled the woman to the side—his smile never fading—and whispered to her, "What the hell are you doing here?"

The two children did not smile at me. They were dirty and tired.

"Did you walk here?" I asked them.

The children didn't answer. They seemed to be swaying in a kind of hypnotic exhaustion. Being forced to march up a mountain had robbed them of individual will. Their spirits, sent away, were not prepared to return to their bodies until they were absolutely certain there would be no more suffering.

"Come," I said, more out of pity than obligation.

I took the children inside and found them bottles of water that they drank wordlessly. I saw Brother Tobias walking back from one of the German trucks and asked him to give the children some food; so they could eat, so I could be rid of them, and so I could eavesdrop again on Pietro and the woman. I felt entitled to be part of any conversation.

I walked back across the Loggia del Paradiso for the exit again, hoping to find Pietro and the woman outside the walls, but stopped when I saw two German soldiers filming the entire operation. With movie cameras against their eyes and other equipment draped around their necks, I knew they were shooting some of those newsreels I'd seen in Rome projected onto municipal buildings. I don't know why they turned their cameras toward me. Maybe because I was a child and the presence of a child during such an event would make it seem routine, safe, and humane. But I didn't want to be on film. I felt as though a film of me would be proof of something I didn't want proven. I didn't want to be seen. Not by God, not *Pippo*, not the police, not Allied bombers, not the Germans, not even the monks.

I ran away from them as though the camera could shoot bullets and I burst out of the exit breathless. That was when I stumbled upon Pietro and the woman almost by accident even though it had been my intention. They were close and engaged so didn't see me. I ducked behind a truck that was idling nearby. What I caught—which was not the beginning—was this:

Her: "—will find me."

Him: "No one is looking for you yet. The Italians don't care about dead Germans. And the German military has its hands full. Look around you."

Her: "I want you to get us on a truck. The bodies are in my scorched restaurant and I am missing. They will be looking for me."

Him: "Okay, maybe they will. But they will search the trucks and they will find you and then . . . who knows. Nothing good."

Her: "You will get us *invited* onto the trucks. You will do it now or I will scream and never stop screaming."

Him: "That would be . . . unproductive."

Her: "You sound like *them*."

He squinted his eyes at her and did not reply because she was right.

Her: "They say my husband was killed in Greece. They did not even return his body to me. I have nothing."

Him: "I'm sorry. But that has nothing to do with trucks."

That was when he noticed a new vehicle stopping by the trucks. The soldiers who stepped out had chains hanging from their necks. He knew exactly what they were.

Also him: "Shit. It's the Feldgendarmerie."

Her: "More Germans. They're all the same."

My attention became split because I heard Pietro talking but I was looking at the men walking toward me—not Pietro—with their hands on their gun holders.

Him: "No, they aren't, because they don't all have the same jobs. Now get inside. I'll think of something. And if you scream I'll push you off the mountain and eat your children."

Pietro took the woman by the hand and forcefully pushed her back toward the PAX entrance, which she passed through and disappeared. I wanted to do the same but I froze like a scared rabbit.

I tried to back away but the two men advanced on me like war machines piloted by a force that knew nothing of the soul. I was anchored to the earth.

Even then I thought Pietro could come for me.

The first one grabbed me. I would describe him but he was not a person. He was a creature or a demon dressed in gray wool that didn't have human qualities, only a human shape. I had seen many propaganda posters from the fascist authorities. All the men were big and strong, their jaws square, their faces fixed and defiant; they walked with rifles over American and British flags.

These men were *those* men. They were *funzionari*. They were devices.

Automatons. The undead. Their absolute clarity of purpose was unchangeable by words or ideas. There is, still, nothing more terrifying than facing faceless power. I would rather beg for mercy from a wolf.

The first one yelled at me. The language was harsh and the tone threatening. The hand was big and it shook me, and I think it could have lifted me off the ground if it had wanted to. If that had happened—if I had become airborne—the man would have known I was not as heavy as a boy. I don't know why I associated being female with being weightless but I did and it only occurred to me then.

Soldier No. 1 pulled me toward his waiting car while asking me questions in German, which I didn't speak and couldn't answer, as Soldier No. 2 walked ahead and opened the back door.

I turned toward the abbey but I saw no one except regular German soldiers engaged in the laborious and mundane tasks of loading crates onto trucks and filling out paperwork.

Of the monks themselves, I saw no one I knew.

And no one saw me.

Soldier No. 2 put his hand on my head and thrust me into the car and then followed me in, sitting next to me as the other got behind the wheel.

"Let me go!" I shouted in Italian, my breath returned, my voice returned, my power as meaningless and useless as it had ever been. I might have been shouting to bombs dropping from the sky.

But at least I shouted. At least I resisted.

I was slapped and it startled me into silence.

How did they find me? How did they even know it was me?

The car started instantly and the driver turned the wheel hard to the left as the car lurched forward to complete half a circle and point us back down the mountain.

I knew instinctively that this moment was going to be my last breath of pure air because they were going to bring me to a building with no name or number, strip me down to nothing, and then fit me with prison clothes like the people in the newspapers. If they did that, they wouldn't believe my name was Massimo.

For the first three turns I tried to think of what to do just like—I'm sure—everyone else ever taken away by goons in the night. I slid back and forth on the black leather seat, and before reaching the fourth turn a thought occurred to me. I had, and only recently, walked up this very road with Pietro after helping murder two men. Much of the walk had been in silence but after my retort about these not being my first dead either, Pietro did give me a warning: "We were seen. We don't know who saw what. But whoever saw something didn't know what they saw either. If caught, do not deny the facts. Accept them all. If they say you were there, say, 'Of course I was there!' If they say, 'We saw you with the chain,' say, 'I should hope so!' And then you make a story out of the pieces. If they say, 'People saw you lock it,' you say, 'What lying Communist pig told you that? I demand to know!' If you are silent and meek they will know you've been caught. We have been trained to accept our capture over here. To submit. So do not submit. Don't be silent and meek. Be loud and hostile! Keep talking, the way you have experienced me talk. If they catch you in a lie, say they misheard you. Insist they look at their notes. They will have no notes because they are not serious about the truth and fear nothing from a child. There is nothing more onerous than talking to fascists who are certain of themselves. They are almost uniquely obtuse."

By the fifth turn, the thought had reached my heart and I found the courage to grab the back of the seat in front of me and shout in Italian, "Where are you taking me? Who the fuck are you, anyway?"

"*Setz dich und sei still*"—the one next to me said, and his meaning was obvious.

"My uncle was a captain in the Italian army and fought the Russians for the glory of fascism!" I yelled, having almost no idea why Italy fought Russia and having only the slightest idea that it had happened at all.

The soldier in the back repeated that I was to sit down and shut up, but I did see the men glance at each other. I crossed my arms, indignant, and tried to imagine how a truly innocent boy would act if he'd been snatched from the monastery without reason.

I tried to think like Pietro and the way he told me stories in the vault as we had worked (rather pointlessly, I then realized, as the Germans were taking away all the art that wasn't painted on a wall).

What was my story? Why had this boy—this *Massimo*—been at the monastery? Because his parents were dead and he'd gone there as a good Catholic. The monks had been sheltering and feeding him.

Yes.

Who took care of him there?

Brother Tobias.

What did he do all day?

He assisted with the art preservation.

Why had he been in the village?

Why not? People go into villages. Why the fuck were you there? Why are you even in Italy? I don't have to answer you!

It was a good start anyway.

This other Massimo would be scared for being snatched away but also eager to get back and do his job, which was to assist the monks in saving all the art, and he'd also be angry that these fools had complicated all that.

Yes. "Indignant" was a good word.

"How long is this going to take? The monks are waiting for me! I'm not supposed to be here."

The one in the back seat turned to me and grabbed my jacket. He squeezed my lapel as though it were my throat and said quietly and slowly, "*Setz dich und sei still!*"

"*Vaffanculo!*" I said to him just as quietly, without taking my eyes off him.

The men both laughed. This much Italian, they already knew.

* * *

THIRTY MINUTES LATER WE ARRIVED at a municipal building on the southern outskirts of Cassino near the Rapido River. The land around it was dry and I could hear the river when I was shoved out of the car. Parked in front were three other cars, all black. The Italian flag—not the Nazi one—hung low over the main entrance, and inside they led me through cool corridors and into a sterile office that looked out toward the western hills.

Inside the office was a desk with chairs on either side and nothing else. No lamp. No mirror. No file cabinet . . . nothing. The windows were barred.

I walked into the room and, seeing how little was there, I turned back to the soldier, still emboldened by Pietro's last advice to me: "What is this? I'm supposed to be up at the monastery helping—" But he ignored me and closed the door.

For a while I assumed they were watching me so kept up the confident facade. I grumbled to myself and walked around, waving my arms periodically and making faces like I was anxious at how long this was taking; like this was unfair; like I had somewhere else to be. I constantly tried to imagine what *Massimo* would be feeling rather than me; the way I tried to imagine what an innocent person would be feeling other than . . . me.

WHAT IF I TRULY WAS Massimo and innocent rather than pretending to be Massimo and innocent?

That notion changed me. It cast a spell.

I WAS NOT HERE. MASSIMO was. Like a character from a novel or a movie, Massimo was a real, complete, and perfect person—as real as anyone else.

A person with feelings and parents. A person with preferences and ambitions, wants and needs. Massimo was a boy and he thought boy thoughts. A fourteen-year-old boy who liked football and cars and pretty girls in bathing suits at the beach and Coca-Cola even if he was told to hate America. Massimo came from Rome too. A rougher part of town than mine. He used to get into fights at school and he often lost because he was smaller but he never gave up and eventually people stopped picking on him because he could be knocked down but never defeated. And there was no fun in that for a bully. The crowd usually turns.

Massimo wasn't very good in school but he had an inquisitive mind. He asked questions and listened to the answers even if he didn't always believe them. He wasn't very trusting of adults. He had an older sister. She was much older. Maybe seven years. Massimo wasn't expected. He was a "surprise from God," his mother had told him, and she tried to baby him and cuddle him, knowing it was the last chance for that, but Massimo venerated his sister and didn't want to be small. He wanted to be big. Big like the father he never met. Big like the boys who tried to romance his sister when she was sixteen and he was only nine. But he wasn't big. He was slender and delicate and beautiful and his fingers were long and elegant, and his skin was soft, and his lips were too red, his eyes too gentle a brown, and his lashes far too long and curly. Massimo was not becoming the man he wanted to be. And it made him angry.

This was now Massimo's story. Massimo's captivity. The "I" in this story stepped into the body of Massimo himself and it was he who began to live it.

I could only hope he would do better than me.

MASSIMO ROAMED AROUND THE ROOM looking for proof they were watching him. They had to be. What else would they be doing? That was the idea Pietro had put into his mind on the hill as they'd been walking back up after "the café"—a term they'd started using to signify an event rather than a simple place. That sort of transference took place all the time. "The war" became a period of time or a social experience rather than a war. "The monastery"—not yet, but soon!—a metaphor for error and cruelty and the inversion of all moral order. By summer there would be more of them. Many more.

He didn't have a watch. Massimo had never really had a need for one. In Rome his parents always told him what needed to be done, or else the movement of the day was certain enough to dictate his actions. On the road it hadn't mattered. There had been daytime and night, and a refinement of those two was provided by the sun. The moon spoke to the rest. At the abbey, Pietro himself had ordered their days. The monks, too, with their Liturgy of the Hours.

Here, Massimo had only the window and the passing of shadows. What structured those hours—and they were hours upon more hours until nightfall, and then a deep night and the rise of the moon, its passage, and then its fall into blackness—was the change of heart he experienced. Even the best of actors, when left completely alone, cannot maintain a character forever. Something of one's own life force begins to assert itself and the spirit refuses to be subsumed into a lie.

By the time he woke from under the table, daylight already illuminated the room. Massimo stood and walked to the window and looked out toward the western hills, which were orange and glowing. They would have been beautiful if he wasn't certain (deep in his stomach) that he was about to be tortured and, afterward, very possibly shot, by the Gestapo or whatever group of people did that sort of thing this close to the front lines.

Torture was a known feature of Italian life. With Mussolini in power since 1922, Massimo's entire life had been lived under fascist rule. When the Blackshirts were alive in the cities and hills they would round up and torture and murder those hostile to the state and Il Duce. Even as a child there was no way to avoid the stories because the political party celebrated it and the children on the playground would joke and mock and imitate.

In the room, though, Massimo's ability to sustain the masquerade failed him. By the time midday arrived and he had not eaten, not drunk, and not used a toilet, he was properly scared. He had heard that people were put into closets so small it was impossible to bend their knees and they'd be forced to stand for days. Other times, people would be frozen to near death and then brought back. Others were cut with knives and bled and still others had their teeth pulled out, one by one, the pain unimaginable and the eyes of the sadistic dentist wide in delight.

When the door did open, Massimo was sitting and praying that it was all a bad dream: that the men in the café were still alive; that he and Pietro had not wandered the hills of Montecassino looking for those beautiful purple flowers in the middle of the night; and that instead *Pippo* had dropped a bomb on that house while the woman and her children were out—maybe at a market a few kilometers away—and they had simply been wiped from existence by a force beyond sight or reason or communication. A force that had either wanted them dead or had simply been in the mood to drop bombs without caring where they landed or on whom. A force that had no mercy for these pitiless mortals but that could, on a whim, lay fault to justice.

The man who walked inside carried no gun, no bag, no papers, only two bottles of water. There was condensation on them and the droplets had collected on the edges of his fingers, cool and wet. He did not close the door entirely.

He was in his thirties. Handsome but not dashingly so. Clean. A gentle face with blue eyes and slightly disheveled hair, which was not typical for a German officer. He carried himself like a schoolteacher.

When he spoke, it was in perfect and melodious and comforting Italian, the sort of Italian Massimo would hear the tour guides speak at the museums he was taken to by his parents on rainy days and who spoke with love and authority about their subjects, and in their every lilt or vocal rise they projected the past and the future of Italy into the present like a song that would never end.

"I am called Jürgen. I only just learned you were here," he said. "I'm so sorry for what you've gone through. Here, here, I brought you a canteen. You must be parched, and famished and in need of the toilet. There's one across the hall. Please. Worry about nothing. Go on, go ahead. Come back when you're done."

The object on the table looked nothing like a canteen, which—as he clearly knew—was made of aluminum with a twist top. This thing looked like a coconut with one strap going around it like a belt, and another going from top to bottom and holding some kind of steel cup in place at the top.

This was how Germans carried water.

Massimo stood, uncertain if this was a trick, and reached for the object. He knew Jürgen was enjoying his inability to open it but he figured it out soon enough. There was a peg and eye at the bottom that loosed the strap when it was opened, and that removed the cup and exposed the twist cap, and the cap gave him access to the water. The thought of poison—of the poetic justice of *being* poisoned by the Germans in retribution for the wolfsbane poisoning—crossed Massimo's mind, and he looked into the bottle for some sign that it was true, maybe some glint of purple or violet in the water that would tell him for certain what was about to happen.

The man stood too and reached out his hand, smiled a sad smile, and took the bottle. He then took a swig and handed back the bottle.

Massimo drank it all. After, he opened the second bottle and—without the proof—did the same.

A moment later he stepped into the hall to find the toilet. There were armed guards sitting casually by the door and all the windows were barred.

He went to the bathroom, closed the door so no one could watch, and relieved this part of himself.

After washing his face in the sink, Massimo looked up at his own reflection. He was entirely unable to recognize himself. He was both more than himself and less. Both taller and shorter. Younger and older. Masculine and feminine. Scared and cunning and powerful and helpless.

Whatever was going to happen here was going to happen as soon as he walked out of this bathroom.

With nowhere to hide, and no way to escape, Massimo exited the lavatory and walked back into the interrogation room.

Jürgen sat on the chair to the left of the desk. The vacant chair on the right was positioned in front of a plate of bread, cheese, olive oil, and prosciutto. He could smell it from where he stood.

"Ah, I almost forgot," the man said, reaching into his pocket, "the salt."

With as much caution or dignity as a hungry squirrel facing a pile of nuts, Massimo sat himself down in front of the man and ate. Out of spite he ignored the salt.

"Good, good. Water, relief, food. You're probably tired and worried. No need to be worried. Nothing bad is going to happen to you."

A schoolteacher with the voice of a serpent.

"We already know what happened. We know who did it. We know everything that's important. This is a formality. You know the Germans. We love our procedures. And paper. But in a war sometimes there are delays. I had to travel and I didn't realize they brought you in yesterday. It was supposed to be today, of course. Why else would you have had to sleep inside a bare office like this?

"I used to be a teacher," he said, surprising Massimo. "It's true. Italian literature and musicology. Italian is my favorite language. I'm so fond of Italians. I like it here. Oh, I know. Fascists and war and all that sort of thing. But the world will settle into a new order, and daily life, like flowers in the spring, will return to its cycle. Until that time we have to maintain law and order. So I'm going to give you a chance to tell me what happened because your words will be more heartfelt and eloquent than mine.

"To start things off, I'll tell *you* something. For example, the woman who owns the café is named Bella Bocci. Her family has lived in the Lazio region for four generations and she inherited the café from her father, who died fighting the Greeks late in 1940 someplace better forgotten near Albania. Across the street from her, and watching you from the window, is Signora Grillini, who was Signor Bocci's mistress for many years. A heavyset woman of limited education, so I suspect the allure lay with proximity and her easy virtue. Grillini, meanwhile, had felt slighted by Bella for being as pretty as her name and she enjoyed fucking her husband out of spite, which probably made her ferocious. She is the one who watched you put the chain on the door. We found someone else who saw you walking up the hill, which leads only to one place, and so we sent—"

"I took it off the door. She's a liar. She wants to impress you."

"Impress me? Why would she want to impress me?"

"So you'll go away before learning that her family joined the partisans."

"The partisans," said Jürgen.

"The Communists. They want Italy to join the Allies."

"Hmm. Yes. I suppose that's true. And she's a strategic mastermind, is she? You're a pawn in her quest to turn the tides of war?"

"I'm supposed to be helping the monks put the art on the trucks. I want to get back and do my job before they miss me."

"Yes. But you are not so strong, are you? You're rather small and frail for a teenager. Not a whisker on you. Strange job for you to have, carrying things. Who told you to . . . adjust the chain on the door?"

"I saw a fire."

"A fire! Wonderful. What is your name?"

"Massimo."

"What is your real name?"

"That is my real name."

"What's your name, little one? It's okay. You're not in trouble."

"Who *is* in trouble?"

Jürgen looked up as though trying to figure out the answer. "Well. It's a good question. There is always an answer, sadly. In this case the answer is the townspeople. They're in trouble. Two officers of the Reich have been murdered and their bodies burned. Can you imagine? We will need to round up the locals and execute a certain number, of course. I will have to check the orders from Berlin. It used to be ten Italian lives for each German, meaning I have to execute twenty random people, but Berlin is becoming angry with disobedience. It might even be a hundred to one now. That's what they were doing in Naples before they tried fighting back. Personally, I think that's why too. The local people understand ten to one. But a hundred to one makes them anxious. I think it's bad policy, myself. I'm thinking . . . twenty-five to one. That seems fair, doesn't it? Lenient? So only fifty. That is how many people you have helped kill today, Massimo. You are a mass murderer now! If you are so keen to carry things, you'll be able to help carry the bodies to the pit. All their pretty Italian faces. Boys and girls, young and old. Your countrymen. All because of you and your decision to lock the doors. Which, of course, was not your decision. It was someone else's. And that's the exciting part. I should shoot you too, of course, but you're so young and impressionable. So soft. This will harden you and help you understand that cooperation with Germany is the best way to live a long and fruitful life. Do you understand?"

Massimo wanted to be aggressive. To shout at Jürgen that he was wrong; that the whore across the street had been wrong; that it hadn't been him at all, and it was all a Communist plot as everything was a

Communist plot! But he had already admitted to being there and holding the chain. He needed to create a story but stories are hard to create. Nothing is easier to understand or harder to make. It is the difference between pointing at an airplane and building one. Massimo was too scared to craft something convincing because fear is the enemy of art.

"There was a fire and people were trapped and I tried to help."

"How?"

"I saw it was locked. I tried to unlock it."

"And you did. We found the chain. How did you do that?"

"I pulled it."

"Another great feat of skinny arms!" he said. "And here you are, the next day, planning to help the monks carry big boxes without a care in the world. Who was there with you?"

"The people trapped inside."

"Be careful, little Massimo. Did I mention you'll be joining us as we pass through town picking out the fifty people we're going to kill to satisfy our quota? Yes. That's hard. Deciding who lives and who dies. But that's what you did! You helped kill two men. Why not fifty more? Killing the children is harder, but we find that if you kill the parents first, it's easier to kill the children after because you think . . . well, how are they going to survive without the parents? What kind of life will they have? It's easier to give them the mercy of a quick death then. Yes, you're doing something good by killing them. You are alleviating the suffering in the world. Really, it is only your own weakness holding you back from doing the right thing. Don't you see that? Did Il Duce teach you nothing? Strength is the only mercy. No, I suppose not. That's why Hitler rules the world and Italy does not even rule itself. Who told you to lock that door, Massimo?"

"I didn't lock it."

"You will pick forty-nine and you will be the fiftieth if I don't get what I want. You have ten seconds. Nine. Eight. Seven—"

There was the sound of feet shuffling in the corridor and both Jürgen and Massimo turned to look through the partly open door. There wasn't much to see but until that moment it had been virtually silent.

Jürgen stopped counting when they both heard Pietro Houdini's voice.

He was nearby. He was speaking German—speaking it extremely quickly and with the timbre of years, authority, and impatience.

What Pietro said was: "*Ich kenne die Geschichte hier und da ist ein mann zwischen mir und dem Führer, also wirst du jetzt zuhören und zuhören wollen.*"

The only word Massimo understood was "Führer."

"Who is that man out there?" Jürgen asked Massimo.

But Massimo didn't answer. He was quite certain that Pietro was going to answer that question himself if he hadn't already.

The German was like a song now: fluid, unbroken, impassioned, almost mellifluous. Massimo couldn't understand it but he could *feel* it: a torrent of words intent on persuasion.

Though the language was foreign, a few familiar words popped out of his sentences that were close enough to Italian that Massimo could piece them together into a sort of mosaic.

Café.

Soldaten.

Partisanen.

Hitler.

. . . and perhaps most strangely . . . *Mussolini.*

Mussolini?

Was Pietro suggesting that partisans fighting against the fascist regime had killed the soldiers at the café? Whatever it was Pietro was saying, he commanded the attention of the military police who may also have been Nazis. Massimo was too terrified to make sense of Pietro's presence or declarations. All he knew was that he was no longer alone and someone had come for him.

He wanted to rush out into the hallway but couldn't. Massimo's feet were cemented to the floor. His strength to act and even run was long gone but the sound of Pietro's voice breathed life back into him.

"Can you hear me?" Jürgen said to Massimo again, snapping his fingers. "Who is that?"

"Pietro."

"Pietro who?"

"Houdini."

"Houdini? Houdini?" He repeated the name, trying to place it. *"Der Handschellen-König?* The Handcuff King from America? My father saw him when he toured in Germany before the Great War. I have never heard of an actual Italian named Houdini. On the other hand, everyone's name here ends in a vowel and a third of the peasants slur. Still . . ." he muttered, and then become lost in thought, a scholar searching for a half-remembered book on a shelf rarely perused. Soon, though, the moment passed and he was back.

"Oh well. Stay here," he added, returning to the matter at hand. "We are going to discuss why the service weapons of my officers were not found on their charred corpses. The wooden and leather bits of their holsters were bound to burn, but guns do not. It is going to be a fascinating conversation given your excellent view through the window and your knowledge of the events inside. The case of the missing guns! A detective story, to be sure. I can't wait to hear it!"

Jürgen's steel chair squeaked across the planks and the man, unhurried, stood to find out what was happening in the hall that was interrupting his interrogation, one that Massimo thought would soon turn into a teeth-pulling, flesh-boiling, fingernail-pulling hell session any moment. Each and every man in the building was bigger than him and there was no way out, not even the windows. The only way out of the building was the one Pietro was forging with words.

Massimo loved Pietro Houdini in that moment the way a child loves Christ.

A moment later the door swung open and the white-haired mountain himself appeared.

"Come on, let's go," he said. "I'm not going to say it twice!"

Massimo didn't move from his seat. The contradiction between what the German had said only a minute earlier and this news was too much to reconcile.

"Fine, you called my bluff. I *will* say it twice. Move it. Now!"

Massimo stood and looked around the room like a schoolboy making sure his mess was cleaned and he'd left nothing behind. With his chair answering the squeak of the first one, he stood and left the room and then—miraculously, unexpectedly, inexplicably—the building itself.

OUTSIDE BETWEEN TWO GIANT BLACK Mercedes cars Pietro opened the driver's side of what could only have been Max Becker's red Fiat *cabrio* that he'd rescued from Sicily after the Allied invasion and the German evacuation.

Borrowed? Stolen? With Pietro there was no way to tell.

The top was down. The inside was beige leather that was a bit worn from the rubble. The wooden steering wheel shined and the steel and chrome glistened, even the parts that were dented. Massimo stood with his hand on the warm handle as though he were being asked to mount a dragon and fly to the moon.

"It's a car. Get into it."

"It's the German's car."

"Before that it was an Italian's car. Get in."

Pietro adjusted the rearview mirror and donned a pair of sunglasses as Massimo placed his hands on his lap, trying not to touch anything as if proof of his presence in the vehicle would bring the mirage to life.

The car fired up and Pietro backed out, turned the wheel hard to the right, and then gunned the little engine to free the stiffness of the front wheels. As soon as they started rolling he heaved the big wheel over with a dramatic spin and they pulled away from the interrogation center, leaving a wake of dust by the river road. Together, the top down, they sped back into town and toward the road to the monastery.

"Are you all right? You look all right," Pietro said, the wind now blowing his white hair around his black glasses.

Massimo had never been in a cabriolet before. It was exhilarating and, after a full day of waiting to die, the feeling of cool wind in his hair and hot sun on his face was too much and he began to cry.

"Oh, *per l'amor di Dio!*" Pietro said, talking to himself, which was his way of talking to Massimo and—in this case—pulling God directly into the conversation. "This is why I didn't have children!" he announced, possibly speaking to all three of them.

"Oh!" Massimo yelled, that shock of emotion and life redirecting itself from relief to rage in the space between two beats of his heart. "You didn't have children so that when you poison two Germans and light their bodies on fire and burn down a building and the Gestapo interrogates your accomplice, you won't have to be bothered to break him out of prison and deal with his tears after? Is that why you didn't have children? That seems like a very specific reason!"

"Oh ho! Look who found her voice! A little time under a Gestapo heat lamp and look what grows!"

They started climbing the serpentine road toward the abbey.

"His voice!"

"Who cares!"

"What's your real name? What's the curse?"

Pietro slammed his hands onto the polished steering wheel, punched it a second time, and then yelled, "Mussolini! My name is Professor Pietro Raphael *Mussolini*, and at the moment, my curse seems to be you!"

It was on the third curve up the mountain that Pietro took a right turn too quickly and they entered it wide at the very moment that one of the Wehrmacht's Opel Blitz trucks was coming down the mountain laden with art. The Fiat was a tiny car with a low and elegant front end whereas the Opel was a beast with massive front wheels and a high bumper. When the two vehicles met, the truck drove up onto the little sports car, shoving the nose to the earth; crushing the front end; sending Pietro and Massimo into the air.

PART II

MASSIMO HAD NO MEMORY—NO COLORS, no shapes, no coherent sequence of events—to explain how he had arrived in the bed. The sheets were white and clean and a heavy gray blanket was lying neatly across his chest. The arrival into this place—having been in the car only a split second ago—was a bigger mystery than his surroundings, which he guessed easily enough: the abbey. The ceilings spoke to that. The emptiness of the place.

He knew from Tobias that the monastery helped the sick. It was part of its mission.

He wanted to remember the accident.

Think.

He saw in his mind the road soaring upward at him to become a black river and he a diver. On his left was Pietro.

The white flash of his hair against the gray of a truck.

Massimo had had the instinct to raise his arms before the blackness of the hard waters enveloped him.

That's all. There was no more.

He guessed the rest. The car and the truck had hit each other. The truck was enormous, filled with the artifacts of Italy. The car was small, filled with a lying murderer and his teenage assistant, who masterminded the assassination. That much Massimo could determine, and once he realized it was all he could possibly know, his attention returned to the room.

"*Bentornato*," said a woman. *Welcome back.*

Signora Bella Bocci. The woman from the café.

They were alone in a massive room—almost a cathedral itself—with one small window at the top of the far wall covered by a black tarp. The room was dark and a single candle beside the bed barely produced enough light to reach the vaulted ceiling. There was a tapestry on the far wall too, beneath the window across from Massimo's bed. In the candlelight, the blood red of the crusaders' battle seemed to flow and the suffering of those under their swords was drowned out by the beating of Massimo's own heart.

There was little else other than dozens of empty cots waiting for the wounded and dead.

Bella Bocci was wearing a shapeless dress several sizes too big. It was, or had once been, yellow with small blue printed birds. Her legs were crossed. A heavy-heeled shoe moved to a slow beat as she looked down at Massimo, who had begun to stir.

"You chose life," she said to him. "A popular choice if not a wise one."

"Where's Pietro?"

She did not answer.

"There is a monk named Tobias who is concerned about you. I take it you know him." It was a question that did not sound like a question.

Massimo said nothing. He looked around for Pietro in one of the other beds but didn't see him.

"Do you trust him?"

"Who?" Massimo asked.

"Tobias."

"Yes."

"He took my children to Rome on a truck."

Massimo wondered if it had been the same truck that hit their car, but that was a wild thought as the Germans were sending a hundred trucks or more back and forth to the Vatican like so many ants on a march. He also suspected that, whatever had happened to Pietro and the car, the truck was surely fine.

She lifted a mug of hibiscus tea from a small end table beside Massimo's bed and sipped.

"I have a sister there," she added.

Massimo looked at her eyes through the steam. They were lifeless.

Bella's Italian had sounds he didn't make when he spoke, and she used words, phrases, and constructions he did not use. Every third word included the sounds of a whisper, and the softness of the vowels felt like an implied threat. He had talked to her before at the café. Twice. Now he listened and heard they were not from the same Italy.

"Tobias said my sister collected them. They were sobbing."

"Why didn't you go?" Massimo asked.

Signora Bocci did not answer him. The mask of death was on her face. It was the same mask Massimo had seen so many times; it allowed a person to walk through the world without contact. Everyone who saw such a mask knew to stay away. Her husband's presumed death had made her a widow and denied her a love she had mistakenly thought was eternal. The Germans had abused her and she had accepted the abuse to keep her children alive.

Until she stopped.

"My parents once begged me to follow them into the hills with the children. Carovilli. A town that barely exists. A farmhouse outside it. 'Come,' they said. 'The crime, the criminals, the Mafia, the shortages, the black markets,' they said. 'The Blackshirts, the Germans, the Allied bombs. Italy was once the place of the Renaissance. Now it is chaos. Lawlessness. Our soul is dead. Cassino is nothing. Come with us.' But I said, 'No, no, what happens when Paolo returns? If I abandon the restaurant and our home we'll lose them. And then what will the children have when the war is over? They'll be peasants.' Now—"

Now, she did not need to say, *the present speaks for itself.* As it always does.

An air-raid siren screeched from the valley. Massimo sat up, noticing for the first time that his left arm was broken and in a cast and his ribs hurt when he moved.

His chest was wrapped.

Who had wrapped his chest? Surely not Bella Bocci. She was no nurse. Who else knew? Pietro knew. Bella knew. Now someone else.

Massimo tried to get out of the bed but it was impossible; his body was broken.

"We have to go," he said in a soft voice that would not shake his pained ribs.

Bella did not move and clearly did not agree. Instead, as the sirens wailed, she reached down to her right and brought up a green pack of cigarettes that Massimo had seen before, at the café: Eckstein No. 5.

She struck a match and the room was filled with light before the match became only a fragile flame to accompany the one candle. She lit the cigarette and Massimo stared—wide-eyed—at the fire as they both waited for the bombs to fall or antiaircraft fire to spark up.

She flicked her wrist in studied fashion, extinguishing the flame before Massimo could protest.

"The cigarettes belonged to the one called Thedrick. He was the one I stabbed." She smoked the cigarette with relish because it had once been his. "The matches too."

"Shouldn't we go?" Massimo asked, waiting for the bombs.

"It'll be over soon," she said. "No one will bomb us tonight."

"Where's Pietro?"

"He's alive. Which is not necessarily good for you. I wouldn't allow my own children to play with him. You can see at least that much, yes? There are still some trucks, Massimo," she said, using his name for the first time. "Go to Rome. This place is doomed. To the south is death and these buildings are a tomb. Even if you get to Naples it will be a city without a heart, a place abused by army upon army. That is not a destination.

It is not a paradise like you think. It is a tortured place. Go north instead. I already sent my children. That should be proof enough."

Massimo didn't want to lie back for fear of the pain to come but he did and the pain came. He didn't want to yell but he did, and rather than anguish he called out—to the accompaniment of the raid sirens—"Pietro!"

Bella Bocci exhaled more smoke than she had inhaled.

"Why can't he hear me?"

"You broke three ribs, your arm, and your clavicle, and there's bruising over most of your body," she said. Her voice remained flat. "The nurse told me. Ada is her name. You think I'm hard because I stabbed a man and sent my children away? That woman has eyes that look like she plucked them from her enemy and uses them for herself out of spite. Some kind of magic seems to follow her. Or maybe it's under her control. I don't know. I work at a café. She told me to sit with you in case you had a seizure or stopped breathing."

"You're trying to scare me. There's no such thing as an evil nurse. They get *mean*, but they can't be *evil*."

"I'm not sure she's evil. I think she's . . . an angel of death. It's not the same. Nurses, though, can be evil. So can doctors. The Nazis have nurses and doctors. Who knows what they're doing? I think this one is trying to prove them all weak and unimaginative. I've seen her look at the Germans. Even their spirits run cold."

"Where's Pietro?" he asked again. The red cherry of her cigarette glowed in the stone room.

That's when he heard the bombers' propellers; felt them in his chest. He swatted for her cigarette to stamp out the glowing end lest they be spotted and the bombers target them.

Bella, though, was quick and leaned back. "What are you doing?"

"I heard the planes. It's *Pippo*."

"The nonsense from the fascist newspapers? There is no *Pippo*. That's a northern superstition. Not to mention, bombers can't see cigarettes. Certainly not inside buildings."

Massimo had had enough of Bella Bocci's mordant tone and fatalism.

"They know who you are!" he said in a loud whisper. "The Germans know your name. Jürgen, the interrogator from the Gestapo. He knows about your husband and the bitch across the street who ratted me out," he said cruelly. "People saw us! They know the guns are missing. They're going to find you. They're going to torture you and they're going to kill us and fifty other people along with us!"

"I have three magazines of eight rounds each. It is more power than I have had in years. If I'm careful I can kill thirty-two more of them. When this is over, Italy will forget the dead and only remember our deeds. The children of the future will need to know we fought back. That we remembered our dignity."

"Where is Pietro?"

"He isn't who you think he is."

"I know who he is!"

Bella Bocci leaned forward toward Massimo in the dark. The air-raid sirens stopped as abruptly as they had started. No bombs had fallen. There were no sounds at all. No people outside. No trucks. No planes. No monks chatting and no soldiers gossiping or yelling to one another. Even the blackout tarp didn't move.

Turning her body to face him, she leaned down and said, "If you do not learn to look into the heart of a man and know what he is, you will not live long."

"Where is Pietro, you witch?"

"Three rooms down. He lost blood. One of his legs is shattered. It will never recover. He may hobble again but never walk. Whatever your plans were, they are behind you. The trucks and Nazis are your best hope. You should go back to Rome. You're just a child."

"Why are you still here?"

"*Ho barattato i miei figli per trentadue proiettili*" is the way she phrased it. *I traded my children for thirty-two bullets.*

Massimo had heard the term *straffete*: the women who resisted the fascists. He did not know what they did or what it meant. He did sense that Bella Bocci had experienced a change and become something else— whether a *straffeta* or not. She was not the woman she had been at the top of the stairs in the café. That woman was sad but purposeful and protective of her children. This woman was someone different. Someone who was no longer here to protect anyone. She was a person with thirty-two bullets.

That transformation had not happened, as best Massimo could tell, the moment she had plunged the blade between the ribs of the German. It had been sometime afterward. Later, he would understand that it was the moment she set her children on the truck and did not turn back to face them as they sobbed and called to her and begged her to come.

THEIR NURSE—THE NURSE ASSIGNED BY the Germans to tend to both Massimo and Pietro with the abbot's approval—was named Ada Solaro. She was Italian and mean and she would not let Massimo see Pietro. Bella Bocci disappeared once Massimo was conscious and alert again. While he healed, it was Ada who looked after him.

Ada Solaro was athletic and strong and if she had smiled she might have been pretty but she had no time and no audience for such matters and, anyway, her store of smiles was long since depleted. Massimo did not meet her over the next few days so much as become the subject of her ministrations and instructions.

During those drugged-out days of recovery, Massimo's knowledge of Ada Solaro increased because she spoke to him as she bossed him around. He did not know exactly why she spoke. Perhaps because she believed there was truly no one listening.

Massimo learned that she had served in the Italian army as a nurse, was drafted from a hospital position in Perugia, halfway between Florence and Rome. When the Germans occupied Italy last month they collected her like a sack of meal and brought her down here to the new promised front. The abbey was not being used as a fortification, per Senger's orders, but they would tend to the wounded and shelter civilians behind its walls. The abbot would not abandon those in need, and the Germans realized early on they'd benefit from that profession as so many were stationed on the mountain. Ada was a solution: a machine part collected and duly installed.

At first she had objected but she learned that more collaboration meant less supervision and less supervision suited her.

Her husband had been collected by the new occupiers too—along with almost half a million other Italian men—to serve as forced labor for the Nazi war effort. Slaves. The Nazis considered it leverage over her because they assumed her love for him was more powerful than her rage. They were wrong.

The more Massimo listened, the more scared of her he became. But he also started to doubt that she was a fascist.

Dangerous, yes. But perhaps in ways he had never heard about.

"They're here and more are coming to me, little one. Wounded Germans. Many, many wounded Germans. What will I do with them, I wonder?"

She confessed this to Massimo. Perhaps it was because she suspected he was a killer too.

DURING THE DAYS HE READ—OR, at least, looked at books. He had never been much of a reader. When he was small, his father would sit beside his bed and read stories to him. Many were old or dull or else approved by the state. The writers who had other stories to tell were cowed into submission so they did not risk bringing joy into the world. In this way, innocence was destroyed and the country conformed and died. His parents wanted to read other stories to him, but they had no way of telling what little Massimo might share with his innocent classmates if he heard the wrong stories—classmates who were already members of the Opera Nazionale Balilla or later the Gioventù Italiana del Littorio. They might tell their own parents what they had heard and who they heard it from.

But there in the monastery, unable to leave his bed, Ada Solaro brought him books far beyond his capacity to understand. After all, she had reasoned, the monastery had a library and it was all going to the Vatican, or to the Nazis, or to the flames. In any case, was it not better for them to be stained and ruined by the hands of a curious child?

Ada dropped them by the armful onto the foot of Massimo's bed because he was short and there was extra space. Some were handwritten books from Montecassino's scriptorium dating from the time that Desiderius was abbot in the mid-1000s. The Nazis had tried to pack everything, but for reasons of their own, they had considered the books less important than the art. So many remained.

What the books said didn't matter. What mattered was how they looked and how they danced in his fever and in the drugs and through the fatigue and the pain and—perhaps most important—the grief over the death of his parents that had opened his mind to seeing magic and coincidence and patterns everywhere.

Most were leather or cloth and all were heavy. None were written in a language he could read and the illustrations did not present seashores and forests, animals and motorbikes, or even princesses in beautiful gowns stranded in the very magical kingdoms we all want to live in. Instead, the books were filled with *illuminations*.

In his loneliness in the giant room, Massimo fell inside the books the way he fell into the stories his parents would tell him before he went to sleep at night in Rome. These were the stories that taught him—at five years old—that before he had memories of his own there had been a past; and sometime beyond the span of his life—beyond his inconceivable death—there would be a future where others would live and he would be part of *their* past. These were stories that took place in far corners of the world where people looked different and spoke other languages and dressed in clothes he had never seen. There, out of sight and beyond the reach of any human voice, these people laughed and cried and fell in love and suffered and created and destroyed and wondered and discovered like him, but also not like him because the world was a wondrous place and people sometimes acted beyond the realm of his understanding.

These were not stories taught at school. They were not the stories Mussolini wanted taught. But families did not always do what they were told and the story of Massimo's parents was not entirely the truth because, like Massimo himself, they too were part of a fiction.

The illuminations were drawn in reds and blues and gold leaf. The monks of long ago had drawn magical animals and mysterious angels and demons for reasons Massimo couldn't dream of. These were the drawings to celebrate the goodness of God and preserve the world's heritage against catastrophe. The pictures were more miraculous because he could touch them. It was as though their final purpose had been revealed: to distract Massimo from finding Pietro.

It worked. But not for long.

"I want to see him," Massimo said to Ada one afternoon when she brought him soup and brown bread and water.

"His leg is shattered. He's grumpy. He's on morphine. He talks," she said. "And talks. And talks. It is incoherent except when it's not. When it's not, it's personal and no one should hear it. Especially you, since you're the only one here who loves him."

"He always talks," Massimo said. "Usually with God."

"Well," said Ada, "he is talking to his wife about his daughter. God is not in attendance."

"He doesn't have any children," Massimo said, painfully propping himself up on his elbows so he could look at the tapestry again as they talked.

"The daughter he doesn't have is fourteen. He says she's strong and brilliant and lonely and scared and lost and doesn't have a father and she needs him to get to Naples with his bag of loot."

Massimo said nothing. This was either new information or Pietro was confused.

"He is arguing with his wife about her," Bella continued, her voice surprisingly sympathetic about Pietro. "The wife is only learning about the daughter. I assume it's a bastard from a secret affair. Either he's making a confession or it's a complete delusion."

Massimo tried to remember what Pietro had said about his reasons for going to Naples. Someone to meet and someone to help? Or was it something else? There were definitely two people and Massimo was sure one of them was Oriana. Did he have a daughter or in his delirium was he referring to Massimo?

Ada lit a cigarette. Her cache of tobacco seemed endless. Maybe she was getting them from Bella Bocci and they had formed an alliance. If so, there was a graveyard full of men who once smoked.

"What he is saying is very unusual, little Massimo. He does not talk about women the way most Italian men do. It is legal in Italy for a man to beat his wife and children to death if it is a matter of honor, did you know that? But Pietro says his wife is a genius. He talks about his wife as a philosopher and a scientist. A rebel and a warrior. I have to admit I found this startling and I thought I was beyond surprises now. If what he's saying is true, Oriana became an intellectual in Turin, which was a dangerous and bold and revolutionary act. She must have broken with him for some deep reason. Something more than infidelity or politics. He sounds quite devoted to her. He must have broken a very deep vow if she left him."

"He talked to me about his wife before. When he was strong," Massimo said, almost mumbling.

"Hmm. You're surprised that I listen to his fever rants? Or are you angry that I have replaced you as his listener?"

Massimo's eyes narrowed. It was high time he got out of that bed.

"He still wants to go to Naples. I don't know why he wants to go. It has something to do with his wife and the Allies and the prison islands. I can't make sense of it. Either way, he can't go," Ada said, standing up and adjusting her clothes. "He also continues to talk about a daughter, which I assume is you because you said he has no children."

"Can I see him?"

"In the morning. Sleep now."

"Is Jürgen going to take me away again?"

"No. Pietro solved that."

"What about *Pippo*? And König? And the Allied bombers? And the wave of fire that's coming?"

"None of that is for tonight. Sleep."

THE NEXT DAY, ON OCTOBER 22, Massimo woke to the sound of trucks and men talking. He knew they were continuing their efforts to move the wealth of nations onto the trucks. Through the open stone window in the infirmary he could hear them talk and argue and sometimes yell at one another. Unlike before, though, he couldn't see. From his bed there was only the pale and glowing hole angled toward the clouds.

The great departure of Montecassino's treasures was happening as sound and he would not see it end.

Ada came in with food and Massimo looked at it as a provocation. He was determined for this to be the last day on his back.

The Black Angel was not in a good mood. After a half week under her care he knew not to antagonize her. Even saying "good morning" could be misconstrued as sarcastic or ironic. Massimo was given two hard-boiled eggs with some salt and a piece of stale bread. She slammed a glass of water onto the steel table beside him.

"Soften it in the water. Food is going to get worse." It was not a prediction. If Ada said it, the truth had already arrived.

On his feet now, chest wrapped tight, Massimo hobbled across the cold slabs to the large archway ten meters away, an exit he'd been eyeing for days. In his weakened state, the doorway seemed to be moving away from him.

With effort he caught up to it and passed from the infirmary into the corridor, which was glowing in sunlit dust like an old painting by a forgotten master. He had not seen the sun in days. The light felt like two thumbs being pressed against his eyeballs. The cloister was green and he tried to avoid looking at it because the glare was too great.

Massimo had no idea what time it was. Late morning, perhaps, but the sacred rhythm of monastic life was now disrupted because of the *project*. The great vaults were emptied, and a million brushstrokes with a billion words were being loaded and hauled, stacked and dropped, mishandled and scratched, boxed and dragged from their former resting places.

Massimo walked through the arches, pushed open a heavy oak door, and went past two German soldiers hiding from the midday sun and two monks muttering in a shared language. It was neither Italian nor German nor English and therefore unrecognizable.

None of that was Massimo's problem. *Their* art—*their* paintings, *their* gold, *their* figurines, their *loot*—was stashed away with Pietro's money and guns in that enormous canvas army backpack that Pietro had placed beneath the flat stones of a basement vault that even the monks didn't remember.

Not that Massimo had actually seen it lately. He wasn't even sure whether Pietro had finished collecting everything he wanted, though with the trucks on their way north with as much as they could carry, he certainly hoped Pietro was done since now—in his injured state—he wasn't going to do much. Still, though, Massimo had seen the smoke in Pietro's room from burning his plans and he still had faith that the plan was working.

He had to. Because if the plan wasn't working, and Pietro hadn't assembled their loot by now, then it meant they had murdered the German officers for nothing and Massimo wasn't prepared to harbor that idea.

No. The sack was deep, deep in the heart of the abbey, at the bottom of a flight of stairs that Massimo was certain descended into hell.

"Not that way," Ada Solaro said to Massimo, coming up behind him and taking his arm. "Houdini's over here."

Down a different and less mystical flight of stairs, into an underground level, and through a large hall filled with the busts of men with no pupils, Massimo was led through a door into a private room the size of two sleeping chambers. There was a window facing west and it glowed like a premonition.

Ada nodded toward a wooden chair, and Massimo sat. Ada closed the door and left the two of them alone.

Pietro looked noticeably thinner despite it having been only four days since the accident. His stubble had grown out and he appeared frail. To Massimo, Pietro was a man from the *Iliad* or the *Odyssey*, as the boy vaguely understood them. This was the kind of Italian that Massimo's schoolteachers talked about as being a *real Italian*. Seeing him weak and undernourished and delusional scared Massimo and Pietro could see it on his face.

"The Germans talk when they think I'm sleeping," Pietro said on seeing Massimo. He expressed no delight at Massimo's presence. He did not beg forgiveness for the accident. He did not sob at knowing Massimo was healthy and strong and safe. "They don't realize I understand them," he continued, his eyes darting around the room. "They don't know I'm from the north and that I studied in Switzerland and I can hear them. Hear how they occupied the telephone exchanges and the mail. How they spy on us. Everything we do." His eyes were wide and wild. Massimo wasn't so much a participant to the conversation as he was a witness to it. Pietro had ideas that—like lines of a poem—had to be spoken and then aligned and assembled once they were external to him. Inside they were no good. It was too dark in there.

"Aren't you going to ask how I am?" Massimo asked.

Pietro looked at him.

"You're feeling unloved and needy. That means you're fine."

"Nice to be asked, though."

"How are you?"

"Where did you learn to drive?" Massimo asked.

Pietro Houdini started to laugh and the laughter caused him more pain than he wanted to show, but what he wanted didn't matter.

"You deserved that," Massimo said.

"More than you know."

He reached for a glass of water beside him and sipped from it. Massimo wondered if it was only water.

"Are we still going to Naples, Pietro? Ada said you can't walk."

"Yes, we're going south," Pietro said. "Only slower. The Germans won't take you north anymore, Massimo. I'm sorry. König is too suspicious of me now. He also knows about Jürgen's interest in you even if the pursuit has ended. I suppose they put their umlauts together somehow and now realize I was at the center of things they can't prove. If we overstep again there are no more tricks for me to play and every day the mood changes here. We will escape, of course, but not in a Nazi truck. Either way, we need to go."

"You're not going to the toilet let alone Naples," Ada Solaro said on entering the room and hearing their conversation.

"You're mean," Pietro said to her. "You're a mean nurse."

"How did you get me out?" Massimo asked. "From the Gestapo."

"I used my best trick."

"What trick?"

"My name. My real name. It often helps me escape, but only me. This inspired my new name. A personal joke. Anyway, this time it helped you escape," he said in front of the nurse, who didn't know his real name but had been listening to his morphine-induced monologues for long enough not to care. "I tried using that trick with Oriana . . ." he said, his voice trailing off.

And then, *allegro*:

"But with you, I walked into the lion's den and threw down my will! This is what the Germans understand. Confidence. A lion's strength. I proclaimed my position. I still have the papers, you see. My secret papers. I explained that I was an ally of the Third Reich—does anyone remember the other two? I don't even remember the other two and I'm an educated man. No one ever talks about the Second Reich. What was I talking about? The Third one. I have always been an ally of your Third-time-is-a-charm Reich! I then pointed to the partisans in the hills as the ones who did this: the ones scheming against the German rule, the ones who had watched their brothers and fathers disarmed and walked, ignominiously, to the trains and transported into Germany as forced labor after Italy's cowardly surrender. It accounts for the missing guns, does it not? It was an excellent lie. You there. Nurse woman. *Shhhh.* Don't tell the Nazis what I said to the Nazis. They didn't hear the sarcasm in my voice at the time and I can't have you explaining it to them. Okay? Okay? We're okay here, yes? Who else would kill officers for guns? I said. And by stabbing them! That's what Italians do! Those little brown-eyed fuckers with their knives and big families and their garlic. How did I know about the guns and the stabbings and you down there at the Gestapo headquarters? I didn't. I went looking for you, I said. You were in the wrong place at the wrong time, trying to save burning Germans.

"The king and Badoglio have fled! They abandoned Italy!" Pietro then shouted, which did not follow in the slightest, but that's what the drugs did to him, it seems. An outburst would remind him of another, more common outburst, and the common denominator was the mood itself. Outrage about one thing bled seamlessly into outrage about another. It seemed like madness but there was a pattern: "Our leaders have abandoned us like bad parents who leave their children behind to be eaten by monsters or fight with kitchen utensils as they go off to save themselves. Now the Germans have said they will kill a hundred Italians for every German killed. A hundred! And we killed two of them, Massimo. And recovered two guns. Two guns for two hundred lives. But I got you out because I knew the magic words. Still. I wonder if the bill will be paid."

"They told me twenty-five to one," Massimo said.

"Ah. You bargained them down. Nothing to worry about, I suppose."

Pietro rolled to his right and lifted his shoulder from the mattress, held it for a few seconds, and then dropped into his bed as though for the first time in days. Sweat had formed on his brow and his eyes stared at the ceiling.

Massimo stood to leave but Pietro reached out a mighty paw and grabbed his arm.

"There's something I need to tell you."

"Something else?"

"On the way to get you from the Gestapo I stopped to make a call. I had to know. I had to . . . know. I called Naples. I had to know. I'm sorry I didn't come sooner. But . . . you don't understand."

"What did you learn?"

"Everything. I learned it all."

Massimo had waited for the answer to his two most burning questions: Was Pietro alive, and what happened at the police station. Now he knew. What he also learned was that Pietro wasn't going anywhere for a long time. And neither was he.

Instead, the south was coming to them.

NOVEMBER WAS A TIME OF waiting. There was rain up above the red tiles of the abbey and there was distant fighting below. Massimo never did board one of the trucks bound for Rome. Neither did Bella Bocci. By the twenty-third the Germans were done. They had picked Montecassino clean and departed for good.

For Massimo, the monastery felt empty and soulless, farther from the eternal than it had been. Until those cold and rainy days, Massimo had never looked on the monks as being depressed. He had learned to equate their solemnity with tranquility. But tranquility and order and stability had now been shattered, and though they accepted the abbot's decisions without rebuke, a heaviness had filled the walls and chambers, archives and museums, and though the abbey was empty it now sat deeper into its mountain cradle and lower under God's sky.

When Pietro was finally on his feet again, with the aid of a cane that had escaped the Nazis' clipboard, he often sat in the former museum at a long wooden table amid the broken glass cabinets, the errant pages of missing manuscripts, and the dust and cobwebs new to fresh air.

The Germans had not deliberately vandalized the monastery, but soldiers will be soldiers, and their interest had been in moving material into trucks as easily as possible so they could end their assignments and eat and drink and smoke and talk and complain. In the end, as best Massimo could tell, every edge had been scraped, every wall had been chipped, every floor scratched, every surface defaced, and several halls and crypts smelled of urine.

Pietro usually sat in the abandoned space staring at the emptiness and, periodically, muttering to himself. One day, a week into this new routine, Massimo appeared and asked if he should listen to Pietro, like before, and relieve God of the distraction. Pietro smiled sadly at him and tears came to his eyes for reasons Massimo couldn't guess.

"God has moved on," Pietro said to Massimo.

"What does that mean?"

"It means . . . I am no longer of any interest. I can feel that the ear of God has turned away. Can't you?"

"What about the curse?"

"What curse?"

"You said life clings to you like a curse."

"Oh, yes. I did, didn't I? I think I said that because everything good that comes near me suffers in the end."

Over meals, such as they were, the monks would talk and share opinions more freely than before the decisions had been made. Then the monks had a say in their futures. Now they talked like life was in the past.

The Vatican had, in fact, received many of the trucks, and their arrival was met with relief by the abbot who had made the deal. The missing trucks with the missing art were not discussed. They had saved what they could from the hellfire to come. No one felt vindicated but some were relieved.

The monks who were most inclined to talk to Pietro, like Tobias and Bartolomeo, whispered to him about the black shadow over the Vatican's uneasy relationship with the fascists, a relationship that even at Montecassino—150 kilometers southeast of St. Peter's Square—filled their hearts with worry and was often enough to silence the sincerity of their prayers.

"It is like Spain," Bartolomeo whispered and the adults understood: a surrender of integrity to evil for convenience.

Massimo knew nothing of Spain.

The first flakes of winter snow arrived soon after the Germans were gone. The days that came were steel and gray and the nights were black and joyless.

Massimo and Bella were not the only laypeople who had come to the monastery for sanctuary, and the monks had made efforts to turn no one away, though there was little they could really do. Food was limited, there was no money for charity, and there was insufficient medical equipment beyond bandages and the advice Ada Solaro managed to provide as she waited for the war to climb the mountain and for the bodies to roll back down.

THE NEWS THEY RECEIVED IN the abbey was scarce. News they could trust even more so. It was known that Vatican Radio was under pressure, and the news from London was hard to receive. Rome Radio had been broadcasting German propaganda. All they could be sure about—because they could see it out the stone windows—was that the Germans were digging in: into the mountain, into the hills, into the mud under the downpours. They were amassing and the men all looked grim.

From his chair in the museum, like a seer, Pietro had a faraway look and he seemed to be able to read the world of geopolitics the way a blind man can tell who is sitting in a room. "They're coming," he said. "Not only the Americans. The New Zealanders. The Indians. Nepalese. Canadians. South Africans. The Free French and their foreign legions from North Africa. Some Italians. And of course the Polish. The Polish are very angry."

"When are they coming?" Massimo asked as though Pietro were looking into a crystal ball and all the answers were there if only Massimo could look in at the exact angle that Pietro did—but that was impossible.

"Soon."

"Why don't we go to Naples first?" Massimo said.

"I can barely walk, child."

"We could go slowly. We've waited so long."

"We are surrounded by mountains and there is only one road south. That's why the Allies are coming this way. They need the road. And winter is coming. The monks have food reserves. No. Now we wait and learn what we can and . . . if you're so inclined . . . you can pray or hope. Personally, I will paint."

FOR THE NEXT WEEK MASSIMO tried to occupy himself because Pietro had nothing for him. There was no art left to protect and no more rants to listen to for the protection of heaven. The monks had no work for Massimo and the mood among them was dour.

At first he started setting traps for the pigeons that now flew into the monastery through damaged or broken windows. Using crates that were left behind or positioning broken chairs on overturned shelves, Massimo created a world of caves and a labyrinth of the mind for the pigeons who occasionally wandered in after a piece of bread. Feeling mischievous and bored, Massimo would close the entrance and declare victory over the creatures, which didn't know they were playing or had lost.

Their refusal to admit defeat, though, took the fun away and so Massimo turned from that occupation to spying on the townsfolk who would arrive at the abbey for protection and he would listen to their conversations, which came to reveal a truth—a glowing and golden truth that sits at the center of war: it was only when looking a man or woman in the eye that one could *sense* the depth of honesty being shared. In this, Massimo learned that trust was the bedrock of survival.

It was a Thursday in the late afternoon under a hard rain when three new members joined Pietro and Massimo's strange group. Massimo watched as they arrived, wet as capsized sailors, to the front door and two were let inside. He would soon know that one was an Italian soldier named Dino Bramante, the second a young woman named Lucia d'Angelo from Termoli, and the third: a brown, limping mule named Ferrari.

THAT DAY THE RIVERS BELOW were flooding and the view from the mountaintop was fogged. Sound travels farther on clearer days, so the iron skies muffled and dissipated the artillery explosions from the south and to Cassino's east. Sometimes the flashes could be seen reflected off the bottoms of the clouds. Perhaps that was why Dino and Lucia's arrival was treated by the monks as a blessed occasion for everyone. Sometimes, even a distraction is cause for joy.

A novice had been the first to meet them and he quickly moved them to the large infirmary ward, where Ada had collected two dozen cots and beds on the assumption that wounded from Cassino, or the nearby hills, or even the monks themselves might need tending in the weeks and months to come. Yes, there had been other townsfolk who had come to the abbey for sanctuary but the abbot had generally fed them and then urged them to return to their families and farms below, where—he said— they would be safe and could wait out the worst of it. "Here is no place for children," he would tell them.

There was something different about Dino and Lucia, however. It wasn't their beauty, though both of them were very beautiful. And it wasn't the softness of their brown eyes or the way each of them seemed to move with the grace of dancers and hold even the most banal of objects— a fork, a teacup, a piece of bread—as if each were a gift given with generosity and received with humility. It was that each of them, in their own way, exuded a gentleness from a warm and glowing heart that was made vibrant because one had the company of the other. Massimo watched them and learned quickly that each was the other's source of strength and civility and, though neither wore a ring, even the monks with their strict codes of modesty never asked whether they were betrothed and no one suggested they should, at any time, be apart. During a war, one does not arbitrarily extinguish a flame.

Ada had them bathed in warm water and dressed them in clean city clothes before nightfall—Dino in blue cotton trousers and a loose-fitting green shirt, and Lucia in a faded red dress with black dots. When they returned from the showers in their new clothes and fluffy hair, they could have been the abbey's own Adam and Eve, each one strong and young and pure and clean.

The abbot himself came to collect them from the infirmary once they'd each rested, and he insisted that they come to supper, fill themselves with the little that the monastery had to offer, and then—if it wasn't too much to ask—share news; because it was already known in whispers that Dino had been stationed with the 33rd Infantry Division—known as the Acqui Division—on an island in Greece and through a gauntlet of terrors had ended up here.

DINO SIPPED FROM HIS BEER that night as if it were tea and would be his last. Lucia was handed an apple—a luxury at the abbey—and received it with a smile of gratitude. Using a long knife, she sliced it in sheets so thin it was possible to see through them. She would place a single slice on her tongue and let it dissolve and offered pieces to everyone around her.

Massimo was the only taker, and watching him receive it had made her smile.

As he allowed the sweetness of the apple to settle onto his tongue, he listened to them tell their story. Pietro, until recently, had continued taking his supper in his room like a recluse, but the isolation had lost its war with his more social side, and now he too ate with the community that—given the chance—once again formed around him.

He had not taken a slice of the apple, but he did sit quietly with his cane and white suit waiting to hear the news he was sure was going to pour out of them both the way it had from Brother Tobias.

"I was in the Italian army. I did not like it," Dino began to explain. "I was stationed on a Greek island called Cephalonia. I suppose we were their occupiers, and for this I felt bad. We had been stationed there without incident for quite some time, or . . . no more trouble than might be understandable under the conditions," he said with a regretful shrug. "And then it all became very strange. As I understand it, Mussolini was deposed and captured and sent to the top of the mountain in exile. But then these German commandos captured the hotel he had been placed in and flew him away. Okay. So then they put him back in power and we have the new Mussolini government called Salò. Okay. But then, finally, they depose him again and the king has General Badoglio take over. Third time, okay. We listened to all this on the radio like it was a distant story as we drank the ouzo, which is not so nice but you can get used to it after a while. The bad politics helps distract you from the taste, believe me. Anyway, Badoglio is in power. Still we are allied to the Germans though the Germans are very mean. The Greeks kept asking us why and we said we didn't know, because . . . Greece and Germany are so far away from each other that it makes no sense for anyone to be angry but . . . okay. We try to keep the peace during the war because that is the only sensible thing to do. And then on the eighth of September we heard the strangest announcement on the radio. We heard that Italy was surrendering to the Allies. But Badoglio then says 'la guerra continua'—'the war continues.' What does that mean? How do you surrender and keep fighting? Whose side were we on? This was so Italian even we Italians couldn't understand it. The Germans, however, are not a questioning people. They are more comfortable with answers. So they jumped right over being confused and turned on us as traitors to our alliance and they attacked us. They attacked us! Right away! Without mercy. Can you imagine?

"We had been friends. I mean . . . moments earlier. Drinking and laughing together. But a voice came on the radio, then some of their commanders spoke, and like heartless creatures for whom friendship and real life meant nothing, they started killing us. We tried to defend ourselves. I suppose. But it was horrible. We fought badly. And when we were captured, the Germans—they murdered *everyone*. In the streets. In fields. Against walls. We were not treated as soldiers. Or even people. We were slaughtered and there was no place to go. I learned later that the Germans called this Operation Achse. They are colonizing us. Taking everything. Guns, food, oil, men for labor. I don't want to discuss the women. And later? Okay . . . much later, I am talking about the time after I escaped, which I will explain, but for now I still have to say: I learned later that some Italians still chose to keep fighting the war *with* the Germans! My mind could no longer contain all these. Okay, I am not a philosopher. But surely there must be some understandable reason for the things we do, no? Well. Not to me. It was chaos. It remains chaos. All of it. There is no way for a sane man to be a part of this and so . . . I am out. This is a movie and I don't like it, and I have taken for the exit."

"The escape?" Pietro said.

"Excuse me?"

"You said you escaped. Which I'm hoping will explain your lady friend and the donkey."

"Lucia and Ferrari."

"Your donkey is called Ferrari."

"No."

"Please tell me it's not the girl."

"No, I mean, Ferrari is a mule."

Pietro nodded and added: "My name is Houdini. Tell me more about the escaping."

"Okay, yes. I see now what you mean. So: I don't know why but the Germans in Cephalonia put me on a steamship called *Ardena* in the port of Argostoli with other prisoners. They put maybe a thousand of us in the hold. This was on the twenty-sixth of September. Many were already wounded. We were beaten. Starving. I don't know even where the Germans were planning to take us. But I have heard stories. Many, already. All the Italian divisions on the mainland—they simply surrendered, not only to the Allies but to the *Germans* who were supposed to be our allies. If there was any resistance against the Germans, they killed everyone. They have taken hundreds of thousands of our soldiers and moved them north into Germany through Switzerland to become slave labor. I think that was to be my fate. They have assassinated our generals. They have now occupied Rome. We are a doomed nation. We have lost this war twice. Twice in one month! And maybe we have lost our purpose and our dignity and our culture all at the same time. I don't know. I just don't know."

Lucia was listening as if from a distance. Massimo watched her face for a reaction but it was clear she had heard it all before. Her eyes were not blank but knowing. Supportive. Empathetic. She followed each word, aware of what was to come and still finding it incomprehensible even in retrospect.

"The ship," she gently said to him, prompting him to continue and perhaps a little faster.

"Yes, of course," Dino said, responding to her touch. "It was on the twenty-seventh. I was in the hold and we were under steam leaving the port. I was not beside a window—"

"Porthole," Lucia whispered.

"Yes. A porthole. I was not beside one of those. So I saw nothing. But only a short time into the sea we struck a mine and the ship exploded. Of this, I am sure. Water started rushing in. Some of the men were tied up and I had to watch them struggle for air and then drown. Others tried to climb out the portholes but the openings were too small and they got stuck. There was blood in the water."

Dino paused and sipped from his beer before resuming.

"They say hell is hot. I assure you it is not. I think now that the deeper and colder water was rushing up as the boat sank, which explains how terrible it was. This was not the water we used to swim in. This cold crushed our chests.

"I fought my way to the back of the boat. Most of the men were trapped inside the main hold but one of the crew had opened the door near me to get himself out and I was able to push my way through before it was closed again. Once on deck I could see how fast the ship was going under. It is a sensation unlike any other. When you're on one of these massive ships the sea looks to be a wide and flat place. It is only when something that big starts to go down you sense—in your body—how deep and dark and expansive the sea really is. It eats ships! It was watching a city erased."

Pietro folded his arms.

"Yes, yes, okay. I'm sorry. The events:

"I found a thick rope that dangled over the side and I decided to climb down into the water. I was always a good swimmer and I thought, 'Okay, better to try to swim away from the fires and guns and the screaming. How far could I be? A few kilometers? I can swim this.' Yes, I know, the Germans were massacring us on the island but what choice did I have? I could only go back.

"It turned out that the rope was attached to one of the *parabordi*—those rubber tubes that the ships use to prevent damage while in the berth. You know them? Well . . . they float. I had slid down the side of the ship until my feet landed on top of one. I couldn't slide farther but the sea was rushing up toward me so I clung to the rope and hoped—no, no, I prayed—that the Germans would not see me and shoot me in the head.

"The bow was sinking fast. It was going down in the front but also starting to list in my direction. Beside me and toward the back I saw a lifeboat come over the side very quickly. There were four Germans trying to save themselves. If they had turned I would have been dead, but they were focused on the water. What happened next was . . . it was terrible. They lowered the boat too quickly and the propeller of the *Ardena* still had a head of steam so as soon as the little boat touched the water they were pulled down. I watched the awareness reach the men before the blades. For what they had done to us, I should have felt nothing or even glee at the justice. But when you see men approach death with their eyes . . . well. I could not look away or feel glee. Some screamed and others faced death in silence. The propeller chopped them apart. Somehow—and I don't know how—the rope I was holding was detached from the ship and . . . I fell. Two meters? Three meters? I don't know. But I dropped and I became a torpedo. I held on to that rope for my very life and all I could think about was the propeller chopping me up. But that is not what happened."

Dino looked at Pietro, the way everyone looked to Pietro: for guidance, for affirmation, for direction. In this case, despite Dino having said something obvious, Pietro refrained from comment out of respect for the story Dino was telling in his own way.

"I sank three meters into the water with the *parabordo* above me," Dino said, looking around the room to all those gathered. He needed them to know. And they needed to hear. "I still held the rope but was now below it. That is when I looked down and saw the ship and learned how deep the sea was. You cannot imagine it if you have never seen it. It was like being next to a sinking city, and as my eyes focused as best they could, I saw this huge hole in the side where the mine exploded and blew open the hull. Still underwater and holding my breath, I watched the front part of the ship rip off like half a piece of paper and it made a sound like a whale dying from sadness.

"From under the water I saw more explosions above. The light. The color. The bullets hitting the water like icicles being used to stab at us. It was seeing but not seeing. I understood more than my eyes were telling me. The Germans—I am trying to explain—were killing those of us who didn't drown. I swam up as best I could, broke the surface for air, and then was pulled far under again. That is when I saw the faces of the men inside the portholes. Only this time I was outside looking in. They were dead. At first I saw only one or two of them but then it was like spirits pouring out of an ancient pirate ship. Hundreds of men. I saw hundreds of men float out through the massive rip in the hull."

Dino took Lucia's hand. "I understood then that the Germans had locked the doors. Why would people do such a thing? That is not war. That is not—"

Dino's beer was gone and he reached for the glass of the wine the abbot had placed on the table. How wine still existed at the abbey was one of its continued mysteries.

"The current of the Ionian Sea is counterclockwise," he continued after downing half a glass to calm himself. "I floated northwest with the *parabordo*. I was too afraid to let go and try to swim. I lost my bearings and didn't know which way to go anyway. I saw the sun through the clouds but as I spun around I lost a sense of its movements.

"I clung to it for maybe ten or fifteen hours. I don't know. It was until well past dawn of the second day. That is when a British commando ship found me. Did you know," he said, wiping away tears, "that the *Ardena* was originally a British minesweeper in the Great War? It's true. The British told me this after they pulled me up and dried me off like a wet dog and watched me eat. It had triple hulls at the bow. It was called an Azalea class. What were the odds that a minesweeper would be sunk by a mine? That we would even hit one from another war? That the Germans who were my allies would kill us and the British who were my enemies would save me? That a man on a balloon floating in the Ionian Sea would be found by another ship at all? It is like an arrow finding another arrow in flight in the dark. Now," he said, smiling for the first time, "here I am telling my story to monks!

"The commandos were from the British 38th infantry brigade. They dropped me at Termoli, which is a pretty little village with a medieval sea wall surrounding the old town with a church in the middle. I'm sure you can imagine it. Like so many places. This was on the third of October. The British were very friendly to me. They showed me how to do this." Dino made a coin dance across his knuckles and then disappear back inside his palm.

Massimo's eyes grew wide.

"They asked me to come ashore and respectfully tell the townsfolk to be quiet and not mention we were there because we wanted to drive out the Germans. It made sense for an Italian to tell them, of course. I didn't realize, though, how desperate people were for news. Before I knew it, I was surrounded by the villagers and fishermen and widows and . . . they *hated* the Germans. It was not only the people on Cephalonia. It was here too. They, too, had heard Badoglio's strange announcement about '*la guerra continua!*' Everyone wanted to know from me why we would fight the Allies when we were being killed by the Germans. This . . . I didn't know.

"I said that the British were nice to me and gave me food and water and clothing and taught me to roll a coin across my hand whereas the Germans were killing Italians. So . . . sometimes life makes things clear, no? That was when I met Lucia. She approached me when the crowd had started to break and she looked at me, and then at my hands, and said, 'Would you teach me to do that?' That was when I knew I was in love and only those events—two world wars, a minesweeper and a mine, the direction of the currents, the kindness of the British, the existence of a coin to use—made our love possible. Can you imagine?"

Pietro grunted. More in recognition and agreement than contempt, though a dash of contempt for the Fates could always be assumed.

Dino's report was long but everyone wanted to hear it. His was the first story they had heard from someone beyond the walls in a long time. It was also the first voice of someone close. Someone they could see, and whose eyes they could look to for sincerity and honesty. Massimo could see the relaxed shoulders of Ada and Bella, of Pietro and Tobias and many of the monks he did not know by name. Their bodies relaxed into the truth. They were not studying the words of the radio for what was not being said.

Dino's face, his eyes, could hide nothing. As Massimo would come to believe: they had never learned how.

The British and Germans fought as he and Lucia escaped, going west into the mountains and staying south of the new German fortifications. Where the roads ended they climbed. Where the summits were exposed to the sky they camped. When the rains came they trudged on like the first humans who pressed ever onward looking to flee danger and settle in peace.

One night they camped at 1,800 meters on Monte Miletto. They avoided the villages when they could because the local *municipi* were usually occupied by the Germans and if they were not, too many eyes saw too much. Another night they were above the tree line and had set up their tent on a ridge because the grassy depression nearby—tempting and sheltered and soft as it was—had proved a basin for rainwater. And so they slept on the hard earth and did not light a fire so they might avoid detection. With the endless sky above them and the mountains to the northwest as far as they could see, it was Lucia who thought of coming to Montecassino. She said she had a dream that they would be received with warmth and kindness by people who would not turn them away.

Four days later they were here. Not only with their soft skin and kind eyes and hard news, but also with Dino's stories and a flute that Lucia brought with her everyplace.

Dino continued: "All worker strikes are forbidden. I heard this from the voice of the new German authorities. Saboteurs will be immediately shot. All mail will be read by the occupiers, and the phone conversations will all be heard. It is impossible to communicate between north and south now. All lines are either cut or too dangerous to use.

"And . . ." he said, suddenly changing the conversation, "how are all of you?"

DINO STOPPED TALKING AND AFTER dinner everyone grew pensive, reflecting on how much was happening and how hopeless it all looked. Pietro did not contribute to the musings and, uncharacteristically—ever since the accident—watched and listened to the mood of the monks and the villagers and the travelers and the peasants. His eyes tracked the speakers. His mind was filled with calculations that Massimo was certain he could hear, like a mechanical adding machine with gears and knobs and white numbers that flicked up with sums and solutions.

When Massimo was not listening to the words, or staring at Pietro, he was watching the patterns. What he noticed was how it was only when the men were choked with emotion that it became possible for the voices of women to soar.

LUCIA D'ANGELO WAS TWENTY-THREE YEARS old. Her hair was black and tied back into a thick ponytail. Her face was pale, her lips were thick, and her lashes were long. Her eyes were exceedingly intelligent: brown, clear, and understanding. It was no surprise to Massimo that when she opened her small black case and removed a flute the dining hall fell into a prayer-like silence.

Without an invitation or introduction, she raised the slender silver instrument to her lips with confidence but did not yet blow.

Instead, she paused when her lower lip rested against the riser of the embouchure. For what, Massimo didn't know. When to begin is something that only a musician can know. In a room devoid of sound, a building devoid of art, a country devoid of hope, she waited for *something* to arrive—something that moved through her—and, once she began to play, it filled that void with everything that was missing.

Into the space came music.

The piece was neither sad nor melancholy, which Massimo had expected on account of the mood. It had been his as well. Born inland, Massimo didn't really know the water, and the open sea held both a fascination and a terror for him. He knew—at least from a map—that Naples was on the sea, and Pietro had described the city to him one night (he didn't like Naples very much), and despite Pietro's generally dour depictions of the Città del Sole, Massimo still felt drawn to it, a sort of morbid push south to the edge of the world and then into the waters and the promise of rebirth.

Dino's story, however, shifted the entire orientation of Massimo's imagination. Before, the sea was far and distant, like a horizon. It suggested finality and arrival. Dino's story made the sea deep and vertical and cold and endless. Not a place where a child could sink forever among lifeless bodies with open eyes. When Lucia placed the flute to her lips, Massimo was certain the sound would capture the sensation of drowning and it would make the air in the room thin.

But she did not. Her music came from the place she wanted to be.

The song she played was the Flute Concerto in D by Luigi Boccherini, a piece Massimo didn't know then but would later recognize and learn to name. Lucia closed her eyes as she played the light, quick piece. As she did, Massimo pictured the notes fluttering over them with the gentleness of butterflies and instead of the dark waters he saw empty fields and intense orange sunlight below dawn clouds illuminating a valley of trees. The music told a story of a coming spring.

Massimo was certain that everyone in the damp, stone-walled room was picturing the same images in their minds and feeling the same emotions. What else? To be in the music was to be in the sun and everyone feels the same in the sun.

If the flute could have spoken it would have told them that the life of the spirit was greater than the life of the body; that Italy's culture was more than its current condition; and that their country was eternal and would someday remember itself as the place that inspired such beauty and grace.

Massimo looked to Pietro and it was clear from his expression—his open eyes, his attentiveness, his posture—that the magic of Lucia's flute had awoken him and turned him outward, turned him away from his inner anguish, his drug-induced journeys, his reflective and dark imaginings. He became present again. Rooted. There.

It was while Lucia played—it was because Lucia played—that the *orso polare* turned to Massimo and asked, "Do you still want to go?"

When was the last time Pietro actually addressed him directly? Weeks, certainly. At least with a question. He'd been talked *at* during that time, but not really *to*.

Feeling distant from Pietro had been painful, and all that time catching pigeons had been a half-hearted attempt to pretend that he didn't feel lonely and rejected and ignored. The problem was that Pietro hadn't been reachable, so there hadn't really been a way to talk to him even if Massimo had had the courage to try, which he didn't. He had felt many things since first coming to the abbey, but until the accident he had never felt abandoned.

Being asked a question with such directness felt like a new beginning.

"Go where?" Massimo asked.

"South. Are we ready?"

Massimo couldn't quite believe the question. While he was happy to be asked about going south—happy to be asked anything—Dino and

Lucia's story had provided such clarity about the situation that even his own young impulses and inherent desire to please Pietro were checked.

"No, Pietro. We are not."

"Why not?"

"Why not?"

"Is it because of my health? My legs?"

"Yes."

"Is that the only reason?"

Earlier, before the accident and the murders and Jürgen, Massimo might have said yes or else stayed silent and waited—like the damaged and scared orphan he was—for the moment to pass as he had under the table in the Gestapo office. Now, however, he was able to muster a different answer:

"No."

"Walk with me," Pietro said.

SLOWLY, WITH A CRUTCH TO support him, Pietro walked out of the room and Massimo followed. They left Lucia and Dino and the music and the monks all behind. Together they passed beneath the portico and beyond the entrance to the former museum where Pietro had whiled away his time. After, they turned left toward the archives that the Germans had not been able to fully empty on account of the sheer volume of papers, books, special collections, scripts, illuminations, and drawings, all of such indeterminate value that it was not worth their time—so said König.

Inside, Pietro chose a brown library desk in a room paneled in wood with glass cabinets that were still open. Paper was strewn across the floor. There had once been rules and order concerning where they could go and what was off-limits. That structure was gone now. In the abandoned space, they collected chairs among the remaining papers as pigeons sat among ruins.

Pietro lifted one sheet from the ground that may have been written in Latin or an old German script. The calligraphy on the old, handwritten pages was precise and had been applied with terrible care. Pietro released his joints to gravity and sank into a chair. Once comfortable, he began fashioning the paper into a boat.

"You remember what I said in the car?" he asked, trying not to crack the brittle paper.

Massimo nodded, also sitting down.

Pietro did too. "I want to explain myself even though it is a month too late. It is true: my name is Pietro Raphael Mussolini. Benito is a cousin. Second cousin, third, I don't even know how it works. Everyone is a cousin in Italy. I met him a couple of times at big weddings when we were teenagers. Perhaps if I had had the foresight to strangle him in the coat closet Italy would never have gone to war, my wife would never have been arrested, and your parents would still be alive. Alas.

"What you need to understand, and what goes against all your education, is that a name . . . is only a name. You were raised in Benito's Italy to think that men pass on magical powers to their sons, and that our blood determines our fates, and that the races are all different from each other and blood is what makes this true, but the fact is, Massimo, the only difference between men is what we look like. Even the differences between men and women—real though some are—determine very little, at least about our minds. The fascists built myths to contain us, but that time is over now.

"You must unlearn all of this. I was never destined to be a certain way because I am a Mussolini. Each of us is unique. Some people are far more intelligent, beautiful, gifted, talented, faster, stronger, or otherwise better than others. This is a fact. But—opportunities notwithstanding— no country, race, or religion has a greater number of these people. The best are sprinkled across the world, and if they cluster in places and at times, it is because those places and times bring out the best in them and attract the best *to* them. Italy was once such a place. Believe it or not,

Germany was too and not so long ago. At other times it was Prague. Or Paris. Or Damascus or Cairo or Baghdad or Delhi or Timbuktu. And the list goes on. Culture can nurture us or crush us. My point is, Massimo, I am named Mussolini. I am not, however, *a Mussolini*. I am *Pietro*. And now? Now I am Pietro Houdini. The escape artist of Italy. I escape from everything and no one escapes from me. It's all very curious. Now it seems we have two more to add to our little group."

"Three."

"Three what?"

"To add."

"Who taught you to count?"

"Ferrari. He is number three."

"Ah. I see. All right. Three it is.

"I have said that I do not believe in the magic of this name," Pietro said. "Mussolini is only a series of sounds, a short opera without a hero. But the Germans find it compelling because, unlike me, they believe in blood and race and destiny and all that nonsense. It is how I convinced them that we were not with the partisans and it would have made no sense for a Mussolini and a teenager to have killed German soldiers for a couple of guns.

"If they lose this war, Massimo, as I think they will, it will happen because they cannot imagine lives that are fundamentally different from their own or that people would be willing to die for that way of life. The same arrogant ideas that got them into this war will be the same ones to get us all out of it. This is how nature finds balance with stupidity.

"There's no need to fear me more because of my name," he finally said.

Though his speech was important, and Massimo had listened carefully, Pietro had not understood the reasons for Massimo's reluctance to leave. It wasn't Pietro's name that scared Massimo. It was—finally—the wave of fire that was getting closer and his worry about what would happen to all these good people when it arrived.

IN THE FIRST WEEKS OF December 1943, Pietro's legs had healed enough for him to start moving around with a new measure of freedom in the monastery. With so much missing now, the place echoed the tiniest sounds and Pietro's tapping cane rang through the halls and stones like a hidden metronome that gradually increased in tempo as time passed. It created a sense of building anticipation and Massimo could tell that the monks felt it too. They seemed to walk faster when Pietro's cane was tapping, tapping away.

That anxious heartbeat usually settled when Pietro entered the empty archives for a rest on his perch or else the former museum, where he would paint.

At first Massimo thought that Pietro had recovered their bag from its hiding place and he was copying the Tizianos for some reason. But Pietro said he was not doing that at all. He had another plan for the paintings but to execute it he needed much more practice because—while he was a good painter—he was used to copying things.

"These three will be Houdini originals," he said.

"What are the subjects?" Massimo said, and Pietro smiled at him.

"I know one. But the other two still elude me. So I am trying to compose this one and make sure I have the hand to fulfill my vision."

"What about the other two?" Massimo asked, still not understanding the relationship between these paintings and the Tizianos.

"I don't know. They have to come to me. I suspect the inspiration hasn't arrived yet."

When he was not with Pietro, Massimo spent time with Dino and Lucia. Aside from a few novices and younger monks, they were the closest to him in age though the decade that separated them was the most formative decade of a life. Still, their vitality and easy laughter in the face of horrors were the best songs inside those heavy walls and their presence warmed the chambers against the harsh winds and early snows coming to central Italy.

One of the monks had said this was going to be the worst winter in twenty years and he worried that the soldiers didn't have warm coats. Massimo hadn't been sure whether he'd meant the Germans, the Allies, or all of them. The statement, though, had sent a chill through him. He huddled more deeply into his own jacket as much for its warmth as its camouflage.

Lucia and Dino's new presence in Massimo's life reminded him of being in Rome when he'd had a certain attraction to his friends' older siblings. Those attractions had not been sexual so much as a kind of hero worship: a desire to be as bold and boastful and beautiful as the teenagers who were already free of their parents, roaming the world and making mischief. Mischief, after all, was so important to children who had been raised to be young fascists.

Being an only child had been unusual. He hadn't known any other single children. Neither Catholicism nor fascism wanted small families, and Massimo was never entirely sure why his mother only had him.

Her.

Remembering his parents reminded him of his real life. The life under the clothes, the illusion, the solution, the strategy . . . whatever he was inclined to call it from one moment to the next. It also meant remembering them. The dinners. The attention. The conversations and arguments and tantrums and their devotion and love through it all. Unlike so many other children, who seemed to run feral through Rome's streets when not in school, Massimo loved being with his parents and they loved being with him. Thirteen years old, he would sit at cafés with his parents and they would sip coffee and he would sip a tea, precocious, and nod knowingly as they discussed the grand affairs of the day and asked him whether he too had any thoughts on the matters in the papers.

That life was a parallel and honest one compared to the other taught inside the schools that always felt forced and imposed and unnatural. Fascism was not only a political system that the grown-ups lived inside; it was also the hard strictures the children were raised in. Fascism was the medals they collected on their uniforms for the right answers to questions, and it was the accolades they received at school for memorizing and reciting its propaganda and for accepting that the highest virtue was confining the soul and giving obedience to the masters.

Especially the girls.

Montecassino was the first place in Massimo's life where all of that was left behind.

MASSIMO, LUCIA, AND DINO WOULD meet in the eastern wing of the monastery in Dino's room, which was a bit larger and had a view that was unobstructed when the clouds permitted. Some days they would play cards and others Massimo would sit and listen to the two of them talk and marvel at them. One day, Lucia put her flute into Massimo's hands.

"I can't play it," he said.

"Not yet," she said with a smile.

"I don't want to."

"Yes, you do. I've seen the look on your face when I start to play."

Massimo wasn't sure if the look Lucia was talking about came from his feelings about the music. He had, if he were to admit the truth to himself, been looking at her lips and her neck and the way she closed her eyes when she was about to blow across the mouthpiece.

On the other hand, he wasn't prepared to say no when she placed the metal—already warm from her playing and smelling of her breath—against his lips.

"Forget the flute," she said. "Blow gently at my nose. I'll do the rest."

In his oversized jacket and itchy gray trousers, Massimo sat on a chair at Dino's desk and looked into Lucia's soft eyes as she knelt on the floor and smiled while pressing the flute to Massimo's lower lip.

"Look at me," she said. "Don't worry. Don't think. Blow. Gently and evenly."

Massimo did as he was told. The sound was only the wind joining more wind outside, a sound that was listless and pointless. That is, until he felt her rotate the flute to change its position on Massimo's lip and in that gentle adjustment—music. A note, soft and pure. A C. Seeing the joy that came to Lucia's face, he continued to blow until he was so breathless that he had to suck in the air like a drowning sailor reaching the surface.

"Good! That was so good!" she exclaimed, and Dino clapped behind her. "Now this time, I'm going to play some notes. You'll be able to tell when it's the right time to take a breath, but just in case, I'll nod. But I'm going to stand behind you because it's hard to do the fingering backward."

Lucia stood, walked behind Massimo, and then crouched down with her arms wrapped around him. She placed the flute to his lips again and Dino watched them both with a fixed thin smile. Massimo could smell the soap in her hair, the one they all used because the monks had stored enough away even with the rationing. On Lucia, however, it smelled better.

"Here we go," she said, and with that announcement, Lucia inhaled deeply. He breathed in too and as she blew out past his ear, he blew across the flute, creating that C note again. But this time, her fingers danced. The flute requires the player to blow harder for higher notes and—knowing that Massimo's skills were limited—Lucia played only the most simple tune for him. Together they created music, and when she was finished, Lucia smiled, Dino started to laugh, and Massimo started to cry.

She was about to say something to comfort him when they heard four trucks pull up outside and then both Germans and Italians start to yell.

"What's this about?" Lucia asked.

A moment later—as though he had been lurking behind the door—Pietro burst in.

"You two," he said, pointing at Massimo and Dino, "need to become invisible. Right now!"

"Why?" asked Dino. "We didn't do anything."

"That's not entirely true, is it?" Pietro said. "You deserted from the Italian army, and the little one . . . has other and more local issues that I'm not sure are resolved even with König gone. Either way, they're rounding up Italian men to make their slave quota or else to force you to fight for the new Italian Social Republic because no one's volunteering for it. Benito is in charge again but Hitler is pulling all the strings now. They might ship you off. They might shoot you for being a deserter. They might shoot you for being a partisan. They might shoot you for being so pretty. Either way, they are not here to help form a quartet! This is war. You fight or hide. Now is the time to hide!

"You," he said, still speaking to Dino. "You come with me. I know a place. And you," he said, pointing to Massimo. "It is time to transform again. Yesterday was a bad time to be a girl. You had my respect and sympathies and support. Today it is a bad day to be a boy. Have Lucia dress you accordingly. If they are looking for men, let them find none. If they are looking for you in particular—they will be looking for Massimo so don't *be* Massimo. The Germans are not lateral thinkers and I don't believe they've read *Two Gentlemen of Verona*. So: time for a dress! Hurry."

"Why not dress Dino as a girl too?" Lucia asked as she stood at the window and looked outside, trying to see who was coming.

"Why? Why? Because there is no time for him to shave and your clothes and shoes are too small and the illusion would not be convincing. *Andiamo!*" yelled Pietro.

Pietro left the room in a rush with Dino in tow, leaving Lucia with Massimo.

Massimo looked at Lucia with incredulity.

"I suppose," said Lucia, "we do what he says."

"Dress me?" Massimo said to Lucia, as horrified by the prospect as he was of the Germans now invading the monastery.

"And quickly," she said. "Take off all your clothes. We only have a moment. We're almost the same size. Close enough, anyway. I'm sure I have something here," she said. "It is a blessing your skin is so fair."

Until then Massimo had assumed this was Dino's room. When Lucia opened the drawer, however, it was clear it was hers.

The last drawerful of women's clothes Massimo had seen were in Rome and they belonged to his mother.

Massimo stepped backward as though looking at a bomb but Lucia pushed him forward.

"Off. Clothes off," Lucia said with the commanding voice of an older sister.

Reluctantly, Massimo stripped down to his underwear as Lucia found a blue dress with yellow stripes that she assumed would be long enough. The waist had a drawstring that Lucia supposed would create the impression of hips. What she was going to do with the rest she didn't know, but her last stub of red lipstick was going to be needed, that much she was sure.

When she turned around, though, she dropped it on the floor and it rolled under the bed. Lucia was not looking at a naked boy but a girl in the Venus Pudica pose: the left hand covering her privates beneath the boxers and her right across her bare breasts.

"Massimo. You're a *girl*."

"I'm a boy."

"You . . . are not a boy."

"I have to be."

"That is not the same thing. For now, being a boy is bad," Lucia said. "You heard Pietro. You have to be a girl because they are looking for men generally and Massimo in particular. They are not sending girls to the army or slave labor camps. They are not shooting girls as partisans. And whatever it is Massimo did? That person is gone now, and so are his deeds. The good news is that what was impossible for me to solve was already solved by God fourteen years ago. It is time for you to become yourself again."

Massimo who was not Massimo said nothing. He simply stood there in the pose feeling utterly exposed.

"You don't need a bra. It would help but . . . you're still young enough. And that underwear . . . *mio Dio*—will have to do for now. Put this on. You slip it on over your head. Hands up. Have you never done this before?"

Massimo slipped on the dress and it hung there, limp.

He wasn't sure what he had expected.

"Did you always dress like a boy? Is this new? We have no time for new. It is best if you can remember."

Lucia dropped to her hands and knees and started crawling across the floor.

"It's under the bed," Massimo said.

Lucia crawled on her belly to retrieve the lipstick. Once it was in her hands, she stood quickly and puckered her lips. "Like this. Do like this. Did you never have a mother? An older sister?" Poor Lucia was becoming exasperated. It was not unreasonable. "Have you ever walked the streets of a city and looked around you? Do what I say. Pucker. Now!" Bending as though to examine a complex and ancient artifact, she painted the girl's lips as she puckered her own for instruction or natural empathy.

Massimo looked into Lucia's eyes and at her face as she did this. She was undeniably beautiful—maybe more so in her frustration.

"What's your name?" she asked gently as she stood back to examine her handiwork, the yelling in the halls coming closer.

"Massimo."

"Your real name."

"Massimo!"

"Massimo is a boy's name. And it's a strange boy's name. You need a girl's name. If you will not use *your* name, then this new girl needs her *own* name and she needs it *now*. Sit. There. On the bed. Feet crossed at the ankles like a good little fascist girl who does what she is told. Hands on your lap. They are coming for us. Oh shit, you need shoes!"

Lucia kicked off her own and placed them on the new girl's feet. Size 37. A perfect fit.

"I want to name you . . . Athena . . . because you sprang out of my head, but that is not Italian. So I hereby christen you . . . Eva. Eva *Something*." Lucia looked down and to the right. She was creating. Concocting. It was as physical for her as molding clay.

"Eva *Ricci*. Your name is Eva Ricci. That's a common name here in Abruzzo. Your parents are dead. You are too shocked to speak, like so many of the soldiers you have seen. I am taking care of you. If they scare you . . . cling to me. I will lie for us both. Eva? Yes? You are listening?"

Eva Ricci—wet from her baptism-by-lipstick—was listening. These were the first words she had ever heard because Eva Ricci was a newborn and the abbey of Montecassino was her birthplace.

EVA RICCI WAS NOT THE girl raised in Rome. She was not Massimo either. She was . . . something apart from the two of them because they were both in hiding.

Eva felt her new dress. Her new shoes. She felt her new legs and her new hips and new breasts and new arms and thinner wrists and longer fingers. She could taste and smell the lipstick. It tasted and smelled like Lucia as best as she could tell. Was this the taste that Dino knew? Did they kiss when no one was around? What more did they do?

She could hear the soldiers' boots approaching in the hallway. Others were pounding on doors demanding entry in German or Italian.

"Stand next to me," Lucia said. "Say nothing. Don't look them in the eyes."

She did as she was told and stood beside the woman who was now . . . what? A big sister? A woman from the village caring for her?

The footsteps grew closer as she stared at the door and wondered: *Who is Eva?*

Unable to accept the possibilities of what might come, and still shaken from Massimo's interrogation by Jürgen, Eva's thoughts turned toward herself and this new life, this new body, this new fiction.

Eva—she decided—always woke too early on the weekends and slept too late on the weekdays. Her father wondered why this was so. Was it because school tired her out so she naturally wanted to sleep in? It was a good theory but it didn't explain why Fridays didn't cause her to sleep late on Saturdays or why Monday mornings were still hard.

What more? What about friends, pets, favorite songs or colors? What did she like to wear even if she didn't have any of it? Had she seen films, read books, watched theater? Did she like museums and ruins and talking with her parents or was she wild and unpredictable and did she sneak out of the house to smoke cigarettes and pretend she was older?

The banging was only three doors away now. There was no time to know herself. There was only time to remember Pietro.

* * *

Pietro had once said that shortly before the Renaissance, the Black Death changed art. During one of his lectures in the archives, months ago, he said that after a third of the population of Europe was dead from the disease, the survivors had lost faith in God and also their fear of the Church. Nudity and eroticism started to appear in paintings and sculptures. He spoke of Donatello's *David*, the first nude sculpture since antiquity dating to the 1440s. David, the biblical slayer of Goliath, was presented not as a muscle-bound Greek god but instead as a delicate, flowing, even feminine figure.

"Donatello saw in his David the body of a gentle soul, one roused to violence out of righteous anger, not an inclination. You see, after a hundred years of death, the West started to restore itself. It did that by remembering itself. Remembering Greece. But also by seeing itself as something that was naturally part of the world. A piece of nature, not something separate from it. That sculpture was a teenager's body, full of truth and life and, yes, even eroticism and sexuality and hunger. The historians say Donatello was influenced by Masaccio's nude painting of Adam and Eve, who left the garden in ignominy, a painting that was not at all erotic. Whether this is true or not, I don't know. But it opened the door for the *David*, a figure on the edge of adulthood. Like you, Massimo. In Oriana's view, Donatello's perspective contained the essence of the degenerate impulse that Hitler would have us destroy. Within his *David* was a full-throated defense of self-expression, exploration . . . and yes, artistic freedom. Adolf really hates that sort of thing."

The soldiers banged twice on the door. Eva grabbed for Lucia's hand and together they stood there as two Italian soldiers burst in.

"Get in," Pietro said to Dino.

Pietro had chosen this crypt for his bag because it was a small, dark, and haunting place. Unlike the others, this one was not connected by tunnels to any other. The paintings on the walls were creepy and the carvings in the rock more so. The ceiling was vaulted and the floor had large tiles. Pietro and Massimo had earlier pried one up, dug out the space below it, and tossed the bag in.

At the time they had dug out much more dirt than necessary for the bag alone, though. Pietro had considered that he and Massimo might have needed to hide in there and he had prepared. So when Pietro brought Dino down the long stairs and into the room that was one ring of hell closer to the center, the hole was big and ready for Dino.

The vaulted ceiling was low. Words in Latin were etched into the walls around them and angels seemed to weep for the decision Dino had to make.

"In there?" Dino asked.

"Where else?"

"There is a bag in there."

"Plenty of room. You lie next to it. Hurry up."

"I don't want to."

"What does that have to do with anything?"

"Something, surely."

"Since when? You didn't want to fight in Albania, did you? But you did. You didn't want to be captured by the Germans and sent off on a ship but you were. You didn't want the boat to sink but it did. Wantwantwant. See how irrelevant that is? Get in."

Dino stared at the hole.

"They're coming. I'm saving your life."

"I don't like confined places. I almost drowned."

"I'll tell you a story to soothe your heart."

"Do you promise?"

"Yes."

Pietro gave Dino a gentle shove. Dino stepped to the edge like a child uncertain if the river current was too strong.

"Dino," Pietro said, as reasonably as possible. "If either the Italians or the Germans find you here, your life is over. We are in a cave with no escape. You need to lie down in the hole and share the space with three of the most important undiscovered masterpieces of the Renaissance."

"Can I see them?"

"No. They're rolled up in tubes and the timing is inauspicious. Get in the hole, Dino. They could come any second, and if they do we die. You have survived too much and gained too much since then to allow fear alone to take it away."

"Tell me about them?" Dino said as he sat and placed his feet in the hole that seemed to have no bottom and put his hand on the slab of rock that would soon entomb him.

Pietro positioned himself to push the slab into place as he spoke:

"The paintings are wonderful. They are three studies from a collection of six paintings called the poesie commission. They were all painted by the Venetian master Tiziano. All were inspired by Ovid's poem *Metamorphoses*. You have *The Rape of Europa*, where Zeus steals young Europa away to Crete. There's the *Danaë*, where Zeus appears like a golden rain to have his way with that maiden. There's Perseus, who saves Andromeda from the sea monster. I could go on. Does this mean anything to you?"

Dino shook his head and dropped to his knees beside the bag.

"They are paintings that would later make other forms of artistic expression possible and acceptable in our culture. You may think that a few old paintings are meaningless. But the happiness we are permitted to feel comes from someplace. Our emotions may be spontaneous, but social acceptance is a product of history, a history reposed on specific acts from the past that changed us all. Acts—artistic ones, heroic ones—that could not be contained by the churches or the kings. That is a very big thought for a very small space. Now get in."

"That is not a story," said Dino, disappointed.

Pietro snorted and nudged Dino again with his foot. Dino lay down and together they moved the floor panel into place as Pietro spoke:

"*C'era una volta*," he began, "the goddess of love, Aphrodite—or Venus, if you prefer—was enamored with an exquisite mortal man named Adonis. They were the most beautiful couple in all of Greek mythology.

"Adonis loved to hunt. One day, Venus had a terrible sense that something was going to happen to Adonis and she begged him to stay. In the Tiziano painting, we see her with her back to us and her arms trying to restrain her lover from leaving her, but he is too strong-willed and too confident of his return and their love for each other. And so he leaves the goddess behind. Soon after, on the hunt, he is run through by a wild boar and is killed. Poor Venus's heart is broken. She is utterly bereft. She mixes his blood with the nectar of the gods and from it blooms a wildflower called the anemone. Around us, for thousands of years, blooms the sadness of the goddess every year for her beloved. Now, a bit more. It is almost in place."

"That is a very sad story!"

"What did you expect?"

"What if they kill you and I can't get out?" said Dino through the thin space remaining.

"I'll worry about it then!" Pietro then unceremoniously pushed the stone into place and sealed it, leaving only enough of a hole for air.

THE SALÒ GOVERNMENT ALLIED TO Germany was composed of third-rate punks. Mussolini, after all, had been ousted by his own fascist council and when he returned to Rome with Hitler's support he had no choice but to execute all the high-quality fascists that hadn't already been killed by the jubilant Italians after Benito's earlier arrest. If there were any useful fascists still around they had run off to Germany or Austria or else had capitulated to the German occupation. Those running the Italian Social Republic, therefore, were the rump administrators, the weak thinkers, the cowards, and the collaborators. The army was made up of the disaffected, self-serving, money-grubbing, or clueless.

To Pietro, this meant that whoever was about to come down the stairs was not going to be the next Galileo.

"Dino, for Lucia. There is no more speaking now."

The problem Pietro had with brushing the dirt *onto* the stone tile and covering over the footprints was that the dust was kicked up by all the movement. By the time the Italian soldier finally did appear about ten minutes later—as was bound to happen—the small room was a cloud as thick as the deception it was intending to perform.

Pietro—rather than pretend the cloud didn't exist—made it worse as the man stepped inside.

"What the hell are you doing?" the man asked. He was of average build and carrying a Beretta Model 38 submachine gun in his right hand as though it were a stick.

"Cleaning out the dust, obviously! What kind of question is that?" Pietro yelled.

"Who are you?"

"Who am I? Why are you looking for me if you don't even know who I am?"

"I'm not looking for you! What are you hiding in here?"

"Hiding? What am I hiding?" Pietro said, looking around him and indicating the nothingness—nothing but a single chair, a broom, a box of chemicals and paints, and a few brushes. "You mean, am I hiding the Secret of Montecassino? Shhh. Don't tell anyone we found it."

The soldier started kicking around on the floor. This was not his first raid and not the first time he'd looked for criminals and convicts and agitators.

"What is this?" he said, running his boot toe along the edge of the slate stone.

"Who is your commanding officer? Do you know who I am? I am Pietro Mussolini. I am the cousin of Il Duce! Get out of here!"

"Il Duce's cousin, huh?" the soldier said, not looking up, and becoming more interested in the edges of the floor. "Why would the cousin of Il Duce be sweeping the floors twenty meters below a monastery?" It wasn't really a question. The man was only voicing his own inner thoughts as his body focused on the stone.

He bent down, placed the submachine gun on his right, and slotted his fingers beneath the stone. A young man, and strong, he lifted the edge and let out the darkness.

Once the stone was as high as the soldier's shins, Dino was able to look up and meet the eyes of the man for almost an entire second before Pietro Houdini placed a 9mm Luger against the back of the man's skull and blew the front of the man's face off from the back side.

The stone crashed down, bumping Dino lightly on the head, as Pietro quickly pulled the body away from the stone, tossed the dead man's rifle onto his own jacket—where he'd later wrap it and hide it—and then worked with Dino to lift and push the slate to the side.

"What did you do?" Dino asked, stunned.

"I solved a problem."

"You made a new one!"

"That's how it works. Do you want the old one back?"

Dino looked indecisive.

"Come out and bring my bag. We have to throw him in."

"What if someone else comes?"

"I don't know. It's unlikely. They don't have enough people to search everyplace twice."

"They may have heard the gunshot!"

"I used his brain to muffle the shot. No one heard anything."

"They'll notice he's missing!"

"So what?"

"So what?" Dino yelled in response. "So what?" he asked, now thinking of it as an actual question. "So what?" he muttered, recognizing that it was not a question at all but—as Pietro had insinuated—an answer. And then: "Actually, that's a good point now that you mention it. Why would they connect his disappearance to us?"

Pietro stood with his smoking gun and rested his other hand on his hip. There was no time for this kind of philosophy but Pietro knew that with his leg and other injuries it would be hard to move the body until Dino came to an understanding of their situation all by himself.

"They wouldn't. Unless . . ." Pietro said, to prompt him.

"Unless . . . they find us standing over the body with a smoking gun," Dino said.

"Welcome after, as the Nordic people say," Pietro said. "Shall we?"

"Okay. Okay." Dino grabbed the soldier and pulled him to the edge of the hole. Once his upper half was folding over, Dino was about to push him when Pietro said, "I wouldn't do that."

"Why not? We have a hole and a body. It feels like a natural relationship to me."

"If you push him, he'll fold at the bottom and then you'll have to climb in and stretch him out and you'll get his brains all over you and then have to lie down and . . . you seem squeamish to me."

"Have you done this before?" he asked, his eyes wide.

"Oh, for God's sake." Pietro hobbled to the body, grabbed an arm, pulled the body up so it was stretched out and lying beside the hole lengthwise, and then he kicked it in. The body rolled down and thumped at the bottom.

Together, they examined their handiwork.

Dino had never killed anyone before.

Pietro had.

"All right," Pietro said.

"I suppose so," Dino agreed.

"Get in," Pietro said.

"What?"

"Nothing's changed. Only now you have less space. Get in. They're still here and looking for you."

"I don't want to."

"We had this conversation already. You're wasting time."

Dino looked at the dead man and the missing front of his skull. It was one thing to kill a man. Another to see the body. And another entirely to crawl into a hole with it and pull a giant rock on top of you to seal you both in under a monastery.

There were sounds from upstairs.

Someone else *was* coming.

Pietro reached down and handed Dino the submachine gun. "Keep your finger off the trigger, please. Now."

Dino climbed down into the shallow grave and Pietro worked quickly to sweep the blood-soaked dust onto Dino and the soldier.

"Oh, come on!" Dino whispered.

"Close your mouth."

* * *

AN ENORMOUS SOLDIER APPEARED IN the doorway and found Pietro Houdini sitting on a three-legged stool using a dry paintbrush to remove grit from the etched name of a saint buried in another chamber. The soldier was also Italian. His jacket was buttoned perfectly and his shoulders were as wide as Pietro's. Across his chest was the same model submachine gun and on his face was a look of disgust.

"What are you doing?" he asked Pietro.

"Trying to please God," Pietro said without looking at him.

"There is no God," said the man with a laugh.

Pietro chose not to pursue that.

"Where is the corporal? I saw him come down."

"He came, he saw nothing he wanted, he went in search of new prey."

The man looked around, studying the walls and the floor and the single lightbulb above them.

"I didn't see him come back up."

Pietro shrugged. He had learned long ago not to offer speculations to solve other people's riddles.

The man started roaming the room, tapping against the walls.

"Please be careful of the mosaics," Pietro said without looking away from his brushwork.

The man walked along, tapping at the walls and stomping on the stone slabs with his foot. When he had almost circled the room he crouched down and placed the muzzle of his gun into a dark patch of dust. He started to move it . . . the viscous mixture dragging through the dust like black lava.

He reached down with his other hand and touched it. It was obvious what it was. Obvious enough that he pulled back the slide on his Beretta.

As he stood and turned, Pietro shot him in the head with his Luger.

The shot blasted through his temple and splattered the stone that covered Dino.

"Shit," Pietro muttered.

Placing the Luger on the stool so it could cool, he grabbed the belt of the dead soldier and pulled him off the stone.

"Go on," he said to Dino, "push it up. I can't be expected to do everything."

Dino pushed upward and over and Pietro positioned the second dead soldier on the edge of the hole, waiting for the right moment, and then—pushed him in. There was a shorter distance to fall than last time and when he landed on the other body there was an audible exhalation of gases from the first.

"All right, all right," Pietro said, looking at the corpses. "Settle back down."

"Are you crazy?" Dino said, receiving the second Beretta rifle from Pietro. He stood holding them like ski poles. "I'm not getting in there!"

"Nothing's changed."

"We murdered two men!"

"We? You've done next to nothing. Get in the hole. I'll come get you when the time is right. There's no space left in there so it's better no one else comes down. It'll be dark when I'm gone. Don't make noise."

"It's much worse now."

"You should be ashamed of complaining earlier. Now get in."

Dino laid himself on the two dead men, his eyes wide with terror and his clothes soaking in blood. Pietro refitted the stone and then panted from the exertion. Lifting had drained him considerably. He was starting to wonder if his heart had been affected by the accident somehow; not only from his phone call to Naples. Perhaps the stress of shooting two men in the head and the fear of being discovered was also a factor.

For a few minutes, Pietro tried to sweep up more of the blood but now the stones were turning red or black and it was becoming clear that the only way to solve the mess was to clean it, and that was beyond both his interests and his strength. And so he opted for the second-best solution, which was to make it all vanish.

Putting the rucksack with the art on his back and the Luger in his waistband under his shirt, which was—miraculously—splatter free, Pietro raised the small stool over his head and smashed the only bulb in the room. Bulbs were in terribly short supply and it was highly unlikely the monks would conclude that this room was worth the use of a new one.

"All right, then," he said, unhappy that his perfect hiding place for the paintings and gold was now filled with two dead bodies and a soldier on the run.

"Please don't leave," Pietro heard as he mounted the first stairs out of the crypt.

"If I stay, I'll have to kill every fascist in the country and we're outnumbered. Counterintuitively, they seem to be attracted to the light. Now stay calm, young man. Think of Lucia."

Pietro mounted another step and through the rock he heard Dino say, "Thank you. For saving my life."

Pietro did not say that he was welcome. If his own shoulders could have slumped even further they would have, but he was already weary. "I didn't do it for you," he said to the blackness behind him. "I did it for the contents of this bag and what they will make possible. They would have found it because it was in the hole with you."

"But . . ."

"I am going to Naples with this bag, Dino. I am also going to get Massimo there safely. I will do what needs to be done to make those things happen. All of this"—he motioned around him though no one could see him—"will end. One way or another. Right now we walk together because our paths are the same, but do not rely on me. I beg you."

"I don't believe you," Dino said. "I think you are a good man."

"You have excellent taste in women, Dino. Maybe the best. But you have terrible taste in men." Pietro looked up the stairs into the light from the cloister. "I hear trucks. Maybe they are starting to leave. Time will tell. I'll get you when they're gone."

"I'm scared," Dino whispered.

"That means you still have your heart and your mind and all is not lost."

THE GERMAN SOLDIER BACKHANDED LUCIA across the face, leaving her lower lip bleeding. He screamed at her in English—a language Eva didn't know and Lucia understood only in common phrases.

It was the Italian standing beside him who translated. He did not speak loudly. His calm tone and clear familiarity with such scenes and events made him twice as scary as the German. Here was a man who was no longer a man. A man without heart or compassion or autonomy or response. He was a tool in the hands of the occupier. A puppet.

"Herr Scholz wants to know where the man is. The one you arrived with. Young. Handsome. A deserter. The monks have already confessed to his presence. Tell us or you will be beaten until you reveal his location. And afterward removed."

Lucia stood up, defiant and shaking in both anger and fear. There were tears in her eyes but she did not make a sound.

Scholz smacked her again, and again the Italian watched.

Eva started to shake. It began as a twitching of her hands and, as though she were being lowered slowly into freezing water, her entire body started to seize and shake too. She couldn't breathe in and when the feeling reached her chest she thought she was about to suffocate.

Eyes wide open, mouth even wider, she quickly inhaled and rather than exhale Eva made a sound so high-pitched and loud that even the Italian stepped back.

It was a shriek. A sound that the walls of the Benedictine abbey had never heard. A sound that traveled through the walls, bursting into the halls and carrying itself through every chamber.

Scholz, at first stunned by the sound, recovered himself. He unsnapped the leather holster on his belt, removed his pistol, and chambered a round. He was about to kill Eva—about to shoot her between the eyes if only to make the noise stop—when three monks appeared in the doorway.

Eva did not stop but Scholz did not shoot because one of the monks was Friar Ryba.

Massimo had known him in passing. They had never spoken but he had a tendency to pat Massimo on the head when they passed each other in the halls and it was done with such a light touch and obvious affection that Massimo had grown accustomed to it and even liked it.

Scholz stopped because Ryba stood over six foot four and had enormous shoulders, and if he had not turned his life to God he might have chosen to become a tank. He wore a close, stylish silver beard cut to the same short length as his remaining hair. A priest from Czechoslovakia, he had fled the annexation of the Sudetenland. Whether it was faith in God, belief in the survivability of his own immortal soul, or simply the weariness that comes from being too scared for too long—a weariness that his frame and constitution had decided to shed—Ryba carried the expression of a man afraid of nothing. When he placed his enormous hand on the top of her head she fell silent as though the monk had flipped a switch.

"You're done here," Ryba said to Scholz. "We are under the protection of General Senger. You were permitted to look for deserters and criminals who attacked your people. You've found a little girl and a peasant woman taking sanctuary with St. Benedict. Get out or be prepared to explain yourself. There is a phone connecting the abbot to the general. You'll be shot before dinner whether or not your confession is heard. And that . . ." he added, "is if you even get that far."

Ryba spoke in German. His voice sounded as though it came from the bowels of a mountain.

Scholz may have been a murderous bully but he was also a calculating one. He holstered the gun, turned on his heel, and left the room without a word.

Outside, four men were loaded onto the trucks. Two were farmers from near Ponte Marozzo. One was a mechanic there with his wife and two daughters who was mistaken for a partisan who had destroyed train tracks near Fontanarosa, the other a laborer who was fingered as a partisan by his wife's lover so he could have her to himself.

FOR AN HOUR, NEITHER EVA nor Lucia left the room. They sat on the edge of the bed holding hands, the blood from Lucia's lip dotting her dress. Eva watched Lucia's toes—bare and dirty—curling and uncurling on the stone floor.

It was after the hour had passed and no more German was heard in the halls, no more shouting accompanied the softer speech of the monks, and the church bell started to ring for the Compline prayer of seven o'clock that Dino burst into the room.

Blood was smeared all over the left side of his face, and his jacket was soaked with it. His eyes appeared extraordinarily white.

Eva watched them standing and staggering toward each other, each looking like the survivors of a bombing. These two miracles of humanity; a couple she had only recently imagined naked together, their bodies soft and their skin touching—lips finding each other across white cotton sheets. Tonight they looked the way Eva had felt when Pietro had pulled Massimo from the gutter after he'd been beaten by the boys in the village.

Dino and Lucia embraced but did not cry. When Pietro entered the room soon after, he looked at Eva. It seemed to take his eyes time to adjust because he had been used to seeing Massimo.

"We need a new place to hide this bag. Come on," he said to the girl who was once Massimo but was evidently not the girl who had become Massimo.

In Lucia's shoes, Eva went to give the Renaissance masters a new place to hide.

PART III

AS PIETRO HEALED HE PAINTED. Not in the crypt, though. The crypt was for the dead, and the smell of the rotting Italian soldiers—which did have an earthly explanation—was treated by the monks as something inexplicable and not in the way they preferred so they stayed away.

November had been wet with cold and gloom. December was worse and Christmas arrived as a day of contemplation and prayer for a peace on earth no one pretended was coming soon.

PIETRO MOVED HIS STUDIO INTO the center of the library and set an easel in a comfortable location by a window in a room that no longer served angels or demons, monks or men.

During the Quiet Period before the Germans started removing the art, Pietro and Massimo had enjoyed the restoration work, as the war was not upon them. The maestro would perform his alchemy and spoke to Massimo so as not to distract God from his pressing affairs. Now was a new time and one they christened the Empty Period because the abbey's treasures were gone and too many black boots had stomped without care through its halls so that now (she could feel it) the monastery's heart was heavy with loss and the emptiness was like the moment after a sad song ends.

Pietro filled the Empty Period by painting among the empty shelves and broken glass. And blessedly, he filled it with words. She listened carefully to every one even if she didn't entirely understand.

"Italy is not a place defined by straight lines in its experience, time, or thoughts," said Pietro one day when the light shone through the high windows and made the dust visible, and he was pleased by this so he could paint with precision and without strain. "There is greatness in Italy, Eva. And reason. And clarity. All to be sure. But little of what makes Italy great is composed of straight lines. Its fashion, its sculptures, its families and language, literature and music are all curved in composition. We are one with the feminine form and men strive to get closer to it. The Teutonics, by contrast, have built a harsher world in a harsher light where the lines of their forests and mountains can pretend not to yield to the horizon as it must for us. If you need proof just look at their cars.

"Linear perspective may have launched the Renaissance from Florence, dear Eva, but it did not launch linearity. Not for us. Perspective is but the canvas. Life itself, as Italy knows, will draw its own lines and few are straight."

This went on for another thirty minutes. She could listen to it all day but if she looked for a point she was probably missing it.

From time to time Pietro would call her Massimo but neither was bothered. To both of them it felt as though Massimo had simply wandered off and—rather than being *gone*—was someplace else and lost in entertainment or exploration in the passageways beneath the monastery.

It was strange behavior, but the strangeness felt like a solution to the pressures of the world around them and so those solutions appeared less strange over time because they were proof of imperfection amid the hardship; and that made perfect sense.

Ultimately, Pietro and Eva were two people who knew each other, and trusted each other, and that was all that mattered.

Consoled that Massimo was still here in the form of Eva, Pietro was content to have a version of his same companion, who now seemed more interested in the paintings themselves than Massimo had ever been. Logically this came down to the mood of the abbey and the disappearance of the Germans. But it was easy to attribute the change to the child: To the boy the paintings had been stolen objects, pieces of a game played against the Germans. To the girl, though, they were artifacts and curiosities.

It hardly mattered to Pietro.

"Come. Come sit," he said, pulling over a wooden chair and sitting her beside the easel.

"I told you—I told Massimo—that the artist is Tiziano. He was Venetian. He painted at the beginning and middle of the 1500s."

It was quiet in the abbey that day. It was a morning between Christmas and New Year. The rain had stopped and the windows caught a few rays of golden light.

"At one point, the young King Philip the Second of Spain commissioned him to create six paintings inspired by mythology. I'm forgetting what I told to you and what I explained to Dino when he was afraid. I'll try not to repeat myself."

"It's okay," said Eva.

"So: Here's what exciting. Tiziano is part of a conversation that life and the expression of life are having with each other. It is not a pedestrian conversation about power or politics; race or religion; or even men and women, although that does seem to be a regular part of it. No. The conversation is about finding new ways to be expressive that will further enrich the soul without undue hindrance from earthly limitations. Said differently: what techniques, what methods, can we employ to open our hearts, and those of others, more directly to the divine? It is a grand question. Not a religious one, but a practical one driven by spiritual hunger. Which brush? Used in what way? Which colors? What moments in time are worth capturing and sustaining and exploring? I love that the greatest heights are achieved through the smallest of gestures and the question is always the same: How?

"That's what art does, my dear child. It opens our hearts to the human condition. It opens the heart of the artist and those of the audience. Fear is the enemy of art because it hinders us from creation. Anyone who uses fear to stop an artist from creating is an enemy of life. If you encounter any resistance to these truths, you tell them that Pietro Houdini said so.

"The three paintings that I found were all studies that Tiziano made of masterpieces that would eventually find their way to Philip's palace."

Since the Germans had gone, Pietro had removed the canvases from the tubes and put them on simple wooden frames so he could study them—or so Eva had thought.

"From time to time you've seen me painting on canvases and even other paintings. All of that is in preparation for a plan of mine that is now taking form. We will need to bring these south. On the way, they will need to be camouflaged, not only hidden. For now, however, we can look at them. I told you about *Perseus and Andromeda* before I met with König. Try to look only at the colors for now. You see the blue paint? We take it for granted now, but Tiziano had access to blue paint only because of the trade on the Silk Road and the power of Venice as a trading state. Otherwise, there would be no blues. And the reds? You see these deep, bloody reds? Those came from the New World. The Mexicans had learned to collect and dry and grind cochineal insects and mix the powder with water to make the dye. It takes seventy thousand dried bugs to make half a kilo! And here we have the deepest reds contrasted to the most vibrant blues. We see it too with *Venus and Adonis*, and also *Diana and Actaeon*. Blues and reds. Trade and learning making new artistic expressions possible."

"Why are you studying them?"

"Hmm?"

"You put them on frames again. Are you studying them?"

"Ah. I see. No, I'm not studying them. I'm going to paint on them. I've been practicing for quite a while now and I think I'm ready. Ready to start, anyway."

"I thought they were priceless."

"They are. I'm going to paint on them but not harm them. I can do that by using water-based colors—a kind of gouache—that will camouflage them so if anyone finds them, they will look like something else. Something worthless. The originals are oil paints and will not be damaged by water."

"Look like what?"

"Well. Something of my own. I now have ideas for two of the paintings I'm going to create to mask the originals. For the third . . . I still don't know. But I feel that I will. It depends a lot on you. Now: leave me to my work, okay?"

THE FIRST GRENADES STRUCK THE walls of the abbey on January 11, 1944. They caused no damage but the realization that the war was now properly upon them sent the monks into a panic.

Explosions that were directed elsewhere still concussed the walls of Montecassino and orange flames rose up from above the walls.

The Allies had attacked.

Inside the walls, as artillery fire grew closer by the day, Eva waited for Pietro to return to the man he had been earlier: the marble god. But he did not quite return. There was some strength again, and his tapping cane provided an upbeat tempo, but in person he looked to Eva like an old building that was sagging under its own years.

Worse than his posture was his moodiness. It was evident that his left leg would never recover, and while his mind accepted this fact, his heart did not. He could not grasp that the rest of his days would be spent limping and walking with a crutch. He was too enormous: His body was too muscular, his thoughts too opinionated, too confident, too *strong* in that classical sense to be diminished by mere pain or injury or age. He could not accommodate the difference between what he knew himself to be and what he was becoming or, perhaps, had already become.

Pietro stayed in the museum and the archives during those first weeks of January and he painted on a Tiziano as the U.S. Fifth Army and the British Eighth Army charged up the Liri Valley and German artillery rained down on them as they came.

He received his meager meals from a fine dish that Brother Tobias brought him nightly along with ale and water, which he encouraged Pietro to drink as he painted.

Eva sat beside him during those weeks wanting to glimpse what he was painting. Pietro refused. She tried making arguments she found quite convincing:

"There are bombs."

"So what?"

"We could die."

"That has nothing to do with you seeing my paintings."

"But . . . they're so unimportant compared to what's happening outside!"

"Not to me!"

Eva decided that if he was going to be a child, then she was going to be the adult.

"People are dying outside the walls," she calmly said. "Thousands of men are at war. The abbey is shaking and you're painting like a modern-day Nero."

"Well, well. Looks who's been listening all these months," he said, not looking past his own painting.

"Why can't I see what you're painting?"

"Because it isn't done and the timing is wrong. Your opinion—even if it is only an expression on your face—will change my feelings about it and then it will not become what it was meant to be. And that won't do, whatever the circumstance. We talked about moments and how they work."

"What if we die?"

"If we die, the perfect moment will never come to pass, which is the essence of tragedy. Tragedy brings us back to drama and therefore life. It's all quite clear in my mind, dear Eva."

There were gunshots outside that worried her but there were no planes. The walls of the abbey, she knew, were as thick as a castle's, and as Pietro continued to paint no matter the noise from outside, she remained calm because his state became her own.

"This is the wave?" Eva said. It was a question.

Pietro paused his painting and looked over his glasses at her. He nodded twice and said, "How long it lasts will depend on the fortunes of war. All that is certain," he explained, "is that the Allies are going to pass through this valley one way or another and at whatever the cost. We must hope that the Germans retreat and the Allies pass through without too much of a fight. I doubt that will happen. They are dug in too well. Hitler is too desperate. The troops here are too well trained. Senger is too stubborn. I suggest hope or prayer. The latter fills the silence better. I think that's why it's caught on."

Eva left to go see Dino and Lucia. She wanted to ask about Ferrari. She knew he didn't like the noise.

LATE ONE MORNING IN EARLY February, when the snows had covered the red roofs of the abbey and outside the walls the Rapido River was filling with blood below, Eva was sitting in the same spot she had been in for weeks and was lost in a novel called *L'esperimento di Pott* by Pitigrilli when Pietro struck up a conversation:

"How are you sleeping these days?" he asked her.

"What do you mean, Maestro?"

"The explosions. The screams. The nightmares. The sense that we're surrounded by lava because . . . we are."

"The fighting usually stops at night."

"Do you sleep? You've never come into my room and you no longer tackle me when you hear the occasional plane."

"I mostly sleep and those are the wrong planes."

"Excellent."

It didn't feel "excellent," though. It felt like Pietro was trying to talk about something that he didn't want to talk about.

"Are *you* sleeping?" she asked.

"Me. Yes. I sleep through it all. It is a kind of iron will I learned in the Great War. Sleep when you can. It is good advice."

"I think you want to ask me something," Eva said.

This made Pietro stop painting and place his brush on the easel he'd made.

"Well . . ." he said. "Yes. I suppose I do. That's very perceptive of you. How should I phrase this? When I collected you . . . or Massimo . . . from the Gestapo, I told you my real name. And then we had the accident. Since then the war has started and everything has changed. Including you, after a fashion. But through it all, we have had each other for quite some time now. I care about you very much. I thought about you a great deal when I was convalescing after the accident. We don't talk as much as we used to and I rather miss it. I suspect it's my fault."

"Do you want me to talk more?" Eva asked.

"No, no. I only feel bad that our time together is more marked by silence than discussion. Do you feel that way?"

"I like reading," Eva said.

"I guess my question is, are you angry at me?"

"I would sometimes come and listen to you when you were on the drugs."

"I was talking nonsense. Ada shouldn't have allowed that."

"She didn't know. I would sneak in. Did you make a phone call?"

"A phone call?"

"You said that you stopped to make a phone call on your way to the Gestapo."

"I said that?"

"Yes."

"Did I say it to you?"

"You said it to Massimo."

"Don't be pedantic."

"Yes."

"I said it directly to you? You didn't just overhear it?"

"You said it to me."

"What else did I say?"

"You said you were sorry you took so long."

"So my judgment was impaired but not my humanity. That's good, I suppose."

"Why did you stop to make a phone call? If the Gestapo had kidnapped you, I wouldn't have stopped to make a phone call."

"I see. Yes, that's a fair question. Is that the question you haven't been asking me?"

"I suppose it is."

Pietro shifted in his chair and stretched out his bad leg.

"I knew that the only way to get you out was to tell them who I was. Telling them who I was might have put my wife at risk if they still had her. I stopped to call my friend to see if that risk had been lifted. I learned that it had, in its own way, and so I came to get you. And I did. I got you. I was, however, in a very bad state and that's why we had the accident."

"What if the risk had not been lifted?"

"You mean, if I had to choose between you and my wife?"

Eva nodded.

"I would have come to get you anyway because you are a child and you are my friend and you were close enough for me to help whereas she was not. Can that be good enough as an answer?"

"So . . . you would have come anyway. But still you stopped and left me longer."

"Only a few minutes longer but . . . yes. Now that you've outsmarted me I suppose I was wrong. But I'm not a perfect being, Eva. I had to know. I told myself that since Becker let me borrow his car I had saved time and I had a few minutes to spare. In truth . . . I couldn't stop myself. Love tears us. It pulls us. It destroys us, Eva. Still: you are right and I was wrong. I hereby ask your forgiveness. I shouldn't have left you there a moment longer than necessary and I should have risked it all. I'm sorry. Will you forgive me?"

She nodded and Pietro nodded back.

"Do you like Pitigrilli's book?" he said, replacing his glasses now and lifting his brush.

"Yes."

Pietro smiled after glancing at the cover. "Sinners here among the saints. Allies and Nazis clashing outside the walls built by the Catholics and you're reading a novel written by an Italian Jew. The world may well be cursed but I'm still fond of it."

"He's a Jew?"

"Depends on who you ask. He was born Dino Segre in Turin. Father was Jewish. Not the mother. Both were Italian. This sounds like trivia—I can see you looking at me—but really it is not. It's more of a well-known fact because he's a friend of my dear cousin Benito's and was an informant for the fascist secret service. So he's an asshole. But . . . then came the racial laws of '38 and his coin was tarnished and no longer good in the better taverns and brothels of our fair kingdom. He's a good writer, though. You can't deny that. We also don't have a great library left. It's a miracle you found a readable book here at all."

"Tobias gave it to me. There are some funny parts."

"That's good. With the monks all silently moping in the other wings of the monastery and the rest of our odd group busy with their lives and helping the townsfolk it's nice to have a laugh from time to time, whatever the source."

DURING THE NEXT TWO WEEKS of February 1944, Eva read her remaining books in Pietro's company and when she was finished she painted on the walls. When painting on the walls was no longer enough she decided to go exploring and watch the war through a series of windows and towers that gave her a vantage point the German army would have envied.

When she was little she knew every room of her grammar school—each classroom, bathroom, and administrative office, the gymnasium, the storage closets, the art rooms, and every hall and window. It was her place. It had no secrets left and every smell and squeak of the floor belonged to her, as though her experiences were more real than anyone else's and her senses could capture sounds and smells and details that no other child could because those children didn't have whatever *it* was that made Eva special. Some kind of magic spark that allowed her to see the world but also look back on it with a suspecting glance and therefore know things in a way that the other children didn't know.

The school was her school.

The government tore her school down two years ago for reasons no one explained and they moved her and all her classmates to another school that smelled wrong. The soap they used to clean the floor was wrong, the sound of her shoes taking a corner in the hall was wrong, the sound of the doors latching closed was wrong. She never became comfortable there and she couldn't explain it to any of her friends because they had all moved on and left the building—left her school—in the past.

Now there was the abbey.

At first the abbey had been terrifying to her. Pietro had almost pulled her up the mountain that first time, and when she glimpsed it through the trees on her way up the winding path it had seem magical—yes—but also intimidating and unwelcoming and haunted. When she entered after being welcomed by the abbot and a few other monks that first day she had felt the majesty of it but she was not at one with it. The abbey was a place that was too old, too foreign, too religious, too massive for her to bond with. This had nothing to do with how she was treated. The problem was the structure itself. She needed to form a relationship with the *rocks*. The walls needed to become used to her presence, and it was only when she started to see the abbey in the way the monks didn't—the monks *couldn't*—that she knew the monastery was starting to accept her.

Some stairs at the abbey creaked, and she learned where to place her feet so she could climb the oldest staircases without making a single sound.

Some chambers let the whispers inside them escape through pipes and holes in the walls, and Eva learned where they were and what kinds of conversations were often had in them and she listened to the monks talk with absolute impunity because she knew the abbey had *let* her listen.

Eva also learned to understand the natural movement of the monks through their day: their liturgical hours and customary behaviors; their chores and responsibilities; their leisure time; and their moments of contemplation. She did not feel closer to them, or come to understand them. They were all grown men in black robes and had made decisions and commitments and vows about a life she could see all around her, and observe, and even participate in sometimes like at meals or when they worked in the gardens, but it was not a life into which she could be invited.

That didn't bother her. The monks were like the tide. She knew when their presence would ebb and flow, when certain rooms would be occupied or else left empty. If there was no logic to their faith, there was a logic in how they expressed it. She came to see their movement as a dance of men that waltzed them from here to there as they discussed this or that, all the while distracting themselves from the war around them by pretending their prayers were in fact the greatest form of attention.

DURING THOSE WEEKS AS THE men outside shelled one another, Eva began to experience the abbey as she had once experienced her school: with all her senses tingling and her memory absorbing everything she saw.

She came to feel that the abbey was somehow alive. Maybe it could not speak, and maybe it was not a person with a consciousness but it had a presence and it listened. And remembered.

Eva was also certain that it was not haunted. To her, Montecassino was not filled with ghosts or even the spirits of the men (and Benedict's sister, Scholastica) who were, in fact, buried down below in the tombs. No. To her it was a place that had a life force, a personality of its own, and she was certain that she was the first person to acknowledge it in a thousand years or more.

When she was little she had an invisible friend. Masha. When she was older, the invisible friend was forgotten but the stuffed animals in her room took Masha's place. When she was older still there was a cat: Roman. Roman belonged to the family next door but Roman preferred Eva's company so it padded across the balconies and would sleep with her or spend days at a time with her.

Whether it was Masha or the animals or Roman, Eva liked to talk to them even though they could not answer back.

Now she spoke to the abbey. No, the abbey did not talk back either, but like Masha and her animals, the abbey listened.

* * *

SOMETIMES EVA FELT ALMOST ALONE there, listening to the noises outside. But that wasn't true. Tobias had once told her that the abbey now had almost forty choir monks and around thirty lay brothers, not including those visiting for study. There was also a lay school for over a hundred boarders and two seminaries with over a hundred students combined. There was some staff, some medical personnel like Ada, and people in the hospital who were injured from the war or else sick. But she never saw any of them because the abbey was so huge and because she and Pietro occupied the spaces no one else could go. Even Dino and Lucia felt far away when she was not with them. That was why she spoke to the abbey.

"I think Pietro is wrong about *Pippo*," she said in a low voice as she followed a long corridor past the courtyard and toward the bell tower. "He says I'm afraid of *Pippo* because it's all-knowing, all-present, and always looking down on me but never showing itself. Pietro said I'm manifesting God in the form of an airplane."

It was one of the last conversations they'd had before Eva decided to abandon him to his paintings and explore. Pietro had told her that he was raised a Catholic—even if they hadn't gone to church—and Catholics don't like spiritual ambiguity. "We confess and after we confess we are certain that we are without sin," he'd said. "The Protestants don't confess. So they have to sit around and worry all the time about whether or not they're going to hell. That's why they work so hard: to distract themselves from their fear of eternal damnation. One might argue that I am adapting these ideas from Thorstein Veblen but there's no one here but us so let's assume they're mine."

It all made perfect sense (to Pietro) and Eva didn't believe any of it. Not for a second.

Pippo was *real*. She *knew* it. And she knew he was *coming*.

The bell tower was behind the basilica and she had to enter it through a very dark and very heavy door that had to be pushed forward from inside a room off the seminary. The door was shaped like an arch and once open there was a circular staircase that led her to the bells. The bell, of course, rang for the prayers, but once they'd been announced—and with hours between them—no one was ever in the bell tower. The only other reason to go up there would be to have an unobstructed view of the war.

The tower's enormous viewing arches had no windows. It was from that vantage point that Eva could see in every direction. It was the spot where she could see the artillery launch from the trees and hills and land on the roads and valley and people below. She would place her forearms on the damp stone and lean forward so she could see better and from there she watched the tanks and the armored vehicles she couldn't name try to secure a crossing for the troops on the other side of the river.

It was too far away to see the soldiers. If she had really seen people and their deaths it might have been different. Instead, it was like watching a storm cloud: the lightning appears in the black with all its drama and noise and then stops as suddenly, leaving only the scars on her vision. She could experience the violence, hear the booms of the cannon, and even hear some yelling in German from soldiers posted nearby, but she felt immune to the results, to the consequences.

There was so much smoke down below. Fires in the village. Vehicles burning.

She was wondering what became of Max Becker and his red car when she finally heard it.

"That's it. That's *Pippo*," she said aloud.

It was growing dark. The snow had stopped and the earth was black mud and bare trees. The sky was an endless sheet of gray and inside that unbroken cloud was the sound of the propeller plane.

Eva stood back from the arch. She needed to go find Pietro. She needed to tell him that *Pippo* was here and it was real and she was not crazy and it was not about confessions and Veblen and doubt and damnation but instead it was a real monster and it lived in the sea above their heads and when it was hungry it came looking for her and her alone.

Eva sprinted down the bell tower stairs as fast as she could, tore through the halls like a wild boar, and hurried into the cloister intent on showing Pietro the truth so that he would know it wasn't all some delusion. But as she was crossing through the slush, Pietro Houdini burst out into the early evening's gloom and hobbled across the courtyard to meet her at the exact moment that *Pippo*—for the first time ever—actually broke through the clouds.

THEY COULD SEE THE PLANE. It was there. It was real and moving under the clouds. They could see it perfectly. And Eva knew it could see them.

EVA AND PIETRO STOOD LOOKING up as the small airplane passed overhead like a black bird. Despite the strange sound and all Eva's earlier fears, what they saw was a single-engine scout that flew slowly over them. Below the fuselage were two wheels hanging down like talons, and though Eva stared at it—paralyzed to her spot—she saw no bombs or guns. What they *felt*, though, were eyes. Eyes looking down at them. Looking *into* them. Looking for their souls.

"Have you lost all sense and capacity to reason?" came Pietro's voice.

Pietro wore a wool trench coat and cap. Behind him were the two German MPs who were usually positioned at the entrance on the orders of Field Marshal Kesselring. They were armed but their weapons were slung and they seemed curious about the plane too.

"What are you doing here?" Pietro asked them in German.

"*Wir waren neugierig, was das Mädchen sah. Wir konnten von dort drüben nichts sehen*," said a twenty-year-old with a shrug. *We were curious about what the girl was looking at. We couldn't see from over there.*

"Stupid kids everywhere I look!" Pietro yelled. "You," he said, pointing to Eva. "We have to get inside."

"It's *Pippo*," Eva whispered. Her voice disappeared like mist but Pietro heard it.

He looked up at the small plane, which was slow enough to look motionless against the mountainous clouds.

Pietro, however, did not accept this: "It's called a *Piper*, not a *Pippo*. That's a Piper Cub. The Allies are doing a flyover to spy on the abbey. They're looking for proof that the Germans are here so they can decide whether to bomb it." Pietro looked at the two Germans, who were staring up at the sky, and then at his own wool coat, which didn't look much different from theirs. "Super. Now we've all seen each other, which means we have to get off this rock. Tonight."

———

Tonight?

The plane passed on.

The clouds closed ranks. A rain came down that turned to a deathly sleet as they stood there. If the clouds had held steady and low *Pippo* would have seen nothing. But he did.

Leave?

The soldiers had left the cloister and returned to their posts as Pietro took her hand in his and stared up into the rain as though the plan he needed was on the other side of the weather.

"We can't leave," Eva said, getting cold now.

"We can't and we have to," he said very calmly.

"But—" she started to say, and then stopped.

Pietro could barely walk and twenty minutes with the cane was usually enough to start him grumbling. He had begun to eat better and Ada was ensuring that he gained back his weight and some of his strength but Eva had often seen Pietro prop himself against a wall or seat himself on a marble bench and start to breathe heavily on more than one occasion; he would catch his breath physically as though it were trying to get away.

And what of the brutal snow they said was coming? And the wind and the cold? Around them in the cloister was the freezing rain and the wind that promised to blow into the center of their bones and freeze the marrow.

He was going to leave the abbey in this?

"And what about food?" she asked. "Where will we get food? People in the cities are starving. Didn't you say people are starving?"

"Yes," he said.

It was on the radio from London. Even the Vatican. There was chaos and crime. The ration system had broken down. People barely had enough for themselves, and the fear of being attacked for what little they had was encouraging even more aggressive and depraved acts.

"And the war?" she asked.

The war. The artillery was flying across the valleys and gunshots were constant by day. The news reports said the Allies were trying to cross the Rapido River and the Germans were cutting them down. Even if Eva and Pietro could evade the soldiers and tanks and bombs and artillery shells, the only way to actually go south was by bicycle or by walking.

There were no bicycles and the ground was snow and mud.

The roads were the prizes of war.

That left only the hills.

And what of the paintings? Could they survive a wet journey that far south? Against theft and murder and wind and weather?

Leave?

Eva thought the monastery was a safe haven in a sea of lava. Leaving was death. Pietro had said so before when it had been abstract. Now that the war was in the valley below, she knew it was fact. Was he saying it was now even more dangerous here? That their island was sinking into the sea of lava and that hours—hours!—from now they would be have to be gone?

And . . . it was nighttime. It was bedtime soon. She could feel the abbey becoming sleepy.

Pietro's face was contorted with hostility. It was directed at the sleet, the clouds, the wind, the plane, this life. Wet and enraged that his hand was now being forced, he stood, turned on a heel, and then puffed his way across the cloister to the covered walkways, marching the child along with him like a delinquent dragged home from school.

With their voices muffled by the weather and the distant thuds of artillery—growing infrequent as the night drew darker—Eva looked up at the basilica they were approaching and then looked with alarm at Pietro. "Are you making me confess?"

The basilica was not off-limits to Eva, but it was the glowing and golden heart of the monastery and inside it was Jesus with his bloodied face, his palms and feet nailed to planks of wood. Eva had been told he took those punishments for us.

Us? Had people been planning to do that to children but stopped because they did it to him?

Eva was afraid of the church and of Jesus.

Pietro stopped and turned on a middle step before reaching the door. Water streamed down his white hair and coursed through his beard. "You will go inside. You will walk to the front, past the chairs, and wait in the pews. I will be back."

"Are you going to tell the others?" Massimo asked.

"What others?" Pietro stood there and for a moment, still like a statue. His blue eyes were gray in the light.

"Ada, Bella, Tobias, Dino, Lucia, and Ferrari." She opened her palms dramatically and shook her head slightly as though to snap him back to the reality of life.

"Who's Ferrari?"

"The mule!"

"It's not a sports team, Eva. We do not have to hit the fields together. Originally, we made plans to—"

"Those plans are smoke."

She crossed her arms.

Pietro was taken aback by her clarity and confidence, the same clarity and confidence Massimo had expressed in saying he was not going to Rome and he was not going on those trucks.

Massimo did not go to Rome, nor did he get on the trucks.

"Why are you bound to these people? Ada is some kind of doctor-warrior I don't even have a name for. Bella is a traumatized killer looking for more blood and the lost children she sent away. Tobias is a kind and gentle monk who will be no use to us in a cruel and violent world. And the lovebirds? They need a nest, not a journey. As for the limping creature—"

"We're together. We stay together."

"Go inside. Say nothing. I need to get our things."

EVA DID AS PIETRO COMMANDED and walked into the ancient basilica, which glowed inside like the lined golden stomach of a dragon. They had no watches and the basilica had no clock. The rain outside continued and what should have been a comforting place, a place of peace, felt more like being inside a crystal ball that was soon going to shatter and all the shards were going to fall around her, cutting her. Bleeding her.

She felt even more alone here than she had in the crypt as she sat on a pew, per his instructions, while the slush from her boots melted onto the marble floor and collected like a tidal basin around her feet.

EVA WAS SHIVERING AND LOST in an imaginary conversation with the abbey about what it would do when she left when Pietro finally returned with Lucia and Dino, Bella Bocci, Tobias, and the nurse, Ada Solaro. Eva noticed that Bocci's purse sagged at the bottom from the weight of something heavy inside, something like a gun.

Tobias placed a black wool cloak over Eva's shoulders.

Pietro threw his bad leg up on a pew and extended his left arm across its back. He was quick and to the point. "We have to leave," he said. "Within the hour."

Staving off the obvious objections, he quickly raised a finger and said, "I realize the townsfolk are coming up here for sanctuary and it creates an illusion of safety, but they are peasants and farmers and simple people who don't know better. I do. If we don't leave we die. I'm leaving and taking Massimo," he said by mistake. "She wants you all to come. I'm indifferent."

"The abbot is staying. All of the monks," said Bella Bocci. "They aren't peasants. They're scholars. Americans won't destroy the monastery. It's the Germans who are the monsters." She lit a cigarette there in the basilica. It was the first in a thousand years. The smoke drifted ever upward, choking Jesus and burning his eyes. No one cared.

"The Americans are pragmatists. They'll do what they need to," Pietro said, his fingers tapping the wood. "They've been fighting their way up this mountain and failing since the beginning of January. It's now the middle of February. Military men become more aggressive when they are denied their objective, and they have been fighting to cross that river for a month. A scout plane looked down on us tonight. Come first light, bombers will arrive. We need to be gone and as far away as possible. We're slow and therefore we need as much time as we can get. Therefore, in one hour, we're leaving," he said.

Whether from pain or anticipation he started to rub his leg.

Bella smoked, Lucia and Dino looked for direction in each other's eyes, and Ada frowned. Brother Tobias looked at Jesus, whose eyes—Eva was sure—were closed thanks to Bella's smoke.

The girl was hushed by the solemnity of the adults. She had already concluded that leaving was impossible and mad. But there they were, considering it.

She looked at Bella Bocci, the woman who had stayed behind to fight. If she wanted to leave the abbey it would not be to run.

Ada Solaro, whom Eva still didn't like, sat motionless.

Above the quiet brood were the ceilings with their painted murals like the Sistine Chapel. Massimo had sat for months listening to Pietro's speeches about the origins of paint. Now it was Eva who looked on them, not as pictures, but as artifacts proving history: trade and commerce, power and divinity, all of it composed of dust and crystal and magic from the four corners of the earth that had crossed all seven seas. They hung there, above them, as proof that everything is connected and the full range of beauty is possible only when we all participate in its creation. It was little wonder you had to break your neck to see it, let alone understand it.

"Go where?" asked Ada, breaking the meditation. "Leaving is one thing. Going is another."

"I will not go back to Cassino," Bella said. "I left my final words in the mailbox. I will not return there unless someone calls me back."

"We can't go there anyway," Pietro said. "It's being bombarded. I'm sorry, but your village will not survive the war. You're lucky the kids are in Rome."

Pietro knew that Bocci had placed a letter for her husband inside the café's mailbox, located down the road with a cluster of others. She had reasoned that maybe—just maybe—when the war was over her husband would find his way home. Finding the café burned to the ground, he would check the mailbox. There was no way to know whether or not he was dead and so it was possible for her to hope and, in Pietro's view, suffer because the grieving never began and so could never end.

Eva had been listening when Bella Bocci told Pietro how she had once witnessed a miracle. A soldier as thin as smoke and as easily dismissed had wandered down the street on a Saturday in late 1942. A child had seen him and soon a dozen children were shouting and running and telling the local priest and the pharmacist that a man was there. When the wife heard and came outside she lost all strength. She was unable to walk and dropped to her knees sobbing. Bella Bocci, who also went to the center to watch, said the tears were so intense they flooded her and there was nothing of her in those moments but salt and sea. Her husband, on seeing her, also lost his strength to walk and collapsed to his knees. And so there they were, each within sight of the other and no more able to touch each other than before.

"We don't take the road," Pietro said to everyone. "There's a footpath through the woods going north to a town called Caira."

"Caira is nothing," said Bocci. "And there are Germans everywhere. Bullets in the day and scared soldiers at night who will shoot at their own shadows."

"Caira is nothing," Pietro agreed, "but it's close enough to get there and it's on the other side of the mountain. There's no fighting there. It's not a magnet for artillery or bombs. If we can get there, we face two circumstances. Either the Allies never break through, in which case we're safe there, or else they defeat the Germans over here and it'll be over by the time they pass through that village. We should be safe there until you all think of what to do next. We, meanwhile, will turn south when we can."

It was Dino who chimed in: "What does that mean? That we will separate from each other? No. We stay together. We are safer together."

"I'm going to Naples with the kid."

"We take the path at night. The Germans hear us. Do they shoot us or let us pass?" Dino asked.

"I don't know," Pietro said.

"What are the odds they don't spray the road with bullets? Fifty-fifty?" Ada asked.

"Yes," Pietro said. "Fifty-fifty."

"We shoot back?"

"If needed, but that's not the idea. We'd be overwhelmed in moments."

"Those are bad odds," Ada said. "Germans are being brought into the infirmary. I can achieve more here."

"Saving lives?" Pietro asked.

"In my way."

"The longer we stay here," Pietro said, "the closer we get to the absolute certainty of death. Fifty-fifty is better than zero."

"If we go," said Dino, "we take Ferrari."

Ada gave Dino a curious look.

"It's the donkey," intoned Pietro.

"He's a mule," replied Dino.

"I don't care if he's a red turtle with a racing stripe."

"Actually," said Ada, "the mule could be a solution."

"To what?" Pietro asked.

"Dying."

He made a face and waved, as though giving her the podium.

"We put one of the wounded Germans on it. From the infirmary. Doesn't matter which one. We leave him in uniform. The priest," she said, signaling toward Tobias, "walks on one side of the mule in his robes, and I walk on the other with the Red Cross on my chest and cap. The rest of you walk behind. The path is narrow."

"Ferrari has a limp," said Lucia.

"Of course he does," said Bella, snuffing out her cigarette directly on the pew.

Eva remembered that Ferrari had not been a happy mule when he first arrived at Montecassino. He did have a limp and he was also undernourished and tired, and—as Eva came to know him better by petting him in the fields day after day—he seemed rather unimpressed by his experience with people. Lucia and Dino had been good to him but Ferrari's was a deeper discontentment. When the fighting and shelling started, Ferrari's reservations about humanity seemed to grow legitimately worse, and even at dusk before the fighting started—when Eva would visit him and tell all the secrets of the day (even secrets she would not share with Pietro)—he was seldom cheered up. The hurt in his leg did begin to heal and he was increasingly able to put pressure on it (much like Pietro himself), but Ferrari's name would forever be sadly ironic. If Pietro's village was not too far away, though, Eva thought, Ada's idea was an excellent one. She hated the thought of leaving Ferrari behind.

"I will lead him!" Eva said. "I can hold his reins."

Ada and Pietro looked at each other. They shared the same thought: A wounded soldier, a priest, a nurse, and an angel-faced child leading a sullen and limping mule. *Would even a Nazi shoot at a scene like that?*

"Even the Bible didn't heap it on that much," Pietro muttered.

Tobias shifted on the pew.

"Oh, for God's sake, what's your problem?"

"I took my vows. "

"Tobias, forever really is over. We talked about this already," Pietro said.

Tobias looked down at the floor without an obvious or even considered reply.

And so this became the plan. They would walk on a path at night to a safe village behind a shield of the most unusual composition.

IN THE BASILICA, THEY ALL agreed that Eva should lead Ferrari through the dark with Ada and Tobias flanking the mule with the soldier on top. Together they would find a path for the rest to follow in the hope they were not cut down along the way.

Pietro stood, signaling that the meeting was coming to an end. He issued his orders: "You two bring your mule to the main entrance. Favor your warmest and driest clothing and that's all. If we live to spring we'll find more. Bring food and extra socks. Water is everywhere. That goes for the rest of you. Ada will collect a German soldier. Choose wisely," he said to her. "If he complains, turns on us, turns us in, or falls off the mule, I'll shoot him myself."

AT TEN O'CLOCK THAT NIGHT the band of refugees met beneath the PAX archway with their packs. It was bitter cold outside and their boots sank into the slush around the edge of the walls. The two German police watched quizzically as the party prepared to leave but they did not interfere, as their mission was to keep soldiers out, not civilians in. For the moment, Ferrari was still unburdened by his future rider. Ada was to meet them around back, on the northern side of the hill, so their new companion—or shield if it came to that—wouldn't be spotted by the other soldiers. Eva held on to Ferrari's reins tightly to comfort them both.

PIETRO WORE A GRAY WOOL fedora with a darker gray band. The rain beaded and rolled from its brim. From beneath it, his cold blue eyes surveyed the scene that he had created and didn't want. He shook his head and thought to himself how he had come to the abbey only as a way station on his journey south to find his wife. While here, he had stumbled on the opportunity to rob the Nazis and, perhaps, use the paintings to save someone else. Instead . . . this: a posse of misfits who had nothing in common but a generic and shared compulsion to keep on living. He glanced at Eva, who was standing beside Ferrari looking tired and glum. Had he done this? Or had it been her?

"*Allora*," he said to them all as he grew tired of thinking and preferred to get moving. It was too cold to think anyway.

He tightened the straps of his backpack, which carried the paintings and his other new belongings, and then turned toward the deadly hills ahead of them. "*Andiamo.*"

With Eva and Ferrari leading the way, and Tobias walking beside the mule in the agreed formation, Pietro fell in behind them with Bella. On their right the stone facade of the monastery—a building that already felt like a ruin—led them forward into the dark. To their left, the fields extended to the trees and then everything fell away down the mountain where the German soldiers had dug in and were pointing their weapons downhill, waiting to kill whatever came up. Ahead were three mules—no friends of Ferrari's—that had been sleeping but woke and stared at them as they all walked past. When the group reached the far northwestern corner of the abbey, Ada Solaro appeared in her full nurse's uniform and a heavy but fashionable coat. She had never worn it before and its pinched waist, belt, and oversized buttons brought an illusion of civility and even normality to the moment. To Eva she looked elegant, as though she were an educated person out for an evening, a woman about to complain and joke about the weather before making her way to a restaurant—the kind her parents used to frequent in Rome.

The moment passed when the German soldier hobbled out from the shadows.

This was the man, they all knew, that Ada had decided to save and use rather than kill and discard down the mountain as she had with others, or so whispered the rumors at Montecassino.

The Black Angel.

Shockingly, comically, the German raised his hand and said in English, "Hi! I'm Harald."

Harald?

This struck no one as a good name for a Nazi.

Even to Italian ears it was clear that Harald was not a very evil name.

He didn't much look like a Nazi either, assuming the look of a Nazi could be determined by the propaganda posters that Mussolini had plastered all around the country in honor of the Pact of Steel.

Harald was in his late twenties. From one angle he looked older because he was gaunt and hunched in the dark. And yet, from another, he looked young because his face was soft and unscarred and he looked like the kind of man who had developed late as a teenager, with no beard, a thin frame, and a gentleness he had always wanted to shed because it did him no good with either men or women. Eva would later learn that his ribs were broken and wrapped and one of his legs had suffered a gash from artillery shrapnel, close enough to the femoral artery that he was almost a goner and would have been if Ada had decided to inconspicuously widen that wound rather than stitch it as she had.

"This is Ferrari. Get on," Pietro ordered.

"Ferrari! *Hammer!*" said Harald in German. And then, in English, "What a *vonderful* name for a donkey!"

"Mule," mumbled at least four people.

No one knew what Ada had told Harald or what he expected when he followed her out of the makeshift infirmary and into the cold, but he had, and when Eva looked at him looking at Ada she knew why. She had seen men look at women like that before. Fourteen years old and previously sheltered from such things, Eva didn't entirely understand but she did know love and devotion and admiration. Harald looked like a man who would have followed her anywhere, for any reason, because doing so would have meant they were together. He was a man smitten by Ada, and though Eva didn't understand it she had seen wounded men look at nurses like that before. Some were hungry and seemed to want to eat the women around them. But others . . . the more gentle souls . . . seemed to look on them as the last incarnations of divine beauty.

Eva could tell that Ada loathed him. Hated the very sight of him. Wanted him gone and erased. And yet she saw that Harald didn't seem to care. He needed to be near her because she was all that remained of art in his world. And so Harald clung to Ada like a curse.

Once settled onto Ferrari, and once Ferrari began walking after Eva, Harald started talking. The more Ferrari's legs moved, the more Harald's lips were powered to move as well, perhaps by the same forces that animated Pietro, though Harald wasn't Italian.

Eva had never thought of Germans as chatty—certainly not Nazis—but there he was, happy as could be. He talked to Eva like they had known each other all their lives, and he had been to every one of her birthday parties and Christmas dinners. He talked about his favorite songs, and why he liked swimming so much, and why he didn't like fishing because seeing the hook stuck through the lips of the fish upset him so much as a little boy he could never shake it. And what do you do with the fish? Hit them over the head? Let them suffocate in the bucket? Freeze them to death in a cooler? There was no pleasant away about it. No, no. No fishing for him.

Etc.

As Pietro directed Eva toward the goat path to the north, Harald turned from Eva and the fish to his own personal story. He informed everyone in a relaxed and easy manner that he was from a town in Germany called Detmold, which was the capital of the Free State of Lippe and, before that, the Principality of Lippe, which actually had a complicated but fascinating relationship with Germany itself and . . .

. . . no one cared.

As Pietro explained:

"If you stay on the mule," Pietro said very loudly because Germans, he knew, were hard of *listening* if not of hearing, "we will return you to your army in due course. If you fall off, we leave you for dead in the snow, assuming I don't shoot you. Are you going to stay on the mule?" Pietro asked.

Harald, who had never seen a mule, said he loved mules and riding them was second nature.

Tobias, who spoke English, laughed at this and Harald smiled at him, infuriating Ada, who scowled.

They pressed forward along the goat path and into the wood.

For five entire minutes of walking through the eerie quiet of the night, with each person placing steps as carefully as possible to avoid unexploded ordnance, land mines, foxholes, booby traps, or bodies, Harald was as silent as the night.

After five entire minutes the silence ended. Harald didn't like the quiet. He found it creepy.

"As I told Nurse Ada," he said, "I don't really want to go back."

"To your platoon?" Tobias asked.

"The platoon, the army, Germany. I am not . . . how do I say this? . . . highly motivated to face the American Fifth Army in order to defend Italy for the future of the Third Reich."

"I can appreciate that."

"Also," Harald continued, "Italians like the Americans more than us."

"I'm sure it's not your fault," Tobias said.

"Yes it is," Ada interjected.

"I meant his fault personally," Tobias said, trying to find peaceful ground.

"When I was a little boy in Germany, it was not like this. People suffered from the other war, yes, of course they did, but before Hitler we were like everyone else."

"How could you have been?" Ada said, injecting herself into the conversation between the men. "How could you have been normal and then turned into this? How? No. It was inside you all and Hitler unleashed it. Made it valid. He allowed you to do what you always and secretly wanted to do!"

"I'm still normal. I didn't turn into anything."

"Germany did. Your normal Germany turned into Nazi Germany. And you fought! You fought for Nazi Germany! For Hitler!"

"They came to my house and they said, 'Get on the truck,' so I got on the truck. They said, 'Run and shoot and sleep and climb,' so I did those things too. Then we got on another truck and all of a sudden I'm here and everyone hates me."

"You wonder why?" Ada asked.

"Not really. Americans have better music, and when they aren't trying to kill you, they're quite upbeat and friendly. I met some once during a cease-fire. We exchanged wristwatches. See?" he said, holding up his arm. "It's a Hamilton!"

THE RAIN STOPPED. IT WAS replaced by a wind that came from the west and blew into the valley below. The shape of the hills pushed the wind up the mountainside and focused it on their faces and fingers and toes until they were so battered they had to lean into it so as not to be knocked over.

"Where is it we're going, exactly?" Harald asked, completing a record-setting forty minutes of not talking.

"Caira," Tobias said, being the only one willing to talk to the German other than Eva, who rather liked him.

"Oh, I wouldn't go there," Harald said.

"You are going wherever we say you're going," Pietro said, his hat pulled down tight on his head.

"I meant, if I had a choice in the matter, I would choose someplace else."

"Why?" Tobias asked.

"Don't ask him why, Tobias," Pietro said.

"Why?" Tobias asked Pietro.

"He's the enemy," Pietro said.

"That's not very nice," Harald muttered.

To everyone's surprise, it was Lucia who spoke. Until then no one knew that Lucia spoke English. Her language was halting and her accent heavy. She had had little practice and much of it had been with British troops to the east on the Adriatic. She had the cadence of a schoolgirl.

"Why should we not go to Caira?" she asked.

"Because," said Harald, glad for the opportunity to let this out, "the Allies will probably bomb Cassino if they cannot break through the line there. I know those German troops. They are paratroopers. They are very good and determined and very serious. Even if they get bombed they will probably fight on even from the grave. They are nothing like me whatsoever. I am very scared of them. Also, Caira is close. It may be hit. But to the west is another *willage* called Villa Santa Lucia. It is maybe five or ten kilometers farther, but it is protected by the hills at the base of the mountain. If you want to hide, I would hide there. In fact, I would like very much to hide there too if you will allow me to join you."

"I don't want you to hide with us," Ada Solaro said.

"I will be very quiet."

"That would be a first," said Pietro.

Bella Bocci lit a cigarette, her hands shaking from the cold. Under her cloak she carried one of the two submachine guns Pietro and Dino had collected in the crypt after killing the soldiers.

Dino, who walked beside Lucia and carried her suitcase for her, studied her face as she listened to Harald describe this village that had her name. He was surprised that she did not react to the coincidence.

THE BAND TRUDGED ALONG THE old goat path into the dark. The thick clouds blocked the stars and there was no moon, only a pale glow.

Eva had never walked far in the cold and snow before. Winters had always been spent in Rome. At other times, excursions outside the city were infrequent. To be in the mountains in the dark and walking on snow as high as her ankles was exotic but also worrying and cold, and inside every shadow were eyes.

The reins in Eva's hands expressed Ferrari's motion with her. The direct line to another living thing calmed her but did not remove the dread as they walked. She felt exposed outside the abbey walls and also felt a sense of longing to return—partly for the safety it had offered but also because she had left it behind. They were just coming to know each other.

Eva turned to Tobias. He loved the abbey too.

"Are you sad to leave?" she asked him.

"I'm very sad," he said, almost in a whisper. "Are you sad?"

"Yes. Why are you sad?"

"Well . . ." he said, thinking of how to explain this to a teenager. "Benedictine monks take vows of stability, fidelity, and obedience. Montecassino is my home and we believe—all of us—that the greatest happiness can be found in committing to one place and one group of people. To leave that place and those people is very sad. But I hope that, in time, I can go back."

"Are all the other monks staying?"

"They haven't had those discussions yet."

"What makes you different?"

"Ada's plan to keep you safe depended on me. And while I take my vows very seriously, the greatest act of devotion is the protection of life. Besides. I would have missed you."

Tobias smiled at her and Eva smiled back.

Ferrari, between them, did not. He did, however, abruptly halt, which jerked Eva's arm.

A stick broke up ahead where the path turned right and dipped farther down into the valley.

For all their preparations, no one had decided exactly what anyone should say or do if they actually encountered someone on the trail.

* * *

PIETRO HAD WARNED THEM ABOUT this, but not prepared them. The Wehrmacht was pounding the Allies from the hills with such ferocity and accuracy that the Americans surely thought the shells were coming from inside the abbey or—if not—at least directed by spotters who were. Since they all knew that the Germans did *not* have spotters or anyone else inside the abbey, Pietro surmised that whatever was in fact happening, the Germans had to be very, very close to it.

"They're German, which—in my experience—means they tend to be quite literal. If the order from Senger was to not be inside the abbey itself, you can assume they'll park their keisters as close to it as they can if they think that's useful. In the end, whether they're inside or just outside the walls may not matter to the Allies. The Americans aren't literal; they're practical. They're the kind of people who'll lock you in a room and throw away the room if they think that's best." Pietro knew the abbey was in danger.

DINO IN BACK AND BELLA in front both had submachine guns. Ada and Pietro were both armed with Lugers in the middle. The path was very narrow and Harald and Eva were unarmed. So was Lucia, who was directly behind Ferrari.

Pietro had also said earlier, in the basilica, that shooting was a bad idea because it was a simple if overlooked fact that guns cannot defend people against other guns. If the other person shoots first it's over. If you're alive you can shoot back but then you're in a hail of bullets. A wall is a good defense. Not being there is the best of all. Pietro knew they could shoot first but they were surrounded by the German army. If it were easy to defeat them, the American Fifth Army would have done it already.

* * *

To Eva, it felt like a very, very long time since the stick broke.

She wanted to scream, and turned to Tobias, who placed a finger over his lips.

Shooting was not going to work and everyone knew it.

Waiting for the Germans to say something was risky.

The solution, chosen by Pietro because it was always his solution, was to talk.

His preferred approach was total and absolute bullshit:

"We're later than expected," Pietro yelled into the woods in English, having no idea what he was going to say next. "I hope it isn't a capital offense," which was an effort at humor.

He'd made a joke to Nazis. It was a bold opening move if nothing else.

Why English? If he had shouted in German and the men in the bushes were American or British or French, they would have killed him. If he had shouted in Italian, no one would have understood and the odds of being shot would have been even. But in English—everyone had to listen. It was the neutral language of war. It was the best language for shouting into the unknown.

From those bushes came a strange reply.

EVA'S FEET WERE SUDDENLY VERY cold. Moving had kept her warm. So had the company and companionship of the adults and Ferrari. Now she stood still with new snow gently falling around them in a way that had earlier evoked peace and tranquility but now felt like desolation and solitude and the kind of weather where Nazis murder people and throw their bodies into ditches that soon flood and the arms rise up with the water—

She stepped backward but it was Ferrari who turned and looked at her. He snorted.

Pietro was waiting for a reply. He knew that anyone could be out there. Germans, Americans, British, the Free French, the Polish, Canadians, Indians, Nepali Gurkhas, the New Zealanders, the South Africans, or even the Italians who now fought for the Allies. All of them were out there, somewhere. All of them scared and armed. It could have been any of them.

But it was the Germans.

They came out—five of them—pointing their weapons at the wounded man on the mule, which stood between a stylish nurse and a teenage girl. They did not shoot (to their credit) because they couldn't figure out for the life of them what they were looking at.

Ada's gambit had worked. But even Ada did not know what she had created. In the basilica they had joked about creating a radical nativity scene. In truth, Ada's plan gave birth to a *notion*. Not a complete one. Not a full understanding. Only the insemination; a virgin birth in the sense of it being innocent.

One German soldier—a bit chubby and very dirty—said, in English, "You are with the mules?"

Pietro had circled around to the front and now stood before Eva to talk to the men or, if needed, block any bullets that might be aimed at her.

Tobias, ever helpful, was about to say something but Pietro put up a finger. He had heard the German's question in a way that the rest of them did not. To him, it was not as a bad translation; it was not as an error or a joke or a fool's query. He heard it instead as sincere and purposeful and even hopeful.

"Yes," said Pietro Houdini. "We are with the mules, yes. All of us."

"Where are the others?"

"Mules?"

"Obviously," said the German.

"Along the way," said Pietro as though it were true, which it might have been. There were mules wandering around everywhere.

"And what about this lot?" asked the German.

"They're needed."

"For the mules?" asked the German soldier.

Pietro rotated his palms to the sky and then back to earth in a gesture they both understood to mean, *what else?*

With that the Germans let them all pass and together they walked on as the light snow continued to fall.

Eva led Ferrari with eyes more keen than a hawk's. She led him over tree roots and around unexpected ditches created by artillery fire. She walked him through encampments of more Germans, who were dug in with mortars and machine guns, and yet who did not ask who they were or what they were doing. None even asked about Harald, who had removed his army hat and wrapped a scarf around his head and insignia. Together they all walked with the tranquility of saints through a gauntlet as if fortune really did favor the brave.

Ferrari never faltered. Never complained. Never objected to the challenges of the trail or the journey taking place long past his normal bedtime.

IT WAS NOT YET DAWN when they dragged themselves out of the woods and their feet first touched asphalt nearby the Chiesa Madonna delle Grazie: a small convent of white concrete that stood alone by the edge of the mountain and faced westward so that the last light of a summer sun would grace it in an orange glow that suggested beneficence. That morning, however, it looked forlorn, gray, and abandoned. It was on their right as they stepped off the goat path and there were no other buildings nearby. Tobias insisted that the company stop there.

He brushed down his robe, fixed his hair, and tried to look presentable. He knocked and waited.

A nun, no older than him, opened the door a crack as though her hesitations alone could have repelled an intruder. He greeted her in both Italian and Latin. Alone at the door they spoke for long enough that Pietro started to become impatient. He knew this was a formality. In their weakened state, he had no objections to kicking in the door and he hoped Tobias understood this.

When the Benedictine was finished he trotted back to the party. Looking over his shoulder as though to check his facts, he said, "She asked about the mule."

"What about the mule?" asked Ada.

"If we were planning to sell it."

Dino, who had stayed out of these decision-making discussions until then, shouted, "No!" from a low stone wall where he and Lucia were sitting and trying to keep each other warm.

Tobias raised his hand for patience. "I said we weren't," he continued, his voice much quieter, "and then she asked if we were planning to eat it."

"That's not a good sign," said Harald, still atop Ferrari.

Pietro gave him a stern look.

"She wouldn't let us in. She did give us an address for a house nearby. She said it is empty and we can stay there."

"It belongs to the nuns?" Pietro asked.

"It belonged to Jews. They haven't been seen since early 1939. She said they're not coming back."

Ada, who overheard, became stone-still at this. Eva felt it like a chill though she didn't know why. It was Ada who turned to Pietro and asked, "Is their door open?"

THE HOUSE ON VIA GIUSEPPE Garibaldi was built of stone with shutters that had once been painted green but had now rotted into a dismal gray. It was shaped like a long rectangle with an orange terra-cotta roof in the style of every other nineteenth-century village house. It squatted, sagging, on a corner that had no sidewalk, having been built at a time when horses alone visited the street.

Its two concrete columns were cracked, the gate was rusted open, and the lock was broken. On the ground level was a sickly green door with iron bars. A rickety outside staircase led to an upper level. Another staircase led downward into a cellar.

Dino and Lucia took it upon themselves to go inside first, where they found the door slightly ajar and subject to the wind and weather. They found the kitchen to be a disaster. Dino saw the damage to the wood and imagined how the open door had been slamming during every storm since the moment the family disappeared. Lucia was looking at the nests and branches and bird and animal droppings from whatever had taken up residence.

They both noticed that the smell of urine and decay was intense. The books on the shelves had rotted from the rain and the furniture was moldy. The bedrooms upstairs were no better.

The basement was worse.

Though exhausted and barely able to stand, Pietro organized them all—including Harald—into a team and forced them to sweep everything they could directly out the upstairs door and let it pile at the base of the stairs to be dealt with later. Out went rotten pots and pans, animal carcasses, the books and paintings and any furniture that wasn't made of wood or steel. Out went the leaves and the branches that storms had blown inside; out went the mattresses that had been home to spiders, flies, and rats.

Out too went the smells and the filth and the impossibility of resting there.

Pietro did not help with the cleanup at first. His concern was the bag and the paintings and the gold and the money. He found that the floorboards in the living room could be pulled up by hand and there was space enough to put the bag in there if he flattened it a bit. The boards were easy to fit back into place.

"I want one of the submachine guns in the back room there," he said, pointing to a bedroom on the ground floor, "and a pistol in a drawer in the kitchen, and then . . . we can figure out later what to do with the rest of them. Dear God, it's freezing in here."

They collapsed onto the dark floors and huddled together for warmth as they waited for dawn.

Outside, Ferrari stood watch over the apocalypse.

* * *

EVERY ONE OF THEM SLEPT until the early afternoon of February 14, when they woke to artillery fire on the other side of the mountain. Bella offered to find food and no one thanked her or objected. She left with a gun. How she would acquire food was anyone's guess and no one cared to ask.

Lucia and Dino were not in high spirits but they wanted to leave the confinement of the house and breathe air that moved and felt fresh and alive despite the weather and mood. Dino said they wanted to explore the village and surrounding area. There was some sunlight breaking through heavy storm clouds that could warm the skin if you caught it in the right spot, and like vacationers, they walked out hand in hand, to discover where they were and what it meant.

Eva put on her boots quickly and followed them out, wrapping the Italian army coat around her shoulders as she went. She had no intention of following them. It was Ferrari she wanted to see.

There was a pile of junk outside the house, material probably rejected by looters. She poked around and found a discarded hairbrush with a broken handle.

It was exactly what she needed to brush Ferrari's coat and smooth his ears.

"How'd you sleep?" she asked Ferrari, who submitted to the brushing.

"I had strange dreams," Eva continued.

She started on Ferrari's left side.

"I had a dream that a giant zipper in the sky opened up and down came two hands that scooped up the monastery like it was a little model made of clay or something. At first I thought it was God—"

Ferrari blinked.

"—but then I thought maybe it was Pietro's hands because they had paint under the fingernails. I also thought he was going to take it up into the clouds and then close the zipper again but he didn't. And *then* I thought he was going to put it someplace else, like maybe on another mountain where it wasn't so dangerous and maybe put it in the sea so it could be far away and safe like Atlantis. That's not what happened. Instead, the hands started shaking the abbey and all the monks and Nazis and townspeople and books and manuscripts and paintings and stuff fell down into the snow."

She walked around Ferrari and worked on his other ear.

"I'm going to find you a blanket. It's cold out here."

Eva turned to the snow-covered mountains. "You've been to the high mountains, haven't you?" she whispered to Ferrari. "You know your way around this whole country. I'm going to take you where it's warm and safe, okay?"

IT WAS ALMOST DUSK WHEN a nun came to find Tobias. She wore her habit and on her feet were heavy Italian army boots taken from the dead. They were at least three sizes too big and she had filled them with layers of socks to fill the space. When she stepped into the doorway upstairs she looked startled. The room was unrecognizable from before. Aside from being clean thanks to Bella's hours of scrubbing with a straw brush, soap, and cold water, Pietro and Dino had spent the afternoon scouring the village for other empty homes and discarded objects of some use if not worth. There was now a simple round table with a broken leg resting on a stack of bricks to level it and a number of wooden crates tilted onto their sides for stools. From the nunnery itself Tobias had collected blankets and pillows because the nuns themselves had extras. Cooking pots with broken handles had been repaired for use in the fireplace that Ada had furnished with wood and branches collected from the nearby forest. Harald had offered to get more, and before Ada could object, he had dashed out the door and come back an hour later with enough to heat them for a week.

The woman called herself Sister Miriam. She carried a cloth sack, and once Tobias invited her inside she reached into it, hands shaking, and handed him a piece of paper.

"What is this?" he asked her.

Miriam was shaking too much to answer. She pointed as though the paper itself would explain.

Tobias did not know any of the nuns and the convent was not Benedictine, but for several hundred years the two had been neighbors and had had a cordial relationship. The nuns never traveled the goat paths and the distance by road to the abbey prevented casual visits, but Montecassino was lord of the region and the pulse of all monastic life. The convent's own priest was dead. The women were on their own.

The paper had a pinkish tint and the text was black, printed in Italian. Without image or adornment it read:

Amici italiani,

ATTENZIONE!

Noi abbiamo sinora cercato in tutti i modi di evitare il bombardamento del monastero di Montecassino. I tedeschi hanno saputo trarre vantaggio da ciò. Ma ora il combattimento si è ancora più stretto attorno al Sacro Recinto. È venuto il tempo in cui a malincuore siamo costretti a puntare le nostre armi contro il monastero stesso.

Noi vi avvertiamo perchè voi abbiate la possibilità di porvi in salvo. Il nostro avvertimento è urgente: Lasciate il monastero. Andatevene subito. Rispettate questo avviso. Esso è stato fatto a vostro vantaggio.

LA QUINTA ARMATA.

Italian friends,

WARNING!

We have so far tried in every way to avoid the bombing of the monastery of Montecassino. The Germans were able to take advantage of this. But now the fight has tightened even more around its sacred precinct. The time has come when we are reluctantly forced to point our weapons at the monastery itself.

We warn you so that you have the opportunity to save yourself. We warn you urgently. Leave the monastery. Leave now. Respect this warning. It is for your benefit.

THE FIFTH ARMY.

As though palsy could be transferred by an object, Tobias's hand began to shake. "Where did you get this?" he whispered.

When the nun failed to answer immediately he dropped it to the ground, grabbed her by both arms, and shouted into her face. "Where did you get this! Answer me now!"

"The Americans. They fired artillery shells near the abbey. They did not explode. They were filled with papers that spread everywhere the wind blew them. One of the monks went outside the walls and collected some. They all said the same thing."

"How did *you* get it *here*?"

"One of the novices ran here with it. We're to tell the townspeople not to go there for shelter. The monks are trying to send people away but they won't go. They insist God will protect them."

"What do you mean, they won't go?"

She was incoherent. Tobias, a calming presence always, drew several deep breaths, took the nun by the arm, and led her inside. Everyone else circled the table to hear. She sat on a crate and Tobias handed her a chipped glass filled with fresh water that Lucia had collected earlier from a stream.

The woman was not winded or thirsty but the normality soothed her.

"What novice?" Tobias asked.

"A young man named Fredrick."

"Yes. From Austria. I know him. Where is he now?"

"He's gone back."

"Gone *back*? It's ten kilometers up a mountain after running the same distance here. And he's running in the direction of the abbey, which they are going to attack!"

"He's gone," she said.

"What else did he say?"

"There are hundreds of people from the villages. Many from Cassino because of the fighting near the river. There are land mines. People don't know where to go so they go to the abbey."

"Are people leaving? Do they believe the Americans?"

"The abbot is staying. Some of the monks. They are going down into the crypts and lower chambers to hide."

"Father Diamare is remaining in the abbey? He can't! He's almost eighty years old. All of them have to go! The Americans aren't going to lie about this. They are going to do it. He has to leave."

"It's done."

The rest of the day was spent in the cold as snowflakes fell and collected on the bottom of the windowpanes.

BELLA BOCCI WOKE EARLY AND restarted the fire, which had died out during the night. Much of the smell of neglect was gone from the ground floor by then and had been replaced by the smell of smoke and unwashed clothing, which was better.

Harald had grown up near the mountains and as a boy had suffered the indignities of extreme poverty after the Great War, when the economy collapsed, the German mark became worthless, and the ground was laid for the Nazis to offer a Faustian deal for dignity and pride and purpose, any purpose. As bad as the conditions were on the main floor of the abandoned house, they never dampened Harald's spirits or challenged his resolve. He was genuinely happy to be alive, fed, and not shot at.

Although his chipper attitude was almost enough to get him killed by Ada Solaro, who reacted to his talking as though she were being zapped by electricity.

It didn't stop him, though.

"If they do bomb the monastery," he said, approaching the chimney with a long stick and some motive, "it'll mean you saved my life. I owe you everything, Signora Solaro."

"Harald . . ." she said, "enough."

The chimney was mostly clogged, so large fires inside were impossible and the iron stove was long since stolen; on the floor were four faded marks where it once stood. The previous day, Harald, in an effort to contribute, as Eva brushed Ferrari, had found a large, broken clay pot outside in the valley that the locals had deemed useless. He placed two large bricks beside each other in the middle of the living room and left a gap between them. He placed the pot on the bricks and in the gap he lit two candles. In less than an hour the pot had become warm and that warmth filled the room. Those who could sleep slept well. Those who could not comforted themselves knowing their companions did.

That morning Bella made herself lukewarm tea by placing a cup inside the pot and afterward went outside to stare at the mountains.

Behind her, to the northwest, was a mountain Harald referred to as Mount Cairo, as the militaries renamed everything; it was snowcapped and over sixteen hundred meters high. There were no paths across it and neither she nor any of their party had the gear—the ropes, the harnesses, the boots, the hats, the gloves, the ice axes, the sunglasses—to forge across it without risking death by exposure or falling into a crevasse or simply sliding off and hitting a rock. She was no mountaineer. But: having run a café and a restaurant in nearby Cassino for years she had heard every tale of glory and tragedy from those who were, and so she knew that to flee to it and attempt a crossing with wet feet was to court death.

Pity. She wanted to look down on Montecassino from that great height. If the Allies really did come and they really did plan on obliterating one of Christianity's most holy sites, it was very unlikely any of her party would have been at risk from that location. They could have watched it with the detachment of the damned.

Bella looked up. Here in the valley it was only some ten kilometers from the peak on which the monastery stood. Around it, the endless fortifications of the Germans, most of them hidden to the scanning eye, visible only when a shell went skyward.

* * *

THE SHOOTING MOMENTARILY DIED DOWN and the muffled sounds of mortar and artillery fire paused. It was replaced by the baying sound of mules.

BELLA HAD LOOKED AT FERRARI, and Ferrari had looked back at Bella. The two had never bonded but they were the only ones there and—as all intelligent creatures look to one another for confirmation—they regarded each other until Bella actually spoke to the creature.

"You hear them too, yes?"

Ferrari snorted.

"Before, there were no mules. Now there are many. Where are they coming from?"

Ferrari looked to the path.

"I think the soldiers are learning that the only way to get things from place to place is the way we've done it since the Romans."

Ferrari looked away.

"Those Germans had asked if we're with the mules. I wonder if this is what they meant."

AT NINE THIRTY IN THE morning, a sound resonated through the valley— like a single note played by a chorus of mismatched instruments that grew louder and louder until the pitch and intensity promised to crack the trees and to split the rocks.

Everyone was inside the house. Pietro and Dino—the only soldiers in the group—debated whether it would be better to be inside or outside when the bombing started. There was no shelter in the village. No obvious safe place to hide. Any safety came from their distance from the target, their denial that death was coming for them, and their faith in the

Americans' determination to obliterate the abbey of Montecassino and not waste a single bomb.

Eva panicked. This was the proof that *Pippo*—the Piper?—had seen her. Had seen *them*; had seen the German policemen in the courtyard when she and Pietro had been standing there with them. Those Germans weren't supposed to be inside the grounds but they were, on account of her. She was the one who had given the Americans the reason they needed to bomb the monastery. She was going to be responsible for the destruction of her favorite place. The place that knew her. That, in its own silent way, loved her and had protected her when no one other than Pietro Houdini had. She had invited death to visit the hundreds of people inside the walls. Little babies in their mothers' arms. Mothers and fathers and their children would have to watch and—

It was too much and yet there was no escape from it.

"We have to go!" Eva yelled.

"We'll be okay," Ada Solaro said. "They are far away though they feel close."

Eva, however, was propelled by more immediate memories. She had listened to Pietro rail against God for his cruelty and false promises and contradictions and distraction. She had been subject to rants about God's immorality of late, and though it was never Pietro's explicit conclusion, she had decided God was sick of them all and wanted them dead. For whatever reason, God had elected to use *Pippo* as His eyes and ears and the Americans as His weapon of vengeance. He was going to destroy the abbey and also Pietro Houdini—the great escape artist—because he had tried to slip out under the cloak of darkness like Odysseus had escaped from the Cyclops. But He was having none of that. He was going to make sure the house was destroyed and all of them too. She could feel it: God was determined to bury them under rubble the way her parents had been trapped. All she knew was one thing and she screamed it into the room: "I'm not dying under rubble like Mamma and Papà! I'm not dying inside! I'm not staying!" and with that proclamation she bolted out the door.

Pietro was in no condition to chase her so he yelled: "Massimo!—damn it—I mean Eva! Come back here!" But the child was gone as the first explosions from the first planes fell on the mountaintops.

In the house everyone watched through the windows as the bombers unloaded their payloads on the nearby mountain. Had the wounded people from Cassino been moved out? Had the hundreds of people who had gone there for sanctuary and to be closer to God believed the sheets of paper dropped by the Americans? Had they returned to their villages? And what of the monks who had prayed there and eaten and talked with them while they were living there?

Would they all be joining the dead Italians in the shallow grave below? Or had they gone into that putrid place with the rotting corpses to hide?

Pietro watched and knew, as a cold calculation, that most of the wounded and the sick and the refugees would still be there, disbelieving to the last what he knew for a fact to be true: that both God and the Americans would ever do such a thing.

FOR THE NEXT SEVERAL HOURS, two hundred and fifty American bombers dropped six hundred tons of explosives on Montecassino—more ordnance than was dropped on *any other single structure* during World War II. It would obliterate the monastery from existence, rake the mountain itself of flora, and had the Germans not moved its treasures from the abbey, so much of the art of Western civilization would have been destroyed by the very Americans who later considered themselves its heroes: Roosevelt and his "Monument Men."

The next day, one hundred and fifty planes bombed it again.

The day after that, another fifty-nine planes bombed it again.

* * *

EVA HAD BEEN TRUE TO her fears. She had rushed to Ferrari and untied him from the fence, and together they had hurried—in their fashion—away from the village and into the hills at the foot of the mountain. There was a footpath there that passed a solitary and enormous tree. Ferrari was not a fast creature despite having mostly healed, and he had no youthful instinct to gallop up hills even if he could have. His was a decidedly contemplative approach of placing one hoof after another and taking his time because rushing had never gotten him anyplace better.

"Come on!" Eva urged him as the two climbed the footpath, higher and higher, on slippery mud and sharp shale.

When they were two hundred meters above the village, as exposed as Abraham must have been above Sodom, Eva sat on a log and watched bombers—lighter then, depleted—fly over their heads on their return run as the smoke and fires rose on the hilltop and other bombs from other planes rained down and down and down on the place that for months she had thought of as home.

IN THE MID-AFTERNOON, WHEN THE bombing had stopped and all she could hear was the sound of soldiers clashing in the far distance, Eva and Ferrari returned to the house. She didn't know that it was troops from far-off India that were trying to take the devastated mountaintop now, or that troops from even-farther-off New Zealand were trying, yet again, to cross the Rapido River. She wouldn't learn that until years later. All she knew was that she was still alive because of Pietro Houdini.

Inside, Eva rushed into Pietro's arms and he held her. There was no yelling and no recrimination. No one wanted to revisit anyone's actions during the attack.

The house was quiet and introspective. None of them could see the damage that had been done or actually hear the cries of those who were surely injured and dying—assuming anyone survived at all—but the weight of loss settled into their hearts.

THE DESTRUCTION OF MONTECASSINO WAS confirmation that nothing was so sacred, so beloved, so old and revered that it would not be dismissed and destroyed for convenience or victory. It was proof that the war knew no limits and love had no dominion.

Eva and Pietro released each other and she stepped into the room to take a cup of water from the pitcher that Dino kept covered to protect it from dust. Ada Solaro was sleeping. She must have tilted her head back to rest but, in the sleep that overtook her, she had slid down and Harald had gently placed her head on his thigh. Eva watched Harald risk placing his hand on her hair.

Bella Bocci had not been in the room when Eva returned and now rushed over, dropping to a knee and taking Eva's face in her hands. She studied the girl, turning her head to each side and checking for wounds, looking into her eyes for responsiveness and awareness, and then turning her around completely to see if she might be in shock from some injury that even she didn't see.

"You scared us to death. Don't you ever do anything like that ever again, do you understand me?"

Eva did not fight against Bella's grip. She wasn't even sure, in that moment, whether Bella was talking to her or else her own children in their absence. Her fear and anger were inseparable and Eva was the only child she could reach.

No one in the room responded to Bella or addressed the bombing.

After Bella released Eva there was a long silence. That was when Eva started to cry. Tears flowed from her eyes, and her mouth cracked into a grimace that couldn't close. A thin drool mixed with the tears ran down her chin and neck. All the terror and fear and self-loathing and guilt, all the images she'd absorbed, rose to the surface and forced their way out.

Bella Bocci, the murderer who had sent her children away so she could kill again, embraced her in a way that felt more to Eva like love than protection.

"You're here now," she whispered. "If the planes return we'll go with you. No more going alone. You hear me? No more being alone."

THE PLANES DID COME BACK the next day and the Flying Fortresses pounded the chalk of the monastery into an even finer powder. When they did, Eva left for her spot again with Ferrari. On that day, it was Bella who went with her to the hill. They sat in silence as they watched.

The day after, it was Ada. But Ada did not sit in silence.

Together, the three of them—Eva, Ferrari, and Ada—watched the now familiar path of the planes as they flew to their target, released their payload, and then carried on, some of them flying directly overhead and then banking to the west to return south to their nests somewhere near Naples.

It was on that third day of bombings that Ada told Eva her secret.

The ground was wet and they shivered in the cold together. Now that watching the planes was a routine, they had come better prepared with a plank of wood and a blanket to sit on and wrap around their legs. Knees up, arms around them, they watched. Eva never spoke during these times and instead looked upward, taking in a sight few would ever see. Sometimes she reached out and touched the front leg of Ferrari for comfort. The mule never objected or moved away.

"My real name is not Solaro," Ada said.

Eva did not turn her head or say anything but Ada could tell her interest had been piqued even in the midst of the spectacle around them. Eva's real name was not Eva either. It was not even Massimo. Pietro's was not Houdini. Who knew about the others?

"It is Pugliese," Ada continued. "Do you know the region? Puglia? It is the heel of Italy. My family is from the city called Bari. I am not ashamed of my name or my region or my people. I did not change it for this reason. But it is on a list. My name was first on a German list and then an Italian list. Not only mine, but my whole family's.

"I was on this list and I knew about it, so I hid. I met a woman while I was hiding and I took her name. We were in a house together. Eight women who had fled one thing or another, who were prepared to do one thing or another for money or safety. I didn't like her at all, this woman—this Solaro. She was mean. She lied. She used foul language of the least creative kind. Her dialect was low-class. Uneducated. Cruel. But I have never met anyone with more fire in her heart to resist those Germans. My God, she hated them. I was very attracted to that hate.

"There was a massacre in our village. She was there. Some of the townsfolk objected to their men being taken away by the German army once Mussolini was ousted and our own army collapsed. They started to chase the German trucks and then one man—an older man, a farmer, a father, I'm sure of it—stood in the middle of the road and raised a rifle at the truck. Where he got a rifle, I have no idea, but I think it was from the army depots that were unprotected when the soldiers all tried to go home. The army left things behind and went. Anyway, the man raised the rifle and like an old hunter put two bullets in the windshield of the truck with our good men in the back. Each shot was true and the German soldiers died instantly. The truck hadn't been going fast so it rolled to a stop and our men got out. Like fools, they started hugging and kissing their loved ones as though a war had been won.

"The Germans then rounded up every male over the age of sixteen, put them against a wall, and massacred them. One hundred and six boys and men. The Nazi commander informed us that we'd gotten off easy because Hitler had said it was going to be a hundred to one. So we should thank him for sparing the lives of ninety-four Italians. He wasn't being rhetorical. Leaving the bodies in the street, he advanced on the mayor's office and forced him—there on the steps of the *municipio*—to thank the Germans for their mercy and restraint.

"The mayor did. You're thinking he was a coward but I was in the crowd. He was no coward. You see, he didn't only thank them. He praised them to high heaven. Said they were God's messengers on earth and how their mothers must be so proud of them, and how they were teaching Italy about the true heart of the German people—it was quite the speech. The commander's name was Heydrich. His smiled faded the more com-plimentary the mayor became until he finally walked off the steps and left the man there to his imagination and poetry. Through everyone's pain—a pain I have no words to describe—they started to laugh.

"It is not a laughter you can easily imagine. It was not a sound I had ever heard before. It came from a place inside the human spirit I didn't know existed. Their children and parents were lying dead on the streets. The blood . . . oh, Eva, the blood . . . it was everywhere. And yet there they were, laughing as the mayor praised the murderers for their beneficence.

"There is a kind of comedy that lies buried deep in the heart of us. A kind of comedy that stirs only when we have been so removed from this earth that we can see it all as a whole. It is there, from this divine view of our circumstance, that we find a place where tears and laughter have never been parted. The mayor lifted us with his praise and his courage to that place above Olympus so that we could look down on these petty tyrants and know—in our grief—that they hold no dominion over the hearts of man."

Ferrari ripped some weeds out of the ground and chewed.

"I'm not a nurse, Massimo. I'm a doctor. A good doctor. A serious doctor. I performed surgeries in Bari and Naples and even Catania in Sicily. I was one of very few women doctors. When I saw what happened that day, and the way the Germans treated regular people—defenseless people, people who were not soldiers, who had done nothing and many even your age—I decided that my oaths were null and void. Why should I do no harm or injustice? Why should I use my knowledge of the body only for neutrality and nonpartisanship, equanimity. These were the virtues of a world the Nazis were seeking to destroy. I alone should carry such a burden? No, no. Missionary work was never the history of my people. I'm a Jew, Eva. Do you understand? I am a Jewish Italian doctor and I will not turn the other cheek. Why should we turn the other cheek? Why should good and right ever give quarter to evil and allow it to advance unchecked even one single step? This makes no sense to the Jewish mind. Allow evil to strike first and meet no resistance? No. That is how we got into this mess. I decided that day to kill as many of them as I could. However I could. I will fight evil until I die, whatever form it takes, and until I am exhausted. I am no doctor now. I have made another vow. I will die keeping it."

The bombers stopped bombing. The last of the empty planes passed overhead. Whatever they had been trying to achieve was over.

"How did you get here?" Eva asked, not knowing what else to ask but also wanting Ada to keep talking. As gruesome as her stories were, she found Ada's voice and her strength comforting.

"I was actually in Campobasso, in the middle of the country, last September when the Germans snatched Mussolini from that mountain hotel. This is when I realized it was not over but was going to start again. The Germans began rounding up doctors and nurses like me and sending us to different locations in preparation for the battles to come. I took it as the invitation I was looking for. I changed my name. I was sent to Cassino and then the abbey. I served them for months in the local clinic. I killed . . . six, I think. Four with the flick of a wrist to expand an artery wound, one with an overdose of morphine, and one was an SS officer. Him I had the pleasure of smothering with a pillow. It took more than three minutes. That doesn't sound like much but it was. I'll tell you something, though: you don't change your mind about killing a Nazi. Once you attack, you commit. I was transferred to the monastery. I don't know why. Once there I had more access to wounded, and less supervision."

Eva had never heard her say this much to anyone. Her story had been horrific but her voice was soothing and humane compared to the mechanical sounds of the planes and the screams of the earth beneath the bombers. She thought of the men Ada had killed. She thought of the monks and the people and the peasants and the German soldiers who had been at the abbey. She considered the monks now buried forever with saints under all the rubble.

"What about Harald?" Eva asked.

Ada looked at Eva. She reached out and touched her face and hair. "We could leave. You and me. Pietro's only staying because his leg is bad and you're only staying because of him. What if we start over? Across from the convent there's a garage and inside it there are two bicycles. I've seen them. Their tires are full. The roads are bad but . . . they would work. We would oil the chains, take some food and a gun, and . . . go. We could make our way to the west coast near Terracina. There is little there. A cathedral, some houses, a beach. It's less than a hundred kilometers from here. It is nowhere near the big roads that the Allies want to use. We'd be safer, I think. We could hide there until the war ends. Everyone needs a doctor. People would feed us. I have a house in Puglia. It is lovely. It has three little bedrooms and a view of rolling hills and a deck. I was planning on returning there when the war ended and I had done my part with honor intact. I know what happened to your parents in Rome. I could take care of you. Send you to school. Help you grow into a strong and proud young woman. Would you like that?"

Eva looked at Ferrari, who had stopped grazing. It seemed as though he had been attentive to Ada's story but of course that wasn't it. Instead he was gazing up the mountain to the northeast in the general direction of Caira—their former destination until Harald had directed them here instead.

Eva looked where Ferrari was looking. Ada, though still waiting for her answer, then turned to see what the other two had spotted.

She heard the answer before she saw it.

Walking toward them at a steady and unhurried pace were five mules and no people. All were saddled with bags and provisions. Without answering Ada and all she had offered, Eva stood up and walked with Ferrari to meet them. In a few minutes all five mules stopped near Ferrari, who made a noise. The other mules made noises too.

On each was a blanket, and on each blanket were boxes and weapons and tubes. The boxes were marked in English and belonged to "The Fifth Army" and New Zealand.

Or they had.

"Well," Ada said to Eva. "Looks like Ferrari has some company."

Eva told Ferrari it was time to go home and Ferrari, who trusted Eva, turned to go. The other mules, however, did not.

Eva—firmly but kindly—instructed the others to come too with an *arr anda* and a *giò* but they didn't budge.

"They don't trust me," she said.

"No. That's not it," Ada said. "I think they don't speak Italian."

Had Ada made a joke?

A joke from Ada Solaro?

At the abbey, Eva had first hated Ada Solaro because she seemed mean and had prevented her from seeing Pietro. Later, she disliked her because Ada seemed cold and unreachable and distant. Once she started looking at Ada through Harald's eyes, though, she began to see her differently. And now, after Ada had finally told her story, she liked her very much. She may even have loved her. But Eva didn't want to go away with Ada.

She wanted to stay with Pietro and Dino and Lucia and also Brother Tobias and—surprisingly, and increasingly—Bella Bocci and even Harald;
Bella, who had stabbed a man to death in front of her and then lit his
body on fire, and Harald . . . well, Harald hadn't done anything specific
that Eva had seen but he wore the same insignia as Jürgen and König and
it was hard to look beyond symbols to the individuals who wore them.

"Let's take them back to the house," Eva said at last.

Ada looked to the mules and then back to Eva. She understood this
as Eva's answer. It made her sad but she'd suffered worse. There was no
way to know whether it was a good choice.

"All right," she said gently and with a kind smile. And then: "Come
on," Ada said to the American mules in English. "Let's go."

The mules came and Ferrari followed.

THAT NIGHT THE COMPANIONS RESTED easy and ate very well from the provisions of the Fifth Army.

They assembled around the clay pot again, and the room became warm. Eva was eating American chocolate and sucking it off her fingers while thinking about whether the chocolate would have tasted any different if she were still Massimo.

Lucia boiled water and cooked pasta. Dino went to the white stone convent with a kilo of sugar and traded it for numerous cans of soup and beans and lentils and coffee and tea that the nuns had been hoarding and willingly surrendered in trade. Bella became the master chef because she was accustomed to making do with rations at the restaurant and was soon put in charge of inventory and making sense of all the provisions that had been strapped to the mules. Among the greatest treasures were five kilograms of salt. At the time, the national ration—when the rations were even distributed—was a hundred grams a month.

Pietro caressed the three Thompson submachine guns that had also been strapped to the mules along with five magazines of thirty rounds each. He instructed Dino and Lucia to put one in their bedroom in back. One he placed on a hook by the front door, and the last he put under a set of floorboards that Tobias had wedged up in the corner of the main room a few paces away from where Pietro had stashed "the loot," as he'd taken to calling it.

The blankets were distributed to everyone and the last was used as a rug.

There was also a radio. They planned to turn it on after dinner and make it an event. But not before Pietro had shared his theory about why the bombers weren't coming back:

"There is a game in America called baseball," he said once dinner was served. He was sitting on the floor and leaning back against the wall, legs crossed, and looking more alive—more vibrant—than he had looked in a month or more. "A man throws a ball and another uses a stick—a bat, they call it—to try to hit the ball. If the batter fails three times, the batter is 'out,' which is a bad thing. What I've learned of the American mind is that they can only see the world though the game of baseball. That means they think in threes. For them, counting to four would be like us counting to six on either hand. On the fifteenth they bombed for hours and hours. Yesterday they came back but it was less. Today they came again and it was less still. Three strikes and Montecassino is out. I think they're done. I think tomorrow will be calm. That is, until they assault the hill by foot. Whatever reservations the German command might have had about occupying the abbey, they will have no qualms about taking the ruins."

"He is right. Tomorrow the bombing may end," agreed Dino, "but if it does, there will be terrible, terrible fighting."

Bella was sitting on a crate at the table, her legs crossed at the ankles. "When it's done, I'm going back," she said.

"Where?" Pietro asked.

"My café."

Pietro raised his eyebrows.

"I know," she said, lifting a finger. "But the land is mine and there is money to rebuild," she said with a glance at Eva that hinted at the gold that once passed between them. "I will bring my children home someday. That is my plan."

"It's a nice idea, Bella. And I wish you luck. I'll . . . help a bit more. We can do that later."

"What do you think will happen in Cassino? To the village?" she asked him. As far as anyone knew, her note was still in the mailbox down the road.

Pietro shook his head in regret at what he had to say: "In January they tried to fight up the mountain and failed. In February they bombed the mountain. Dino's right. They'll try to take it again. But after that? If they fail? The third time? They're going to destroy everything, Bella. They will bomb anything and everything in their way because—until they cross this valley—they can't get to Rome, and until they get to Rome, this war won't end. Rome and Berlin and Tokyo. Complete surrender. Those are their three objectives and there are too many dead to change them. How that will be dealt with is beyond my imagination. But I fear for Cassino."

"So we will all rebuild and I will not be alone."

"That's the spirit," he said.

"Lucia and I are going back to her village. On the coast. Where we met," Dino said.

"Yes," Lucia added. "My parents live there. My cousins have a house and I think we can live in it. There is a view of the sea, which Dino doesn't like, but we decided that we can turn the bed in the other direction."

"You're going to turn the bed so you can't look at the water?" Pietro asked.

"No," Dino said. "We are going to turn the bed so I don't have to look at the water. I don't like how wet it is."

"My mistake."

"Me?" Tobias said, responding to the new attention. "Yes. Well. Last October a number of our monks left in a kind of exile from Montecassino. I'm sure they joined other monasteries and that was one of them. I have heard wonderful things about it. Being a monk is a way of life and I like it. I will stay there until they rebuild the abbey."

"Rebuild it?" Harald asked.

"Yes. Of course. You see . . . the plans were among the documents sent to the Vatican on the German trucks. It will be rebuilt. I am sure of it."

"Will you go back to the fatherland, Harald?" Ada asked.

"The Germany in my heart is not the Germany here on earth. If it changes and calls to me, I'll go. Otherwise, I will assume that—like so many fathers do to their children—I have been abandoned. Where are you going?" he asked.

"Why?"

"No reason."

"What about you, Pietro?" Tobias quickly interjected.

"Me? Me what?"

"We know you're going south. We know you have a magic bag we're not to touch, and we respect that because you have saved our lives. But tell us. What is your plan when the war ends?"

"Perhaps we'll speak of it someday, my friend, but this is not the moment."

"We are sharing our dreams, Pietro."

"And you all have my deepest respect, support, and sympathies. But for me . . . my secrets are still too raw. My dreams are not fully reassembled. This is not the moment."

"Can we listen to the radio?" Eva asked.

"Oh yes," said Lucia. "I'd like that. Is there music?"

No one had heard music on the radio in months.

"First the news," said the *orso polare*.

PART IV

THE SOUNDS OF FIGHTING DID start again the next day and once they started they were interminable. In the weeks ahead the Germans would occasionally drive by on the road at the edge of town and the survivors could hear the distinctive engines of the trucks as they approached and then passed by and vanished, bringing reinforcements and supplies to the front.

The battle was for control of the high ground and, ultimately, Route 6, which was three kilometers to the south. In this way the companions were safe if they stayed away from the road and if Allied artillery didn't overshoot its mark and land on their heads.

DURING THOSE MONTHS OF FEBRUARY, March, April, and into the beginning of May, everyone in the house found a rhythm to keep one another sane, fed, cleaned, calm, and patient. There was always the risk that the war on the other side of the mountain would crash down on them. But the longer they stayed, the longer they wanted to stay because they knew that the mountains and the road were death and their house was, every day, proving itself a sanctuary.

Along with the shelling and the shooting and distant yelling came the stranger night sounds of mules. Once there were hundreds in the hills. Now the Allies had brought in thousands—maybe tens of thousands—from lands all across the Mediterranean because experience had taught them what history knew: mules and only mules were able to carry the logistical loads over the winter mud, through flooded roads and fields, and up the very sides of mountains.

Are you with the mules indeed.

Ada had been right. Both the mules and the mule drivers who spoke to them were conversant in a dozen languages or more, from Greek to Arabic, Spanish to Slovenian. And the mules themselves needed veterinarians and shoemakers and harness makers, and handlers they trusted.

Mules, as it happened, were smarter than horses and therefore more stubborn: they would do only what made sense to them.

Who were they, this motley and unexpected group of survivors? When they fled the abbey after seeing *Pippo*—or the Piper—they were refugees. Now, with the American mules and Ferrari, they were *mulers*. That was their lie if anyone asked. They worked for the Germans if anyone wondered. They did what they were told. They were not political. They just wanted to live.

Ada Solaro? She was the vet.

Pietro and Dino were harness makers and shoemakers.

Eva helped walk and train the mules.

Bella and Lucia fed and cared for them.

Harald was there to supervise and be German.

Tobias was a monk. There was no accounting for him nor was there a demand.

THIS MADE SENSE TO THE people of Villa Santa Lucia, a tiny village of some eight hundred people, with a municipal building and a short commercial street with a central store. On the hillside, the smattering of houses were the homes of conservative farmers and their wives, all living lives that had been largely unchanged for two hundred years. Only now, the geopolitical center of history was a few kilometers from their front doors and nothing they had known, experienced, or seen in a nightmare could have prepared them for the war they watched reflected from the heavy clouds of winter and spring above them.

The story of the mulers in their village was a truth they could understand, and if it was a lie it was the best kind: a mercy to those who heard it.

When food became more scarce, the companions—now the *mulers*—actually did perform work for the Germans who occasionally passed through demanding supplies from the community and stripping them of whatever they needed. It was Harald who managed to keep the group alive; he negotiated with the army, and explained that their presence here was keeping the Allies from shelling the entire valley. Taking too much would cause them to flee, which would be no good for anyone.

The Germans were highly susceptible to logical arguments about pragmatism even if they were fallacious and no one had the time or inclination to think beyond the obvious because they were at war.

Pietro's mulers helped the soldiers haul food and ammunition up the passes in return for rations. The regular German soldiers never wondered where these people came from. An attitude—a mood—had settled among the combatants that anything that worked wasn't to be questioned, and a time without questions became a world without mysteries. This was the nature of their certainty and such is the eternal truth of war.

WHEN THEY WEREN'T WORKING FOR the Germans they would stay close to the house. Repairing it was a constant battle. The former owners (the actual owners) had clearly not been wealthy, and everywhere they looked— the rafters, the roof, the plumbing, the chimney—there was evidence of a good-intentioned and hardworking hand trying, without much skill, to patch the place together. Some of those repairs proved effective and creative. Others were poorly considered and slapdash. The colder and wetter the days, the more the building revealed itself, forcing everyone to stop the leaks, find the drafts, and otherwise hold the place together.

Pietro had hidden the paintings but he constantly feared for them. He'd completed two of them back at the abbey in the archive room long after it had been stripped bare and left as hollow as an old log. Those had been calm days compared to these even though the orange flashes of battle were sometimes reflected off the windows and through the stained glass. Because these two were finished they were covered in watercolors that could run and therefore reveal the masterpieces below. They needed to be kept dry—not that the originals didn't need extraordinary care as well, but the companions were not living in a museum and there was no curator here to help.

Ironically—or perhaps inevitably, which might be an irony of a higher order—Pietro was indeed elevated to the post he once claimed as his own. There, in Villa Santa Lucia, he became the *maestro di restauro e conservazione*. One week he needed to remove the paintings from under the floor because he feared a leak. Another time he had to move the sack and tubes away from the wall where the wind and cold was coming in that might cause the oils to crack. It was an endless battle and Pietro was the general, always outflanked by Mother Nature and always on the defensive.

Those were the two paintings that Eva was never allowed to see.

The last painting, however, was another matter.

On days when the sun did shine and the rain did stop, Pietro engaged in an extraordinary act of discipline. His final piece, he told Eva, was being done in a style known as pointillism. In these paintings, he explained, the image was produced by applying only dots to the canvas. Thousands of them. Tens of thousands. The closer one stood to the canvas, the more the figures and meaning disappeared. It was distance that provided perspective, and meaning required the participation of the viewer to bring the points together and help create the visceral and living scene that, Pietro thought, "might prove even more touching than the realistic ones" because of the understanding of how hard the artist toiled to bring that moment to life. "In this case, a moment in the future," he said.

"You want to toil?" Eva asked him one day when the makeshift easel was set up and she was *still* not allowed to see it.

"I even want to suffer."

"But . . . it will have to be destroyed later so they can see the real painting underneath it."

"These three paintings—not Tiziano's but mine—are not regular paintings, dear Eva. They are a form of theater that in some ways is the opposite of painting. You see, every painter—wittingly or not—paints for eternity. Oh yes, we know in our minds that nothing will last forever, but we expect our paintings to last in the way we expect our children to live on for eternity once we're gone. Theater people—performers—do the opposite. They perform, the audience watches, there are laughs and tears and cries of astonishment and then . . . poof. It's over. Gone. Nothing but the memory of it and the love that remains. That will be the case with these three paintings someday. No one says that the actors should not toil or that the dancers should not sweat. They must because performance is life and life is performance and we toil and we sweat and in the end nothing may remain but the mark we place on others and knowledge that we participated in something of value that in turn kept it alive. Writers and painters want eternity, Eva. Performers know better. They are more honest with themselves. That is why my painting is more like theater. So much philosophy in stabbing a canvas with a tiny brush!"

"When can I see it?" Eva asked.

"Eventually. The moment will present itself. We had this conversation already. At least, now that I think about it."

"How will it present itself?"

"You'll know because . . . seeing them will feel like the most natural thing to do in that moment and not looking at them will feel odd. Don't rush it. You can only experience things correctly once. There's no point in wasting it."

Eva would watch him paint while she sat on the floor and used a very small pocketknife to carve small animals from pieces of wood she'd pulled off the walls of the house. Tobias had taught her how and she liked it because it gave her something to do while Pietro painted.

There were no books left to read, and aside from the radio (which was on all the time) and Lucia's flute playing (which was reserved for the nights so something could be special), there wasn't much else to do for entertainment. Caring for the mules was satisfying but she loved only Ferrari, and talking to all of them didn't work because they spoke English.

What changed was that Pietro started to talk again. And in his words and stories and anecdotes and lies and exaggerations, color began to return to her life as spring started to spread over Italy.

He started talking one afternoon in March about an hour after lunch when his final painting was almost done and his remaining paints were almost dried out anyway.

They were in the living room, in the corner where he had commandeered about four square meters that he considered his own sovereign territory because the light from the unbroken window was excellent.

He sat back and rubbed his leg.

"At the abbey I told you about Perseus and the Ethiopian princess named Andromeda," Pietro said. "I think I also explained Venus and Adonis, where the goddess loves the young man but he does not obey her when she begs him to stay and so he's tragically killed on his hunt. The one I'm covering here is the saddest, I think. It's about Diana and Actaeon. Actaeon was a beautiful and innocent boy. Sort of like our Dino. One day Actaeon accidentally wanders into a grove where Diana—the virginal goddess of the hunt—is bathing. She's surrounded by naked and lush nymphs. It is every young man's sexiest dream. For this intrusion, however, Diana is outraged and turns Actaeon into a stag. You know what a stag is?"

Eva did not.

"A deer with big horns. The poor boy never intended to find her or spy. His actions were not lascivious. So this punishment by Diana is very unjust. But that isn't all. Actaeon, now a stag, is then pursued and ripped apart by his own hunting dogs in a grisly death. Tiziano does not show us the transformation into a stag. He does not show us Diana's transformation into rage. Instead, because he was a great artist in his soul, not only in his hands, he shows us the moment where the young man pulls back the red drape in the forest to reveal overwhelming beauty and sensuality and joy. Tiziano is saying to us, 'Look! If only that one moment could have lasted an eternity, it would have been an eternity of wonder and possibility. An eternity that was serene and full of potential and desire. And yet, that is not what happened and everyone seeing this picture, so long ago, would have known the story. The picture is known not for the horror it shows, but rather because we see the beauty that will soon be lost. In my opinion, dear Eva, Tiziano chose that moment wisely and immortalized that pause between the two extreme states of being."

Eva did not know why but Pietro's description of the painting scared her. It made her look around the room as though this moment too was a pause rather than a solution to staying out of the war. Pietro had been saying for months that the wave of war was coming to them. Somehow, despite all they had witnessed and endured so far, that prophesy did not yet seem fulfilled and hearing about Tiziano proved it to her.

ONE NIGHT, DEEP INTO APRIL, when the rains had stopped and a nearly full moon shone through the cracks in the curtains, Eva woke in darkness with a terrible feeling of panic.

She rolled onto her side considering what to do. At night, Pietro, Tobias, Harald, and Eva all slept in the main living space, which included the fireplace and the kitchen. Pietro was on the bumpy sofa. Tobias and Eva had their own lumps of cloth and blankets that served as beds, and Harald was in a corner where he had hung a white sheet for a modicum of privacy, a sheet that signaled surrender in case anyone wondered about his state of mind.

Lucia and Dino shared a room in the back. Ada and Bella shared the second bedroom. Including the bathroom, that was the house except for the lower level, where they rarely went and found unsalvageable due to mold, broken windows, and floor damage.

Eva thought of going to Tobias. As always he would have been supportive but she knew it would be from a sense of obligation to his faith rather than a sincere interest in her. Pietro was twitching, which meant he was deep in sleep, and if she did wake him, he would be disoriented and in pain because of his leg.

She considered the women. If she woke Ada she would ask her too many questions, probe too deeply into her mind, make her talk about what was still formless inside her that she didn't really want to bring into the light by naming. Bella would either yell at her and send her back to bed or coddle her and cuddle her as though she were her own missing daughter.

No. It would have to be Lucia and Dino. They were less wordy, less intense. Less like parents than older siblings. They could be a comfort.

Eva stood up from her mattress on the floor and walked barefoot out of the main room and into the hall, which was pitch black as all the doors were closed. Lucia and Dino's door, she was surprised to see, was actually framed in blue, as though from a spell.

Rather than knock she crouched low and looked through the glowing blue keyhole of their door.

Inside the room was like an aquarium. The moonlight flooded in and cast a glow on every surface. The bed across from her, the desk, the lamp, the dresser, the two people inside—all seemed to be floating and moving in the slowest of motion in the light that could have been water.

Across from the door was the double bed. There, completely naked, Lucia was kneeling on the left and facing Dino, who was kneeling and facing her to the right. Eva's view was framed and unobstructed. The curve and texture of their forms was visible and illuminated.

They were not kissing each other but instead facing each other. Dino's penis was erect and Lucia had placed one hand on it. With the other, she cradled the rest of him from below. Their foreheads touched and he seemed to be leaning into her as though in a trance.

Eva could see that his eyes were closed and hers were wide open.

Dino's penis glistened with olive oil as Lucia stroked him. Drops of the oil spilled through her fingers and fell onto her own thighs. Dino's hands touched the backs of Lucia's upper arms, not to guide them but as though to support himself lest he float away or fall over.

The moonlight shone on his back and, because of the mirror on the wall across the room, it was also reflected on Lucia's. Together, barely moving, they were immaculate and paired, fated to be there in that perfect moment.

Eva had seen nude bodies before. But she had never seen sexual ones; erotic ones; sensual ones. The words Pietro had been using to explain the paintings had not really made sense to her until now. She had never seen two people touch in this way. She had had no idea that a man could be entranced by it or that a woman could be so in control of a man.

Without warning, Dino let out a tiny sound, and a moment later, cloudy moonlight burst from his penis and sprayed over Lucia's stomach.

She did not flinch.

Lucia's smile grew pronounced. The tension in Dino's shoulders and neck relaxed and he seemed to fall into a meditative calm.

As if underwater, Lucia brought her lower hand up to his neck very slowly and then pulled him to her. Together, in architectural stillness, they embraced. Still. Timeless. Blue.

EVA EXPERIENCED THE BEGINNING OF May as a fitful dream. The war and the fighting continued, brutal and cruel, concussive and terrifying, as it had always been, but for four and a half months none of it had touched the village. Their story about being mulers became easier to sustain every week because every week they more fully *became* mulers; and because spring's promise touches our faces and enters us through every breath, it was impossible not to be lulled into a sense of tranquility as life returned to the hills and the springtime seemed to suggest a future peace.

Routines formed and their relationships deepened and evolved. Most of it happened over meals because growing, gathering, buying, and preparing food—like an ancient tribe—required everyone and so the meal itself was the moment that everyone shared.

They always ate together.

One balmy evening, Harald told them a story about how he had been caught in a firefight with the British a few days before he was wounded and sent up to the abbey. At one point, after an intense firefight, a British soldier came out from behind an outcrop of rocks with a makeshift white flag. He was all alone. Harald and his three companions didn't shoot. The man put the flag down, and then his rifle, and all by himself he walked fifty meters across the exposed ground to collect one of his wounded companions and pull him back behind his defenses. The soldier then did this for two other men. It took almost ten minutes and all the guns were silent. When the man was done, he picked up his rifle, turned in the direction of the German soldiers . . . and saluted.

"He actually saluted us. For not shooting him. For being honorable," Harald said.

Harald said that moment changed him. He couldn't get back in the mood of killing people after that. The pageantry was too at odds with the consequence of it all. As one of his companions said, "The problem is that the humanity keeps getting in the way."

These stories, and Harald's general disposition, were usually welcomed by everyone—even Dino, who had experienced the very worst of what the Germans could deliver—but it was Ada alone who responded by withdrawing, much to Harald's sadness, because it was obvious to everyone that his stories were always for her.

No one but Eva knew that Ada Solaro was really Ada Pugliese; that she was a doctor and not a nurse; that she was Jewish. To Eva, she was just Ada: the nurse who scared her at the abbey and prevented her from seeing Pietro and then became, over time, the woman who loved her and wanted to adopt her and help her grow up, safe and hopeful.

Eva was not the only one who saw Ada's struggle, though. Harald himself saw it too when she withdrew from his company at the very moments everyone else seemed to embrace him. On this point, at least Eva understood why—as best she could.

Eva understood from the abbey—and from chats with Pietro about the subject—that all soldiers loved nurses. They were soft whereas war was hard. They were mothers and healers. Their voices were kind when men's voices were angry. Their touch was the only touch of comfort they had felt in months or maybe years. They were usually clean and smelled good and soldiers were often young men—some still teenagers themselves—and their fantasies were robust and expansive and absorbing.

When Ada bathed and her black hair was down and her shoulders were perfect, she could have broken many hearts. Ada's eyes were the deepest of browns and her lips were full and red. She was, by all accounts, a stern beauty. How could Harald not have loved her? She had saved his life and was now his companion. They lived together. Every aspect of their lives was intimate.

And the only other women in the house were Bella and Lucia. Lucia too was lovely but she was accounted for and there was no such connection between them. Bella was mercurial and damaged and not nearly as intelligent. It was natural for Harald's eyes to follow Ada alone around the room.

Ada wasn't going to fall in love with Harald. But she did warm to him. There was a lightness to the way he navigated suffering and hardship, and there was a natural camaraderie to his approach to daily tasks: cooking, cleaning, collecting, mending. He liked being around people. He was curious and never bored. This almost childlike affection he had for Ada irked her because her hatred for the Germans—the look of them, the sound of them, their presence, their very smell—was not only personal but political and philosophical and historical. To see an exception, to experience a single person as unique and apart from it all, was jarring.

Lucia and Dino continued their nocturnal activities, quite often, and Eva watched (quite often). Sometimes Eva saw how their roles were reversed and it was Dino whose eyes were open and Lucia whose eyes were closed, her hands squeezing his shoulders. Those moments were a revelation because the fascist world of Eva's childhood did not allow for men being soft and generous toward women.

Their uncomplicated love was a kind of comfort to all of them in the house. It was their relationship that felt most natural and expected. They were a proper match.

Bella was the most solitary of the lot, and for that reason, when she spent time with anyone other than Eva, it was usually with Tobias, who liked to be outside as much as he could, most often in the garden he had created around the house after laboriously clearing the small plot of land of the garbage and rotting machines that had cluttered it. From the abbey he had taken seeds for basil, mint, rosemary, thyme, and sage as well as tomatoes and aubergines. The basil and mint had grown after a month, and the thyme and sage after three. The rosemary was slower and the vegetables too but watching them flower and grow and enter the world—fresh, innocent, perfect—was inspiring and a pleasure for them all.

The other presence in the house for Eva was the one beneath the floorboards. As much as it was intended to be a benevolent presence, as often as Pietro discussed and described Naples, told her what they would do there together, and why the contents of that bag were for her benefit too, she nevertheless felt that the bag carried with it a dark and pervasive power.

At the abbey, the lowest and most sinister chambers held the bodies of the dead. The first bodies those of the saints: of Benedict and Scholastica. Others were added to the tombs over the centuries, and the last two placed there deliberately had been the Italian soldiers, courtesy of Pietro Houdini and a German Luger. As much as she had loved the abbey and had relished her time exploring its halls and chambers, climbing its stairs, and viewing the entirety of the world from its windows and portals, she had always known it was built on the bones of the dead.

Here, it felt much the same. Every day that the owners didn't come back and stand at the door in surprise at their unexpected guests was another day that the war and death announced themselves. Even Pietro's own cavalier decisions had contributed to this mood, if unintentionally. When the Germans were moving all the material out of the abbey they had brought their own Nazi packing material. Pietro had liberated three cardboard tubes from their stash and placed the Tizianos into them. The swastikas on the tubes pulsed like black hearts under the floorboards.

The Germans—said the radio—were finally falling back. In January the Allies had launched an amphibious invasion at Anzio to the north

and west but failures of leadership and bad luck had stymied the operation and the Germans had recovered the initiative. There on the Gustav
Line the battle too had been steady since January but now it looked like
the German forces were going to collapse. It was a time of hope. If not for
the abbey, then at least for themselves, for Italy, for Europe, and perhaps
for the world, which would find peace when Rome, Berlin, and Tokyo
yielded.

The Liri Valley was about to open, and with it the road to Rome.
Once that happened, the Allies would wash past them like the surf, and
then quickly Eva and Pietro could proceed—with caution, but without
fear—to Naples.

Eva was getting ready to go.

She had heard all their stories, all their plans. She knew that her
friends—her family—were ready too.

She even held out hope for the art; not the art they'd stolen but the
rest of it.

Originally it had been Tobias who gave her that hope. He had explained that he and the other monks who had returned on the trucks saw
deliveries made to the Vatican with their own eyes. They suspected that
many of the best pieces had been diverted but they saw firsthand how
much did reach Rome, including a few documents that were of no interest to Germany but would prove essential for the lifeblood of Italy and
the Catholic Church: the plans of the abbey that had been recently drawn
up—as though by providence—by Don Angelo Pantoni, a monk who
had been at Montecassino for years and had left only in October of '43
while the Germans were loading the trucks. Tobias knew Pantoni well, as
they'd lived at Montecassino for years together. He had been a graduate of
engineering from Padua and in 1940 he had carried out a general survey
of the monastery's buildings that would someday be among the papers
that Schlegel and Becker had packed up and sent to Rome.

What she did not know—could not know, because the remainder of the art's story hadn't happened yet—was how the rest of it would indeed survive, even the art that the Nazis had stolen. Even—in its own way— the abbey, which was now dead.

PIETRO'S RANTS AT GOD DURING the Quiet Period at the monastery were usually about Benito and his Blackshirts; about fascism and evil and war and duplicity; about intolerance and shortsightedness and man's incapacity to take Prometheus's gifts and his sacrifices seriously.

"Long before Jesus suffered for our sins, Prometheus was tied to a mountain, where his liver was eaten out by an eagle every single day for hundreds of years because he stole fire from the gods and gave it to us. Humanity! Prometheus was tasked with molding us from clay. He gave us forethought and the means to build a better world and for this Zeus gave him hell. We were not meant to succeed, Massimo. We were not created to create. Our successes are all rooted in sins; whether it's Prometheus stealing or Eve plucking the apple, there is no version of this story where goodness and foresight and kindness are not inexplicably linked to cruelty, torture, and hell. This war is about good and evil, Massimo," he said at the time, "but good might just kill us all before it wins."

The Allies came from the west and with them came the unspoken promise the mulers had felt from the green sprigs and fresh rains of spring, a promise that they would soon depart from one another only to reunite with others: Bella with her children, Tobias with his brothers, Pietro with his wife. No one in Villa Santa Lucia had any idea that the Moroccan part of the Allied forces and many Arabs and Berbers had been fighting for the French in North Africa and Sicily and here. But they were welcome because of what they were: heroes of Montecassino.

Eva knew nothing of Arabs or Berbers. If the terms were even used in Rome when she was a child they evoked images of shopkeepers and camel riders and sheiks from *The Seven Pillars of Wisdom* or perhaps *Arabian Nights*. That Morocco was nowhere near Arabia had not been part of her education.

The Moroccan legions were an important part of the war effort. They were a chapter of Italy's glory and its pain; they were heroes to democracy and they were a plague that the gods unleashed.

Part of the French Expeditionary Force, they were called the Goumiers. They had been attached, at first, to the pro-Nazi Vichy government. When the Allies took Morocco, they surrendered without firing a shot and switched sides.

The Force Expéditionnaire Français was created from Moroccans, Algerians, Tunisians, and Senegalese—more than a hundred thousand men divided into four divisions. But it was the Moroccans who fought at Montecassino.

These men came from the Rif Mountains and were united by tribal ties. There were around eight thousand of them and they wore the Arabic burnous of green wool and carried their own daggers.

They fought hard for the Allies for reasons of their own. After the North Africa campaign in 1942, the Goumiers fought eastward. They were mountain people who had grown up in the harsh hills long occupied by Spain. They fought in Tunisia and Corsica and Sicily and Elba. When they reached the mainland they traveled up the leg of Italy until they arrived at Montecassino.

They were under the command of the French general Alphonse Juin. He had been born in Algeria and had served the Vichy too and then the Allies, just like the Moroccans.

In May, these mountain warriors climbed over Monte Petrella to the southwest and not far from the coast. The Germans had considered it unpassable and so had left it undefended. From there they marched across the Polleca Plateau in the direction of the town of Pontecorvo not far from Villa Santa Lucia. On the way the Goumiers met the Germans in the village of Esperia. It is said the Germans jumped into a ravine, to their own deaths, rather than risk being beheaded by the Moroccans. It is said the Moroccans used their knifes, the *koumia*, to carve off body parts as souvenirs.

The Polleca Plateau was also where many women and children were hiding. The Italian men had been sent off to slave labor in Germany after Italy was occupied, or else they were already dead: killed in Russia or Albania or Greece.

The Moroccans laid waste to the plateau and the people there. Then they approached the Germans at Montecassino.

For the Allies, this was the breakthrough they needed. The Goumiers helped secure the victory in the south of Europe. But for the women and children and remaining men of Italy, it was the beginning of a new terror.

LUCIA WAS SLEEPING LATE AND Dino and Pietro were inside discussing sports. Both were football fanatics and the topic was the FIFA World Cup of 1938, when Italy and Hungary made it to the finals after Italy beat Brazil 2–1 on June 16. On the nineteenth, three days later, Italy faced the Hungarians and beat them 4–2. Pietro was trying to convince Dino that Italy's victory was the last happy moment they had all experienced as a country. Dino agreed, only to shorten the lecture, and once Pietro was placated Dino said that he was trying to imagine what it must have been like to have been on the Italian team during those days in between.

Eva had not heard the game on the radio like the rest of them and was not interested in football. But she loved watching Dino get excited about things that no one else thought about.

"You win on the sixteenth and then it's quiet," he had said. "So quiet. Too quiet. Everything is anticipation. Do you celebrate and rejoice and allow fate to decide the final outcome, or do you focus your mind and become disciplined and harden your soul for the last and final fight yet to come? I would have exploded. Three days is too much. I would have been too happy," he admitted. "I would have kissed every girl, hugged every man, drunk the wine, eaten the food! I would have become an embarrassment to my nation and a threat to my friends—such would have been my happiness at coming that close to victory. I would have been so happy to be that close I would have ruined it. This . . . I am sure of. I am not proud of this, but I know myself."

"What would have been your position?" Pietro asked Dino.

"In football? Midfielder, I think. I'm small and fast but I was never a good striker because . . . I miss."

"That's not a good feature in a striker," Pietro admitted.

The women were upstairs and so was Harald.

When the men's conversation turned to the technical aspects of football Eva grew bored and skipped out of the house to find Tobias, who had moved on from the herbs to flowers. Despite the absence of the former owners, the tulips had still bloomed and Tobias was keen to leave the property better than they'd found it (a point they had all passed long ago, but the notion was less a measure for Tobias than the continued expression of a commitment).

"Do you like it here?" she asked him.

"Well," he said, pausing his work to consider her question, "I don't like what brought us here, and the circumstances are terrible, but meeting you all and spending time together has been a blessing I never expected. Also, I get to sleep much, much later."

"That's true. But there's more cooking," Eva said.

"But for fewer people. See? You can usually find something. Like these tulips, for instance."

In the midst of so much destruction, he said, even the planting of flowers was a kindness because the bees needed pollen for their honey and along with the deaths of so many people had also come the devastation of the natural world and all the flowers. We don't need to mourn the flowers like we mourn the people, said Tobias, because they don't have immortal souls. But they are God's creation too and so we set about bringing the land back to life by planting seeds and tending to the garden because God told Adam to do that and we can assume he meant the rest of us too.

"And they're pretty," he said. "Which cheers us up."

Eva started to help. Tobias directed her to dig little holes to a certain depth and line those holes with the darkest and most nourishing soil she could find. This was not hard because there was plenty of topsoil. Together they poured in fresh water using Tobias's favorite blue jug (the handle was broken, but the bird on it was lovely). When the soil was moist ("not a puddle," instructed Tobias, "just wet the dirt") they dropped in the seeds and moved on.

THE MOROCCANS CAME FROM THE ROAD.

They arrived by foot up the Viale Europa, which was a street Eva had always avoided because she remembered Pietro introducing her to the Tiziano paintings and she knew what happened to the poor princess. She saw the Moroccans spread out, unhurried, along the Via Roma, the Via Napoli, the Via Umberto, the Viale Dante Alighieri. There they walked with their weapons, their swords, in that tiny village of no significance.

There was confusion at first and even rejoicing. They did not look like American troops but these were the Allies! With the Allies came the promise of democracy and an end to the Germans and the fascists. They had broken through the front and now the path to Rome was going to be easier for them. Their presence was proof of the beginning of the end.

The Battle of Montecassino was over. The war was not, but the Nazi back had been broken and now it was a matter of time. They all knew it. They could *feel* it because life follows the rules of drama.

Eva stood in the herb-and-vegetable garden near the back of the house and looked down the road. A local policeman approached four of the Allied soldiers. They were all armed with the same Thompson guns she and Ada had found on the mules. He raised a hand in greeting and then . . . they shot him in the stomach.

Eva couldn't believe what she was seeing at first. She assumed it had been a German sniper or an accident.

Then they poured petrol on him and lit him on fire.

"Get inside," Tobias said. He said it very softly. "Tell the others to hide. Go now."

Tobias started walking away from her and the flowers and Ferrari and the blue jug with the bird on it and toward the Moroccans.

Eva couldn't move. She was uncertain of what was happening. Had the Allies just shot and then burned a man alive? Why was Tobias approaching them?

The policeman wasn't dead yet. He was still burning alive and the men weren't even looking at him anymore.

Eva heard many more screams from houses and streets she couldn't see. Her legs shook.

Up the road that led to the diminutive municipal building she saw a woman standing in front of her daughter—Eva's age or maybe younger—as five of these soldiers in their green-and-white-striped tunics stood in front of her. They talked for a moment but Eva couldn't hear what was being said because it was too far away. The woman then yelled at the man who was talking to her. Without hesitation or expression he pulled out a knife and slashed her throat. When she dropped to the ground, clutching it, the other men took the little girl inside.

Eva turned back to Tobias.

The Benedictine monk, the gossiper, and the grower of herbs had his hand up in peace or pleading or supplication. Eva couldn't see his face but she knew him and she knew what he was doing: appealing to them. Looking for their mercy, their humanity.

When he was close enough two men started to beat him.

At the very moment Eva was about to scream she felt a hand on her mouth.

The hand was big and strong and the other hand reached around her waist, pulling her backward to the front of the house.

Every muscle in her tensed, and then, rather than freezing and waiting for death, she started to flail: elbows jabbing, head slamming back—

"Calm down. Not a sound," Pietro whispered into her ear. "Not a single sound."

Her body went limp.

Pietro had been outside too, watering the mules on the other side of the house. He backed her into the front door, which was open, the screams and the gunshots and the smoke from burning bodies fixing their attentions outward for danger and not noticing what was behind them.

Eva backed into the house with her eyes fixed on the two men beating Tobias until he was weak and rubbery as two others unfastened their belts and trousers.

Pietro pushed Eva inside and then turned to close the door without looking, without seeing.

Eva, however, did see and when she did she froze in place.

Five of them were already there.

One was beating Bella Bocci and on her face was a rage Eva had never seen. She kicked and punched and scratched, and the more the man was hit and the more he bled, the more he beat her while dragging her by the hair toward the back bedroom. He seemed to delight in her struggle.

Eva heard two gunshots and looked at her own body to see if she'd been hit but the bullets had not been for her.

Pietro had moved—as fast as his leg would let him—for the kitchen and the Luger in the drawer but he was too slow. The bullets hit him twice: once in the stomach and once in the leg. Eva watched him fall against the sink. His free hand reached for the open drawer as support but he was a big and strong man despite his age and the drawer gave way and he fell to the floor.

So did the gun, which Pietro immediately picked up and used to shoot the Moroccan in the face.

Eva watched his head explode out the back.

That had been the last bullet in the gun. After all these months they had failed to reload it with a fresh magazine.

Dino's pants had been pulled down to the ankles and he was bent over the sofa. One man held his arms and the other was behind him. Eva saw the man's erect penis but still could not believe what she was seeing.

Dino's face was so badly beaten that he looked lifeless.

And Ada? And Harald? Where were they?

In the next five seconds, everything would change again:

When the other two Goumiers reached the door of the main bedroom—one with Bella's hair in his fist—the door opened for him.

And there was Lucia: holding a .45 Thompson gun.

EVA'S NAME WAS NOT EVA. That name had been given to her by Lucia.

Her name was also not Massimo. That name had been given to her by Pietro.

No one she knew south of Rome and north of Naples knew her real name. And yet, she had been Massimo. And she had been Eva. And she had also loved them both as though she had known them. The people around her had known both Massimo and Eva and loved them too. They were her and also not her. She had become them but had also been apart from them. They had protected her from harm and now, here in the hellscape at the crest of the wave of the war, she needed to save them as they had saved her, as she could not save Tobias or Dino or Bella or Pietro.

IN THAT MOMENT OF UNDERSTANDING, both Massimo and Eva appeared before her as separate children. No longer herself, but complete and unique, and beloved.

THERE WAS NO TIME IN real life for what came next and yet it happened all before Lucia pulled the trigger on the Thompson.

"MASSIMO," THE GIRL SAID ALOUD to the boy she had been. "You have to go. You have to go now. And never come back."

"I know. I love you," Massimo said to the girl.

"I love you too," she said to him. "We will always be together." Massimo grabbed the girl's hand, turned into light, and vanished.

That left Eva, who stood before the girl from Rome.

"Go with him," the girl said to Eva.

"No," she said. "We can do this together."

"You were there for me. You did your part in this war. Now it is my turn. Like Bella. And Ada and soon Lucia. Go with Massimo. He is more fragile than he seems. Stay together. Always. We'll see each other again someday. I feel it."

"I love you," said Eva.

"I love you too," the girl said.

Eva too faded into nothingness, as had Massimo, at the precise moment Lucia pulled the trigger.

THE BULLETS FROM THE THOMPSON submachine gun pierced the air where Eva and Massimo had been standing in front of the girl.

She was not experienced with the powerful weapon. The bullets found their own targets.

The men near her who had been holding Bella were the first to die. One .45 bullet blew off the top of the head of the one who'd been pulling Bella by the hair. Three more bullets exploded out the back of his partner.

Another bullet hit the hip of the man behind Dino, dropping him to the floor in screams of anger and pain.

Three more bullets punctured the corpse Pietro had created by the refrigerator.

The door burst open and the girl saw Harald holding one of their pistols, guarding Ada, who was behind him.

It was Ada, though, who spoke first because she knew what he did not and could sense the future he could not see.

"Harald!" Ada shouted. "Wait." She reached for his arm to hold him back, but Harald was only interested in the hunt.

A doctor, her hand was not strong enough to stop him from charging into the room with the courage of a lion and the love of a brother.

Three steps in, one of Lucia's bullets hit him in the head, killing him instantly.

HARALD'S BODY FELL BACK ON Ada, who caught him, and two more of Lucia's bullets hit his chest, which shielded Ada from being shot herself.

Under the weight of his body she dropped to one knee and held him for a moment like Michelangelo's *Pietà* that Pietro had described to Massimo in the vaults under the abbey that was no longer an abbey.

When Ada did stand she did not call out in agony or even look angry. Instead she took the Luger from Harald's hand, passed through the room with the lightness of a dancer, and executed everyone who wasn't supposed to be there. One by one she shot them starting with the two who had attacked Dino.

Bang.

Bang.

Bang.

TIME, AFTER THOSE EVENTS, DID not function as it had before; the way one event is expected to follow another sequentially, with cause preceding effect. That rule was broken because time is the first real casualty of war.

WHEN EVERYONE WAS DEAD, ADA left to face whatever was happening outside. Bella was alive but barely conscious. So were Lucia and Dino, but Dino's mind was . . . away. Some part of him was beyond reach. The girl could not approach any of them, even to help.

There were still sounds from outside but there was now complete silence within. Lucia was beside Dino and the hot weapon hung from her shoulders. The girl stood in her place, not knowing what to do until she saw Pietro waving to her.

"Over here," he said.

The girl stepped to the cooking area and sat beside him. His breath was shallow and he was in pain. He had been hit once in the side of his belly and once in the leg. He had removed the headscarf and long dagger from an attacker and was using them as tourniquet. She couldn't measure the severity of his wounds and he was not interested in discussing them. He had other things to say:

"First we killed the Germans in the café," he said to her. "Then the Italians in the crypt. Now we're at war with the Allies in the house." He sat up a bit higher against the cabinet door and grimaced as he moved. "I warned you," he said. "I warned you that it was all madness. That it was chaos out there. But I couldn't save you."

"I'm fine," she lied.

"A flame deluge," he said, momentarily drifting off. "That's what it is. All of it. No place to stand anymore."

The girl did not reply because the words had not been for her.

"The paintings," he said, returning. "The money. The bag. The loot. There are more bullets for the gun. You know how to load it. Everything is yours now," he said, tapping the floorboards.

"But your wife," the girl said. "Oriana."

"I have one last story for you," he said.

Pietro repositioned himself again. He instructed her to ignore his wincing and listen carefully. He was no longer speaking to God. He was speaking directly to her:

"My wife and I decided not to have children. I told you this, too casually, too aggressively, in the car before the accident, but it's true. It is the reason for everything that has happened here, including why you and I are sitting on this floor.

"Oriana and I came of age at a time when the fascists told women their lives were worthless; their ideas pathetic; their role to spread their legs to put things in or take things out. To serve men. This is the world you were raised in, and it is little wonder to me that you chose to wear trousers and cut your hair when you needed to feel more powerful. I was moved by your courage. Where did it come from? I wondered, looking at you in the gutter in Cassino. How deep did it run?

"Our decision not to have children—children that would grow to be saddled with the name Mussolini—was complex. In one way, it was a rebellious and political act. Oriana's body was being colonized by the fascists, and she fought back and refused to be politically raped in this way. I admired her fortitude. If they wanted her to be a baby machine to make more soldiers, they would have to suffer disappointment because her body would be for pleasure only, she decided. And not theirs. Not mine either. Hers. She would use it for movement, for dance, for intimacy, for joy, and for transporting that brilliant mind of hers from place to place. I agreed to all of it if I could share that joy and that mind.

"That was the idea. It was all very youthful and bold and inspirational, but . . . we have only one life and when any person makes an irrevocable decision, it is a profound and somber matter. To make such a decision out of rebellion is to be forever defined and controlled by what you hate. If Oriana was not going to have children because of fascism, it meant that fascism had succeeded in snuffing out her drive to live; to create; to be fully a part of the cycle of life and death. It would be a terrible defeat. I once told her this but she wasn't interested in hearing it. And by the time she left me, it was too late because her child-bearing years were behind her.

"I told you before that I am a bastard, a proper son of a bitch. It's true. I may have agreed to our plan not to have children but by the time I was in my forties—if I'm honest—not having children felt like I had weakened myself. It felt as though I had not fought for life. I had surrendered, and no man wants to surrender. So out of this weakness I had my affairs and my lovers. You are a child so you think infidelity is serious. It is serious, but there are things much more serious. You see, what I had really done was break from the sacred adventure Oriana and I were on—the one we had agreed to."

Pietro checked the scarf on his leg. There was blood but no leaks. No arterial splatter. No slow death. What was happening inside his belly, though, the girl could not say and Pietro would not discuss. He was going to finish.

Pietro gestured toward one of the dead Moroccans and the girl understood. She retrieved a Colt pistol, checked that it was loaded and chambered, and handed it to Pietro. He rested the barrel on the floor in the general direction of the door in case anyone he didn't like tried to enter.

Stable for now, he continued:

"Here's what I want you to know. One day, last year, we were at the Caffè Zanarini on the Piazza Galvani in Bologna. It is a well-known place. It was sunny and we were under an umbrella by the table. Oriana had a glass of prosecco and I had a beer."

He breathed more heavily. His wheezing became more intense. Speaking was an effort.

"There was rationing, of course, but . . . money still worked and the enterprising found a way to deliver. Money I had. I still have. A good amount. A lot of it is in the bag with your paintings.

"We were drinking and talking about the suffering of the architecture from the war. We had been reflecting on how much had already been lost because of the insanity of these people. And then—from nowhere—she asked if I regretted not having children."

Pietro shifted on the ground out of a discomfort caused more by the memory and confession than the bullet holes.

It was in that moment the girl realized she was taking Tobias's place. She was hearing Pietro's confession.

SHE LISTENED BECAUSE SHE WANTED to be the listener Pietro needed. But what does a child know of an adult relationship that bears thirty years of weight, not to mention the gravity and promise of old age, geopolitics, and war?

He went on:

"You must understand, Oriana did not phrase her question as being about *us*. It was about *me*. She was probing into my mind. In that moment—that precious moment—I didn't respond. I groped for words and somehow—because we had been together for thirty years—she saw that I was not confused about how to answer her, but whether to answer at all. My pause was too long and she filled it.

"'What are you afraid of?' she asked me. Oriana knew that the only thing I feared in this life was the loss of her love. Guns, bullets, and ridicule; loss of reputation, fame, and fortune—these things meant nothing to me. I was a bull. Losing her love was the only thing that scared me because it was all I ever needed, and therefore the most that could be taken away. Drawing a straight line between those two points, she created her answer and then said it: 'You don't regret it because you *have* a child.'"

The girl had heard Pietro Houdini's confessions before. At the end, there was always relief. He would emerge uplifted and pat her on the head and—even after murdering the Germans—he would be aligned with himself and the stars. In this moment, however, Pietro had no hope of relief in either his body or his soul. No, it was not a confession. It was a *reckoning*. Pietro was an immortal discarded to the earth and now subject to the immediate decline of old age. There he was. Old. Lame. Bleeding. Not a god but a man. Not marble but flesh. In those moments Pietro Houdini needed to be the best man he could with the life he had left.

* * *

"I SAID NOTHING IN RESPONSE to Oriana's observation," he said, his voice low, his tone distant as if describing an episode that belonged to someone else from long ago. "My failure to reply was, of course, deafening. In my silence, in my cowardice, I had confessed to betraying our marriage vows, but much more. I had betrayed our covenant to each other. I had betrayed the very life we had deliberately crafted together. I had betrayed the revolution and the rebellion. I had made a mockery of her and what we had built. Her life was not as she had thought it had been. She was not in the story she had committed to. Ours was no longer a partnership among equals. I had betrayed her in ways far deeper than infidelity and sex. The marriage that was both behind her and in front of her had turned to smoke.

"Oriana Beatrice Mussolini—the damned woman had taken my name before knowing the consequences—stood up from our table, removed her linen jacket from the chair, and walked away from me without a word. I never saw her again."

He shifted again. He asked for water and the girl gave it to him.

He finished:

"She didn't return to the apartment that night. Or the next. Or the next. Two weeks later, without a word in between, the police arrived and said she had helped blow up a railway line that the Germans were using to transport goods through Switzerland. She had already been sentenced to a prison on an island off the coast of Sicily. I was told the only reason she had not been shot like the others was because of our name. Mussolini.

"You see how life toys with me? I abandoned our personal rebellion against fascism, so she went to find partisans of her own. The fascists killed the rest of them but not her. I needed to get to her. I was going to her when I met you."

He tried to sit up higher but couldn't. There was blood on the floor around him now.

"You're going to live," he said to the girl. "These paintings are key. At first I wanted to hide them to infuriate König because infuriating König was fun. But then I had an idea. I was looking at you when it came to me. I came up with the idea that I would somehow find my daughter in the south and give the paintings to her, and someday after the war she could return them to the government and be a hero and enter society with a medal and money and help find a new path, not one saddled with a father named Mussolini.

"Ah. You're shocked. Well . . . yes. Yes indeed. There's a daughter. That's what I accidentally told Ada after the accident while I was on the medications. She thought I was talking about you but I wasn't. Oriana had been right. I did have a daughter and the mother wrote to me periodically about her welfare over the years. I sent money in return and burned the letters to keep the secret from Oriana. I probably burned our plans back at the abbey out of habit. Anyway. I have never even seen her. Not even pictures. Sitting here I now realize I was dreaming and you are the only real daughter I have ever had. I should have done it all for you from the start. But I'm a slow learner. What I'm saying is, everything is for you. It's yours. Those Tizianos will lead you to freedom. I know you had good parents but they are gone and so, if only for a moment, I hereby adopt you. That medal will be yours. In return, you are my witness. You watched me fight to get to Naples, to get to my wife's remains. To apologize for abandoning our vows to each other. Not the marriage vows. The others. The unspoken ones."

"Her remains?" I asked.

"When I stopped at the Esso station in Cassino on my way to the *municipio* to save you from Jürgen I called a journalist I know who worked at *Corriere di Napoli* when he was young. Later he became a professor."

Pietro coughed and shook.

"His relationships are a spiderweb throughout Naples. He told me that when the Allies liberated Sicily, they freed the political prisoners on the islands as I suspected. Oriana did get to the mainland before the invasion. There was a Nazi in charge of the city. Colonel Walter Schöll. Scum of the earth. The city couldn't take his executions and murders and indignities anymore. They rose up and fought to the death against the Nazis for four days. Naples rose! Like the Jews of Warsaw, we rose! On the second day, Oriana was caught with a backpack full of ammunition. They knew who she was and this time the Germans shot her in the head. They shot her and left her body on the street. A woman named Mussolini fighting for the partisans? It was a dangerous game and she lost, but at least she lost playing the right game. Word got back to my friend. He made sure she was buried. He told me on the phone. That's why I was so angry at you. I wanted to get to Naples to kneel at her grave and pray for forgiveness. I needed to beg the dirt—"

Pietro coughed blood.

He pointed: "My friend's name is inside that bag. And directions. You should memorize them in case you lose the bag. It's time to go."

"I'm not leaving you," the girl said to him.

"Take Ferrari. And the guns. A big one and a little one. Kill anyone who gets in your way. Really. Anyone. If they look at you sideways, kill them. It doesn't matter anymore. If there is guilt, suffer it later in life. The paintings will serve you just like you serve them. Remember the stories I told you. They are all around us all the time. They will guide you."

"I love you," she said to him.

"Do I call you Massimo? Or Eva?"

"They're gone. I sent them away."

"Who remains?"

The girl told him her name.

"I love you too," he said to her, and used her name.

He pulled her down and kissed her forehead and then once on each eye for Massimo and Eva, who he also loved.

"Go now. Eyes down. Spirit up."

"Is there a God?" she asked him.

"I'm afraid so," said Pietro Houdini.

THE GIRL DID AS PIETRO said and collected the backpack and guns. She left Bella unconscious on the floor and said nothing to Lucia or Dino, who had retreated to the bedroom.

Ada was gone. Harald was dead. And Tobias . . .

She loaded Ferrari, who was more than eager to leave, and she freed the other mules. Were the Moroccans still in the village? She wasn't sure. What mattered was that she was set on a path, and because she was set on a path, the world around it grew hazy and out of focus. There was only where she was going because only that attention allowed her to forget where she had been.

Ferrari was shaky but in the girl's presence he calmed. Together they walked. The way she chose her direction was to follow the bodies of the dead Moroccans.

There were still fires raging and people screaming but the Goumier corpses were a comfort, each one unable to do any more harm and also leading her away from the village and toward their executioner. Someone who was on her side and not theirs.

It did not require much imagination to know that it had been Ada who killed them all.

And wherever Ada had gone was the right way to follow.

Before turning into the steep hills along the goat path, she and Ferrari came upon that huge and magnificent tree they'd often passed before. Around it was low brush and bare rock. It was a tree that had watched over the Roman world, and since then, generations upon generations of people had passed beneath it.

It was there the girl found Ada's body.

She was lying on her back, her legs crossed at the ankles, her own gun in her hand, and a bullet through her brain. The girl looked down at the woman, whose face was still beautiful and timeless in death. At first it made no sense. It was impossible to shoot someone like that. It would take years before she came to a settled understanding: that Ada Pugliese had wanted it known—to whomever was left—that she had done it to herself, and that she never surrendered, never gave up, and did not fail.

The slide was open on the Luger. It had been her last bullet.

At first, standing there with Ferrari, the girl thought Ada had been overcome by the horror. And then she thought about Harald's death and how, maybe, Ada had loved him though it was unlikely. It was also during those intervening years that she came to a more mature conclusion: that Ada had used her last bullet on herself because her soul had been torn and tattered beyond human endurance by *contradiction*.

She had once been a doctor committed to saving lives. All those lives had been Italian because she was Italian and those were the people around her. Her neighbors. She had lived and worked in Italy and those were the people who had been sick or in danger and needed her. Then her own country turned on her and stripped her of her nationality and identity and purpose and said that she was *not* a cure to life's ills but a virus.

She lost her family.

For what? For some madman's arbitrary theories about blood and race.

So when the Nazis took over, Ada had started killing them; she was a doctor no more. But then, out of necessity, she saved one, and came to know his kindness and humanity, as Tobias knew she would. Did she come to hate herself for killing the others? Who were the others? Nazis? Soldiers? Killers? Jew haters? Or were they just boys? There was no one left alive to answer.

So she and Pietro and Bella killed the Germans, who started the war and killed millions.

And then Pietro killed the Italians, who were fascists and had sided with a devil.

And Pietro and Lucia and Ada killed the Moroccans, who were allies and murderers and rapists.

THOSE WERE THE GIRL'S THOUGHTS in the years to come, when she became an adult and was able to place the dead in the sweep of history. But that day she turned away from Ada, angry at her for not staying alive to take care of her as she'd offered to do that day on the hill as they watched Montecassino burn, and wanting only to go south. To Naples.

To the sea.

PART V

AT NIGHTFALL, THE GIRL LEFT the remains of the village and traveled into the mountains toward the ruins of the abbey. She wore a long coat with a Luger in the pocket and she carried a Thompson across her chest. The four magazines were secured in a leather ammunition bag that she wore like a purse. Across her back in the bag were three priceless Renaissance paintings, ancient Greek gold, and a wallet filled with five hundred thousand lira. She had four German watches strapped to her wrists that Harald had said she could hawk for thirty thousand each. On her feet were leather boots she'd pulled off a dead Moroccan who was the right size and beneath her was a limping mule named Ferrari.

She saw no living Germans as she approached the ruins of the abbey. She saw no monks. The soldiers standing around were Polish and American and British. Most were smoking. None smiled at her and none challenged her. The expression on her face was a warning and her finger on the trigger of the Thompson was the bullhorn announcing it in case they were hard of hearing.

The hilltop was a pile of rubble and in that rubble was the blood and the entrails of those who had fought to make it their own or had hidden there with faith in God's love. The ruins had been taken by the Polish forces and the German line was broken. The Axis forces had either died or retreated to fight farther north. None of this was the girl's problem anymore. The wave had come, like Pietro said. It had broken on them and she had lived. Now there was nothing to stop her between here and Naples except bad luck.

"THE NUMBER ONE KILLER IN human history," Pietro had once said to her. "What is?"

"Bad luck. You can't see it coming but sometimes you can smell it."

A CALM HAD SETTLED OVER the debris like a dusting of snow. What she smelled was cigarette smoke and gunpowder, car exhaust and the acrid sulfur of artillery and explosions. The coldness of her eyes created a path for her down the mountain. The men she saw around her were not the men from down below. Whatever had possessed them was not here. These men were glad to kick stones down the hill and bet on how far they could go.

The girl and Ferrari approached the edge of the pass she had once descended from the monastery with everyone else but now had to stop because the way forward was not the place she had once been. In front of them, the forest was completely nude. The bombs and fires had scorched the land and only a few dozen blackened tree trunks remained, all of them sticking out of the ground at grotesque angles. The earth itself was now a powder as thin as ash.

The girl and Ferrari could see up the mountain from here because nothing obscured the view. The mountain that had once been lush with life was now a mound of gray sand. The abbey—once a fortress—was now a set of shapeless hills. The surface had a few remaining edges and corners where the walls had not collapsed entirely, and there were openings where there had once been doors or windows or hallways. Most of those that remained were arches because of their unique capacity to withstand enormous loads. The only part of the building that was even recognizable was the corner with the PAX entranceway. But that was far from her and she could not see if the Latin inscription had survived. It would have meant nothing either way.

It was no longer there. It could no longer hear her. It was dead.

She stood there staring for so long that she was approached by a young soldier wearing a cap rather than a helmet and smoking in such a way that he seemed to be imitating a movie actor.

"*Ciao, como stai?*" he asked her.

His Italian accent was strange. Possibly English. She didn't know.

"*Qualcuno è sopravvissuto?*" she asked him.

"Huh?" he said.

"*Vivo? Vivere? Chiunque?*" she said, pointing at the abbey and using the easiest words she knew, like talking to one of the mules who didn't speak Italian either.

"Oh!" he said. "*Sì. L'abate. E alcune persone,*" he said in a way that hurt her ears.

"*L'abate?*"

How anyone had survived the bombardment she couldn't fathom. But somehow the abbot and "some people" survived. Around her, though, she knew that hundreds of others were dead and their bones were now ashes and dust as scripture has promised.

Though not curious and not in the frame of mind to wonder such things, she did remember the beauty of the mosaics Pietro had so carefully restored with nothing but lemon, water, and cotton balls. Perhaps the angel's wings or Mary's hands were still there, deep underground, and in the dark.

She and the mule turned to another path as the soldier called out to her but she was no longer interested in talking to him. He had seen her guns and so perhaps his decision not to follow had been judicious.

She and Ferrari circled the mountain because the way over it was now destroyed and crawling over the debris was impossible.

* * *

AFTER TWO HOURS OF WALKING she encountered more Allied soldiers. She recognized some of the flags on their uniforms but not others. The Poles and the British were there. They ignored her and the mule entirely and none looked on her Thompson gun as a threat or concern, given what they had recently faced and the work they had yet to do.

Eventually she reached the serpentine road from the ruins to the remains of Cassino, which was pockmarked now from the fighting and presented the girl and mule with vehicles lying twisted and wrecked along the way. Some bodies had been removed but parts remained.

The May weather was temperate and no rains had washed away the war.

Below, through the trees and tall brush, the village—such as it was— came into view. It too had been wiped away and scorched by the bombers and was now nothing but rubble. The note that Bella Bocci had placed in her mailbox for her husband to find had most likely been incinerated.

Two mules looked at Ferrari and he ignored them.

In the wreckage of Cassino she met up with the main road. She rode Ferrari south and passed the U.S. Fifth Army walking north.

Rocking to the sway of Ferrari's awkward gait, she rode through a thousand soldiers who were trudging toward Rome and more fighting up north.

Never once did they utter a word to her, and never once did she question her decision to ride against the tide.

NAPLES WAS A HUNDRED KILOMETERS away if she and Ferrari continued on the main road but the girl turned off it and made for the coast instead. If the soldiers were here, she reasoned, they may not be there. Fewer eyes and guns around her was better. Sane people would recognize her for the threat she was but there would always be someone to try his luck.

Ferrari ate the rough forage of the spring land and the girl ate what she had brought while learning to search the packs of the dead soldiers for rations. When the bodies and packs and mules became scarce she would walk into towns like a gunslinger and buy dark breads made with sawdust. Farms had some apples and pears and apricots and strawberries. She stole what she needed and was prepared to deliver an answer to any questioning she faced.

When she entered the town of Mondragone, on the coast, she saw more debris from earlier fighting. Remembering Pietro's monologues about the evils of man, she took heed of his warnings and tried to touch nothing. There were booby traps and land mines in the haystacks and olive groves; there were mines in the ditches and riverbanks.

HAD SHE CHOSEN THE MOST direct route, the march to Naples could have taken her thirty hours of riding, or two to three days. Pietro had shown her this on a map long ago but it had been too hard to believe. The realization that Naples had been only a three-day ride from Montecassino—after all those months of waiting and recovering and planning and suffering—was too outlandish to comprehend. Montecassino had not been a church to her but an island, one in a sea of leviathans with teeth and red eyes ready to devour them. And afterward, the house in the village had been their rowboat, far out in that sea as she watched the island burn.

It occurred to her that Becker's red Fiat could have covered the distance in a leisurely afternoon, music playing through the radio, as the driver and a friend told jokes and chatted about the weather between songs.

She did not choose the direct route. Instead, she quadrupled that distance and allowed the journey to take almost two full weeks by following the coast and taking the off-road paths where she would encounter fewer people and have the upper hand if they met.

The girl and Ferrari had plenty of time together and—as Pietro had talked to Massimo in the abbey—she talked to Ferrari. She ranted and complained and confided. She also questioned, and for that Pietro would have been proud of her. The mule was a good listener but a poor conversationalist. If Pietro had been with her she would have asked him what had possessed the minds of the Moroccans and the others who did the same. She had seen Dino's body respond to Lucia—to her kisses and caresses and tenderness and erotic movements. But she had also seen the other men grow hard to the sounds of screaming and begging and the sight of brutality and blood.

There was no sensible way for her to reconcile what she saw through the moonlit keyhole with what she saw on the other side of that same door.

Is the range of man truly so vast?

Is it only men?

On the tenth night the stars were set across the moonless sky. *Pippo* was only a memory now and there were no more bombers or bombings because the war was north and she was beyond the breakers. The planes that did fly overhead now—recon, logistics, troops—had no interest in her, and she had no interest in them.

It was cool that night so she lit a fire inside the ruins of a small house without a roof in an overgrown field. Everything inside it was blackened from fire. Ferrari grazed outside. He never wandered far and she didn't bother tying him up; if she was killed, it would be better that he ran. From her bag she pulled out a C ration from a case of them she'd collected earlier, a box probably dropped from a truck or else tossed there by a soldier who wasn't in the mood to carry them any farther.

The label on the can read: BISCUIT, CONFECTION, BEVER-

AGE, and KEY FOR M UNIT ENCLOSED but the girl didn't know what these words in English meant. She pried off the key from the bottom, lifted the tab, and slotted and twisted the ribbon around the top. Inside were three candies at the rim of a cup containing powdered coffee. Around it were cubes of sugar in brown paper. Beneath the cup were five biscuits, round with little holes in them. She heated water in a steel cup, poured in the powdered coffee, and added two of the sugar cubes. Ferrari would eat the third later. He'd tasted them before and liked them.

The biscuits were not enough for a meal but dipping them in the weak coffee was tasty and satisfied her stomach before bed. Tomorrow, or possibly the next day, she would reach the outskirts of the city and would have to change her appearance to fit in.

SOMEONE YELLED.

It was a girl.

There was a silence deeper than the night had been before the sound. The girl stood and reached for her rifle, waiting for any proof that the yell had been real and her mind was still her own.

"*Aiutami!*" It was a call for help.

The girl left the can and fire behind and ran to Ferrari's side; he was already looking in the direction of the voice. She could make out the faint shape of a structure, a house or a building, on the far side of a stand of trees.

She started walking, crouching low as though on a hunt, the taste of the coffee and biscuits still in her mouth. It was not immediately clear to her why she felt compelled to respond. In Villa Santa Lucia, she had watched others be killed and done nothing. On the road here she had passed children without shoes whose fate was clear.

She moved because the compulsion was real. It felt immediate and personal. There was no *reason*. There was only instinct. A pull toward an event that had to be faced because she was already a part of it.

With the Thompson across her chest and Ferrari far behind, she jogged as quietly as she could along a narrow and worn footpath through the dark brush and scree. The land sloped downward into a depression where she saw a house similar to her own camp. The roof was partly blackened and burned away and the stone walls were tilting and weak. She saw no lights. Instead, she felt only a gentle evening wind behind her that carried the smoke from her own fire.

It looked haunted or possessed, not occupied. Her place was a respite: a place of rest. This—only a few hundred meters away—looked like a house of the damned.

Stepping as softly as she could in her army boots, she advanced along the path with the weapon pointed forward into the darkness. The breech was already open and the safety off. A squeeze of the trigger would send the bolt forward, firing the gun. The Thompson had two levers and four settings: Safe and Fire, Single and Full Auto. She liked the idea of it working automatically.

"*Aiutami!*"

It definitely came from inside.

The girl crouched low now, like the soldiers did when they moved through cities and villages. When she reached the wall she placed her shoulder against it as they had done, and she stood up very slowly until she could look into the frame of the window and through the sliver of glass still embedded in the soft wood.

On the remains of a sofa was a girl. The two of them might have been the same age but she looked younger and fragile. Her dress had once been white and now was as gray as the filthy room. Around her upper arms were chains that pulled them backward and each leg was bound at the ankle. She was not crying. Instead, her face was blank and she sat like a mannequin in a window of horrors. The girl wondered how this lifeless creature could have called for help. But she had.

There was no entering the house through the window because it was too high and full of glass shards, so the girl stayed low and close to the walls as she circled around to the back in the hopes of finding a collapsed wall or hole.

As she crept to the edge of the house she peeked around the corner and almost pulled the trigger when she saw two enormous black eyes with freakishly long eyelashes looking back at her.

"Ferrari! How did you get here? Be quiet!"

Ferrari had been quiet. He continued to be quiet.

The back wall was half rubble. With the butt of the Thompson against her shoulder and the barrel forward she stepped into the room and looked around. Seeing no danger, she ventured a whisper.

"I'm here." It was barely loud enough to be heard. But it was.

The front door was across from her. The windows on either side had been blown out and she could see through their empty sockets the bushes beyond in the direction of the distant road. The wind was blowing the brush around her and she wasn't sure what she was hearing. For the moment she didn't care.

What did that girl on the floor by the sofa see when she finally looked up and saw another version of herself there? A girl wearing boots and a coat and carrying a submachine gun? Maybe she saw what the girl herself could not: someone beautiful and strong whose hair—once cut short like Massimo's—was now shoulder-length and framing the elegance of her young face that could no longer be hidden. Her cheekbones were graceful and high and arched downward until they disappeared under wide cheeks that were fuller at the jaw. Her hair was black and her eyes were darker than a crow's. The bridge of her nose was wide and—had an adult been in the room and looked at her—it would have been clear that her body was going to grow thin and graceful as the baby fat left her in her twenties, and by her thirties she would arrive at her own natural prime that would stay with her through her forties with no effort.

Whatever the girl on the floor might have seen, what she said was "*straffeta*."

Straffeta. Partisan. An Allied assassin. A Communist infiltrator. It was the word used for Ada and Bella: A word used for a woman.

For the girl chained below the sofa, the girl in front of her was not a girl at all but something larger. Something powerful and determined and confident.

"Don't speak."

The chained girl obeyed.

The chains were looped around each arm and twisted at her back, and then went around the sofa itself to be fed through the space at the bottom and attached to her feet. Two locks behind the sofa secured the chains together and it was all fastened to a bolt on the floor. Whoever had done this had planned it, wanted it, and then stalked a victim and relished his success.

"Where are the keys?"

"He has them."

"Where is he?"

"He's coming back. Soon. He comes back with food for me."

"Does he always have the key?"

"Yes," she whispered, and the girl with the gun knew why.

"Where is your family?"

The girl didn't answer.

"Do you have someplace to go?"

"Yes."

The poor child had matted hair and her face was blackened from the soot of the sofa where she rested.

A brief look at the chains and the locks and the iron loop on the floor proved that it was useless to try to free her. Maybe, perhaps, she could have shot off the locks but if the monster was close the sound would alert him and they would both die.

Across from the sofa, in the corner, was a pile of rags and blankets that were partly burned. They had no color and so the girl went to them and crawled inside as though she were a mole. They did not cover her completely, but with her knees up she became one with the cloth and the shadows.

They waited in silence and barely breathed.

As she waited there on the dirty floor for the man to return, she thought of everything that could go wrong. He could return with other men. Maybe the girl was going to be sold. Or . . . rented. Maybe they had had enough of her and they were coming to kill her, maybe to strangle her, or shoot her, or cut her throat. The Moroccans had burned men and women to death. Maybe it was something these men had learned to do too.

One scenario emerged from her fears fully formed:

"Give me the key," she might say to him in a voice that has never been threatening.

The man, calm and deliberate and knowing he was talking to a teenage girl, would smile and then take out a big knife and approach her. This was a man who, like a spider, had woven a web and then waited for a child to capture and wrap in chains.

How many steps were there, for a large man, from the door to her throat?

Ferrari was outside. He was a quiet soul but he made noise. He moved and shuffled about and he could sense danger. Mules have a tendency to whisper and Ferrari spoke Italian. What if someone passed that way first and heard him? He'd know someone was inside.

A wooden handle. A long, straight blade, sharp on one side, and only half-sharp on the other. That was what he'd be carrying. The memories of the Moroccans came back to her as she crouched, cowering, in the corner.

Their green-and-white-striped cloaks. Their curved knives. Their beards. The expressions on their foreign faces.

Maybe this man's blade would be curved too.

After time without measure she heard hooves outside. It was a horse, a pony, a mule. She heard someone dismount. As he walked toward the front door she could hear that he had a limp like Pietro.

She looked at the terrified girl, who stared at her, which was a mistake.

No, no, don't look at me, she tried to say.

She pointed to her own eyes and then at the floor.

No. There was no comprehension in her face. Maybe she was soft in her mind from her ordeal. Maybe she was stupid or a fool or too afraid to think and reason. How long had she been in here? What had the man already done to her?

"*Ora di cena, piccola bellezza*," he said in a voice as rough as smoke, and which sounded more German than Italian. *Dinner time, little beauty!*

The front door was locked, despite the windows being open and the back wall demolished. He fussed with the lock and then stepped in. He was bearded and very large with vascular muscles in his neck and forearms and an underfed and gaunt look. The derangement on his face was greater than the frenzy of what she'd seen in the village. Those had been evil but purposeful men. So too was Jürgen, who'd wanted to arrest her, torture her, and kill her after the events at the café with Bella and Pietro. But Jürgen did not have a crazed face. What had scared her about him was his cold rationality and utter faith in the virtue of his actions.

But this man looked . . . otherworldly. His eyes were strange. His glances were hectic.

On his hat was a large, colorful pin. It was bright green and looked like a child's drawing. It was shaped like a laughing swordfish with a happy smile and a black eye. It was incongruous and therefore mad.

She looked to the girl chained to the sofa and to the green sea monster and immediately she knew that she was *inside* the Tiziano painting. Andromeda was tied to the rock, where she was going to be eaten alive by the sea monster, and was saved only because Perseus arrived and, with a knife of his own, flew down on the wings of Hermes and beheaded the beast.

THE PIN WAS NOT AN illusion. It was from the German 9th U-boat Flotilla, based out of Brest, France, on the Atlantic coast. She would come to know this in time because soon it was going to become hers.

THE MAN LOOKED AT THE girl on the sofa, who was not staring at the floor like she was supposed to but instead was peering into the shadow of death in the corner of the room.

The man looked at her and then followed her eyes and looked into the corner too.

"What is that?" he said loudly. "Is that a little rabbit in there? Or do we have another visitor to join us? Another little sister for us to play with?"

Three steps. That was the distance a man that large needed to reach her in the pile of cloths.

He got one.

In a fraction of a second and with a single twitch of her finger, twenty-two automatic rounds of .45 caliber ammunition carved his head off at the neck and shredded his torso to meat.

With the smell of sulfur hanging in the still air and her ears ringing from the burst of gunfire, she stood and looked out the window to see whether they were alone. Convinced they were, she bent down and approached his head and body. In a state of tranquility, as if surrounded by divine protection, she bent down and searched his pockets. There they were, the keys, shiny and clean and new. Palming them, she stepped to the man's head and removed the smiling green swordfish pin from his hat and placed it in her pocket.

The girl on the sofa stared at the dead body. She did not cry and was not visibly moved by emotion.

The locks opened easily and the chains were heavy to untwist and move but with effort and some time they were finally removed.

"Thank you," said the little girl, who was, when seen up close, indeed younger.

"You're welcome."

"I'm going home now."

"Come," said the older girl, the fresher air now entering the stale death chamber on a night breeze.

They walked outside together, one barefoot and the other in French army boots. Ferrari had feared the gunfire and had walked himself up the dark path of dirt and rock in the direction of the first house, where he waited once free of the woods.

He recognized the girl as she approached. He shook his head and whispered something she didn't understand.

Reaching beneath his belly, she unfastened the harness that held her gear to him and then she heaved it off and set it to the ground. Without allowing herself too much time to consider her choice, she scratched the mule's ears and said to the girl in the dress: "This is Ferrari. He has a bit of a limp but he is the best mule in Italy. He is kind and brave and loyal and works hard. I am going to the city. He can't come with me. I am giving him to you. Will you take care of him?"

The girl reached out her hand and gently touched Ferrari, who didn't respond. Her fortunes were changing too quickly for her to speak.

The older girl hoisted the younger onto Ferrari's back. She then filled a backpack with two C rations, a can of Spam, and a bottle of water. "This should get you home. Ferrari eats whatever he wants from the ground. He isn't picky. But he needs water. Find it in rivers or puddles. He likes it when you talk to him. Someday, if you can, give him sugar."

Confident in her decision and holding back any thoughts but for the future, she nodded to herself to close the chapter.

"*Fai la brava*," said the older girl to the younger, and with a pat on Ferrari's rear, the two rode off and were gone; not like Europa, stolen away by Zeus as a bull, but instead as a girl freed from being a plaything of the gods.

SHE RETURNED TO HER HOUSE and lay down. Without Ferrari nearby it was harder to settle but the cinders of the fire were still red and she was able to add two logs and start it again. Knowing the body was not far away did enter her thoughts but once she slept it did not haunt her dreams. The silence of the dead was no longer a source of fear. If anything, the dead were a comfort.

EVENTUALLY SHE DID FALL ASLEEP. She had a dream about Bologna, where she had never been. When she awoke at dawn, partly rested, she was certain that Pietro Houdini was still alive.

HER JACKET AND FACE AND hair were covered with a cold morning dew. Her first thought went to Ferrari and she recalled that he was gone. With that sad memory the pieces of the night returned to form the story she had experienced but even now barely believed. The harness and supplies and backpack with the paintings were all safely beside her.

She reached into her pocket and found the pin of a green and smiling swordfish.

Through the open roof she saw an iron-gray sky. There would be glare as she walked today and she'd need to squint for hours. She had no appetite. Once properly awake, she reorganized the provisions so that she had one smaller satchel hanging at her side and the big black pack with the paintings in the tubes on her back. The Luger, as always, she carried in her pocket. The Thompson she slung across her chest.

Napoli, according to the last bullet-riddled sign she'd seen, was forty-three kilometers away. That meant two days of walking and only one more night of travel.

At the main road she glanced down at the other house on the off chance that the sea monster's horse was still there for her to use but it was not.

She walked.

THERE HAD BEEN LESS FIGHTING this close to the coast. Less evidence of a war. She felt like a refugee or maybe a lost soldier like Dino after the shipwreck, but all around her was the odd sense that nothing strange was happening here. Like maybe there was . . . peace.

Above her, seagulls squawked and complained to one another and from the west she could smell the Mediterranean.

Over the next half a day she was passed by horses, wagons, donkeys, mules, and several bicycles, but no motor vehicles. Children, much younger than her, stared as she walked by and for the first time she considered that she might look a bit odd carrying a machine gun across her chest. The front line of World War II was far north of her now, pressing toward Rome according to the radio she listened to when the crickets came out.

She walked.

SHE SMELLED ROTTING FISH. THE land was flat and if her own feet hadn't carried her down from Montecassino, she would have thought she was in a different country.

Her coat started to feel heavy. It had helped her become Massimo, and Massimo himself had loved this coat. Once Bella Bocci had cut his hair and draped this over his shoulders, he'd felt like a young man for the first time and he'd never wanted to abandon that feeling. That was why putting on the dress with Lucia had felt unnatural and uncomfortable, as though he were being forced to become a girl and he was not a girl. Now, however, Massimo was gone and so too was Eva. The coat became only a coat: not a symbol, not a cloak of transformation, not a camouflage. She wondered whether it might be time to let it go. It would not be that cold again. Her time in the mountains and hills was over, and soon it would be June, when the sun would only beat down further on the hot rocks and asphalt of Naples.

By the side of the road she removed the coat and tossed it into the bushes. She also ejected the magazine from the Thompson and tossed it far into the woods. The gun itself she hurled in the other direction.

From now on the Luger would have to suffice.

———

"COME ON, GET IN!" THE boy yelled from the back of the fruit truck.

The girl had slept under a tree, eaten a large breakfast of C rations that contained "frank and beans," some canned fruit, and a chocolate bar. It did not make her feel good, but she did feel full.

The boy yelling at her was one of four teenagers on a truck and two of them were girls. She'd been walking for two hours as the day was growing warmer and hadn't seen a sign for Naples in a very long time. She was becoming hot, bored, and agitated. All of which was better than afraid and freezing but her body cared nothing for the self-awareness.

She considered his offer while looking at the girls, who seemed jovial and chatty.

"Where are you going?" she asked.

"The Gallery," he said.

"I don't know what that is."

"In Naples?" the boy said.

"Oh." Pietro had mentioned something about this. A lot had happened since then.

"You don't know it? Galleria Umberto Primo. We sell our fruit there."

"And a lot more," said the other boy.

The girls laughed.

"Why not come?" he added.

The girl had memorized the address of Pietro's friend as she'd been told to do, and her plan was to find the old castle by the water as her start-ing point. Even so, she did not understand the city.

The girl did not want to say where she was going. She only consid-ered that a ride to the center would be helpful having already walked so much.

Why not come?

What a question. Maybe he hadn't seen what she had seen.

The girl considered that they would be easy to kill if it came to that. Her hand was already gripping the gun and she could shoot through the lining of the bag if she needed to.

Her boots were hot.

Al diavolo.

"All right," she said.

Climbing up the back, she sat herself on a crate the way the other four teenagers had. The truck started moving almost immediately.

The two girls carried themselves like they were older. Knowing. In charge of something—but she couldn't imagine what. The boys felt some-how electric. There was a buzz to them.

"What are you all so happy about?" she asked.

The driver brought the vehicle up to speed—thirty or even forty ki-lometers an hour. The last time she'd been in a car she was Massimo and Pietro Houdini was driving Becker's Fiat up the serpentine path to the abbey, having recently learned that his wife was dead. The wind was in his hair and the smells of the forest and hills were all around them like a song. At the time, as Massimo, she hadn't known about Oriana and it had been a wonderful relief leaving Jürgen behind even if Pietro was angry at her. She might have expected the pleasurable sensations to bring back the fear of the crash but they didn't. The crash had been an accident. Terrible, painful, but not deliberate. It was malice she feared now, not happen-stance. It was good to be moving this fast again.

"We come into the city only once a month. The rest of the time we work outside. But now we get three days in Naples. Do some *business*. Make some *money*!"

"Steal some *shit*!" said the other boy, and they all laughed.

"What's in the big bag?" said one of the girls. It was obvious she'd washed her hair for this outing. On her feet were her mother's high heels, at least a size too big, and the edges were cracked. Her sundress was too loose; she'd lost weight or else it wasn't hers to begin with. The edges of her breasts looked soft, their shape firm, and her body alluring. It seemed she wanted it this way.

"Some paintings my uncle made."

"Show us," she said, an arm over the side of the truck.

"Too hard to roll up again. They're not good anyway."

"Why are you carrying them around?"

"I miss him."

"I'd like to see. Anyone else want to see?"

The other girl changed the conversation. She was more plump, and voluptuously so. Where she got the food to fill out like that, the girl couldn't guess. It was the kind of ruddy health she hadn't seen since the early days in Rome when women would sit out and eat cakes and sip coffees on the piazzas talking about family and men and politics and how the world was terrible, just *terrible*, having had no idea that being able to sit there and complain was a luxury.

"We'd have to clean you up, but you could make some money," she said.

The girl didn't understand what she meant. There were hundreds of thousands of lira at the bottom of her bag. She didn't need money. She needed a ride.

"The Americans have all the money," the other girl went on. "Ours is worth less by the day. All the Neapolitans keep jacking up the prices for the GIs, so regular people can't afford stuff anymore."

There was a dialect to their speech. The girl couldn't follow it entirely.

Pietro had said that Italy was never one country. It was unified only in its suffering. "Later, the past will either hold it together or rip it apart," he'd said. "Time will tell."

"I got a guy who'll pay two thousand lira just for the easy stuff. Clean you up, bathe, get a new dress on. You're pretty enough, not that they care too much. Right age. Most of those GIs don't like the mothers wandering around looking all sad and pitiful. Makes them think of their own mammas back home and that doesn't do the trick most of the time. They like to remember those girls back in school. The ones they were afraid to talk to, and now, for five thousand, they can look down and see two of them looking up with four brown eyes. Same cost as ten bottles of booze to them. Usually only takes ten minutes with these guys and that's if you stretch it out. You good with your mouth?"

"I don't need a job," the girl said.

"What makes you different?"

"I have people waiting for me."

"What kind of people?"

"You ask a lot of questions," the girl with the gun said.

"Don't need to take offense."

She said nothing because nothing came to mind. She hadn't needed to talk her way out of a conversation since the interrogator in Cassino. Since then it had all been bullets and knives.

"All right, tough girl," one of the boys said. "Don't get high-and-mighty with us. Selling pears and apples to restaurants in the Gallery isn't going to do it, you follow? You don't sound like you're from here. Where you from?"

"Cassino."

"Where's that?"

"Far. Bottom of the hill under the abbey of Montecassino."

"The abbey of what?"

"Doesn't matter anymore."

"Is that why you're on the road?"

"I'm not used to talking so much," she said.

"People here talk all the time except when it's too hot. Then they drink vermouth and hide inside. You do understand that the entire Allied army is wandering the streets of Naples, right? And they're drunk and stupid and they're buying whatever they want if they don't just take it and they're selling all their stuff from the PX that they get for next to nothing, and they're selling it to the Neapolitans, who have nothing but who buy it anyway so they can sell it to the rest of us for whatever they can get. You know where you're going, right? Because if you decide to just wander down the Via Roma in the middle of the night, they'll be fishing your body out of the water the next day and blaming it on black marketeers if anyone cares enough to blame anyone at all. You ready to walk into that?"

"I've walked out of worse."

"It's different from getting *bombed*," the buxom girl said. "We've all been *bombed*. This is personal. Meaner."

"I know about mean."

The boy wanted to change the topic again. The truck was moving fast now. Fifty kilometers an hour over bumpy roads. Some parts were damaged. Some parts were smooth. The truck moved like it knew the road all by itself having driven the route a thousand times. "I'd want to see those paintings."

"Nothing to see," she said, looking at the passing trees.

"You don't carry something like that on your back for hundreds of kilometers because it's nothing. What are you hiding?"

The other three were looking at her. They hadn't thought much about the tubes sticking out of the top of her canvas bag, but now that the boy had started talking about secrets they were curious. There was a hunger in their eyes as though they had stumbled on money.

"Family stuff," she said. "I'm not going to show you on a moving truck. As I said, nothing to see because you've seen it a hundred times. Family portraits. That's all."

"You've been out in the sun a lot," he said. "On the road. You don't scare easy. You don't seem like the sentimental type."

The girl didn't like his tone. He was talking himself into something. The others moved and swayed to the rhythm of the ride. They were neither in this yet or out of it. A word could turn it.

She had enough bullets.

Would Pietro want her killing four kids?

He would not. But he'd want her safe at all cost, that much she knew.

"I'm not sentimental. And you're right. They matter to me. They matter a lot. They matter to me more than you do. Or her. Or them."

The girl moved the gun in her pocket enough so the others looked. They did not see it, but they saw enough to wonder.

"I survived the bombing of Rome. Saw my parents buried alive. I was beaten by a gang and left broken in the gutters at Cassino. I helped murder two German officers so we could get their guns, and later my people killed all kinds of Germans and Italians and Moroccans and whoever else was in our way so we could survive. I've been beaten, kidnapped, interrogated, assaulted, shot at, and run over. I'm one of the last of our group still alive. What do you think all that says about me and my interest in showing you my paintings?"

They did not answer her.

The truck slowed and then stopped. There was traffic. Up ahead, what passed for the local authority was taking bribes from the vehicles trying to enter the city limits.

Quickly, and without preliminaries, she stood and hopped off the back of the truck. It had been higher than she'd expected and she twisted an ankle when she landed, which hurt.

It was starting to feel like everyone had a limp.

"Thanks for the ride," she said to seal off any talk.

"You're making a mistake," said the thinner girl. "We could have been useful to each other. We could use someone like you!"

The driver couldn't hear the conversation and didn't know his cue. He pulled up ahead before the conversation was over and the four of them became smaller and smaller and then only specks against the backdrop of a city that absorbed them like particles of dust in a sea of rubble.

THE HEAT WAS CHOKING BY mid-afternoon as she saw the first tall buildings and felt the commotion and vitality of the occupied city. The sky was powder blue and there were seagulls squawking above. She smelled southern pines and the strong waft of the sea as well as diesel fuel from the ships. Ahead, the concrete buildings were separated by narrow passages where faded clothes drooped from sagging lines.

She stood by the side of the increasingly busy road watching American trucks drive by as she tried to decide where to go: to her family, who were not expecting her, or to Pietro's friend, who was also not expecting her.

"The city," Pietro had written in his instructions for her, "will be . . . unrecognizable. I have no idea what remains. I have no idea if your aunt and uncle's building will still be standing or whether they will be alive or dead. I'm sorry to be blunt but you need to consider this. The same is true for my friend. The Allies bombed the city, the Germans gutted it, the natives revolted, and now the Allies are there *en force* to molest it because all these people used to be their enemies despite the Italians feeling liberated. From the moment Giacomo put the receiver down I was cut off from the city's fate."

This was part of his preamble to the actual instructions, which were mercifully brief and easy to remember.

The decision she needed to make was not about the odds of the buildings still standing, though. It was about the consequences of showing up at all. If she went to her family, she figured, she'd be received and loved. The money in the bag would be a relief to them. They were never rich—no more than her own family in Rome. They would protect the paintings even if they didn't understand them.

But: What if one of them was dead? Her aunt? Her uncle? The child? If any of that happened it would be a place of overwhelming grief and the money might be a relief but not a balm. And even if none of that happened her presence would bring grief because she would bring the news of her own parents' deaths.

She walked.

The girl saw street children with no shoes, their faces filthy, their clothes in tatters. She saw soldiers walk past them with the same disdain they would give to sewage rats. She saw clean men talk to hungry women, and rather than offer food, they haggled the price of their remaining dignity.

She passed Italian men—some with mourning bands on their lapels—who were weak, powerless, defeated, and unable to protect themselves let alone the women they loved, assuming they were capable of love at all. If they wore suits they sweated and the elbows were worn to a shine.

The girl recalled Pietro's instructions:

"You will go to the water because there will still be a sea. You find the Castel Nuovo, because even if it was attacked it will still stand because it is a castle and has already stood for six hundred years. Once you find the castle on the sea, you go *north* on the Via Medina. It becomes something else, I forget the name. You keep going. It becomes Toledo. On your left—that hand—you turn onto Pellegrini. The ground floor is nothing but shops. You need to find the actual entrance. Its archway. You go in, you find the doorway, you try to get to apartment number nine on the second floor." He had drawn a diagram to make it easier to remember. "It's not so far from the university. My friend's been there for ages. Castle. Medina. North. Turn left on Pellegrini. Number eighteen. Don't trust the bell to work. There may be no electricity. You may have to wait. Maybe for days."

Family or friend? She wanted to be with family but the choice was really no choice at all after what she'd been through. No. She would not be the bringer of death. Not to unsuspecting innocents. There would be time to find her family and share the grief if there was any time left at all and anyone to share it with.

NAPLES DID NOT LOOK OR feel like Rome. It was neither old nor new, alive nor dead. In Rome, the past was venerated and tourists and school-children were taught reverence even if the history was incomplete or crafted to serve Il Duce. Here, it was something to crawl over like the carcasses of the dead, and the people walked over stone and rubble as though it had never been anything but. There was graffiti on the walls. It was a place without self-respect or unity. It was a wonder they rose up together at all.

It was also confusing. There was a waterfront that was still intact, and after midday, in the early summer heat, people walked (and pushed and yelled and lingered and loitered) along the Via Francesco Caracciolo, over the plaster from the building facades that had not yet been washed out to sea by rains or wind. That waterfront, though, was no center. The city, for the girl, lacked an order because it had no structure she could understand. It was not like other Italian cities or villages. Naples did not radiate outward from a church and a piazza. It felt as though it had started at the water and, over time, pushed back and back and back again into the hills and then, from time to time, Vesuvius would rebel and force them away again.

As she walked, half of the buildings around her were on the verge of tumbling down and from them—as though willing to accept their fates—

people stood on their balconies looking at her. As their eyes tracked her and no one said hello or wished her a good day, she felt as though she were the stranger here and not the tens of thousands of Allied soldiers in uniforms.

Liberty boats bobbed on the water. Empty landing craft were docked or anchored or beached. The heavy yellow sun pressed everything downward and lower into the earth except for the sea itself, which shined like a mirror between the Italian ships that had been sunk in their berths.

Walking, she knew the city was looking at her. Not with curiosity. Not even with the deliberateness of a human gaze. It was more like an animal taking in its surroundings so that it was aware in case anything decided to pounce.

The Americans were busy moving objects from one place to another and, unlike the Italians, they ignored her. The proximity to so many men, however, scared her and for a time she wished she could have been Massimo; that he would arrive, as he did before, to face the world and its hardships for her. As the feeling came, so too did Eva's voice. Not as words but as a mood. A kind of hummed melody that reminded the girl that the old ways were behind everyone now and there was no substitute for fortitude.

The farther into the city she walked the hotter and clammier she became. The mountains had been war and smoke and murder. But there had also been trees and birds and wind and the freshness of the forest. It was no compensation but it provided moments of respite and escape. Here there was none of that. She was inundated by car exhaust, sweat, dead fish, and urine. The coat would have been useless here; the machine gun would have been impossible to carry.

It was strange how the rules of a place can be learned so fast and without instruction.

As she walked along the sea, hoping she was going in the right direction, she looked at men and boys fishing in the rubble with sticks and lines for food or something to sell. The kids in the truck had been right: everyone had an angle, had a need, had a hustle to survive in a constant jockeying of bodies against others.

PIETRO HOUDINI HAD BEEN RIGHT too. The Castel Nuovo was still standing. It was a beast of a thing. Three black, rounded turrets and pieces connecting them that looked like they came from other buildings. The girl knew nothing about fortresses, but compared to Montecassino it looked to have been built without love or dignity or even a plan. It was a monstrosity that lived on through centuries and wars and bombardments and became the worse for it. The longer she looked, the less she wanted anything to do with it.

She looked for the road going north.

The tall buildings formed canyons and she watched British soldiers pour gin on the pedestrians below and laugh and yell at them in English—those "greasy bastards" who were their enemies only a month ago.

Mangy and listless dogs lay in shadows.

The name of the street was luckily still attached to the side of a building that, somehow, remained erect. The number of the man's apartment was coming up. The apartment blocks were three or four stories on either side with iron balconies. People were constantly hauling baskets up and down from the street on ropes and pulleys. Bread and food and money and bottles and bags. They looked at her as she walked by and said nothing. Had she been attacked or stabbed she was certain they would have done nothing and considered it another instance of bad luck: the universal killer.

A child—five years old at most—was sitting on a step at the entrance to the professor's building. She was stripping cigarette butts and placing the last of the tobacco in a tin. Beside it was another tin for the papers.

That one was overflowing but she placed the new paper on the pile anyway and it rolled down and collected on the asphalt around her.

There wasn't an adult in sight.

The backpack was feeling heavy and her feet were hot again. The girl realized she hadn't drunk water in a long time. Ignoring the little girl, she placed the pack in the corner and then sat, leaning against it as if it were a pillow. She kept the smaller bag containing the gun around her shoulder and removed a little bottle of water. She drank most of it but couldn't avoid the wordless longing in the girl with the black fingers and soulless eyes.

She handed the remaining water to the kid, who drank it without a word of thanks.

That was the last thing she remembered before falling asleep.

"GET OUT OF MY DOORWAY. There's nothing for you here," said a man's voice using an Italian much like Pietro's: beautiful, fine, crisp, and intelligent.

She opened her eyes. The right side of her face hurt because she'd slept with it pressing against the concrete frame beside the entrance. The kid was gone. The backpack was still wedged into the corner behind her and she realized that she could have lost everything—*everything*—to falling asleep.

The man's shoes and trouser legs were inches from her face. They were fine and formal shoes, black and leather, but the uppers were coming unstitched from the soles. The trousers were frayed at the bottoms.

"Wake up," he said, nudging her with his foot. "Move along."

"Are you Professor Giacomo Ambrosio?"

Tired and hungry, she nevertheless stood up and pulled on the backpack. When she was in school in Rome the girls were all growing faster than the boys. Most of the fourteen-year-olds towered over their male classmates. The same must have happened to her, without her noticing, because she stood almost eye to eye with the skinny man in front of her. The army boots helped. She stood tall and strong.

"How do you know that name?" he said.

The left arm of his glasses was attached to the frame with a long pin.

"I am a friend of Pietro Houdini. He sent me."

329

The man chuckled at the teenager and then turned away. Shaking his head, he slid an iron key into an ancient hole and turned it in order to enter the building. "There's no such person," he said over his shoulder. "What a ridiculous name. Go away. I don't care why you know my—"

"Mussolini. Pietro Mussolini. Husband of Oriana, who is dead, and he knew this because you are the one who told him by telephone. And I know because he told me."

The man stopped turning the key. It was clear that he could not think and move at the same time. It explained to her why he was so thin: too much thinking, not enough movement. It was a lucky thing that Pietro never suffered such an affliction.

"Come in," he whispered. "Before anyone sees you."

She followed the professor through the doorway and into the interior courtyard, which was as shabby as the exterior of the building. He led her up a staircase that smelled like the plaster that was crumbling, dry and lifeless, from the walls. They arrived at his doorway on the second floor.

"Don't expect much," he said.

It was tidy inside. The main room was decorated in reds and hunter greens and browns. There were floral prints on the furniture and drapes and there were hundreds of books and a beautiful player piano against the wall; the sheet music on the stand was carefully marked and the edges were soft from years of handling. On the walls there were tasteful paintings and several portraits of family members long dead. The dining room table was being used like a research library with several open books around a typewriter that was loaded with paper.

"Sit," he said, pointing toward the sofa in the middle of the room, across from two wingback chairs, one of which was worn and the other clean. There was a table between them. She placed both of her bags beside the table, sat on the sofa, and waited.

A few minutes later he emerged from the kitchen with a pitcher of water, some biscuits, a small bowl of olive oil, and a larger one of cold and weak soup on a tarnished silver platter. He placed it all on the coffee table and sat.

"Where is he? Is Pietro dead?"

"He was still breathing when I left him," she said.

The man nodded his understanding.

"Where were you?"

"Villa Santa Lucia."

"Where is that?"

"Below the abbey of Montecassino."

"You were at Montecassino?"

Her look was the answer.

Parched, the girl drank an entire glass of water, refilled it, and drank another. Though her fingers were filthy she ate a biscuit and sat back on the sofa. She would have washed them if she'd had the will to stand.

"He told you to come here? To me?"

"Yes."

He leaned back on his worn chair and crossed one leg over the other. He ate and drank nothing.

The biscuit was stale.

"You can stay," he said, leaning back. Resigned. "It's safe enough, I suppose. But . . . I have almost nothing. There's been no work. I write articles I can only hope to publish someday. The Americans can't decide if they liberated us or have occupied us. They have not created any solutions for—"

There were more words, more explanations of what he could and could not do, but she was uninterested. She removed the platter from the table, almost tipping over the olive oil onto the carpet as she did, and made space on the coffee table for what mattered. Opening the large pack, she started removing the contents and placing them on the table:

The three paintings in their Nazi tubes.

The sack of ancient Greek gold.

The paper with the man's name and address, which, she now realized, she'd forgotten to destroy like Pietro had told her to. He picked that up and examined it as though it were an archaeological relic.

The girl then poured five hundred thousand lira onto the table, where it overflowed and rolled onto the floor. Pushing some of it away to make space, she placed ten cans of C rations, five of which had meat. There were other sundries too and those she placed on the threadbare rug beside her one change of clothing.

Deciding that there was nothing to lose now, she unpacked the smaller satchel and put the Luger and its two full magazines on the table beside three packs of cigarettes Bella Bocci had insisted be stuffed in there, "to make friends."

The professor's eyes were wide. He looked at the pile of money, the sack of gold, the tubes of mystery paintings. The gun.

"May I have one?" he asked, pointing at the German cigarettes.

"Yes."

It may have been too much too fast but it was done.

He lit the cigarette with a shaking hand. When he inhaled, his shoulders slumped even lower. A relaxation settled over him that was long awaited.

"There's food in the cans," the girl offered.

"What's your name?" he asked.

The girl shook her head.

"How long have you been alone? Since you left Pietro?"

"A while."

Not sure of what to do next, she opened the bag of gold and poured it onto the table too beside the C rations.

Fifty pieces? Seventy? More? Pietro had said they were worth far more than their weight if one knew how to sell them. The professor's eyes narrowed, trying to get closer to them without moving. It was not greed in his eyes but awe. He was facing a cosmic change of fortune that was either arbitrary or preordained. Either way, it was as unfair as any other.

He removed his eyeglasses and replaced them with a set of reading glasses from the inside pocket of his wrinkled jacket. Finding the courage to lean forward, he picked up one of the coins at random and studied it.

"Where did these come from?"

"Syracuse," she said, repeating the word Pietro had used. "And then Naples. The museum sent them to Montecassino. The Nazis were going to steal them. We stole them from the Nazis."

"They're pieces of a history and a story that—" He stopped himself, perhaps remembering where he was. And when.

He placed the single coin back on the table.

"He gave me that money," the girl said, pointing at the lira. "I didn't steal it."

"I believe you," he said, glancing at the gun.

The professor sat back again and removed his glasses. He twitched them in the direction of the tall tubes that held the last mystery. "What are those?"

"Do you know anything about art?" asked the filthy child of the professor.

At this the professor started to smile and then he choked because he accidentally laughed with smoke in his lungs. He was clearly out of practice either laughing or smoking. The coughing made him laugh more because he was an intellectual and therefore defenseless against absurdity and irony.

When he was almost finished coughing he raised a finger to signal that it was nearly over and to ask forgiveness.

"Thank you for that," he said, barely alive but happy to be so, and perhaps for the first time in a while. "Fascists aren't funny. Neither are Communists while I'm on the topic. You, however . . ."

The girl hadn't actually intended to make a joke.

"Why do you ask?" the professor—the journalist, the piano player—finally managed to say.

She pointed at the tubes.

He looked at the gold and then at the tubes and drew the obvious conclusion, as outrageous as it may have been.

"What's in them?"

"Three of the six poesies by Tiziano. Pietro said they're studies from the commission by that Spanish king. He said no one knows they exist except us."

"You're telling me," he said very slowly, "that there are three undiscovered paintings from the Renaissance master on my table?"

"And some other stuff."

"And some other stuff. *Sì, naturalmente.*"

She waited.

"Have you seen them?"

"Yes."

"Which ones are they?"

"*Venus and Adonis. Perseus and Andromeda.* And *Diana and Actaeon.*"

He looked at the tubes.

"May I see them?"

"No."

"Oh," he said, a bit startled. "Okay. I'm curious why not, if you don't mind."

"Pietro painted on them."

"Pietro painted *on* the paintings?"

"He used watercolors. Or gou—something. He said they'd wash off. He thought it was the best way to protect them in case anyone saw them."

"I see. Well . . . that sounds like him, I suppose. You've seen Pietro's handiwork, I suppose?"

"He wouldn't let me."

The girl explained how she and Pietro had arrived at Montecassino and the lies that brought them there. She described the Quiet Period of restoring the artwork on the walls and cataloguing the ones on the shelves. She talked about the café and Bella Bocci and her children. She told the story of Jürgen and Truman König and how they both seemed to vanish like apparitions once the war actually came, though she always felt they were going to reemerge based on some law of the universe that said villains never go away and always show up again at the end. She said that, even here, it felt like König might be looking for the paintings and Jürgen might be trying to solve the mystery of the two murdered officers.

"It doesn't work like that in war," the old journalist said. "The threads of our stories burn. People vanish. Others take their place. What we expect to come does not. And what we don't expect does. It isn't like regular life or the stories we tell about it. Everything in war is shattered. To expect coherence is to not understand the essence of the phenomenon."

Bella's cigarette smoke hung in the air, still as a cloud over a tiny island of limitless treasure.

She thought of the smoke in Pietro's room after he burned his plans.

"We went to school together," he offered. "We've known each other since we were children. About your age, I suppose. He became a scientist. Chemistry and physics. He was very clever. He surprised everyone with his strange mix of muscles and brains. A real ladies' man when he was in his prime. A Renaissance man when he was older. I went the other way. Arts and history. We met in the middle with politics and painting, I suppose. We'd set up easels in his farmhouse outside of Bologna. Oriana was a painter too. She'd join us. We'd challenge one another to use a certain style one day, a different one the next. We'd work and argue and scheme about setting the world to rights. Words and colors and shapes. Perspective was the unifying concept."

The room was dark and the windows were closed. She could smell the furniture. The trappings of domesticity enticed her and she felt as though life in the apartment were suspended like the very dust.

The edges of the blackout curtains burned with mid-afternoon sun. She could smell the outside heat.

"All right, then. Let's see what you have there, shall we? I think the moment has come for you to know your own mysteries and burdens. Don't you?"

The three tubes were indistinguishable and neither Pietro nor the girl had bothered to mark them, as they were to be carried and joined as a piece.

Ambrosio snuffed out the cigarette on a chipped dish and then reached for the first tube. He gently shook it until the edge of the canvas was exposed and then he pulled it with the gentleness of a man removing a scroll from an Egyptian pot. It scraped against the cardboard. The pitch increased as it slid out.

"Whatever it is, we should probably not place it on the olive oil. Not this close to the finish line, as it were."

Professor Ambrosio walked with the single rolled painting to his giant worktable. With patience, he collected his books, placing bookmarks in the relevant locations, and stacked them at one end. He then walked around the table and lifted the heavy black typewriter that had been there so long the feet seemed melted to the spot. With effort he placed it under the table so he wouldn't trip on it later. With a nod of his chin he asked for help, and the girl stepped to the end of the table and—the professor at the other—they lifted the faded green tablecloth, folded it, folded it again, and folded it a third time. He then took possession and stacked it at the far end by the books. The table itself was slightly dusty but shined and was extremely smooth and almost without blemish.

Reaching into his pocket he withdrew a handkerchief and dusted down the surface until it was worthy of its task.

"Are you ready?" he asked.

"No."

"Ah. Do you want to prepare yourself somehow?"

"I think I want to change," she said.

"Into new clothes?"

She didn't answer but the professor looked at her hands and her face and her hair. Compared to the lovely grains of the walnut table she was slovenly.

"The shower is over there. There's a clean towel in the washroom. A bit ripped but perfectly serviceable. My wife was a little taller than you but . . . the clothes in there will do. They're in the closet and the drawers on the left. Take what you like. Don't be shy about it. They have no owner now."

She left him there as he unfurled the first canvas and then set about freeing the two others.

In the bathroom of faded white tiles, the girl turned on the water and waited a few minutes until it ran hot and the steam clung to the glass. The pressure was low but the heat was good. Stripped down, she stepped in and hung her head, watching the water at her feet turn black and run like ash from Vesuvius down the drain.

There was a bar of Palmolive, which was ubiquitous in Naples because it came from the PX stores of the U.S. soldiers. It smelled good and it worked so she scrubbed herself and washed her hair with the suds three times until the water ran clear down her shins and between her toes.

After, she worked on her nails and face.

When the water began to lose its heat she turned the faucets and dried herself off with the towel, which was as thin as a scarf and as stiff as paper, having dried in the sun too quickly. But, as promised, it was clean and the abrasion felt renewing.

In the master bedroom she opened the drawers and found women's underwear only slightly too big. There was a small bra only a size too large. It was the first time she had ever worn one.

In the closet were dresses of many kinds and shapes and colors for an array of occasions. There was no sartorial code for the events to come, so she found a blue skirt that fell to her calves and an ivory collared shirt that buttoned up. The skirt was a little too big so she removed a brown belt with a bright brass buckle from a hook inside the closet and fitted it into place.

Everything was soft and clean and smelled like mothballs, which to her smelled like permanence.

On the inside of the closet door was a full-length mirror. The girl stood there and looked at herself.

She had not seen herself—not *as* herself—since before the bombing in Rome. Before her parents died. Before taking that butterfly clip, which she now fixed into her hair; not only because it reminded her of her mother, but because it felt like home.

There she was. One day shy of her fifteenth birthday.

"Welcome back," I said to myself.

BAREFOOT, I RETURNED TO THE living room and found Professor Ambrosio sitting at the table and looking at the three pictures. He'd placed them in a triangle with two at the bottom facing himself and the other just above them and centered.

He looked up at me and appeared shocked.

"I took a long time. I'm sorry."

"I barely recognize you."

"I feel better."

I'd left the Luger on the table and had simply walked away and showered. I saw that it hadn't been moved; nothing had. I still don't know whether I felt a kind of fatalism at that point, in that dark room, or whether I already felt safe. I am old enough now to realize the two are related. Solving that paradox remained ahead of me.

"Can you see them from there?" he asked.

"No."

"Come look," he said.

I walked around the table and stood beside him so I could examine them properly.

I suppose the professor really wanted to see the paintings beneath the ones Pietro had made but those didn't interest me. I'd seen the Tizianos and experienced all the trials they portrayed, as Pietro had predicted. I didn't need to see them again. It was Pietro's paintings that interested me more.

"He really improved these past few years. I have to hand it to him," the professor said. "Do these mean something to you?"

I looked and when I did I couldn't help but smile. Because they did. They meant a great deal to me.

On the bottom left was a view from the Chiostro del Bramante if you had been standing between the statues of St. Benedict on one side and his sister, Scholastica, on the other. Pietro had used the tools of linear perspective to create a Renaissance-like picture of architectural naturalism. In the picture, standing hand in hand, were a man with white hair and a boy with short and dark hair wearing an overcoat. Together they were looking over the greens of the valley as the dusk turned it a tranquil orange.

"For Massimo," it said, in place of a signature.

On the bottom right was a bucolic picture—more impressionist than realist, inspired by the French school—of a beautiful young girl with medium-length hair leading a mule up a mountain pass toward a man in the distance who was waving in greeting. She had a kindness in her eyes and a butterfly clip in her hair. There was a bandage around the mule's foreleg and around them both was a sea of flowers.

"For Eva," it said.

The final one sat above the other two. It was, perhaps, the most startling of all. It was painted in a dreamy pastel pointillism and it had taken Pietro ages; he started at the abbey and didn't finish until the spring in Villa Santa Lucia. Of course, we had *had* ages together before the Goumiers came and I had watched him, day after day, work on it. Until now, though, I hadn't seen it. The amount of work involved was far beyond any mere effort to cover the Tizianos from prying eyes. This had been a labor of love.

It was a street scene and there was a café. The name of the café was the Antico Caffè Greco, both written on the awning and etched into the window. It was a beautiful and well-lit place. Through the windows I could see other paintings hanging there but I could not see their details. Outside and in front of the café were tables. In a playful nod to Michelangelo's *Last Supper*, I could see all of us. The *orso polare*, of course, was Jesus and he was smiling, seated in the middle, and holding a drink. Beside him on one side was Massimo, who was eating a chicken leg, and on the other was Eva, who held an elegant glass with ice cream. To Eva's right I saw Dino and Lucia and Bella at the end. To Massimo's left were Ada and Harald and Tobias. Ada had her hand on Harald's shoulder, and Tobias was smiling and yelling something at Pietro, who was surely not listening. Everyone looked jovial.

Behind Pietro was a woman with long black hair. The style of the painting obscured the details of her face but she was elegant and tall and confident. Her hands rested gently on Pietro's shoulders with the affection of . . . a wife? No. A daughter; a grown daughter, maybe thirty, in the prime of her life, who had come to visit her beloved *papà*. For a fleeting moment I thought it might be his daughter. But then I saw the dedication.

"For you," it said.

He did not even know my name during the months he painted this. He didn't know my name until he was dying on the floor near Harald and the Moroccans in Villa Santa Lucia.

For you.

"They're really very good," the professor said. "I am having a hard time believing that he painted these over three priceless oils that history doesn't know exist but . . . I suppose I've seen crazier things lately. Possibly even today. You do understand that to reach the master works below, we will eventually have to wash away and destroy those he painted above?"

"If we do," I said to him, looking down on these gifts, "the moment will present itself."

THAT NIGHT I SLEPT IN peace in the guest bedroom, which was soon to become mine. In the morning I woke late and when I did we both drank my coffee and ate the food that was now ours.

When we finished eating he sat back and indulged in another ciga-rette. He was not one for conserving them. I had heard they go stale after a time but I suspect his reasons were more simple: "Smoke 'em if you got 'em," the Americans GIs used to say.

"What about this family of yours?" he finally asked me. I had men-tioned them but not explained much.

I liked to imagine their warm embrace. I relished the thought of rushing into my aunt's arms and looking into her eyes, which were so much like my mother's. I'd have been happy to be surrounded by my family, my people, my community, my blood. I would have liked to sense I was home and that the journey was over.

Only, it didn't feel over. I couldn't imagine going back to the arms of adults and to be treated like a child again. What would happen to my gun? To Pietro's plans for me?

"Not yet," I said.

* * *

IT WAS UNDERSTOOD WITHOUT SAYING it that we would remain together for some time. I found him simpatico though I felt no deep bond to him as I had with Pietro. We were like distant family who had met at a funeral and were joined together by our love for the dead and this was enough. I was a child and he was a grown man but I was older than a normal child because of what I had seen and done and knew. Ours was a camaraderie that was uncomplicated. We didn't know it but we had enough money (and ammunition) to last us the rest of the war.

When the honking began I turned to the window. I couldn't see out because of the thick curtains. The honking grew and multiplied and soon it sounded like the entire street—and then the entire city—was honking.

And . . . yelling? Cheering?

For a brief and melodramatic moment I thought the entire city of Naples had remembered my birthday: June 5, 1944. On that day I was fifteen years old. No one knew that other than me, though. I looked to the professor for a more plausible explanation.

"I don't know," he said. "We should turn on the radio. The only way a whole city can learn something all at once is by radio."

The merriment grew louder as he raised himself wearily from his kitchen table and bent over the radio knobs to turn it on and increase its volume. As Vatican Radio spoke, the approaching thunder of voices made me turn from the announcer to the thick red velvet blanket covering the exit to the balcony that overlooked the street.

Pushing the curtain open would reveal a world of wonders that were calling to me. I could feel the draw from the other side.

The radio was a wooden box and the man inside it was talking fast. We did not hear the beginning of the talk but the subject was clear: the Allies had reached Rome. The Germans were pushed back to the far north. The fighting continued and the war was not over but fascism in Italy was over. Rome was liberated. Something new was coming. Whatever it was had already started to form beyond that red velvet cloth in front of me.

Professor Ambrosio looked to me as though wondering what we should do.

I could have stood and pushed aside the red curtain to expose the mystery beyond.

But I already knew what happens to those who do.

PART VI

IN 1964 I WENT BACK to Cassino for the reconsecration of the rebuilt abbey by the Pope. Among the artifacts that Schlegel and Becker did, in fact, have shipped to the Vatican were the original plans of the building, including the survey conducted by Don Angelo Pantoni. That is how they rebuilt it. Standing at the new PAX entrance I was stunned by the reappearance of what I had once known and seen destroyed. The craftsmanship, the illusion, was dazzling and as I passed into the cloister to see, everything was disturbingly accurate. The textures were all wrong, and the color was gleaming and fresh, but the lines and carvings and even the stairs were perfect. I was able to stand where Massimo and Pietro had looked out to the west and toward California (as absurd as that now seems). The arches were the same. The stone. The view. But the abbey was silent now. It no longer had a voice, and though I whispered to it when I was alone, I felt no presence there able to hear me.

I left before the Pope spoke. He had nothing to say I needed to hear.

I was an adult by then and I had a car of my own so I drove down the newly rebuilt road that snaked to the new village of Cassino. It was a 1961 Alfa Romeo Giulietta Spider Veloce. Red, of course. It sounds exotic now, but it was a cheap red convertible and as close as I could reasonably come to the car that Becker had collected in Sicily and Pietro had wrecked.

I hadn't planned on buying such a car. For almost twenty years the idea never occurred to me, but then Sophia Loren won an Academy Award and everything changed.

In 1960, Vittorio De Sica directed *La Ciociara*, or *Two Women* in English. It was based on the 1957 book by Alberto Moravia and it told the story of the Marocchinate, or "the deeds of the Moroccans." It was a story of a mother and daughter who were raped in a church in 1944. The girl was my age at the time. It was a way for Italy to speak about and recall what happened. The French helped fund it. Sophia Loren would win the Academy Award for Best Actress in a Leading Role and the film would be nominated for the Palme d'Or at Cannes.

The world now saw what I had seen. It made me feel less alone. I realized then that it was one of the feelings Pietro had wanted me to understand about art.

So it followed that I bought Becker's car.

It sounds foolish but time travel is a remarkable experience.

I didn't return to Rome after leaving the abbey, though. Instead I drove to a little village I had never heard of called Castro dei Volsci. I had read in the newspaper that a monument was raised there, a monument the Pope should have visited, and the prime minister, and the French president, and the American president because they all should have placed a flower and murmured their apologies for remaining silent, thereby forcing art—and art alone—to speak.

The statue is called the Monumento alla Mamma Ciociara. It is marble and shows the curvaceous form of a scared but resolute woman pressed against the hellfire winds of fortune itself, trying to protect her daughter, who rides and clutches her back. It is one of the most beautiful yet gut-wrenching sculptures I have ever seen. The etching on the plinth "recalls the many daughters of this land who, in obedience to their homeland traditions, faced death with heroism in defense of their honor and their freedom: June 3, 1964."

I appreciate that it is there and that it is carved in stone to bear witness to our continued and relentless wars on the innocent; it is another tile in the mosaic first sketched in *The Women of Troy* by Euripides, a Greek man who could not stomach what his own people had done to the women of the vanquished and who had no choice but to stage it in Athens in 416 BC so they might understand the horror of war itself and not only its glory. And yet, 2,380 years later, we carve another rock.

I drove back to Cassino, which I assumed was rebuilt with Marshall Plan money from America. I was surprised to see that the building with Bella's café had been reconstructed and there was—once again—a restaurant there.

I parked and went inside for a drink because Sophia Loren and the Pope and the statue and the abbey all required me to confront these stations of the cross, as it were.

Inside, my order was taken by a man of perhaps thirty. His accent was closer to mine and I suspected that he was either from Rome or had lived there for a long time. I did the arithmetic and took a guess.

"Are you Bella's son?" I asked.

He said he was and smiled. He looked strong and healthy and had an intelligent face.

"How is she?" I asked. "I knew your mother long ago."

"Oh, very well, thank you!" he said to me. "She's traveling now. She has a friend in Elba so I'm afraid you've missed her. How do you know each other?"

"The war. I remember you and your sister going off to Rome with the Germans."

This started a long conversation. The sister was now married and well. There was going to be a child soon. The biggest surprise was that their father had returned home. He had not been killed but had walked all the way back from . . . where, I don't know. One of Dante's rings. The letter in the mailbox had survived much like the statues of Benedict and Scholastica survived the bombing of the abbey and the Genbaku Dome survived the bombing of Hiroshima. There is no accounting for it. There is only the knowledge that it is true and the wonderment it creates.

I told the man my name (he was only a few years younger than me but I felt much older at the time) and left. I suspected that Bella had either swallowed her stories or divulged only what she needed to so that a livable balance could be maintained. Lies can be a mercy.

That left Villa Santa Lucia.

I didn't want to go but I did.

The Alfa's small engine rumbled and I left Cassino behind me on one of the new roads built after the war. The surface was perfect and the little engine's character put me in mind of dear Ferrari.

RECORDS OF DEATHS IN SMALL Italian communities are kept by the church and the local authorities. It was a Saturday in the early afternoon so the *municipio* was open. Around me there was no evidence that anything bad—anything inhuman—had ever happened here. I explained to the woman behind the counter why I was there. I spared nothing and I could see on her blank face that she understood everything.

Yes, they did have records. Yes, I could look and I did. But of the *orso polare* there was nothing. Nor Lucia or Dino. But I did see Ada Pugliese and they did record her name properly. I found Tobias, whom the nuns had brought back to the abbey.

OVER THE NEXT FEW YEARS I looked for Pietro at the university in Bologna and in Switzerland, where he studied. Giacomo Ambrosio did know the name of his daughter: Sofia. He did not know the name of the mother, though, and without that Sofia was invisible. I had wanted to tell her about her father. About what he did and how much he loved me and that whether he was a good man or not I couldn't say, but I loved him too, with all my heart. I stopped looking because the search only reminded me of him, and of what he'd said.

In the end I was his daughter, not her.

PIETRO HOUDINI, LIKE HIS NAMESAKE in America—the Hungarian, the American, the Jew, the illusionist—disappeared. And like Harry Houdini's widow, I waited for him to miraculously escape from death and return to me but he never did. And yet—even though he would surely be dead now from old age—a part of me is certain he survived and lived and made trouble, and yelled at God, and God listened and together they would wrestle; and beneath them continents would form and islands would rise from the sea and flowers would grow from the ground and what had once been cursed became blessed by the struggle if not the victory.

As for the paintings: I cheated.

In the summer of 1972 I hired a wedding photographer in Rome with a Hasselblad and he took perfect, well-lighted photos of Pietro Houdini's three paintings. I had these enlarged to their original size and then framed and placed on the wall in my house. My daughter grew up with them. I kept them in the divorce.

The Tizianos are now on the walls in Naples, where they belong, as I explained earlier. And the gold? That has been returned to Montecassino. Well . . . most of it anyway.

When Pietro sat on the edge of my bed he said to me, "We will need to lie, cheat, steal, fight, kill, and sin our way to Naples. We will hold our own lives as precious above all others. We will trust no one but each other, and we will try to remember that in this country, at this time, there is no way to tell friend from foe."

And so we did.

I am, therefore, as he helped to make me: a liar, a cheat, a thief, a fighter, a killer, and a sinner. I became more too. A wife, a friend, a mother, a lover. So too a writer and a journalist: a columnist and a provocateur, despised by the political left and the right in equal measure for speaking my mind and forming my thoughts in words against which they have no response; for refusing—always, always—to submit to orthodoxies that restrain us rather than set us free. Why? For the spotlight? No. Because I saw what I saw. I experienced what I experienced. I know what I know, and I owe a debt to the dead and I will truly be damned if anyone tries to stop me from repaying it.

Pietro Houdini would have accepted nothing less from me.

I RECOVERED FROM THE WAR at the same pace as Italy, and like Italy, I never came to terms with my internal contradictions and tensions and passions but somehow held it together all the same. If nothing else, I am now able to trust again and tell friend from foe. In this way I may have outgrown my country.

I AM REMINDED, AT THE end of my story, of another: of Anna Maria Enriques Agnoletti. The Nazis shot her in 1944 and Italy later gave her the Medaglia d'Oro al Valor Militare for "outstanding gallantry" in not giving up her countrymen under Nazi torture. The words spoken in honor of the award are engraved on my spirit: "*Immemore dei propri dolori, ricordò solo quelli della Patria* . . . "Forgetful of her own pains, she remembered only those of her country."

Anna Maria was a Jew.

One of her torturers was a Benedictine monk who played piano while she screamed.

And so: We are cursed and yet cling to life. We are rejected and yet fight on. We love when we are hated. And the universe that is indifferent to us cannot resist the force of life and be drawn to it.

Pietro Houdini said that life clung to him like a curse because he loved living, and his curse was that his own enthusiasm—despite it all—attracted life to him; each of us was a universe bending in his direction. And because he was a flawed man but a good one, he saw the harm he caused more than the good he did.

He loved me like a son.

He loved me like a daughter.

He helped me become who I am.

Since then I have also come to know *what* I am.

I am the life that clung to him.

I am the curse of Pietro Houdini.

This book is dedicated to my friend Michael Kim
because time is precious.

ACKNOWLEDGMENTS AND DENIALS

IN MY SECOND NOVEL, *The Girl in Green,* I wrote that the book was "inspired by many actual events." It turns out that my later novel *How to Find Your Way in the Dark* was too. Now too is this one. A pattern is forming.

For certain kinds of writers—writers like me—a project begins more with an impulse and a sense of wonder than a plot. I started this novel after completing my science fiction epic, *Radio Life.* That story was partially inspired by (or, as I prefer to say, is in conversation with) *A Canticle for Leibowitz,* by Walter M. Miller, Jr., who—during World War II—had been one of the aircrew who dropped the bombs on Montecassino, obliterating it from the earth.

I knew, after *Radio Life,* that I was not done with Montecassino. Something was drawing me toward it. I knew it was old. I knew it was magical. I knew it was a storehouse for treasure and history and art. I knew that we Americans dropped more bombs on it than any other single building in all of World War II. Beyond that, I didn't know anything.

Sometimes, for a novel, that is enough: a sneaking suspicion that there is a story there.

I knew nothing of Julius Schlegel or Maximilian Becker, of the abbot who survived the bombings, of the trucks that ferried the art away to both the salt mines and the Vatican alike, and I knew nothing of the Allied Moroccans and the rapes and the murders. Instead, I wrote the first line and once I did the entire landscape opened up and all unfolded and then took a new form as I moved back and forth between fact and fiction in the context of the reality

357

of events. Consequently, it was never my intention to find what I did, or even to write about what I did. I was always left—like a historian—with a simple choice: attend meaningfully to the truth of events or not. I did my best.

And so:

Although this is a work of fiction, the following all happened more or less as portrayed in the story—if not to my characters, at least to somebody: The bombing of Rome by the Americans; the transfer of Naples's art to Montecassino; more or less everything about Montecassino (including the reference to Don Quixote, the history of the Moors and the Jews, and everything else unexpectedly interesting); the story of *Pippo*; the Piper plane itself flown over Montecassino by the Americans, who were looking for Germans; all the atrocities of the Germans; all the noble, complex, and confusing acts by them too; Becker and his Fiat (I have no evidence that it was red but . . . it had to be, right?); the atrocities committed by the Moroccans, with each incident I described having been taken from a database compiled by the Associazione Nazionale Vittime delle "Marocchinate" o Goumiers (the locations were adjusted to suit dramatic purposes); the stories of the poesie paintings and their history (though I made up the three pictures that Massimo and Pietro saved); the bombing of the abbey itself and the abbot's survival and the civilian deaths.

There really were a *lot* of mules.

A FEW APOLOGIES:

While the situation, history, life, and experiences of the abbey are accurately presented (within reason), the interior halls were a bit of guesswork. The abbey itself didn't reply to my queries and I couldn't find a floor plan.

At some point Pietro uses the term "keisters." Americans, via Yiddish, did use the term by the 1930s. It is not German and it is unlikely

Pietro (an Italian) would have known it. But . . . it was just the perfect thing for him to say and I couldn't help myself.

I used the term "football," which Americans call "soccer." I could not in good conscience use the term "soccer" in this book set in Italy. Sorry if that confused anyone.

Given the vast range of subjects addressed in this book—from the history of the abbey to Renaissance painting, battles of World War II, the Marocchinate, and the Moorish occupation of Spain—it is not impossible I might have made a mistake. If so . . . sorry.

A FEW ACKNOWLEDGMENTS:

My thanks to the monks at Glenstal Abbey—a community of Benedictine monks in County Limerick, Ireland—for answering my questions about daily life at an abbey. Normally I make jokes about who is to blame for my errors, but in this case I accept that they are fully mine and mine alone.

Thanks to Professor Alan R. Perry at Gettysburg College for his scholarship on *Pippo* the plane, which introduced me to the phenomenon, and for our subsequent correspondence. This part of the story would not have been possible without him (and was a nice reminder to me of how all good scholarship matters, even if the subjects appear modest).

Many thanks to Angela Carpentieri, who consulted with me on Italian translations and appropriate term usage, though any errors are mine.

Thanks also to Julie Lindahl (author of the brilliant *The Pendulum: A Granddaughter's Search for Her Family's Forbidden Nazi Past*) for similar support with the German. All errors there are also mine.

The term "flame deluge" was respectfully borrowed from Walter M. Miller, Jr. Readers of my science fiction novel, *Radio Life*, will know why this was on my mind.

Acknowledgments

Pietro's distinction between "*chronos*" and "*kairos*" is accurate, but to the best of my knowledge the distinction wasn't fully appreciated in the twentieth century until scholarship in the 1950s, so even an overeducated git like Pietro probably wouldn't have known this. However, it was too perfect not to use and I request forgiveness. I thank Jennet Kendra Sepúlveda for bringing that wonderful distinction to my attention and therefore Pietro's.

Pietro's speech to Massimo ("the function of tragedy") is inspired by and paraphrased from E. V. Rieu's September 1949 introduction to his own translation of *The Iliad*.

The nickname *orso polare* was inspired by Mark Helprin's *Memoir from Antproof Case*, in which the Brazilians called Oscar Progresso the same thing.

Thanks to Matthew Adams for "*Der Handschellen-König*" and confirming that Jürgen *would* likely know about Harry Houdini (a fact doubted by my esteemed British editor, who is rarely wrong).

The quote from Euripides was translated by Edith Hamilton, who called *The Trojan Women* "[t]he greatest piece of anti-war literature there is in the world . . . Nothing since, no description or denunciation of war's terrors and futilities, ranks with *The Trojan Women*, which was put upon the Athenian stage by Euripides in the year 416 BC." I was deeply moved by that play, and my decision to face the traumas of the women unapologetically was inspired by that literary tradition.

My mental image of the girl is partly inspired by a photograph I saw of a fourteen-year-old named Jeanine Nicole Heimer, included with the other pictures, as explained below. All I know about her is that she was born in Paris on June 25, 1929, to David and Suzanne Margulis Heimer. On October 28 she was deported from Drancy, France, to Auschwitz with her parents and older brother, Maurice, where they were murdered on October 31, 1943, because they were Jewish. The photograph haunted me, and what I can only imagine to be her spirit infuses this novel. I would dedicate this book to her but the idea makes me too sad.

ABOUT THE AUTHOR

Derek B. Miller is an American novelist, international affairs professional, and windmill jouster. He is the author of six highly acclaimed novels. *Norwegian by Night* won the CWA John Creasey Dagger Award among other accolades, and *How to Find Your Way in the Dark* was a finalist for the National Jewish Book Award and a *New York Times* best mystery of 2021.

Miller is a graduate of Sarah Lawrence College (BA) and Georgetown (MA), and he earned his PhD summa cum laude in international relations from the Graduate Institute in Geneva with postgraduate work with Rom Harré at Oxford. He was the founder and director of the Policy Lab in 2011; is currently connected to numerous peace and security research and policy centers in North America, Europe, and Africa; and he worked with the United Nations in Geneva for more than a decade.

He has lived abroad for more than twenty-five years in Israel, the United Kingdom, Hungary, Switzerland, Norway, and Spain.

Miller is a mediocre guitar player, a decent cook, an avid motorcycle rider, and an enthusiastic father with aspirations for greatness.

In the story I made reference to numerous images that you really should see. If you follow the code below, you can see the six poesie paintings that play such an important part in the story and are also part of the novel's cover. You will also see *Il monumento all Mamma Ciociara*, which is one of the most moving sculptures I know, and also the photo of Jeanine Nicole Heimer. Thank you for joining me for *The Curse of Pietro Houdini*.

—Derek B. Miller, Sitges, Spain, 2023

You can also access this content at CurseOfPietroHoudiniBook.com

Avid Reader Press, an imprint of Simon & Schuster, is built on the idea that the most rewarding publishing has three common denominators: great books, published with intense focus, in true partnership. Thank you to the Avid Reader Press colleagues who collaborated on *The Curse of Pietro Houdini*, as well as to the hundreds of professionals in the Simon & Schuster advertising, audio, communications, design, ebook, finance, human resources, legal, marketing, operations, production, sales, supply chain, subsidiary rights, and warehouse departments whose invaluable support and expertise benefit every one of our titles.

Editorial
Lauren Wein, *VP and Editorial Director*
Amy Guay, *Assistant Editor*

Jacket Design
Alison Forner, *Senior Art Director*
Clay Smith, *Senior Designer*
Sydney Newman, *Art Associate*

Marketing
Meredith Vilarello, *Associate Publisher*
Caroline McGregor, *Marketing Manager*
Katya Buresh, *Marketing and Publishing Assistant*

Production
Allison Green, *Managing Editor*
Jessica Chin, *Manager Copyediting*
Samantha Hoback, *Senior Production Editor*
Alicia Brancato, *Production Manager*
Wendy Blum, *Interior Text Designer*
Yvonne Taylor, *Desktop Compositor*
Cait Lamborne, *Ebook Developer*

Publicity
David Kass, *Senior Director of Publicity*
Alexandra Primiani, *Associate Director of Publicity*
Rhina Garcia, *Publicist*
Katherine Hernández, *Publicity Assistant*

Publisher
Jofie Ferrari-Adler, *VP and Publisher*

Subsidiary Rights
Paul O'Halloran, *VP and Director of Subsidiary Rights*
Fiona Sharp, *Subsidiary Rights Coordinator*